G·A·HENTY

PERCY THREATENS TO SHOOT THE FERRYMEN.

THROUGH THE SIKH WAR

A TALE OF
THE CONQUEST OF THE PUNJAUB

BY

G. A. HENTY

Author of " Beric the Briton," " The Dash for Khartoum," " Held Fast for
England," " With Clive in India," &c.

WITH TWELVE ILLUSTRATIONS BY HAL HURST
AND MAP OF THE PUNJAUB

NEW YORK
CHARLES SCRIBNER'S SONS
1902

PREFACE

MY DEAR LADS,

Among the many wars by which, province by province,^" the Empire of India was won, few, if any, were more brilliant and hard fought than those which terminated in the annexation of the Punjaub. It is satisfactory to know that the conquest of the Sikhs—a brave and independent race—was not brought about by any of the intrigues which marred the brilliancy of some of our early conquests, or by greed for additional territory, but was the result of a wanton invasion of the states under our protection by the turbulent soldiery of the Punjaub, who believed themselves invincible, and embarked upon the conflict with a confident belief that they would make themselves masters of Delhi, if not drive us completely out of India. It was fortunate for Britain that the struggle was not delayed for a few years, and that there was time for the Punjaub to become well contented with our rule before the outbreak of the Mutiny; for had the Punjaub declared against us at that critical period it would assuredly have turned the scale, and the work of conquering India must needs have been undertaken anew. I have endeavoured, while keeping my hero well in the foreground, to relate the whole of the leading incidents in the two Sikh wars. Yours sincerely,

G. A. HENTY.

CONTENTS

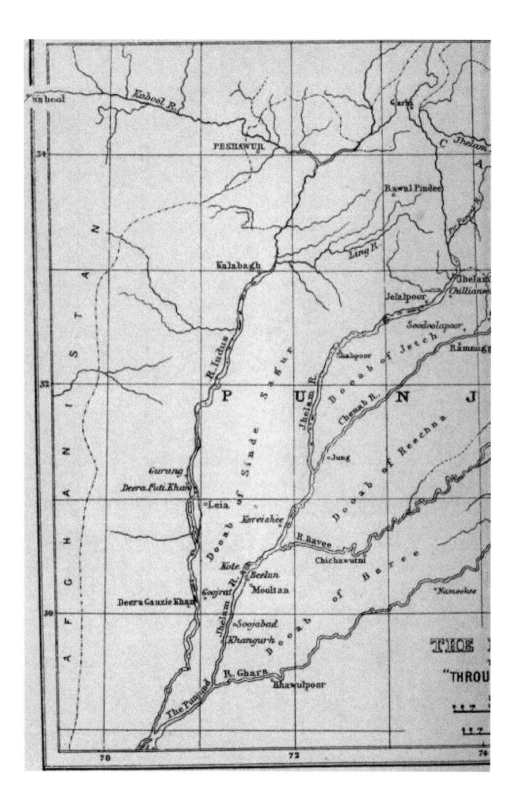

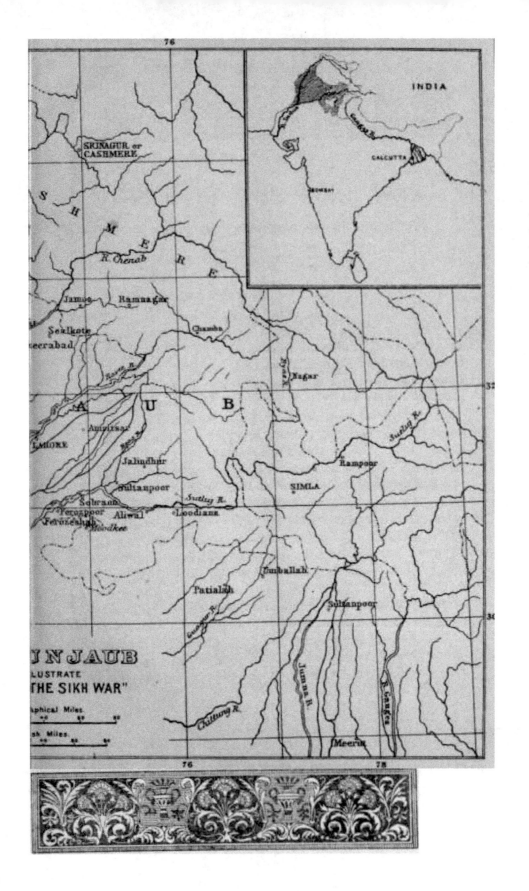

THROUGH THE SIKH WAR

A STORY OF THE CONQUEST OF INDIA

CHAPTER I

EASTWARD HO!

GROVES, here is a letter for you," Dr. Bubear, the head-master of a large school at Dulwich, said, as the boys rose from their places to leave the school-w room at the conclusion of their work. The lad addresseT, a boy of about fifteen, went up to the desk.

"It is from your father's lawyers, Messrs. Sims & Hammond. I have received one from them myself. I think you will find it satisfactory," and he nodded kindly. "You had better stop in here to read it, for it looks somewhat bulky, and I fancy contains an inclosure."

Percy Groves returned to his seat, and did not open the letter until he was alone in the school-room. It was a long time since he had received one. Fifteen months before he had lost his father. Major Groves had returned on half-pay a year before his death, being obliged to quit the service from the effects of a severe wound which he received at the storming of Ghuznee. His regiment had been absent several years from England, and after he had left the service and taken a house at Dulwich, he had made but few acquaintances, spending most of his time at the military club to which he belonged.

Percy, who was an only child, had been born in India—his mother dying when he was five years old. His father had kept him three years longer with him, and had then sent him home to England to the care of his grandfather, who had, however, died a year later; and from that time Percy had known no home but Dr. Bubear's, until his father returned and took up his residence near the school. A few days before his death Major Groves had a long talk with his son.

"I am troubled about you, Percy," he said. "Besides my half-pay I have but three thousand pounds—a sum sufficient indeed to finish your education, pay your expenses at the University if you decide to go into one of the learned professions, and to help you a bit until you make your way. I have written to three or four of my old friends, who will, when the time comes, do their best to procure you a commission in the army, in case you have a fancy then, as I know you have now, for soldiering. Lastly, there is my brother. We have never kept up much correspondence, but we have always been good friends; he was in the army himself, but sold out after only serving a year, as he saw that there was very little chance of active sevice in Europe. He knocked about the world for some years and then went out to India, and the next I heard of him was that he had entered the service of Runjeet Singh, the leader of the Sikhs, who had great respect for European troops, and employed a number of foreign officers—Italian, German, and a few English—to train his troops on our method.

" I have not heard of him for some three or four years, but when I did he was still in the Sikh service, and held the rank of colonel, and was, I heard, high in favour with Runjeet Singh, and there I have no doubt he is still, that is if he is alive. No doubt he is married to some dusky princess, and has probably accumulated a fortune. These adventurers, as Europeans in the service of native princes are generally called, either get murdered soon after they get out there, or else accumulate large fortunes. I have no doubt that if he is alive he will take charge of you.

"The life is an adventurous one, and I do not say that I should advise you to adopt it; but in that respect you must decide for yourself, when you reach the age to do so. If your uncle is able to push your fortune out there you might do worse than stay with him; if, on the other hand, when you get to the age of seventeen or eighteen, you do not care to remain in India, you must come home and get the officers to whom I have written to use their influence to obtain a commission for you, which they will, I have no doubt, be able to do, as the son of an officer forced to retire from the service in consequence of wounds is always considered to have a claim.

" In that case the knowledge that you will obtain of Indian methods and languages would be a very great assistance to you. But mind, if you do go out to your uncle it will not be possible for you afterwards to choose one of the learned professions, for however much you may try to educate yourself out there, you will not be up to the mark of lads who have gone through the regular course of schooling here."

"I don't care for that, father; I have always made up my mind to be a soldier, as you were. I should like very much to go out to my uncle if he will have me."

The major was silent for a few minutes.

"I don't know that it is a wise step," he murmured to himself; "but the boy has no friends here—my old comrades will do what they can for him when the time comes, but until then he will have but a lonely life.

"Very well, Percy," he went on, turning to his son, "I will write to your uncle. It may be eighteen months before you get an answer from him—that is all the better. Work hard at school, lad, and learn as much as you can, for you will get but little learning out there. If your uncle does not care to have you, or thinks that things are too disturbed and unsettled out there for him to undertake the responsibility, you must fall back on the other plan and remain at Dr. Bubear's until you are seventeen. I have written letters to the friends who promised to see after your commission; you will find them in my desk. Keep them by you until you are leaving school, and then post them, that is if your wish to go into the army is unchanged. If it should be changed, Messrs. Sims & Hammond, my lawyers, will put you in the way of carrying out your wishes in whatever direction they may lie."

There had been several such talks between father and son, and Percy knew that he should not have his father long with him. He listened, therefore, gravely to his words, but without showing emotion; for although when alone he often gave way to tears, he knew that the major, himself a quiet and self-restrained man, was adverse to any display of feeling. The boy did not think the end was so near, and though prepared in some way for the blow, it was a terrible shock to him when his father, five days later, expired. He had again become a boarder at Dr. Bubear's, remaining there during the holidays as well as in school-time.

Two or three times old friends of his father had come to see him, and had taken him out for the day. This was the only change he had had, but he had worked hard and risen considerably in his place in the school. In accordance with instructions from Messrs. Sims & Hammond he had gone regularly to a riding-school, as the major, knowing the Sikhs to be a nation of horsemen, had thought it desirable that he should learn to have a good seat on a horse. The lawyers had also arranged that he should twice a week have lessons in Hindustani, and he was allowed to work at this instead of Greek. His progress was comparatively rapid, as after a time the language he had heard spoken for the first eight years of his life came back to him rapidly. He had hardly begun to look for a reply from his uncle when Dr. Bubear handed him the letter, which he doubted not contained the answer. He had hardly hoped that it would be favourable, for during the

intervening time he had learned something of what was going on in the Punjaub, and knew that since Runjeet Singh's death there had been many troubles there, and that things were in a very unsettled state.

This information he had received from one of the boys whose father was a director of the East India Company. The doctor's words, however, gave him some hope, and when alone he opened the letter with less trepidation than he would otherwise have felt. Messrs. Sims & Hammond wrote as follows :—

"We have pleasure in forwarding to you a communication from Colonel Roland Groves, which was inclosed in one sent to us. In the latter he expressed his readiness to receive you, while pointing out that the position of affairs in the Punjaub was unsettled in the extreme. He doubtless speaks further of this in his letter to you. As our late client, your father, instructed us that we were to be guided entirely by your decision in the matter, we leave it in your hands, observing, however, that in the face of your uncle's statements with regard to the country, it appears to us that to go out to him at present would be an exceedingly ill-advised and rash step. Should you, however, decide upon doing so, we will, upon hearing from you, take the necessary steps for obtaining your outfit and securing your berth. A client of ours in Calcutta will, we doubt not, arrange on your arrival there for forwarding you up the country to your uncle."

Having read this, Percy broke the seal of the inclosure and read as follows:—

"Mv DEAR NEPHEW, —I am filled with grief to learn from a letter, forwarded to me after his death, that your father is no more. It is many years since I saw him; but we were always capital friends, though as unlike in disposition as two brothers could be. He tells me that he has no friends in England in whose charge he could place you, and asks if I will have you out with me until you are of an age to enter the army at home,

THROUGH THE SIKH WAR

if, indeed, you do not decide to follow my example and take service with one of the native princes.

"As far as taking charge of you goes, I am perfectly ready to do so—indeed more than ready; for it will give me great pleasure to have poor Hugo's son with me and to treat him as my own, for I am childless. But the sort of career I have chosen is pretty nearly closed. The Company have most of India under their thumb, and allow no English except their own officials to take service with the protected princes. At present the Punjaub is independent, but I don't think it can remain so much longer. Since the death of the Old Lion, as Runjeet Singh was called, things have gone from bad to worse. One ruler after another has been set up, and either dethroned or assassinated. The army is practically master of the country; and one of its first steps was to demand the dismissal of all foreign officers, and the greater part of us were accordingly discharged.

"Some of them left the country; others, like myself, are living on the estates granted us by Runjeet Singh, and on the pickings, which were considerable, that had come to us during our term of service, and we are waiting to see what may be the next turn of the wheel. Life here is something like that of a baron of old in England. My house is, in fact, a fortress perched on a rock. I have a garrison of several hundred picked men, and as I am a much easier master than most of these Sikhs, who wring the last farthing from the cultivators, I could raise a thousand more at a couple of days' notice. Still the place is not impregnable; and in the present disturbed state of the land, where there is practically no law save that of might, I might be besieged by some powerful Rajah, and in the event of the place being taken there is no doubt what my fate would be.

" However, at present the great men are too intent upon quarrelling with each other to trouble about me, especially as they know that the place is not to be taken without hard

knocks. Moreover, although we who take service with foreign princes have no claim whatever for protection from our own countrymen, the fact of my being an Englishman is to some extent a safeguard. However, I want to put the case fairly before you; and if you come out here I will do my best for you—I will try to fill, as far as I can, your father's place. At the same time I warn you that the position here is a perilous one, and that there is no predicting how matters may turn out. My own opinion is, however, that our people can never permit the state of things that prevails here to go on, and will be forced to interfere before long. The Sikhs think that they are fully a match for us. I know better. They are brave, but so impatient of discipline, that although they look well enough on parade they would become a mere mob when fighting began.

" I need not say that the annexation of the Punjaub by the English would suit me admirably, but there will be a time of great trouble and danger before that can be accomplished. I daresay you wonder that I do not come home, having made, as you may suppose, a fortune amply sufficient to live upon there. But I do not think 1 shall ever do that; I have lived too long in India to settle down to English ways. Now that your poor father has gone I have not a single friend in England, and the humdrum life would kill me in no time, after having for four-and-twenty years lived in an atmosphere of intrigue, excitement, and danger.

"Now you know all about it, Percy, and can judge for yourself. By the time you get this letter you will be almost fifteen, and, as your father tells me that he has talked the matter over with you, capable of forming some sort of an opinion. As far as money goes, do not let that influence you one way or the other. The Old Lion was one of the most liberal of paymasters; and although one spends money freely out here, I took care to transmits considerable portion of the presents I received and the money I earned to a firm who act as my agents in Calcutta, so as to be in safety if at any time I

THROUGH THE SIKH WAR

had to make a bolt of it. That money will some day be yours whether you come out to me or not, for I have no one else to leave it to; and I am, by the same messenger who carries this letter to the British agent at Loodiana, sending instructions to my agents that in case of anything happening to me, the money is to be transferred to your name, and they are to communicate with the firm who are, as your father tells me, his lawyers in London.

"I don't know whether I am acting altogether wisely in agreeing to your coming out; and I certainly should not have done so if it had not been that your father, who must have been perfectly aware of the disturbed state of this country, evidently wished that it should be so. Well, if the life has its dangers, it has its advantages. In our army at home an officer is but one bit of a great machine; his life is a routine, and in peace time as dull as ditch-water. Here a man has, every day and every hour, need of his brains, his courage, quickness, and spirit. In war-time we fight the enemies of the Maharajah; in peace we have to combat the intrigues of our enemies and rivals, to guard against the dangers of assassination, to countermine the approaches of the enemy, to be ready for instant flight, or sudden favour and promotion.

"It is a man's life, Percy, and to a man of spirit worth a hundred existences at home. If I knew you personally I could form a better idea as to whether I ought to say to you, stay where you are, or, come here. Your father says that he thinks you have a fair share of pluck and determination, and that he considers you to be as sharp and shrewd as most boys of your age. As he was the last man in the world to speak one word beyond what he considered due, I take it that his estimate of your character is in no way too flattering.

" Think it over yourself, Percy. Can you thrash most fellows your own age ? Can you run as far and as fast as most of them? Can you take a caning without whimpering over it? Do you feel, in fact, that you are able to go through fully as

much as any of your companions? Are you good at planning a piece of mischief, and ready to take the lead in carrying it out? For though such gifts as these do not recommend a boy to the favour of his schoolmaster, they are worth more out here than a knowledge of all the dead languages. It is pluck and endurance, and a downright love of adventure and danger, that have made us the masters of the greater part of India, and will ere long make us rulers of the whole of it: and it is of no use anyone coming out here, especially to take service with one of the native princes, unless he is disposed to love danger for its own sake, and to feel that he is willing and ready to meet it from whatever quarter it may come. However, there is no occasion for you to make up your mind at present upon more than the point whether you will come out to me for three or four years; when it will be time enough to make your final decision. In any case you may always consider me your affectionate uncle, ROLAND."

Percy read the letter through very carefully, ft was something like what he had expected, for his father had in his last days spoken much to him of his brother.

"He was cut out for the life he has led, Percy," he had said to him. " He was the leader in all mischief at school; he had any amount of energy and life. He would not have made a good officer in the king's service; for he was impatient of authority, and would have been at loggerheads with the adjutant, and perhaps with the colonel, in no time. Once he set his mind to do a thing he would do it, whatever it was; and his straightforwardness and loyal nature would certainly win for him the confidence of any of these Indian princes, accustomed as they are to being surrounded with intriguers ready at all times to take sides with the most powerful, and to sell themselves to the highest bidder. He will tell you frankly whether he thinks you had better come out to him or stay at home. But mind, if you do go out he will expect a good deal of you, and if you don't do credit to him as well as to your-

self, he will have no hesitation in packing you off home again at an hour's notice."

Percy was pleased to see that, although he warned him of the difficulties and dangers of the position, his uncle clearly did wish him to come out to him, and he had no hesitation whatever in making his decision. After reading the letter for the third time, he placed it in his pocket and went across to the doctor's.

"I expected you, Groves," the latter said, when he was shown into his study. " So your uncle is willing to receive you, but leaves the choice entirely to yourself. That is what Messrs. Sims & Hammond said in their letter to me. Evidently they think it a very foolish business, but say that as they are bound by their instructions they have only to carry them out if you decide to go, but they hope that I shall use my influence to induce you to decide upon remaining here. I have no intention of doing so. It was for your father to make his choice, and he made it. He knows the country and he knows your uncle's character, and as he thought the opening a good one for you, I do not feel that it lies within my province to influence your decision in any way. I need hardly ask what the decision is. I know that you have been looking forward to the receipt of this letter, and the ardour with which you have worked at Hindustani, as your master tells me, shows that your wishes lay in that direction. So you have made up your mind to go?"

" Yes, sir. My uncle does not try to persuade me to come, but he says that he will be very glad to have me with him. He lives in a fortified castle with a lot of retainers, like a feudal baron, he says."

"Then I am quite sure no more need be said," the doctor replied smiling; "I don't think any boy could withstand the prospect of living in a fortified castle. And now I suppose you want to go and see the solicitors? "

"If you please, sir."

"Very well. I will give you leave off school this afternoon. If you find that there is a ship sailing shortly you will have many preparations to make, and as I am quite sure your thoughts will be too occupied to think of lessons you may consider them at an end. If, however, you find it will be some little time before you are able to sail, I shall expect you to put the matter altogether out of your head until the time approaches, and to work as hard as you can; though we will give up Latin, and you can devote yourself entirely to Hindustani. Let me see you when you return from the lawyer's. You know the way to London Bridge. You cross that, and anyone you meet will then direct you to Fenchurch Street. You had better have your dinner before you start."

Messrs. Sims & Hammond did not conceal from Percy their opinion that his decision to go out to join his uncle savoured of lunacy. "We are willing to carry out your father's instructions," the senior partner said, shrugging his shoulders. "We considered it our duty to express our opinion frankly on the subject to him. Having done that without avail, our duty in the matter is at an end. We find it a not unusual thing for our clients to prefer their own opinions to ours, not unfre-quently to their own cost. Since we have received your uncle's communication yesterday, we have made inquiries as to the vessels loading for Calcutta, and find that the India-man the Deccan will sail in ten days' time. That will, I take it, be sufficient time for you to make your preparations. One of our clerks will at once go with you to take your berth, and then accompany you to some outfitter's to get all that is requisite. Your father left with us a list of the clothing and other matters he considered would be required in the event of your going."

Five minutes later Percy set out in charge of an elderly clerk, and by the close of the afternoon the passage was taken and the whole of the outfit ordered, and Percy walked back to Dulwich quite overwhelmed at the extent of the wardrobe that

his father had deemed necessary for him for the voyage. Several suits of clothes had, in accordance with the instructions on the list, been ordered, of a size considerably too large for him at present. Major Groves had appended a note to the list, saying that he did not consider it necessary that a large stock of such clothes should be provided, as there would be no difficulty in having them made in India, and that, moreover, Percy would probably, to some extent, wear native attire.

The ten days passed rapidly. Percy, although nominally free from the school-room, nevertheless worked with ardour at his Hindustani.

"You have made great progress, Groves," his teacher said on the last day. " I should advise you strongly to work several hours a day at it during the voyage. Some of the passengers who are returning to India are sure to have with them native servants and ayahs, and you had best take every opportunity of speaking with them. You must remember that there are a large number of dialects, and even of distinct languages, in India; and it is probable that you will find your Hindustani of little use to you in Northern India. Still, it will greatly facilitate your learning the other languages, and most of the educated natives understand it, as, like French on the Continent, it is the general medium of communication between the natives of different parts of the country.

Possibly you may find among the servants on board a native of Northern India, and may be able to commence your study of Punjaubi with him."

Two days before the vessel sailed Percy went by appointment to the lawyer's office, and Mr. Hammond took him to the shipping office and introduced him to the captain of the Dec can..

" I will give an eye to the lad as far as I can, Mr. Hammond," Captain Grierson said; "though, to tell you the truth, I would almost as lief have a monkey as a boy to look after. Still 1 don't feel the responsibility as great as that of my young

lady passengers. Do what I may, they will indulge in flirtation, and I have to bear the brunt of the anger of the relatives to whom they are consigned in India, when they discover that my charges have already disposed of themselves on the voyage."

During those last days Percy was the object of the greatest envy and admiration of his school-fellows. To be going all the way out to India by himself was in itself splendid; but the idea that he was to live in a castle with armed retainers, and the possibility of a siege and all other sorts of unknown dangers, seemed almost too great a stroke of good fortune to fall to the lot of anybody. Most of his effects had been sent direct on board the Deccan, but he had obtained from the store where they had been deposited, the cases containing his father's rifles, double-barrelled gun and pistols, and the fact that he was the possessor of such arms greatly heightened the admiration of his companions.

But even the knowledge that the pistols were in his cabin, and the other arms stowed below with the greater portion of his belongings, scarcely sufficed to keep up his spirits as he stood, a solitary and rather forlorn boy, on the deck of the great ship as she warped out through the dock-gates.

The doctor had come down early to see him on board, but had been obliged to return at once to his duties at the school, and everyone but himself seemed to have friends to see them off. The entrance to the docks was crowded with people waving their handkerchiefs and shouting adieux to those on board, while many who were to land at Gravesend were on deck chatting with their friends. The captain stopped good-naturedly by his side for a moment as he passed along.

"All alone, Groves, eh? You will soon make friends, and I think you are really better off than those who haven't got over saying their last good-byes yet. I always think it is much better to finish all that sort of thing at home, instead of prolonging the pain. Here, Harcourt," he called to a young

fellow about sixteen, in a midshipman's dress, "you haven't anything to do just at present. Give an eye to this youngster; he is going out to join an uncle in India, and is all alone on board. Introduce him to the other midshipmen when you get an opportunity. I have told the steward to mess him with you; he will be much more comfortable there than he would be with the people in the cabin aft. You will like that arrangement, won't you, Groves? "

"Very much indeed, sir," Percy said, feeling as if a great load had been lifted off his mind. Harcourt led him down between decks to the ward-room, as they called it, where the third and fourth officers and the four midshipmen messed.

"This is our palace, Groves. A bit of a hole in comparison with the saloon, but a snug little den, too, when everything is going on well and everyone is in good temper. I will tell the others that the skipper has made you free of it. The third and fourth officers are both good fellows, and I think you will find it comfortable. If you don't, you have got the saloon to fall back upon."

"I am sure to find it comfortable," Percy said confidently. " I have come fresh from school, you know, and am not accustomed to luxuries; I should find it miserable among all those grown-up people. I only wish I was going out as a midshipman instead of a passenger, so as to have something to do."

" Ah, well, you can talk to the skipper about that. Perhaps he will put you on a watch if you ask him. I don't say the work is very lively, for it isn't; but I know that I should be very sorry to have to make the voyage with nothing to do but walk about with my hands in my pockets. However, I must go on deck now. We had our breakfast long ago; we dine at two bells, that is one o'clock. If you can't hold on until then I will get our steward to bring you a biscuit."

" I can hold on very well. I had a cup of tea and something to eat before I left."

Percy followed Harcourt on deck again, and feeling now more settled as to his position, was able to look on with interest and pleasure at what was being done around him. The passengers had settled themselves a little; some had got out their chairs, and were seated chatting in groups, but the ladies for the most part were below arranging their cabins. Men in couples walked up and down the waist smoking, or leaned against the bulwarks discussing the voyage and their mutual acquaintances. Most of the sails had now been set, for the wind was favourable, and the great ship was running fast down the river and was just passing Woolwich. A sailor, barefooted and with his trousers turned up to his knees, was sluicing the decks with water. Others were coiling up ropes. Others again, dressed more in accordance with Percy's ideas as to the neatness of a sailor's costume, were standing at the sheets and braces in readiness to trim the sails to port or starboard, as the sharp turns of the river brought the wind on one quarter or the other.

Percy was surprised at the silence that reigned among so many men, but he understood the reason when the sharp orders were shouted from the quarter-deck where the first officer was standing by the side of the pilot. Then there was a hauling of ropes and a creaking of blocks, and the towering pile of yards and sails swung over. Now and then the ship's course was suddenly changed to avoid some barge or smaller craft that got in her way, sometimes missing by the smallest margin running them down. On one or two of these occasions a mate shouted angrily down at those in charge of these craft, and these shouted as angrily back again. Once past Erith the river widened and the dangers of collision ceased, for the craft were all proceeding in the same direction; for the stream was now running too strongly for the barges to attempt to make their way against it, even by hugging the shore and keeping in back waters. At twelve o'clock the luncheon bell rang, and the passengers disappeared from deck. But Percy was -so

absorbed in watching the shore that he was quite surprised when Harcourt touched him on the shoulder and said:

"There are two bells, youngster. You must keep your ears open or you will be missing your meals; for they do not ring for us, and anyone who does not turn up to his grub goes without it."

The voyage was a very pleasant one to Percy Groves. The captain did not allow him to act as a volunteer midshipman; but it was not long before he ceased to regret this decision, for he found among the four or five native servants returning to India with their masters one from the Punjaub. The man's duties on board occupied but a very small portion of his time, as he had little to do except wait on his master at meals; and he was very glad to arrange, for what seemed to Percy a ridiculously small sum, to spend five or six hours a day in conversation with him. Accordingly, after breakfast and dinner the two took seats up in the bow, Percy on a low stool, the native squatted beside him, and there spent hours, at first in learning the Punjaubi equivalents for Hindustani words, and then, as time went on, in conversation.

The native knew a little Hindustani, and could get on fairly in English, so that they were able from the first to comprehend each other; and as Percy's former studies helped him materially, he picked up Punjaubi quickly, and by the end of the voyage was able to express himself in it with considerable freedom. He was always up early in the morning, and until breakfast-time chatted with any officers or midshipmen off duty, and sometimes with the early risers among the passengers— two or three of whom, when they found that the lad was a first-class passenger on his way out to India to join an uncle, became very friendly with him, being struck with the steady way in which he passed the greater portion of the day in preparing himself, as far as possible, for the life he was about to lead.

"Why don't you come aft, Groves?" one of them asked him.

VKKCY LEARNS THE PUNJAUBI LANGUAGE,

" I should feel altogether strange, sir. The two officers and the midshipmen are all very kind and friendly, and we live very well there, and I feel much more at home than I should do with the ladies. I have not been accustomed to ladies. I do not remember my mother, and for years I lived altogether at school. After my father came back, and I lived at home with him, only gentlemen came to the house. I like it all very much, and should not like to change. Besides, if I got to know a good many passengers, I might not be able to spend so much time in work; and I do so want when I join my uncle to be able to be useful to him, which I could not be if I did not know anything of the language."

" Well, I am sure, Groves, your uncle ought to be pleased when you join him to know how hard you have worked. It would be a very good thing if every young cadet and writer who went out would do as you do, and prepare himself for his work out there, instead of wasting six months in lounging about, trying to make himself agreeable to the women on board. He would not only find it very useful out there, but he would find it very profitable. For a young fellow who, on arrival, was able to speak one of the languages pretty fluently, would be certain to attract the notice of the authorities, and would find himself in a responsible and well-paid berth, while the others were kept at desks in Calcutta or Bombay, or sent out as assistants to unimportant posts.

" It is my servant who is teaching you, and he tells me that you are making wonderful progress, and that you already know as much of the language as many officers who have been in India for years. I can tell you, too, that you could not have taken up a more useful dialect than Punjaubi. At present, of course, the Punjaub is independent, and the consequence is there are very few officials who have taken the trouble to learn the language; but no one doubts that- the time is not very far distant when we shall have to interfere there, and in a few years we may have to take it over altogether.

need hardly say that there will be a great demand for officials able to speak the language; and should you enter the Company's service, you would have every chance of obtaining a post there of greater importance and profit than you could hope to reach after years of service under ordinary conditions.

" I myself am stationed in the province south of the Sutlej, which the Sikhs at any rate consider to be a part of the Pun-jaub, and am pretty well acquainted with what is going on at Lahore. I don't know your uncle personally, although of course I know him well by reputation. He was one of the best of the European officers in the Sikh service; and although, like all the others, he was dismissed at the bidding of the mutinous soldiery, I have always heard him spoken well of. He was popular among the men of the two regiments that he commanded, and bore an excellent reputation among the natives generally, abstaining from the high-handed exactions by which some of the foreign officers amassed large sums of money. He is said to have been prompt in action, to have maintained excellent order amongst his men, to have protected the natives against any acts of plunderng or misconduct, and the districts where he was stationed were contented and prosperous.

" Like most of the other foreign officers, he held himself altogether aloof from court intrigues. Doubtless they were perfectly right in doing so; but for all that, as matters have turned out, it might have been better for the Punjaub had these officers gone beyond their duties and thrown their whole weight into the scale in favour of some strong man who would have put a stop to the dissensions that if they continue will certainly bring ruin upon the country.

"However, their position was a very difficult one. The Sikh chieftains were always adverse to Runjeet Singh's policy of Europeanizing his army, and were extremely jealous of the favour he extended to the Europeans in his service; consequently the position of these officers was, from the moment of

V>

his death, an extremely delicate one. Moreover, it is probable that the Indian authorities would have viewed with considerable disfavour the passing of the affairs of the Punjaub into the hands of European adventurers, of whom only two or three were English. The foreigners, of course, would have had no sympathy whatever with our aims, and would indeed have been formidable opponents in case of trouble, their interests lying entirely in the maintenance of the present state of things in the Punjaub.

" You are going out to the most troubled portion of India, youngster; and I almost wonder at your uncle allowing you to come, for there will be a great convulsion there before matters finally settle down."

" So he told me when he wrote, sir. I am only going out to him till I get old enough to either go into the army or to enter the Company's service, if my father's friends can obtain a commission or a writership for me."

" Get a writership, my boy, if you have the chance. The civil service is vastly better paid than the military. Well, it may be that we shall be thrown together again out there. It is nearly time for our commissioner at Loodiana to go home for his furlough, and I think it very probable that I shall be appointed to his post during his absence, in which case I am pretty certain to be in communication with your uncle; and it may be that when the time comes I shall be able to lend you a helping hand to enter the service. If you stick to work as you are doing now, I shall certainly feel justified in recommending you as one who would prove a valuable young officer in the Punjaub if we become its masters, or on the frontier if the country still maintains its independence. In the meantime, if there be trouble in the Punjaub and you have to fly for your life, remember you will find a hearty welcome at Loodiana."

The voyage was free from any incidents of importance. The Deccan rounded the Cape without experiencing any

unusually bad weather, and except for one or two minor gales the weather was fine throughout the voyage.

Most of the passengers were delighted when she dropped anchor at last in the Hooghly, but much as Percy longed to see the wonders of India, he was almost sorry when the voyage came to an end, for the time had passed very pleasantly to him. This had been especially the case towards the latter portion; for his studies had increased in interest as he acquired a knowledge of the language, and by the end of the voyage he had come to know a good many of the passengers. His first friend, Mr. Fullarton, had spoken warmly to others in favour of the quiet lad, of whom they caught sight when they happened to stroll forward to smoke a cigar, occupied so intently upon his conversations with the native beside him.

"I hate book-worms," one of them had said when Mr. Fullarton had first spoken to him on the subject. "Give me a lad with pluck and spirit, and I don't care a snap of the finger whether he can construe Euripides or solve a problem in high mathematics. What we want for India are men who can ride and shoot, who are ready at any moment to start on a hundred-mile journey on horseback, who will scale a hill fort with a handful of men, or with half a dozen Sowars tackle a dacoit and his band. What do the natives care for our learning? It is our pluck and fighting powers that have made us their masters."

" That is all very true, Lyndhurst, and I thoroughly agree with you that of all ways of choosing officials for India examinations would be the very worst; but this lad is not a book-worm at all in your sense of the word. He knows that it will be of great advantage to him when he arrives in India to be able to speak the language, and he has accordingly set himself to do it with a dogged perseverance that would do credit to a man. Look how he has utilized the voyage, while the cadets and ensigns and young civilians have thrown away six months of their lives in absolute idleness. Besides, I am

sure the boy does not lack either pluck or spirit. I am up a good deal earlier than you are in the morning, and I see him going about the rigging like a monkey. He is quite as much at home up there as are any of the midshipmen, some of whom have been four or five years at sea. I saw him sky-larking the other evening with two or three of them, and I can tell you he quite held his own. He is certainly a favourite with all the officers. I should be ready to wager that when the time comes he will turn out well, whatever circumstances he may fall upon. He is a merry fellow too, and has one of the most infectious laughs I ever heard; he is no more like your ideal book-worm than I am."

The only time that Percy came aft and mixed with the other passengers was when they practised rifle or pistol shooting, sometimes at empty bottles thrown into the sea, sometimes at bottles swinging from one or other of the yardarms. This amusement was practised three or four times a week, for it was a matter of importance to every man, military or civilian, to be a good shot. It was useful in the hunting of tigers and other big game. Life might depend upon proficiency with a pistol if attacked by a fanatic or in a brush with dacoits, while for men likely to be engaged with the fierce tribesmen of the hills, or in conflict with Sikh, Beloochee, Pathan, or Afghan, a quick eye and a steady hand were essential.

Encouraged by Mr. Fullarton, Percy got out his pistols on the first day when the practice began, and never missed an opportunity afterwards. "Never mind the rifle," his friend said; "you are not likely to do tiger-hunting at present, and you will have plenty of time and opportunities for that later on. Stick to your pistol practice; you are going among a wild set of people, where the knife is readily drawn in a quarrel, and where men do not hesitate to rid themselves of a foe or a rival by assassination. Practise with your pistols steadily on every occasion here, and keep it up afterwards; it may be of more use to you than everything you have learnt at school from the

day when you first went there. You know I approve of your sticking to your Punjaubi, but you can well spare an hour three or four times a week; and although it may do you more good in your future career to be a good linguist than to be a good pistol-shot, the last may be the means of saving your life, and unless you can do that, your study of languages will be so much time thrown away."

And so by the end of the voyage Percy became a very fair shot with the pistol, and indeed there were few of the passengers who could break a swinging bottle more frequently than he. He was surprised, when the anchor dropped, at the eagerness evinced by the majority of the passengers to get on shore. He himself looked on quietly, for the captain had said to him early that morning, "There is no use in your hurrying ashore, Groves; you know no one there, and an hour earlier or later will make no difference to you. I shall be going off this afternoon and will take you with me, and after I have been to the shipping office I will go with you to the people you have letters for. I know them personally, and an introduction from me will probably interest them more in you than will the formal letter those lawyer fellows are likely to have written."

The captain's introduction was of great benefit to Percy. The agent took an interest in him, and put him up at his house for a fortnight. At the end of that time he arranged for him to take a passage up country in a native craft that two or three officers had chartered to convey them to Delhi, beyond which town there would be no difficulty in hiring a boat to the point at which he would disembark, and thence travel up by road. He enjoyed his journey much, although it occupied a considerable time. He could have gone very much faster by road; but time-was no particular object, and the agent thought that he would be cheated right and left in his bargains for vehicles, and might not improbably have some of his baggage stolen. Percy greatly preferred the passage by river, and when finally he had to take to a close vehicle, he congratulated himself that he had accomplished the greater part of the journey free from the dust, heat, and inconveniences of land travel. He learned that he would have done much better had he taken his passage from England to the other side of India and ascended the Indus, but he supposed that his uncle had directed him to come via Calcutta because his own agent was there and could make the arrangements for him, and he perhaps considered that the passage thence by water would be much safer than one through the recently-conquered province of Scinde.

This was indeed, as he afterwards learnt, the reason why Calcutta had been chosen instead of Bombay. There had, about the time his uncle wrote, been a number of robberies, sometimes accompanied by murder, of persons travelling up the Indus in boat, and it was for this reason the longer and safer route up the Jumna had been chosen. He left the boat at Sultanpoor, and had about a hundred miles of travel thence through Umballah and Sirhind to Loodiana, a station in what was known as the protected district. Here on the frontier of the Punjaub were stationed some British troops with a Resident, whose special duty was to keep the government informed of what was going on upon the other side of the Sutlej.

The agent had advised him on his arrival at Loodiana to go straight to the Residency.

"It is probable that your uncle will have written to the Resident about your coming, and that instructions as to the best course for pursuing your journey may be awaiting you there. It is a long way from Loodiana to his place, which lies quite in the north of the Punjaub, and but a short distance from the Afghan frontier. He will know about what time you will arrive, and may even have sent down one of his officers to accompany you on the way. He could not, of course, guess that you would know any of the languages, and it would be

THROUGH THE SIKH WAR

impossible for you, speaking nothing but English, to make your way alone through the Punjaub. Even as it is, I should advise you, should you on arriving at Loodiana find no one there from your uncle, to send up word that you have arrived, and to wait quietly, even if it be a month, till you hear from him."

CHAPTER II

THE SHADOW OF WAR

T EAVING the cart with his luggage a short distance away r L* Percy entered the office of the Residency, and giving his name to a clerk said that he was desirous of speaking to the Resident.

The clerk on his return from the inner room requested Percy to follow him. An officer was sitting at a desk. He iooked up with a smile as the lad entered, and Percy was astonished to see Mr. Fullarton, to whom he had said goodbye on board the Deccan.

"You did not expect to see me here, Groves?" he said as he shook him cordially by the hand.

" No indeed, sir, I had not the slightest idea that you had left Calcutta. I am glad indeed to see you."

"I only stopped there a few hours," the officer said. "As soon as I got to Government House I was told that Macpher-son was ill, and that I must travel up at full speed to relieve him, so I started next morning and travelled as fast as horses could take me up the country. I have been here for more than three weeks. I have not forgotten you, and as soon as I arrived here I sent off a chit to your uncle to tell him that you had landed at Calcutta, and would probably be here in the course of a fortnight or three weeks. Two days ago one of his native officers with an escort of sixteen men turned up

here. They are encamped on the plain over there. You will know the tent by a blue flag flying before it.

" I told your uncle that I had made your acquaintance on board the ship, and that I thought he would be very well pleased with you. I did not tell him anything about your having picked up so much Punjaubi, but left it for you to give him a pleasant surprise. Of course you will put up here for to-night. I shall be knocking off work in a quarter of an hour, and in the meantime you may as well go and have your bath, after which you will feel more comfortable. I will send a man across to your fellows to tell them you have arrived, and will be ready to start in the morning. By the way, I think it would be as well if you went over there at once ; it would please them, and there is nothing like making a good impression. My buggy will be at the door in ten minutes, and I will drive you out there. So you had better have 'a preliminary wash now, and can take your bath after we get back."

Touching the bell a servant entered. Mr. Fullarton gave him orders to take Percy to a room, to have what boxes he required carried up there, and to pile the rest in the hall. By the time Percy had got rid of some of the dust of travel, and changed his travelling suit for another, the Resident was ready, and they were soon driving over the sandy plain in a light trap drawn by a wiry-looking native pony. In a few minutes they reached a small tent, before which waved a blue flag. As they approached a stir was seen. A native officer ran out of the tent, ranged his men in military order, and placing himself in front of them saluted as the Resident drove up.

"Good afternoon, Nand Chund; I have brought the colonel's nephew over to see you. He has just arrived, and will be ready to start with you to-morrow, but even before eating he wished to see the officer whom his uncle had chosen as his escort."

The Sikh raised his hand to his cap in salute to Percy, and said in his native tongue: "All happiness to the nephew of my good lord! "

"Thank you, Nand Chund," Percy replied in the same tongue, " I am sure that you must be an officer in whom my uncle has great trust and confidence or he would not have chosen you for such a mission."

The Sikh looked greatly surprised at being thus answered in his own language.

"I did not know," he said, "that the young sahib had acquired our tongue. My lord told me you would not understand me, and that I should have to explain to you by signs anything that it was necessary for you to know."

" I speak your language but poorly at present, but I hope to do so well before I have been long with you," Percy answered. "My uncle was well, I hope, when you left him? "

" He was well, sahib; though much troubled by the machinations of powerful ones who are his enemies; but his heart was light at the news that you would soon be with him."

After a little further conversation Percy drove off with Mr. Fullarton, after having, at a hint from the latter, handed to the officer twenty rupees, to be laid out in providing a feast for the troopers.

"They will all be as drunk as hogs to-night," Mr. Fullarton said; " the Sikhs are one of the few races in India who drink to excess. They do so from the highest to the lowest. The Old Lion himself used to be drunk every night. However, as they will have a good meal before setting-to at the liquor, you will see that they will all be as fresh and bright in the morning as if they had touched nothing stronger than tea. They have wonderful constitutions, and after a few hours' sleep shake off the effects of a carouse that would make an Englishman ill for three or four days."

After an hour's drive they returned to the Residency. As they entered the house Percy was greeted by his former instructor, who had been out when he first arrived, and who now conducted him to his room.

"It is far better here than on board the ship, sahib," he said. "There Ram Singh was of no account, even the common sailors pushed and jostled him; here he is Fullarton Sahib's butler, and gives orders to all the servants."

"No doubt you feel it in that way," Percy laughed. "I feel it is better because here is a great cool room and quiet, and a bath ready for me without having to wait for an hour for my turn. It is certainly very much more comfortable, but there are drawbacks too. There was no dust on board ship, no occasion for an armed guard, no fear of disturbance or troubles."

"That is so, sahib; but what would life be worth if sometimes we did not have a change and adventure. As I have told you, I have had my share of it, and now I am well content to be the head servant of the Burra-sahib. But my lord is young, and it is well for him that he should learn to bear himself as a man, and to face danger."

" Well, it may be so, Ram Singh, but just at present it seems to me that I should prefer a peaceful life for a few years."

"The sooner a cockerel learns to use his spurs, the better fighting bird he will turn out," the man said sententiously.

"Yes, that is all very well," Percy replied. "But if he gets "badly mauled when he is a cockerel he is likely to shirk fighting afterwards."

After taking his bath and dressing himself in a suit of white linen, Percy went down to dinner. He was pleased to find himself alone with Mr. Fullarton, who in the course of the evening told him much more than he had hitherto known of the state of affairs in the Punjaub.

"Things look very bad," he said. "But it is possible that they may go on for months and even years before the crisis comes. As to this, however, your uncle will be able to tell you more than I can. Mine is, of course, the official view of matters, gleaned from the reports of men in our pay at Lahore and other places in the Punjaub. The reports of such men.

however, are always open to grave suspicion. .As they take bribes from us they may take bribes from others, or may be are in some way interested in deceiving us. Your uncle will doubtless be much better informed. Although he has taken no active part in the plots and conspiracies that have been continually going on ever since the death of Runjeet Singh, he must have been more or less behind the scenes throughout, and will certainly have tried and trusted agents at Lahore.

" At present you are only interested in these matters as far as they concern the safety of your uncle and yourself. Still it is always useful in a country like this to have an insight into what is going on around you. Should there be trouble, remember that the Sikhs value courage, quickness, and decision above all things. I am not supposing for a moment that you are likely to show the white-feather, still you may be involved in danger that would shake the nerves of hardened men. The thing to remember is always to assume an air of courage and coolness. To show weakness would forfeit the respect of your own people, and would in no way alter the fate that would befall you if you fell into the hands of your foes. You know the old saying—'Assume a virtue if you have it not.' That you should be alarmed in such a position would be only natural, but you must if possible conceal the fact, and must nerve yourself to put on as great an air of coolness and indifference as you can muster. Remember there are very few men who do not feel horribly uncomfortable when exposed to great dangers, and that bravery exists not so much in having no feeling of fear as of concealing all expression of it.

" When you hear a man boasting that he has never felt fear, and that he enjoys being under fire, take my word for it he is a liar. In the heat of battle, and especially in the excitement of a cavalry charge, the sensation of fear is lost; but in the preliminary stage I never knew a man yet who, speaking honestly, would not confess that he felt horribly nervous. I will not keep you up any longer, you have had a long journey

to-day and must be early in bed. You will be called before daybreak, for you may be sure your men will be here before the sun is up, and they will be gratified to find that you are prepared to be off. I need not repeat now what I told you on board the ship, that should you have to fly for your life you will meet with a warm welcome here."

It was still dark when Percy was aroused by Ram Singh.

"It is time to get up, sahib. I have water boiling, and there will be a cup of tea ready for you as soon as you have had your bath. The bheesti is outside with the water-skin."

"All right! " Percy said, jumping out of bed. "Send him in."

Taking a bath consisted of squatting down in the corner of the room, where the floor was made to slope to a hole which carried off the water poured from a skin over the head of the bather. As he dressed, Percy drank a cup of tea and ate a couple of biscuits, while Ram Singh packed up his trunk again. He had just finished when he heard the trampling of horses. He at once went out.

"You are in good time, Nand Chund."

"It would not have done to have kept the sahib waiting," the Sikh said, " though we scarce expected to find him ready for us so soon."

He then ordered the baggage-horses to be brought up, and four strong ponies were led forward. Percy's trunks, which had all been made of a size suited to such transport, were firmly lashed one on each side of each saddle. When this was done a handsome horse was brought forward for Percy. He was about to turn to enter the house to say good-bye to Mr. Fullarton, who had the night before told him he should be up before he started, when the Resident made his appearance.

"I always rise before the sun," he said, "and take a drive or a ride, and am back before it gets too hot for pleasure. Then I have a bath, change of clothes, and am ready for my work. Early morning and evening are the only times that life is enjoyable here, and unless one takes exercise then one cannot expect to keep in health. Good-bye, Groves. Tell your uncle to keep me informed of what is going on whenever he gets an opportunity. Take care of yourself, and, whatever comes, keep your head clear and your wits sharpened. Many a life is thrown away from want of prompt decision at a critical moment."

Percy shook hands with his kind friend, and then leapt into the saddle without putting his foot into the stirrup, a trick he had learned at the riding-school. A murmur of approval ran through the men, who muttered to themselves, " He understands a horse; a brisk young fellow, he will do no discredit to our lord." Then he took his place by the side of Nand Chund, waved his hand to Mr. Fullarton, and started. His companion at once put his horse to a hand gallop.

"Surely you do not mean to travel far at this speed?" Percy said. "The pack-animals will not be able to keep up with us."

"They will follow, sahib. You see I have left four men in charge of them."

"Yes, and you have eight men here. Where are the other four, for I counted sixteen yesterday? "

"They started before dark, sahib, with the four other baggage animals. Two of them we shall find when we halt for food, when the sun gets high. They will have pitched a tent in the shade of some tree, and will have the meal cooked in readiness for us. The other two will have gone forward to the point where we shall rest for the night. They have another tent, and will have the evening meal in readiness. So it will be each day. They will travel by night, we by day. At the end of three days we shall have reached a point where care will be a necessity, and will then travel in a body."

"But from whom have we reason to fear danger?" Percy asked.

"We do not fear danger," the Sikh replied, "but we prepare to meet it. In the first place there are robbers—bands of men who acknowledge no master, such as deserters from the army, fugitives who have excited the enmity of some powerful chief, and criminals who have escaped justice. Such men form bands, rob villages, plunder well-to-do peasants, and waylay, rob, and murder travellers. These are the ordinary foes; all those who journey have to prepare for them, and they are not really dangerous to a well-armed party. Then, again, there are the bands by profession robbers, but who are for the time hired by some powerful or wealthy sirdar who wishes to gratify a private spite. Openly perhaps he would not dare to move, and he therefore remains in the background, and hires bands of robbers to do his business. Such bands are far more formidable than those composed of ordinary marauders, for they are of a strength proportioned to the object they have to accomplish, and may even number hundreds.

" It is these against whom we have to take precautions. My lord your uncle has powerful enemies, and these doubtless employ spies, and are made aware of all that passes in his stronghold. Should they have learned that he was expecting your arrival, they would of course see that your capture would be a valuable one, as they could work on him through you. At any rate the departure of my band is sure to be noticed, and though we travelled by a circuitous route we may probably have been tracked to Loodiana. Besides, they might think that I had some important mission to the British Resident there, and that I may be the bearer of some letter that might enable them to work my master's ruin, and so will spare no pains to wrest it from me.

" For the first three days we do not follow the route leading to my lord's stronghold, consequently there is little fear of an ambush; but during the last five days of the journey, when we are making for the fortress, we shall have to sleep with one eye open, to travel by unfrequented roads, and for the most part

by night. The colonel would have come himself to meet you, but in the first place his visit to Loodiana would be seized upon by his enemies as a proof that he was leagued with the British, and in the second his presence is required in the castle, where, so long as he is present, there is little fear of any sudden surprise or attack, but were he away some traitor might corrupt a guard or open a gate, and thus let in the troops of an enemy."

" But there is no civil war, Nand Chund. How then could a chief venture to attack my uncle? "

"There is no war," the Sikh repeated, "but the sirdars never hesitate to collect their followers and attack a rival when they have a chance. Even in the days of Runjeet Singh this was so; for although his hand was a heavy one, it was easy to bribe those about him to place the matter in a favourable light, and a handsome present would do the rest. But since the Lion has passed away there has been no power in the land. The government has been feeble, and the great sirdars have done as it pleases them, so there is everywhere rapine and confusion. Those who are strong take from those who are weak: the traders who prospered and grew rich in the old days now fly the land or bury their wealth, and assume the appearance of poverty; the markets are deserted, and towns flourishing under Runjeet are now well-nigh deserted."

" But why have they a special animosity against my uncle? "

"First because he is a European, secondly because he is wealthy, thirdly because those who fly from the extortion or the tyranny of others find a refuge with him, lastly because the district under his charge is flourishing and prosperous while others are impoverished. Merchants elsewhere clamour for the rights that he gives those under his protection, and for taxes as light as those imposed by him in his district."

"But I thought that all Europeans had been deprived of commands," Percy said.

"That is true, but in this country a man only surrenders a

profitable post when he can no longer hold it. Even Runjeet Singh's orders to governors to surrender their posts to others were often disobeyed, and he was obliged to march armies to enforce them. It is far more so now. Three years ago my lord was nominally deprived of his command of the district as well as that of his troops by the orders of the court at Lahore, but he was too wise to obey. Had he opened the gates he would assuredly have been taken a prisoner to Lahore, and there have been put to death; so he held on, and none have cared to undertake the work of turning him out.

"Still the man appointed as his successor is, we may be sure, only waiting his opportunity. He belongs to the family of one of the most powerful of the princes—one who could put ten thousand men in the field; but the colonel has nearly two thousand good soldiers, and such strong walls that with these he could repulse an open attack by three times that number. Besides this all the district is in his favour. They dread nothing so much as that another should take his place, and the news that an army was advancing would at once swell his force by three thousand fighting men. Moreover, he has allies among the hill tribes who have never, save under the pressure of force, acknowledged the authority of Lahore. It is not until his rival's relations have made some compact with another sirdar equally powerful that they are likely to attack us openly.

"Treachery, however, is always to be feared, and still more the knife of the assassin. We believe that the soldiers can be trusted to a man; but who can tell? Gold is very powerful, and among two thousand there must be some who would sell their dearest friend were the bribe sufficiently large."

" But they say that the power of the nobles is broken, and that it is the army that is master," Percy remarked.

"That is so. The soldiers are the lords of the Punjaub. Runjeet Singh's policy was to strengthen the army, which under its foreign officers was always faithful to him. After

his death there was no strong hand, and the force which the Old Lion had trained to conquer his foes turned upon the country and became its master. They clamoured for the dismissal of all foreign officers, for increase of pay, for the right to choose their own leaders, and all these things they obtained. There is no longer discipline or order. They oppress the people, they dictate terms to the court, they can make or unmake maharajahs. If at present they are quiet, it is because they have everything they can ask for. Thus then there is no one to control the sirdars, who can do as it pleases them, if only they keep on good terms with the leaders of the army. That would matter but little, but when they wish to attack each other they have but to buy the services of a regiment or two and the thing is done. There lies the danger of our lord.

"Those most hostile to him would not dare to attack with their own followers, but they will sooner or later obtain the assistance of some of the military chiefs; the more so that these are hostile themselves to our lord because he is a foreigner, and at present the cry is, death to the foreigner. It is only because the colonel had so good a name in the army, —for all knew that although nowhere was discipline more strict, he was always just and kindly, that no man was punished without cause, that he had no favourites, that he oppressed none, and used all the influence he possessed with the old maharajah to obtain the pay for his men regularly,—that the military chiefs have so far failed to get the soldiers to consent to any movement against him.

" Besides, the troops are aware that he is a brave leader, and know that his men will die in his defence. Therefore, it would need a higher bribe than usual to induce them to risk their lives in a struggle from which they would gain nothing. It is far easier to revolt for extra pay than to obtain the money by an attack on the colonel's fortress. Thus, for aught we know, it may be years before serious trouble comes. It will depend upon what events occur. At present the soldiers are well content to do nothing but eat and drink at the expense of the people. In time they will become restless, and then, who knows, they may attack and plunder the strong places, or they may make war upon the English. They believe that they are invincible. They have an immense number of guns, and they think that because the Sikhs have conquered Cashmere and wrested territory from the Afghans, and hold all the country north of the Sutlej, nothing can withstand them. I know nothing, I am but an ignorant man as to all things outside our country; but I know that the English conquered Scinde although its sirdars and soldiers were many and brave, that they made themselves masters of Afghanistan, and even after their great misfortune there came back and again took Cabul and punished the Afghans; and I say to myself, Why should the Sikhs want to fight this people, who do not interfere with them, and who have always respected the treaties they have made with us?

"The Old Lion, who feared no one and who spread his rule far and wide, always kept friends with thc English, although most of his chiefs would have taken advantage of their trouble in Afghanistan to go to war with them. He knew the power of the foreigners, and was always ready to engage white officers to teach his soldiers. He had a wiser head than any of the soldiers who are now ready to raise the cry of war with the English; and I know our lord's opinion is, that should we engage in a struggle with his people we shall assuredly be beaten. But what avail are these things with men puffed up with pride, and with the belief that they are invincible. It is certain that some day or other the army will clamour for war with the English, and who is there to say them nay? Not the boy, Maharajah Dhuleep Singh, nor the Ranee, his mother and guardian. Then we shall see how things will go."

"There is no doubt how things will go," Percy said. "The English will conquer the country, as they have all the other parts of India that have tried their strength with them."

"They have never fought a country like ours," the officer said a little proudly. "The army is a hundred and fifty thousand strong, and the chiefs must all join, so there will be two hundred thousand at least, and all good fighting men. They are well armed and have vast stores of guns and ammunition: they have been taught to fight in European fashion. We are told that if all the British troops in India came against them they would number scarce fifty thousand."

"That may be," Percy agreed, "but they would win—they always have won, and often against odds quite as great. Besides, when your two hundred thousand men are in the field you would have your whole fighting power, while if it were necessary England could send out army after army as strong as that now in India. How far is it to our first halting-place ? The sun is beginning to get very hot."

" It is three hours' ride from Loodiana. Going at an easy pace we shall be there in another hour."

Percy was heartily glad when his companion pointed out a yellow speck under a clump of trees and told him it was the tent. " I brought with us only small tents, such as the soldiers use on their expeditions," he said, "so -as to excite the less attention; they are mere shelters from the sun and night air."

"That is all we want, Nand Chund."

" They weigh only a few pounds, sahib, and can be carried by a horseman in addition to his ordinary baggage. We have three or four of them with us, so that we can at any time pitch one should we arrive at a halting-place before the baggage animals."

A quarter of an hour later Percy was lying under the shade of the tent, the sides of which .were tied up to permit the air to pass freely through. In a short time tiffin was served, consisting of an excellent pillau of fowl, a dish of meat prepared with savoury condiments, followed by an assortment of delicious fruit. The drink consisted of water cooled in a porous jar, flavoured with the juice of a slightly acid fruit.

" I would have brought wine," the officer said apologetically, "but my lord your uncle said that you would not be accustomed to it, and that, riding in the sun, it was better you should take only cooling liquors. He has sent, however, a tin filled with an herb that with hot water makes a drink of which he is very fond; it is sent up to him in a chest from Calcutta. He said you would know what to do with it. He calls it tea."

"I am glad of that," Percy said. "There is no difficulty in preparing it. It needs but boiling water poured over it. I will have some this evening. I am very fond of it too, but I am accustomed to drink it with sugar and milk."

"We have sugar," the man said, "but milk will be difficult to obtain. Our master never uses it with his tea."

"I shall get accustomed to it," Percy said, "though I am sure I sha'n't like it so well at first. At what time do we move on again?"

"In about six hours, if it so pleases you. It is ten o'clock now, by four the sun will have lost some of its power."

" How many hours' ride shall we have? "

"Three hours at a canter. We are doing but a short journey to-day, as it is the first. After this we shall never be less than eight hours in the saddle; that is, if it is not too much for you."

"Oh, it is not too much," Percy replied, "but I shall feel rather stiff for the first day or two, after not having ridden for so many months; but I certainly should be glad to travel as much as possible in the evening."

" We can do that, sahib, for we shall have a moon for the next week."

"How may days will it take us altogether? "

" We are now but half a mile from Aliwal, where we shall cross the Sutlej, and shall encamp to-night near Sultanpoor. As I told you, we are to-day travelling as if going to Lahore. To-morrow we shall strike north and shall camp near Adinana-gar. The next morning we shall cross the Ravee, and shall then turn to the north-west, pass by Kailapore and Sealkote, cross the Chenab and Jhelum rivers, then ride north some forty miles, where we shall strike the hills and reach our lord's district, which extends some thirty miles either way among the hills. This is the route by which I hope to travel, but if I hear of danger by the way we shall of course strike off to the right or left as may be most convenient. The journeys are from thirty to forty miles a day. Our horses could, of course, go much farther, but we must regulate our speed by that of the baggage animals. We shall be fully a week upon the road. Coming down we did it in five days in order to be in time for your arrival."

"Those eight trunks are not all filled with my things," Percy said with a laugh. "You must not think I travel about with all that luggage. Four of them are mine, the other four are filled with things my uncle wrote to his agents at home to get for him and send out with me. I have no idea what is in them."

"The baggage is nothing if we were travelling in peaceful times," the Sikh said, "but at present the lighter one goes the less likelihood of being meddled with. As it is, you will not know your boxes when we come up with the baggage animals this evening. It would never have done to be travelling through the Punjaub at present with boxes of English make; they would be looted by the first party of soldiers who came across them. I had them measured the evening you came to my tent, and carpenters were at work all night to make boxes that would contain them. Then the boxes would be sewn up in matting before the animals started this morning, and marked with native marks to the address of a merchant in Jummoo. The road for the first four days is the same as if we were going there. Thus if the matting is cut, the native box will be seen inside.

" The four men with them are dismounted, and their horses

led by those who came on here ahead of us. Jummoo was the safest place that we could choose to address the packages to, for Ghoolab Singh is one of the most powerful of our chiefs; the most powerful perhaps. He is brother of Dhyan Singh, who was Runjeet Singh's chief counsellor, and uncle of Heera Singh, who succeeded his father after his murder by Ajeet Singh. He it is who is your uncle's principal enemy, as it is his son who obtained the appointment of governor of the district. Baggage directed to a merchant in Jummoo is therefore less likely to be interfered with than if intended for another town, as complaints laid before Ghoolab by an influential merchant might cause inquiries to be made and punishment to be dealt out to those who have interfered with his goods in transit. Ghoolab's name is still powerful, even with the soldiers, and his influence among the leaders is quite sufficient to obtain some sort of redress for injuries committed upon those wealthy enough to pay for his protection."

" It seems a curious state of things to anyone coming straight from England," Percy said, "where the law protects everyone, and where the richest and most powerful dare not wrong the V__poorest peasant."

"That is good," the Sikh said thoughtfully, twirling his moustache, "but in that case how can the rich obtain any advantage from their money? How, indeed, can they become rich?"

"By the rents they obtain from those who cultivate their estates; from mines and from money invested in public funds or companies."

"And what do they find for their retainers to do? "

"They have no retainers; that is, no armed retainers. Of course, they have servants who do the service of their houses and look after the stables and gardens and so on, but they do not carry arms themselves, nor do any of their servants."

" But if they are wronged by a neighbour, what do they do then?"

"They simply go to the courts of law for redress, just as anyone else would do. The cases are heard and the decisions given by the judges, and the richest man has to obey them just the same as the poorest."

"It sounds very good," the Sikh said thoughtfully, "but it seems to me that your country must be a very bad one for fighting men and those who live by adventure."

" Those who want to fight can enter the army and fight the battles of their country abroad, while those fond of adventure can go to sea or can visit wild countries, or can go out to the colonies, where it is a hard, rough life, but where an active man can acquire wealth."

" Now the sahib had better lie down and get a sleep till it is time to be moving," Nand Chund said rising. "My men are all asleep already, it is getting too hot even to talk."

CHAPTER III

AT THE CASTLE

FOR four days the . journey was pursued without incident. They had brought with them a sufficient store of provisions for the journey, and travelled by by-paths, avoiding villages as much as possible, halting for five or six hours in the middle of the day, and performing the greater portion of the distance after sunset. Just as they had started for their evening ride on the fifth day two horsemen overtook them and reined up as they did so.

"We have missed our path," one said, "can you tell us how far it is to a place where we can find shelter for the night?"

"Ten miles farther you will find yourselves in the main road, a mile from Sealkote."

" If you are bound thither we shall be glad to ride with you for protection," one said. "There are many parties of bud-mashes about, but they will hardly interfere with so strong and respectable a company."

"We travel slowly," Nand Chund said, "and shall not reach Sealkote to-night. When the beasts are tired we shall halt."

" We are in no hurry, and do not care whether we reach the town to-night o* to-morrow morning, therefore if you have no

objection we will share your bivouac. Far better to lose a few hours than to run the risk of having our throats cut."

"As you will," Nand Chund said. "You are very welcome to stay with us, if it so pleases you."

As they rode the strangers chatted with Nand Chund, Percy reining back his horse and riding among the men. After travelling about five miles Nand Chund ordered a halt, the baggage animals were unloaded, a tent pitched, and two of his men began to prepare a meal, while the others looked to the horses. The two strangers also dismounted and spoke for a time together, then one said to the Sikh officer:

" You will think that we do not know our own minds, but we have concluded that as the moon is bright and our horses fairly fresh we will push on to Sealkote."

"It is for you to decide," Nand Chund said. "You are welcome to stay with us, and free to ride on if you prefer it." After a few inquiries about the way the two men mounted and rode on. As soon as the sound of the horses' hoofs became faint Chund spoke to one of his men, who immediately left the party and glided away to the right.

"I have sent him to watch them," Nand Chund said to Percy; "I warrant they will halt before they are gone half a mile. My man will keep in the fields till he gets near them, and will bring us word if they move on."

"What do you suspect them to be? "

" I have no doubt they are enemies. They may have been on our track since we started, or only for the last day's march, but they are watching us no doubt."

"What makes you think so, Nand Chund?"

"Many things. It was unlikely that they would be upon this by-path instead of on the main road. That they should offer to stop with us when they were so well mounted, was singular, also their change of intentions when they found that we were going to halt. Their conversation too was not that of honest men."

"What did they talk about?"

" They said they were coming from Lahore, and talked of all the doings there."

"What was the harm in that? " Percy asked in surprise.

" Only that it was natural when falling in with a party like ours that they should have asked many questions. Whence we came, and whither were we going? What merchandise we •carried? Were we trading on our own account, or were we carrying goods for some trader? How was it that I had such a strong armed party with me ? These are the questions honest men would ask, but they spoke only of their own doings and asked no word about ours. I have no doubt whatever that they know who I am and who you are, and that all they really wanted to learn was where we intended to stop. Now they are, I am certain, watching us, or probably one may have ridden off to carry the news and fetch their band, while the other remains to see that we do not move our camp."

"What are you going to do, Nand Chund?"

" I shall wait till Ruzam returns. If they should have ridden straight on we shall move at once; if they both remain on watch, and it seems that they are likely to do so till morning, I shall, when Ruzam returns, go off with four of the men, and making a circuit come down upon them from behind and despatch them. If one goes and the other remains on watch, Ruzam can be trusted to give a good account of him before he returns here."

"But it would be terrible to kill two men who have nol; actually harmed us," Percy said, shocked at this, his first experience of the customs of the Punjaub.

"They have not done us much harm yet," Nand Chund said grimly; "but they are endeavouring to draw us into an ambush, which will cost us our lives and you your liberty, and perhaps our lord his fortress and his life. Therefore I shall have no more hesitation in killing them than I should in shoot' ing a lurking tiger."

Three hours passed, and then Ruzam glided into the camp.

"What is your news, Ruzam?"

"They have just left," the man said; "I have been close to-them all the time listening to their talk. They have been watching you from a spot half a mile away. They would have come up to hear what you were saying, but neither would stay behind alone, saying what was true enough, that we also might be watching them, and if they separated they might be taken singly. For the same reason neither would stay while the other rode forward. I could have shot one, but I could not have been sure of killing the second before he rode off, and so thought it better to be quiet. At last they concluded that you had really encamped for the night, and that they could safely ride off with the news. It was unfortunate that the moonlight was so bright, for it prevented my crawling up close enough to attack them before they could mount."

" Did you hear what roads are likely to be beset? "

"No, they did not enter into particulars; but they said that they would be sure to have you, as there would be parties on every road. It is the young sahib they are anxious to capture; and the orders were strict that he was to be taken unharmed, and that all the rest of us were to be killed or taken prisoners."

"We will delay no longer," Nand Chund said. "We will leave the tent standing and put some fresh wood on the fire. They can be at Sealkote in an hour, and perhaps will return with a party without delay. Load up the horses and let us be off. Did you hear them say where they have come from, Ruzam? "

"Yes, sahib, there were six of them at Loodiana. They must have got news from someone in the fortress of the- object of our journey, they arrived there on the day after you did. The morning we started one man was sent off with the news while the others followed us, not together but singly, so that every road we could take should be followed and our steps

traced. Each night one man has been despatched with the news of our halting-places."

"You see, sahib," Nand Chund said to Percy, "I was not wrong in saying that our ride would be a dangerous one, and truly so far our enemies have been more than a match for us; now we must see if we cannot double upon them."

As soon as the baggage was packed the party mounted, and to Percy's surprise the officer led the way back along the road by which they had come.

"It is of no use our going forward," he said. "Doubtless they will take some little time in getting the members of the band, who are at Sealkote, together and making a start—we can calculate on at least an hour for that—but that only gives us three hours' start. They will, I hope, make sure that we have continued our journey, and will ride on fast so as to overtake us before daylight. We will go back for a mile and then turn off across the fields by some country track, and we may hope before we have travelled very far to hit upon another leading in the direction we want to go. We shall have the moon for another five or six hours, and after that we will travel by torchlight. We have brought some torches with us. One will be enough to show us any ditches or nullahs when we are proceeding across country, when we are on a road we can do without it."

Two of the men dismounted, and giving their horses to their comrades went on ahead searching for some track across the fields. After half an hour's riding one was found, it was a mere pathway used by peasants, and turning off on it the party followed it in single file.

"Would it not be better to leave the baggage behind us," Percy asked the officer. "Then we could go on at a gallop. It would be a nuisance to lose all the things, but that would be of no odds in comparison to our lives."

"No, sahib, the colonel's boxes may be of importance. And at any rate, it has not come to that yet. If we are

attacked and have to ride for it, of course we must leave them, for whatever may be in the boxes the colonel sets your life at a much higher value. But I hope now we shall outwit them. The road we were travelling will be known to them, and it is along that they will be gathering, therefore we may well give them the slip. We will cross the Chenab at daylight at Gazerabad, and cross the Jhelum by boats a few miles below Jetalpore. They would be on the watch for us there. Then I think we shall be safe till we get near the colonel's fortress. That of course will be the most dangerous portion of the journey, since they will know by whatever road we travel it is for that point we are making. We will halt in a grove, and I shall send t\vo of the men off on horseback by different roads. We may calculate that one of them at least will reach the fortress, and the colonel will then send out a force sufficient to beat off any attack likely to be made, for, as our strength is known, some thirty or forty men will have been considered ample for the work."

"That seems a very good plan," Percy agreed. "I wonder that they should dare to venture into my uncle's district, where, as you say, the people are all favourable to him."

" There are many valleys and nullahs in which they could conceal themselves; besides, much of the country is uncultivated, and they could lie hid for a fortnight without much fear of being discovered if they took provisions with them and encamped near water."

All night the journey continued. Percy was so sleepy that he several times dozed off in his seat, and woke with a start, finding himself reeling in the saddle. At times, however, he was obliged to pay attention to their course, for it was often a mere track, that even the men walking ahead had difficulty in following. There were deep nullahs to be crossed, and once or twice wide water-courses, dry now, but covered with stones and boulders. These were, as Nand Chund told him, foaming torrents in the wet season, and at such times quite

impassable. Occasionally the track turned off in a direction quite different to that they were following; and they then directed their course by the stars, a man going ahead with a torch until they came again upon cultivated ground and struck upon a path leading in the right direction.

The two rivers were crossed safely, and they then rode north for two days.

Percy felt thankful indeed when, after pushing on all that last night, Nand Chund, upon arriving at a clump of bushes, decided to halt just as daylight was beginning to break in the «ast. The two best-mounted men received their instructions, and at once rode on at a brisk pace, while the rest entered the bushes and dismounted, the men with their long knives clearing a space sufficiently large for the party. A fire was lit and food cooked, then four men were placed on watch at the edge of the thicket, and the rest threw themselves down to sleep. It seemed to Percy that he had hardly closed his eyes, but he knew he must have slept for some hours, from the heat of the sun blazing down upon him, when Nand Chund put his hand on his shoulder and said:

"All is well, sahib. A party of horse are approaching, and I doubt not that the colonel is with them."

Percy leapt to his feet and made his way to the edge of the thicket.

"They are our men," Nand Chund said; "they are riding in regular lines." A minute or two later he added, "There is the colonel himself at their head—the officer with the white horse-hair crest to his helmet."

Unless so informed Percy would have had no idea that the tall bearded man in silk attire was an Englishman, until he leapt from his horse beside him, exclaiming heartily, " Well, Percy, my boy, I am glad indeed to see you safe and sound. I have been in a fidget about you for the last week; for I have had news that bands of strange horsemen had been seen on the roads, and there were reports that some of them had

entered my district, though where they had gone nonc knew. However, all is well that ends well. I was delighted when two fellows rode into the fortress this morning, within a few minutes of each other, with the news that you had got thus far, and were hiding here till I came out to fetch you-. You may imagine we were not long in getting into the saddle. Well, this has been a rough beginning, lad; but your troubles are at an end now. You may be sure that there is no foe near at hand who will venture to try conclusions with four hundred of the best troops in the Punjaub. I hardly fancied that you would have come, Percy. I don't know when I have been so pleased as when I received the letter from Mr. Fullar-ton at Loodiana, saying that you had come out with him, and would probably be there in a few days."

" I was very glad to come, uncle,—very. It did not take me five minutes to decide about coming after I had read your letter."

"You are something like what I expected you to be, Percy, although not altogether. I fancied that you would be more like what your father was at your age. It seems but yesterday that we were boys together, though it is so many years ago. But I don't see the likeness—I think you are more like what I was. Your father, dear good fellow as he was, always looked as if he had a stiff collar on. Even from a boy he was all for method and order; and no doubt he was right enough, though I hated both. Well, you may as well mount, and you can tell me about your voyage as we ride back. You have done your work well, Nand Chund. I knew that I could safely trust the boy in your charge. Have you been troubled by the way? "

"Only once have we absolutely seen them, sahib; " and the officer gave the colonel a short account of the incident of the pretended travellers.

"So they were at Loodiana the day after you arrived? Then someonc must have sent off word of the object of your

mission as soon as you started. We must find out these traitors, Nand Chund, and make an end of them. However, we will talk that over afterwards."

By this time the horses had been led out from the thicket. The colonel watched Percy critically as he mounted, and nodded approvingly as he sprang into the saddle.

"That is right, lad; I see that you are at home on a horse. We shall make a Sikh of you before long. How have you got on with him, Nand Chund ? You must have been quite in a fog, Percy, as to what was going on. Your tongue must have had quite a holiday since you left Loodiana."

"The young sahib speaks Punjaubi very fairly, colonel, and we had no difficulty in understanding each other."

"Speaks Punjaubi! " the colonel repeated. "You must be dreaming, Nand Chund. How can the boy have learned the language. I suppose you mean Hindustani—though how he could have picked that up in an English school is more than I can understand. There was no such thing heard of when I was a boy."

"It is Punjaubi he speaks, colonel, though he told me he could also make himself understood in Hindustani," the officer said in the native language.

"Nand Chund tells me that you can speak Punjaubi, Percy, but in truth I can hardly believe him."

" I don't speak it very well yet, uncle, but I can get on with it. I worked five or six hours a day on the voyage out with a Punjaubi servant of Mr. Fullarton. I thought it would be of great use for me to know something of the language when I arrived. As to the Hindustani, I have had a master at school twice a week for more than a year before I sailed."

" I am delighted, Percy. You must have worked hard indeed to speak as fluently as you do, and it does you tremendous credit. I own I should never have thought of spending my time on board ship learning a language. You do take after your father more than me, after all; it is just the sort of thing

he would have done. Well, I am pleased, boy,—very pleased. Mr. Fullarton spoke in very favourable terms about you when he wrote. I wondered then how he should know anything about a boy of your age who chanced to be a fellow-passenger, but thought it was merely a bit of civility on his part, and meant nothing. I suppose he heard from his servant that you were working up the language with him, and so came to take an interest in you. Perhaps you sat near him at table?"

"No, uncle; I took my meals with the second and third officers and the midshipmen. The captain offered to put me there; it was so much nicer than going among a lot of grown-up people, and of course it gave me a great deal more time for work. But towards the end of the voyage I came to know most of the passengers. Mr. Fullarton was the first to be kind to me. He used very often to come forward to where I was working with Ram Singh—that was the name of his servant,—and he would explain things about the grammar that I could not understand and Ram Singh could not tell me, for of course he didn't know anything about grammar."

"Well, you can ride, you can talk Punjaubi fairly, and you know something of Hindustani. That is a capital beginning, Percy. Have you any other accomplishments? "

"Nothing that I know of," Percy laughed, "except that on the way out I practised pistol-shooting; and before we got to Calcutta there were not many on board who shot much better. Mr. Fullarton made me practise from the first, and told me that to shoot straight was one of the most valuable accomplishments I could have in India."

"He was perfectly right," the colonel said heartily. "A quick eye and hand with the pistol are invaluable, especially in a country like this, where assassination is the most ordinary way of getting rid of an enemy. My pistol has saved my life several times, and the fact that I am a dead shot has no doubt saved me from many other such attempts. Even the most

desperate men hesitate at undertaking a job which involves certain death; for even if they planted a dagger between my shoulders before I had time to lay hands on the butt of a pistol, they would be killed to a certainty by my men. You. must keep that up, lad, till you can hit an egg swinging at the end of a string nine times out of ten at twelve paces. It is very seldom that you want to use a pistol at a longer range than that. Now, am I at all like what you expected me to be?"

" I don't think I had formed any distinct idea about you, uncle. Father said you were taller than he was and bigger, and of course I expected you to be very sunburnt and brown, and that perhaps you would have a beard, as most of the Sikhs have beards; I thought too, that perhaps you would dress to some extent like a native; but I did not expect to see you altogether like a Sikh."

"We all adopted the native costume to a great extent," the colonel said. " Of course there was always a prejudice against us, and anything like a European dress would have constantly kept it before the minds of our men that we were foreigners. The dress, too, was lighter and more easy than our own in a climate like this, and I don't think anyone could deny for a moment that it is a good deal more picturesque."

The colonel was indeed in the complete garb of a Sikh warrior of rank. On his head he wore a close-fitting steel cap, beautifully inlaid with gold. A slender shaft rose three inches above the top, and in this was inserted a plume of white horse-hair, that fell down over the helmet. From the lower edge of the steel cap fell a curtain of light steel links, covering the forehead down to the eyebrows, and then falling so as to shield the cheeks and the neck behind. In front was a steel bar, inlaid like the helmet. This was now pushed up, but when required it could be lowered down over the nose almost to the chin, so as to afford protection against a sword-strokc from the side. A robe of thickly quilted silk fell from

the neck to the knees. Round the body were four pieces of armour, of work similar to the helmet. One of these formed a back, and the other the front piece, two smaller plates cut out under the arm connected these together.

Across the back was slung a shield of about eighteen inches in diameter, also of steel inlaid with gold. In action it was held in the left hand, and not upon the arm like those in use in Europe in the middle ages. The arms themselves were protected by steel pieces from the elbow to the wrist, the hands being covered by fine but strong link-mail, kept in place by straps across the palm of the hand. The legs were covered by long tightly-fitting white trousers reaching to the feet. The sash of purple with gold embroidery bristled with pistols and daggers. All the armour, although strong and capable of resisting a sword-cut or a spear-thrust, was very light, the steel being of the finest temper and quality. The costume was an exceedingly picturesque one, and showed off the colonel's powerful figure to advantage.

The officers were very similarly attired. The soldiers were for the most part dressed in chain-armour, with shields larger than those of the officers, but of leather with metal bosses; some wore turbans, others steel caps.

"What do you think of my men, Percy?" the colonel asked, as he reined in his horse and watched the horsemen trot past four abreast.

"They are fine-looking men," Percy said doubtfully, "but they would look a great deal better if they were all dressed alike."

" Ah! that is your European notion, Percy. No doubt to an English eye, accustomed to our cavalry, they do look rather 3. scratch lot, but dress makes no difference when it comes to fighting. From the first the Maharajah's European officers had to abandon the idea of introducing anything like uniformity in dress. The men clothe themselves; and in addition to the expense it would be to them to get new clothes on

joining, their feeling of independence would revolt against any dictation on such a subject. It has all along been very difficult to get them to submit to anything like European discipline, but to attempt to introduce uniformity of garb would produce a revolution among them. There is no such thing as uniformity even in the attire of the most highly-favoured troops of the native princes, and the appearance of their escort and retinue is varied in the extreme.

" Richly-dressed nobles ride side by side with men whose armour and trappings have come down to them from many generations. Some carry lances, some matchlocks, some only swords; some are pretty nearly naked to the waist, others are swathed up to the eyes in gaudy-coloured robes. So that a man's arms are serviceable, and he is willing to learn his drill, is obedient to discipline and of good behaviour, I care nothing for his clothes; though as far as I can I discourage any from dressing more showily than the rest, and of course insist that all are fairly dressed in accordance with their notions. You must remember that until the days of Marlborough there were nothing like uniforms in European armies, especially among the cavalry. And even in his time there was very considerable latitude in the matter of dress."

"I suppose I shall have to dress in Sikh fashion, uncle?" "It will be certainly better, lad. Indoors their dress is easy and flowing, and you will find it comfortable. Your European dress will at once mark you out, and should there be troubles your chances of escape would be vastly greater in Sikh costume, than in anything which would at once point you out as a European. In the course of a year you will speak the language like a native, for, as you may suppose, you will hear nothing else, except when we are alone together. And indeed to me Punjaubi now comes much more naturally than English. If it were not that I have always made a point of getting a box of European books sent up from Calcutta whenever an opportunity offers, I should almost have forgotten

my native tongue. There, that is the fortress. It looks fairly strong, does it not? "

They had just ascended a brow, and as they did so the stronghold came suddenly into view. It stood on a rocky spur, running out from the hills behind it. This broke suddenly away at the foot of the walls, and seemed to Percy to be almost perpendicular on three sides.

" It looks tremendously strong, uncle. Surely nobody could scale those rocks? "

"No; except by treachery it is impregnable on the sides you see, or at any rate on two of them. On the side facing us it is very steep, indeed almost inaccessible. There is a footpath cut for the most part in the rock. It zigzags up the face, and there is a small gateway, though you can't see it from here, by which the fortress is entered from this side. There are three places that can only be -climbed by ladders, and when these are removed nothing, unless provided with wings, could get up. The weakest side is, of course, that which we don't see, where the spur runs up to the hills behind. I have taken every pains to strengthen it there, and have blasted a cut thirty feet deep and as many wide, at the foot of the wall across the shoulder. I have, indeed, very largely added to the strength of the whole place since I was first appointed governor ten years ago. At that time I only resided here occasionally, sometimes moving about in the towns and villages, at others absent, often for months, with my three regiments, on some military expedition. But I foresaw that there would be troubles at Runjeet Singh's death, and quietly and steadily piepared for them.

" I knew the weak points of the place. For when I was first appointed, my predecessor, as is often the case, declined to hand over the fortress to me, and I had to capture it. It was no easy matter then, but I managed one night with a hundred picked men to scale the rock unnoticed, when a storm was raging. Then we threw up a rope with a grapnel to the top

of the wall, drew up a rope-ladder, and so got a footing; we crept along the walls with scarcely any opposition, for the sentries were cowering under shelter of the parapet, and we reached the gate before the garrison had taken the alarm. The rest was easy; we threw open the gates, fired a couple of guns as a signal, and the main body of my troops, who had moved unperceived to a point a quarter of a mile away, hurried up, and we were speedily masters of the place. I at once resolved that I would do my best to avoid being turned out in so summary a manner. So far I have succeeded. There have been two or three attempts to take the place, but none of them were serious, for I take care that my sentries don't sleep at their posts, and it would need a regular siege by a large force to take it; I mean, of course, by Sikhs. The British have proved over and over again that rock fortresses considered impregnable can be taken without serious difficulty by determined men."

"How large is it, uncle?"

" It is about a quarter of a mile from end to end, and at the widest point it is about two hundred and fifty yards from wall to wall. So there is plenty of room not only for my troops but for a large number of fugitives from the country round. 1 have grain stored away sufficient for a year, even if the strength of the garrison was doubled. Water was of course the principal difficulty. There were some large tanks when I took possession, but I have greatly added to them. Of course all the water that falls on the roofs in the rainy season is carefully collected and stored; and in addition, I have constructed troughs to a streamlet six miles away in the hills. This brings me down sufficient water for our daily needs without touching the supply in the tanks, which is stringently preserved in case of a siege, for, of course, an enemy would as a first step intercept my supply from the hills.

"The supply in the tanks is certainly ample for many

months, and would of course be replenished in the wet season, so I have no anxiety on that head. I always keep a considerable amount of salt in the magazines, and on the approach of an enemy, cattle would be driven in, slaughtered, and salted; but in fact meat is a matter of minor necessity here, for although the Sikhs have no objection to eat it, they can do very well without it, and are perfectly content if they can get plenty of the native grain and a proportion of rice."

The road wound up the valley under the foot of the rock on which the fortress stood, and then climbed the hill by zigzags cut at an easy gradient until it reached the level of the shoulder, which it followed down to the castle, a quarter of a mile away. The wall on this side was much higher than that on the other faces. The gate was flanked by two massive stone towers, and two others rose at the angles. A drawbridge was lowered as they approached, and over this they crossed the deep fosse that had been cut by the colonel. Ten cannon were placed on the wall and four on each of the towers.

"It would be a hard nut to crack, Percy," his uncle said, as they rode into the gateway.

" It would indeed, uncle. No wonder you have been left here unmolested."

Passing through the gateway they were faced by another wall, which extended in a semicircle in front of them. Four cannon frowned down on the gateway from embrasures, and the parapet, which was very high, was closely loop-holed for musketry. Turning to the right, they rode between the end of this wall and the main one, and then turning sharply to the left rode into the town. Percy had expected to find only a barrack, but there was a main street with shops on either side, where commodities of all kinds were sold. Behind these were the buildings where the troops were lodged, and in the centre of the town stood a large and handsome stone building, the residence of the governor. Everything was scrupulously clean and tidy. Women-were drawing water from conduits, children played about unconcernedly, and everything looked so quiet and peaceful that Percy wondered vaguely whether the inhabitants shared to any extent in the doubts that his uncle had expressed to him of his ability to hold the place against such a force as might possibly be brought against it.

AND HIS UNCLE ENTER THE ZENANA.

CHAPTER IV

A RAID FROM THE HILLS

AS the party rode through the street the people looked up in surprise at the young European riding by the side of the governor. It was evident that though the secret of his coming had reached the ear of an enemy, it had been well preserved in the town.

On his alighting at the entrance to the governor's house the colonel said, " Now I will introduce you to my wife. She is most anxious to see you, and is quite delighted at the thought of your coming."

Passing through the great hall, where the colonel received visitors, listened to complaints, and administered justice, they passed through a richly-carved doorway into an inner room. Here was a table and writing-desk, with a large English arm-chair.

"I never could fall into the Eastern custom of sitting tailor-ways and writing on a pad on my knees, but have kept, as you see, to a table and comfortable chair. This we may call my private business sanctum."

Drawing aside a heavy curtain in one corner of the room he entered an ante-chamber, whose walls were covered with elaborate carvings. A cushioned divan ran round it, and there was a thick carpet over the greater part of the marble floor. Another curtain was drawn aside, and they then entered the principal room of the zenana. A lady some forty years old was seated on a divan, and rose at once as they came in.

"Welcome back, my lord," she said to the colonel. "I knew that with the force you took with you there was no reason for anxiety, but in spite of that I was anxious. I always am when you go beyond the walls. One can never say what will happen."

"You are a great deal more nervous for me than you are for yourself," the colonel said. "This is my nephew, who has come so many thousand miles to be with us. You can speak to him in your own tongue, for I find, to my astonishment, that he has studied it on board ship during the voyage to such good purpose that he can get along very fairly."

"I am glad of that," she said, holding her hand out to Percy. "I have been wondering how I should talk with you when my lord is not here to interpret, and how I should be able to manage things when you understood nothing that was said. I am very glad you have come. I have no children, and hitherto my lord has not cared to follow our custom and to adopt one. Not that I have been lonely for eight years, for since the death of Runjeet Singh my lord has always dwelt with me, and I have never been alone, except when he made short tours through his district. Now you will be as a son; and even when he is away I shall feel that there is someone whom I can trust entirely to look after the defence of the fortress during his absence."

"I am sure there are numbers of my officers whom you can trust entirely, Mahtab."

"There are many whom we think we can trust, Roland; but who can say with certainty? Have we not seen at Lahore how one after another proved faithless to their benefactors? Who can say of another man that he cannot be bought? Percy is young yet—he is but fifteen, you tell me— but in another three years he will be grown up, and will become your right hand, providing he is not tired of our life here."

"Oh, there is no fear of that!" Percy broke in. "There will be heaps for me to do. In the first place, I have to learn to speak the language perfectly, then I have to acquire the manners and customs of the people and how to drill troops. I hope, uncle, you will begin soon to teach me to ride as well as the Sikhs do."

"That part is not difficult, Percy. The Sikhs may be called a nation of horsemen, but it would be more true to say that they are a nation of men who ride horses. I admit that they have firm seats, and can sit their horses up and down hill in the roughest country, but as for taking a leap either wide or high they would not be in it with English cavalrymen. What with their peaked-up saddles and their short stirrups and sharp bits they check a horse's speed and spoil his temper, while they themselves have no freedom of action, and could no more stand up in their saddles to deliver a downright blow than they could fly. I had a fair seat on horseback when a boy, and used to ride to hounds, and during the short time I was in the army rode more than one steeple-chase, but I was certainly nothing particular as a horseman. Here I am considered extraordinary. I hope in a short time to make you as good a rider as I am. Nor will you be long in learning your drill, for that is simple enough, being little more than forming from column into line and from line into column.

"A regiment that can do that is considered as fairly competent. I have got my men to charge in fair order, instead of each man going off at a bat as fast as his horse can lay foot to the ground, and with that I am satisfied. It is useless to teach them skirmishing and outpost work, for these seem to come naturally to them. Therefore all the drill that there is to be learnt may be acquired by a sharp fellow in the course of a week. Indeed, recruits generally take their places in the ranks at once, and soon get hustled into knowing what they have got to do.

I

" As to the language, I grant that it will take some hard .work before you learn to speak like a native, still as you will hear no other tongue you will pick it up naturally and without much regular work except to acquire the niceties of the language. Nand Chund speaks it very correctly, and I will give you into his special charge, and if you talk to him and he corrects you for a couple of hours a day it will be quite enough in the way of work. You may also, if you like, go on with your Hindustani. I have a factotum, a sort of secretary and steward rolled into one, who speaks it fluently; and it would be as well that you should understand it, for although it would be no use to you here, it may be valuable if in the future your lot is cast in other parts of India. You will every day do a little sword exercise. Nand Chund is a good swordsman. When you have learnt all he can teach you I will put you on with some others so that you may learn a trick from one and a trick from another. Your pistol shooting you will of course keep up."

"And when you have nothing better to do," Mahtab said, " I shall always be glad to have you here. Two or three of my maids are wonderful story-tellers, and know among them, I think, all the stories of the history of the Punjaub. I don't say that these are all strictly true, but certainly they are all founded on fact, and as they are all about war, and love, and stratagems, and wonderful exploits, imprisonments, and escapes, they will amuse you, and at the same time be good practice."

"I shall like that very much, aunt. Do you speak any English yourself? "

"A little," Mahtab said. "I can hardly talk it at all, but my lord taught me so that if he wished to write to me, or I to him, we could send letters to each other, and should these fall into others' hands they would not be understood."

"We have found it useful several times," the colonel said. "She has sent me warnings that have enabled me to avoid

falling into traps; and once, that was before I was governor here, I was able, when engaged on an expedition three hundred miles away, to warn her of a plot to seize her in her house. The messenger I sent was captured, but as there was nothing upon him save a scrap of paper with a few words they did not understand, they tossed it with contempt on the ground. My man was a sharp fellow, and happened to be bare-footed, and presently he managed to shift his position so as to stand on the piece of paper and grasp it with his toes. He was led off a prisoner, but made his escape in the night and brought my chit to my wife, who, being warned, assembled some friends of mine, and when the fellows came to carry out their design beat them off handsomely."

" I can see that it must be very useful in that way, uncle, and that it would be just the same as a secret code. Does aunt remain shut up here, or does she go about as ladies do in England?"

" Not quite so freely as that, Percy, but she certainly does not remain shut up. The Sikh women have much more liberty than those in other parts of- India, and naturally I have persuaded her to adopt our customs in that respect to a considerable extent. It is true that when she goes out she is always veiled; but that is a concession to the general feeling. In fact her veil is no thicker than that worn by English ladies, certainly no thicker than a widow's, and even that she throws aside when travelling with me outside a town."

" I am at home in this district," the lady said. " My father was a rajah, and was lord of this territory until Runjeet Singh's troops overcame him. He was killed in the defence of his fortress; not this, but another thirty miles away. Your uncle was in command of one of the regiments, and my mother and I were sent to Lahore under his escort. He saw and took a fancy to me. He was so kind and considerate on the journey, that in spite of his being an enemy I fell in love with him. When we arrived in Lahore Runjeet Singh asked

him what present he should make him for his good services, and when he said he should choose my hand, Runjeet gave it willingly, and with it a jaghir —that is," she added, seeing that Percy looked puzzled, "a grant of land—of a considerable portion of my father's territory. It was partly on that account that some years afterwards he was chosen as governor of the district, and I doubt whether, valiant as he is, he would ever have taken this fortress, had it not been that two of my father's old retainers, who had lived here for many years, acted as guides, and showed him a way up the rock they had been in the habit of using as boys."

"And now, wife," the colonel broke in, "we are both of us forgetting that the boy has had nothing to eat this morning, and I only swallowed a mouthful before starting."

"It is all ready, Roland, though I had forgotten all about it."

She clapped her hands, and on an attendant entering gave orders that a meal should be served. Four young women brought in a table, which they placed before her divan. Two English chairs were set beside it, and in a minute or two a variety of dishes were placed on the table.

" I suppose you would rather have a cut off a joint, Percy, than all these messes," the colonel said as they did justice to the meal.

"I don't know, uncle. They are very nice, but I don't think there is so much flavour in the meat as there is in an English joint."

"Certainly there is not, as a rule, in India; but I think that our sheep, which pasture right up among the hills, make as good mutton as we have at home. Still I don't pretend to be a judge; I own that I have quite forgotten the flavour of English meat."

The next six months' life at the fortress was, with one exception, uneventful. Percy worked steadily at Punjaubi, and had come to speak so well that he could pass as a native

in an ordinary conversation. He had learnt his drill, and now took his place regularly in the ranks of the cavalry regiment as an under officer. An hour a day was devoted to sword exercise and pistol shooting, and for an hour he worked at Hindustani. The hot hours of the day were generally spent in Mahtab's company, talking to her, or listening to the long stories of her attendants. When it became cool he mounted his horse and rode down to the plain with his uncle. An escort always accompanied them to prevent a surprise. There he went through a course of horsemanship, his uncle teaching him to leap over substitutes for hurdles, or across a wide trench dug out for the purpose. After he had taken these obstacles a few times one of the best Sikh horsemen would take him in hand, and he learnt to perform the feats of leaning over and picking up a handkerchief or a javelin from the ground, carrying off a ring hanging from a string, or lifting a tent-peg from the ground at the point of his spear.

One day a mounted man rode in at full speed. He dismounted at the door of the colonel's residence, and the servant took in word that he had brought news of importance and begged to be allowed to see him at once. The man was covered with dust, and had a bandage stained with blood round his head. He made his salaam and then stood waiting to be questioned.

"Where do you come from? " the colonel asked.

"From the village of Jaegwar, your excellency."

"What has happened there?"

" Last night, sahib, the Turgars from the hills came down upon us. They burnt the village and killed many. They have carried off the cattle and the women. Three of the villages have been destroyed. We did our best, but we were taken by surprise, and but few of us escaped. I myself got a deep graze with a bullet as I rode off. I have come to pray for your lordship's protection, and that it will please you to punish these robbers and to recover the women and stolen property."

THROUGH THE SIKH WAR

"I will do what I can," the colonel said quietly, "and can promise you that I will teach these mountain robbers a lesson. Whether I can recover what they have carried off is another matter." He struck the bell and a servant entered.

"Let this man's horse be put in the stable and well fed. See that he himself has food, and tell the hakim to see to his wound. Send an orderly to Nand Chund, Sohan Verdi, and Lai Boghra, and beg them to come here immediately."

"Who are these Turgars, uncle?"

" They are a tribe of hill robbers on the other side of the river. The country nominally belongs to Cashmere, but the government at Sirinagur has no more authority over these hill tribes than it has over the Highlanders of Scotland. Jaegwar lies forty miles to the north, and it will be a troublesome business to punish these beggars, who differ in no respect from the Pathan hill tribes along the whole range of mountains on the northern side of the Indus. It is some years since I had trouble with any of them, for on the last occasion I punished them so heavily they have been quiet ever since. No doubt some reports have reached them of the state of confusion in the Punjaub, and they think to take advantage of it. However, they will find out their mistake. I am just as much bound to protect my district as if I were still a dutiful servant of Lahore; as indeed I am, save in the matter of resigning my governorship, for only ten days since I sent off the annual amount at which the district was taxed when I took charge of it.

"The sum is not a large one; for at that time it was, I should say, the poorest district in the Punjaub, though now, thanks to the fact that life and property are both secure here, the population has increased fourfold, and the revenue tenfold. Still I have no doubt the amount I send is very useful at Lahore, where the treasury is said to be empty; and it enables my agent there to urge that I am faithful to the government, though I refuse to resign my post, where I was placed by

Runjeet Singh, or to hand over the people he entrusted to my care to men who seek only to extort their last penny from them and to grind them into the dust."

The servant now announced that the three officers were in attendance. They were at once shown in, and the colonel informed them of the news he had received. " These robbers must be punished, and punished heavily," he went on, "for if they were permitted to plunder my people without retaliation we should have half a dozen of these hill clans following their example. The question is, what force can we send without unduly weakening the garrison here? Cavalry would be of little use, but I will take fifty troopers. We may find level bits of country where they can be made useful. Of course I will take the four mountain guns and the ten camel guns, and the ist Company of Artillery, to whom they belong. But our chief dependence must be on infantry. I should say we could spare four hundred very well; that will leave an ample force against any sudden attack on the place; as to a serious expedition, I should certainly have warning from Lahore in time to return before it could arrive here. I shall myself accompany the expedition, and, Sohan Verdi, you will take the command of the fort in my absence. I know that I need not tell you to be vigilant. Nand Chund will go with me in command of the troop of cavalry, and you, Lai Boghra, of the infantry. Take No. i and 2 Companies of each of the regiments. As Rundoop Koor commands the Camel Battery, he will of course be in charge of the guns. Let the troops cook a meal at once and parade in an hour."

The officers saluted, and were about to retire when he added, "We will take no tents with us, or baggage of any kind, but I will see that there is an ample supply of grain and flour. Anything else that we may require we must take from the enemy."

"You will let me go with you, I hope, uncle?" Percy exclaimed as soon as the officers had left the room.

"Certainly, Percy, it will be a good introduction for you to mountain warfare."

"Thank you, uncle; it will be a splendid change, and I shall enjoy it immensely. Can these Turgar fellows fight? "

"They can fight in their way well enough, but they are no good against disciplined troops."

"What is their way, uncle?"

"Their villages are all fortified, for when they are not engaged in plundering the villages of the plains they are constantly having petty wars with each other. Otherwise their only idea of fighting is to make sudden rushes down upon a column or a convoy struggling along some defile or up some breakneck path. These rushes are formidable enough against unsteady troops, but disciplined men who keep their heads and show a bold front can beat them off again easily enough. I need not say that one has to be careful on these expeditions, for a man who straggled away from the main body, under the belief that there was no enemy near, would be cut off to a certainty; so you will be pleased to remember that whatever happens you are to keep near me. Now I will go and give orders about the bullock carts and the provisions; there is no time to be lost. You had better go in and see Mahtab, and tell her what has happened. Ask her to get us something to eat before we start, and to see that provisions for our private consumption are put into the carts."

Percy was rather nervous at the mission, as he was afraid that his aunt would be alarmed at the thought of the colonel going into danger. She, however, took the news very coolly.

"We had many such expeditions when we first came here," she said. "Of course there is danger, but it is very slight; and the colonel has so often been in great danger and has come out unharmed, that I have ceased to worry about small things. The cannon generally do the work, and the tribesmen run before the infantry can attack them. The real danger is from surprises, and your uncle has "had far too much experi-

ence to be caught unawares. But you must be careful, Percy, not to wander away, or to get excited and dash on ahead; you must keep near to him."

"So he has ordered me, aunt, and I shall be very careful."

"I hope you will," she said seriously. "There is no glory to be gained in these hill fights, but foolhardiness may very well cost anyone his life. These tribesmen have plenty of courage, and are quite reckless of their lives if they can but cut down an enemy; they are as patient and watchful as wild beasts in pursuit of prey."

The preparations were soon made; the troops who were to take part in the expedition fell in at the appointed time, and the colonel, after making a careful inspection of them, placed himself at their head and led the way through the gate. Percy rode beside him, and immediately behind came the troop of cavalry; the artillery followed. The little guns were carried on the backs of the camels, the four mountain guns each drawn by as many animals. The infantry followed the battery, twelve bullock carts bringing up the rear.

"I am going to send the horse straight on, Percy. It is pretty certain the hillmen will have recrossed the river and be up in their villages before this; their tactics are always to strike a blow, collect their plunder, and be off again to the hills long before a force can be collected to oppose them. Still the cavalry will give the peasants confidence, and they will return to their homes when they hear that a force, however small, has arrived for their protection. They will be there by midnight, and will be able to gather news from the peasantry as to the villages these robbers came from, and inquire about roads and guides, so that when we get there to-morrow night no time need be lost about those matters. It is an important thing with these hill tribesmen to strike back as quickly as possible. I found when I first came here that nothing impressed them so much as the promptitude with which they were chased and punished. It was so different to

the dawdling way in which native operations are conducted, that it took them completely by surprise. You know the old saying — he who gives quickly gives twice, and it is just as true of a blow as it is of money."

Half the journey was accomplished that day. The night was cold enough to render blazing fires most enjoyable, and Percy when he lay down felt the comfort of the long Sikh coat made of sheep-skin with the wool inside, and the outside decorated with patterns worked in coloured threads. The following evening they reached Jaegwar, and the colonel took up his quarters in the principal house in the village, to which some of the inhabitants were now returning. Nand Chund made his report as they were eating their supper.

"There were about five hundred of them came down, colonel, in seven different parties. As far as I can make out about three hundred of them were Turgars, and the others were Nagas and Kotahs. They killed about eighty men and carried off seventy or eighty women, and four or five hundred head of cattle. They burned four villages, and set on fire two or three houses here. Fortunately there was no wind, and the flames did not spread."

"Now as to the road, Nand Chund."

"The track, for they say it is nothing more up to the Turgar villages, crosses the river about two miles north of this place. There are five villages, all lying within a circle of about three miles. The nearest of them is six miles beyond the river. The fighting force is put as from twelve to fifteen hundred, but of course if the two other tribes aid them it would more than double that. There are some steep places on the road, and one very deep and narrow valley, quite a ravine I should say, to be passed through. If they get to know of our coming that is no doubt the place where they will fight. If we get through there before they can gather to oppose us they will, of course, make their stand at their villages, which are all high up on the hills."

"The men have made two marches of twenty miles each," the colonel said; " it would be as well that they should have a day's rest before we advance, for it will be a heavy day's work. Besides, I would rather that the Turgars should hold the ravine or any other strong points they may have. Were we to march through these before they were ready to oppose us, they would say afterwards that we could never have got through had they known we were coming, but if we show them that they can no longer rely upon being able to arrest the advance of a column, it may be a long time before they venture upon another raid like this. However strong the place is, you may be sure we shall be able to turn them out of it. That rocket tube will astonish them. Besides, however strong the valley is we ought to be able to outflank it. Another advantage of a fight there is, that if we turn them out with a good deal of loss we shall carry the villages more easily, for it will shake their courage if they find they are unable to hold the place they had relied on as the main defence of their villages."

Accordingly the force rested the next day, and on the morning following started before it was light, and reached the ford across the river just as day was breaking.

"I have no doubt they are prepared for us," the colonel said, as he watched the troops and guns making their passage. "They would hardly have expected that a force would make its appearance here so soon, but they are sure to have placed scouts on the hills to give them warning."

" It is a wild-looking country," Percy said, as the increasing light enabled them to see hill rising behind hill.

"Yes. A battery or two of horse artillery, knowing the country well and taking post on the hills, would make it vary hot for us. Fortunately there is no fear of anything of that sort. The wall pieces are all they have, besides muskets and matchlocks. The road seems to go straight up the hill and over the crest," he went on, after examining the ground with his field-glasses.

"Ah! I can make out a group of three or four men, just to the left of that bush there. Do you see the smoke?—they have just lighted a fire. That is a signal, I have no doubt; as you see, the smoke is getting thicker and thicker."

Three or four minutes later two other columns of smoke were seen rising, one two or three miles to the right, the other as much to the left.

" Take a dozen of your troopers, Nand Chund, and skirmish up the hill; a company of infantry shall follow you. If you find only a handful of men there, drive them off; if they are in force, get near enough to draw their fire and find out their strength, and then fall back again upon the supporting company. We shall not be far behind. But it is hardly likely that you will be pressed, they will not be able to gather to offer any serious opposition until we get some miles further."

The little party of cavalry rode on, a company of infantry following close behind them. Colonel Groves waited until he saw the rest of the force cross the ford, and then set forward again. He had handed his glasses to Percy, who sat watching the advanced party as it ascended the hill. The horsemen had scattered along the hillside, and were several hundred yards ahead of the infantry.

"They are firing, uncle," he exclaimed presently. " I don't see the smoke, but I heard the sound of shots. There! I saw a puff of smoke just now."

"How many guns did you hear, Percy?"

"Five or six; I should say that is about all there are. I saw three standing up, and there may have been two or three more engaged in making the fire."

" It is hardly likely that they would have more than five or six men on watch. Even if they knew yesterday that we had come to the village, they would hardly keep more than a lookout here."

This was evidently the case, as the horsemen were seen to pass over the crest, and one of them soon reappeared and galloped down the hill.

"Nand Chund reports, Colonel," he said when he arrived at the head of the column, "there were but four men, they fired a few shots at us. When we reached the top of the hill they were half-way down the other side. There is a good deal of bush and some wood down there. Nand Chund says that he will not advance further till the company in support joins him, as there might be a force hidden there."

" Quite right. Tell him that at any rate he is not to mount the next hill until we come up."

When the force arrived at the crest they saw Nand Chund and the footmen drawn up beyond the bush in the hollow.

"It is a good deal steeper beyond, uncle."

"Yes, a great deal steeper. There will be some little difficulty in getting our guns up; and if I mistake not, there is a body of men on the opposite crest."

A trooper was sent on to Nand Chund telling him to advance no farther until the whole force came up. When the force was united the colonel said: " This hill is too steep for you to act with effect, Nand Chund. Ride along the valley with the troop for a mile or so, climb the hillside, and then come back along the crest till within a quarter of a mile of them, and as soon as you see them begin to fall back before our advance, charge and take them in flank if they are not too strong, and chase them down the other side, but do not pursue too far."

The cavalry at once rode off. Two companies of infantry were then thrown forward in skirmishing order, the rest of the force followed two or three hundred yards behind them. When the skirmishers were half-way up the hill the enemy opened fire. Orders had been given to them to pay no attention to this, but to keep their muskets slung behind them, and to press forward. When they arrived within a hundred yards of the enemy they were to lie down and return their fire until the column came up. The order was carried out; but just as the colonel reached their line he saw Nand Chund's horse-

men coming along the top at full speed. " Forward, men, at the double!" he shouted; and the troops, leaping to their feet, climbed rapidly up the hill. But it was over before they reached the top. The hillmen had not awaited the arrival of the cavalry, but had fled down the hill behind, the sowars pursuing them and cutting down several before they reached some very broken ground at its foot; from this they opened a sharp fire, and the cavalry at once retired up the hill again. The track now, instead of ascending the next rise, followed the valley down.

"You see," the colonel said when he reached the crest, " the valley makes a sharp bend half a mile down. No doubt that defile lies up there. You can see that the next hill is very much more lofty and rugged-looking. Well, Nand Chund, what force was there ? "

" Somewhere about a hundred, colonel. I should not have charged them, but I saw they were beginning to make off."

"They are gathering like a snowball," the colonel remarked. " I expect that when we reach the defile we shall find their whole force there."

For another two miles they followed the valley, which grew narrower as they advanced, the sides being more and more precipitous. Parties of men had been seen moving about higher up, and presently a scattering fire was opened. The colonel ordered two parties, each a hundred strong, to make their way up the hill on either side and then to advance along it, keeping abreast of the column.

"If the opposition is serious," he said, "I will aid you with the guns."

In a short time the hillsides were dotted with puffs of smoke. Little could be seen of the enemy, who lay behind rocks, occasionally running back and then dropping again behind fresh shelter as the troops advanced. The fire on both sides momentarily became hotter. The four mountain guns now opened fire, throwing shell high up on the hillside.

The natives could be seen bolting from their shelters, and the two flanking companies, which had been almost brought to a standstill, resumed their advance.

The valley narrowed more and more until it was but some ten or twelve yards wide at the bottom. The sides were covered with great boulders and jagged rocks, with bush growing up between them; from these a fierce fire was opened. The four mountain guns had been left behind at the spot where they could still assist the flanking companies; but the camel guns, guarded by the cavalry, advanced along the bottom, keeping up a rapid fire against the invisible foe. The infantry were directed to clear the rocks on either side. The fire was very brisk, and the reports being echoed and re-echoed from the hills, the sound seemed continuous.

It was evident that the enemy were far superior in number, and progress was very slow until the two flanking companies appeared high up on the hills, and advancing along them opened fire on the enemy below, who, although hidden from those in front of them, could be seen from above. The effect was immediate. The fire slackened, and the force pushed forward as rapidly as the nature of the ground would permit, and in a quarter of an hour issued out at the other end of the ravine. Numbers of men could be seen ascending a hill in front of them, and on this, as the colonel had learnt before starting, the first of their villages was situated. There was a halt until the troops were again assembled and the mountain guns came up. The advance was then renewed.

CHAPTER V
RETRIBUTION

UPON resuming his march the colonel divided the infantry into three bodies of equal strength. The first, which was accompanied by the guns, was to move by the path straight up the hill; the others, between whom the cavalry force was divided, were to ascend it a few hundred yards to the right and left of the central column, so as to flank the village on either side. For a time the enemy kept up a fire from the brow of the hill, but this died away as the troops, pressing rapidly forward, neared them, and in a short time the top of the hill was gained. The village stood a quarter of a mile away. It was surrounded by a high wall, above which could be seen the tower of the chief's fortalice.

"These little four-pounders will not be of much good in breaching that wall," the colonel said. "We must attack by the gate and batter that down. Percy, do you ride round to the column on the left, and see if there is any gate on that side. Do you, Nand Chund, do the same on the right. If there are gates there I will send some of the camel guns to try and beat them down. If they can't do it the gates must be blown in, there are men with powder-bags in each column. Let the cavalry work round behind the village, and see what the ground is like there. It looked to me as if it broke away on that side. If there are no gates in the side walls, let the

right column move round to assist the cavalry to cut off the enemy's retreat. Let the infantry of the left column join us here for the attack on this gate. The fellows are evidently in strong force."

Indeed the wall was fringed with smoke, and the bullets were pattering round thick and fast. The men, however, had at once been placed in shelter behind a stone wall, and remained inactive for half an hour. When Percy and Nand Chund rode back within a minute or two of each other, their reports were similar. There were no gates in the side walls, while behind the wall on the other side there was a deep precipitous ravine, with but a few feet between its upper edge and the wall. The colonel gave the order that fifty of the infantry should remain on either side to fire down into the ravine as the enemy retired across it, and the rest should join him. The cavalry were to take post just out of fire on both flanks, to cut off any fugitives who might drop from the walls, and endeavour to escape from the top of the hill.

The time had not been lost, for the four mountain guns had kept up a steady fire at the gates in front, which were, when the two bodies of infantry came up, already torn and splintered, one of them being evidently thrown off its hinges. Then two of the companies advanced through the inclosures in skirmishing order, and when within fifty yards of the wall opened fire at its defenders, aided by the whole of the guns. After waiting for five minutes to allow the fire to have its effect, the colonel gave the word and the column ran forward towards the gate. A heavy fire was opened through the broken planks.

"Don't wait to return it," the colonel, who was riding at the head of column, shouted. " Throw yourselves against the gate, your weight will burst it down."

With a cheer the men rushed on, and as they reached the gate there was a crash. The shattered gate fell, and they poured into the village.

The resistance was slight, for as soon as the column began to advance the fire from the wall had suddenly ceased. Ten or twelve men were shot or bayoneted at the gates, but as the troops spread through the village they met with no more antagonists. The doors of the houses stood open, but the hearths were cold, and the women and children had evidently been sent away early in the morning. As soon as he entered the gate and saw that resistance was over, the colonel shouted to the men behind to follow him, and rode straight through the village for the gate behind. He was, however, only in time to see the last of a crowd of men hurrying out through it;

but an outbreak of firing both to the right and left showed that the parties posted there were harassing the fugitives in their retreat.

As soon as the men behind him came up he led them through the gate, bade them spread along the edge of the ravine and to open fire on the tribesmen, parties of whom were already beginning to mount the opposite side of the ravine. The fire was maintained with considerable effect until all were out of range, then the various detachments were called in by the sound of the bugle, and the troops ordered to cook a meal. While this was being done a thorough search was made through the village. In the chief's tower a considerable quantity of gunpowder was found stored, and as soon as the troops had finished their dinner fire was applied to every house in the village, and a length of fuse thrust into the powder. As they marched out through the gates by which the enemy had retreated, there was a heavy explosion, and the tower fell in ruins.

They then moved towards the next village, in which direction the enemy had retreated. They crossed the ravine, and then kept along a valley to the foot of the hill on which the village stood. The ground was covered with scrub and bush, and they were half-way up when there was a tremendous yell, and on either side a great number of half-naked figures sprang

up, poured in a volley of matchlock balls, arrows, and spears, and then flung themselves upon the column.

Against younger troops the sudden assault might have been successful, but Colonel Groves' meri were all old soldiers, and though taken by surprise faced both ways without confusion, and poured withering volleys into the enemy. Many fell, but the rest came on, and for a minute or two there was a fierce fight—bayonet against sword or spear; but the tribesmen in vain attempted to break the lines, and soon, in obedience to a shout from their leader, sprang away and threw themselves down among the bushes, vanishing almost as suddenly as they had appeared. The troops now assumed the offensive, and pouring volleys into the bushes as they advanced, swept through them, bayoneting all they found, until the Turgars again leapt to their feet and fled. The march was now resumed up the hill, and the village, which was found deserted, was taken possession of. Here the colonel determined to halt for the night. Sentries were placed at the gates and on the walls, and the troops fell out and scattered among the houses.

"I fancy that there will be no more fighting," Colonel Groves said to his nephew, who had ridden close beside him throughout the day. "They have had a tremendous lesson. I counted over fifty bodies as I crossed the ravine, and at least three times that number must have fallen in the attack upon us. We have destroyed one of their villages, and this is in our hands, and they must see that, unless they submit, the others will share the same fate. They have done their utmost and failed. I think they have had enough of it."

Late in the afternoon, indeed, a mounted man, accompanied by two foot-men, one of whom carried a white flag, was seen approaching the walls. Colonel Groves ordered them to be admitted, and they were brought before him.

"We don't want to fight any more," the chief said.

"I daresay not," the colonel replied, "but we are perfectly ready to go on fighting. You began it, and we have no intention of stopping yet."

"What conditions will you give?" the chief asked.

"The only conditions I will grant are these—the return of all the captives taken away, of every head of cattle, and of all articles stolen; the payment of a fine of five hundred cattle; and the delivery into my hands of the eldest sons of your twelve principal chiefs to hold as hostages for your good behaviour in the future. If these conditions are not accepted I shall burn your villages, and destroy your plantations and crops."

"We have not got all the prisoners," the chief said; "there were others with us who have taken their share."

" I shall reckon with them afterwards. I am only asking you to give up .the prisoners and spoil you have in your hands. I shall find, when I have punished the other two tribes that were engaged with you, what captives they have, and if any are missing I shall return here and burn your villages over your heads."

"We cannot pay five hundred cattle."

"Oh, yes, you can! I know pretty well how many you have, and five hundred will not leave you altogether without some. I will not abate one from my demand, but I will consent to take the value of any deficiency in gold and silver ornaments, taken at their weight in metal. Those are my first conditions and my last, and you can carry them back to your chief."

"The three principal chiefs are killed," the man said, "but I will take your message back to my tribe."

"You had best return with an answer to-night, for at daybreak we shall fire this place and advance against the other villages."

" Will they agree, do you think ?" Percy asked when the chief retired.

"They will agree," the colonel replied confidently. "The
threat of destroying their plantations will induce them to yield. Their houses they can soon build up again, but, with the greater part of their cattle gone, the destruction of their plantations would mean starvation to all."

The colonel was not mistaken. There was no reply that night, but at daybreak on the following morning a procession was seen approaching the village. It consisted of more than half of the women who had been carried off, four hundred cattle from the plains, and five hundred of the little hill cattle. There were also twelve lads, a few of whom were almost men, while others were but four or five years old. Ambassadors soon arrived from the Naga and Kotah tribes. These had, as the colonel learnt from a captured native, sent contingents who had taken part in the fight on the previous day. Similar conditions to those imposed on the Turgars were demanded, except that the fine for each tribe was fixed at three hundred head of cattle only, the colonel knowing that they were poorer in this respect than the Turgars.

For two days messengers went and came, and it was only when at last the troops were upon the point of starting against them that they yielded, and on the following morning the captives, hostages, and cattle arrived at the village. The chiefs of all three tribes were ordered to attend that afternoon. The colonel addressed them, and severely admonished them as to their behaviour in the future. "If again," he said, " there is any outrage whatever upon your peaceable neighbours on the other side of the river, I warn you that no mercy will be shown you. Your villages will be destroyed, your plantations rooted up, your crops burned, and your country made desert from end to end. I punished your neighbours ten years ago, and I have punished you now. The next time I have to bring a force across the river I will root you out altogether."

The chiefs all gave the most solemn assurances that they would in future abstain from forays across the river, and in
order to mingle clemency with justice, and to disembarrass himself of the trouble of looking after a number of prisoners, he restored to each of the tribes eight out of the twelve hostages that had been handed over, retaining only the sons of four leading chiefs. Upon the following morning the expedition marched back, two companies of the infantry and the guns forming the column, while the cavalry and the rest of the infantry looked after the great herd of cattle that had been collected, and escorted the rescued women, many of whom were completely prostrated by what they had gone through. The total loss of the column was but fifteen killed and fifty-three wounded.

" I am glad to be back again," the colonel said as they rode across the river. " It has been a very successful little expedition, and the lesson has been so severe that I do not think we are likely to have any more frontier trouble for some time. The other tribesmen will all be awed at the punishment we have inflicted."

"What will you do with the hostages, uncle? "

" I shall keep them for three or four months, and then send them back with a message to the effect that, feeling the tribes have been sufficiently punished, and being assured that they can now be relied upon to abstain from giving trouble, I am willing to trust them, and will therefore no longer deprive the chiefs of their children. Such clemency will aid the effect of the sharp lesson we have administered."

The joy of the villagers at the return of their wives, daughters, and cattle was unbounded, and blessings were showered on the governor, who had shown himself so zealous and powerful in protecting those under his rule.

Another two days' journey took them to the fortress, where their arrival with the eleven hundred captured cattle was hailed with lively satisfaction by the garrison.

Things returned to their normal state. Percy studied, rode, and drilled during the day, and spent his evenings in the

zenana with his uncle and aunt, and from the former received a detailed account of the course of Sikh politics since the death of Runjeet Singh.

Up to the time of the death of the maharajah in 1839 the most friendly relations had been maintained between the Pun-jaub and the British. He was succeeded by his son, Khurruk Singh. He was a weak man, who possessed neither the firmness nor ambition of his father, and the real power was in the hands of Nonehal Singh, his son. He was a fiery young man, and shared to the full the hostility felt toward the British by most of the Sikh chiefs. His father died, and there was a general idea that the young rajah would speedily declare war against the English. He was, however, killed on his return from his father's funeral, by the elephant on which he was riding running against a beam supporting some stonework, which fell and killed both Nonehal and another prince who was riding with him.

There was little doubt that the affair was not an accident, but that the mahooth&& been bribed by the adherents of Shere Singh, a reputed son of Runjeet Singh, who had many powerful supporters in his claim to the throne. The chief of these was Dhyan Singh, the prime minister of Runjeet, who had been removed from his office by Khurruk Singh, and who, with his two brothers, had been all-powerful during the later years of the Lion. A number of the chiefs, however, were by no means disposed to again submit to what was practically the rule of Dhyan and his brothers. Shere Singh had the advantage that, like Nonehal, he was very popular with the army, and for the moment he obtained possession of Lahore. He was, however, expelled by the mother of the late Nonehal, an able and ambitious woman. She, however, made the mistake of refusing Dhyan any employment, and the ex-vizier soon organized a party sufficiently strong to recall Shere Singh.

The ranee ordered the gates to be shut, but General Ventura ordered the soldiers to open them, and the ranee fled. As

soon as Shere Singh was seated on the throne, he handed over the entire management of business to Dhyan Singh, and gave himself up to hunting, and drinking, and other pleasures. Dhyan was greatly offended at the conduct of the prince, who owed his elevation to the throne to him, and endeavoured to persuade him to act in a manner more worthy of his position, assuring him that the Sikhs would never submit to be governed by a prince who neglected all public affairs, and was habitually drunk. The prince was offended at the remonstrances of his minister. His boon companions fanned the flame of anger, and persuaded him while in a fit of drunkenness to sign an order for the execution of Dhyan Singh. The latter, however, was kept well informed by his agents in the maharajah's household of what was going on, and saw that his oiily hope of safety was in striking the first blow. He therefore gave orders to Ajeet Singh that the rajah should be killed. The officer was more rapid than the agents of Shere Singh, and the latter was shot immediately, and his son was at the same time murdered. Ajeet, however, either from disappointment at not receiving from Dhyan a reward equal to his expectations, or from some other cause, shot him in the back, and he fell dead a few hours after the murder of the maharajah.

Heera Singh, Dhyan's son, a great favourite with the troops, knew that the death of the maharajah had been determined upon by his father, and had left the city and gone to the camp of General Avitabile, another of the European officers of the Punjaub army. When the messenger arrived with the news that his father too was dead, he was in the act of haranguing the troops and preparing them for the news of the death of Shere Singh. Heera ascended to the flat roof of Avitabile's house, and sent messages to all the sirdars who happened to be in Lahore, begging them to come to him. On their arrival he unbuckled his sword and handed it to them, saying, " I am left alone and fatherless, and I throw myself on your protection. Either kill me or give me your support."

The sirdars at once declared that they would follow him. Heera then harangued the soldiers, and offered them an increase of three rupees a month in their pay if they would declare for him. Ventura and Avitabile both espoused his cause, and with their troops marched against Lahore, where Ajeet Singh had caused Dhuleep Singh, a child of four years old, and the only lineal descendant of Runjeet left alive, to be proclaimed maharajah, and himself vizier. It was night when Heera arrived in Lahore. His guns blew open the Delhi gate of the town, and then a desperate battle commenced in the streets. Both sides had artillery, and the battle raged until the morning with terrible slaughter. Heera's troops were victorious; the fort was stormed, and Ajeet killed by a soldier as he tried to escape. Every man in the fort was killed and the city given up to plunder, and horrible cruelties perpetrated upon the connections and friends of Ajeet Singh.

Heera had no intention of grasping the dangerous position of maharajah, and as soon as the fighting was over he went and saluted the child Dhuleep as maharajah, assuming himself the position of prime minister his father had occupied. This was in 1843. At that time the British were occupied in conquering Gwalior, and the signal overthrow of the Mahrat-tas on the fields of Maharajaypoor and Punniar served for the moment to abate the eagerness of the army for a war against them. They were, however, as usual, mutinous and clamorous for still further increase in their pay, and the treasury at Lahore being empty, Heera Singh had the greatest difficulty in complying with their demands, and in order to do so he caused an uncle, who like Dhyan and Ghoolab had amassed enormous possessions, to be murdered, and used his wealth as a means of quieting the troops. These, however, soon advanced fresh demands, and Heera being unable to satisfy them was murdered.

At his death Dhuleep Singh's mother appointed her brother Juwaheer as vizier. The choice was not pleasing to the sol-

dtr~

diers, who invaded the palace and murdered him before the eyes of his sister and her child. Ghoolab Singh, the last sur-rivor of the three great brothers, was invited to take the office of vizier, but he wisely declined the dangerous post. His possessions were vast, and his power almost equal to that of the ruler of the Punjaub. He was virtually supreme in all the northern territories that had been conquered in the time of Runjeet, and from his residence at Jummoo ruled over all Cashmere, together with the country stretching up to the borders of Afghanistan.

He it was who was the mover in the intrigues against Colonel Groves. One of the first demands made by the soldiers upon the accession of Heera Singh to power had been the immediate dismissal of all the foreign officers in his service, and greatly against his inclination, for he knew that these men alone had the power of keeping the mutinous soldiery in any degree of order, he had been forced to accede to it. Most of them had left the country at once, knowing that murder would speedily follow dismissal; but Colonel Groves having, since the death of Runjeet, successfully defeated all attempts to turn him out of his governorship and fortress, had determined to await the end, being sure that ere long the hatred of the Sikhs against the British would bring about a war that might entirely change the position.

It was a few months after Percy's arrival that Ghoolab refused to accept the post of vizier.

"That is good news, uncle, is it not?" he asked, when a messenger arrived bearing a letter containing the news, from a member of the court at Lahore who was in the colonel's pay and interest.

"I don't know, Percy, I rather think it would have been better if he had accepted the post. In the first place he would have had his hands so full that he would not have had time to give much attention to my affairs. Then if he had sent strong bodies of troops to attack this place, as likely

as not they would have said that they were being sacrificed in his interest, and it would have been an occasion for a fresh mutiny. And lastly, the viziership has of late been fatal to its holders, and Ghoolab might have formed no exception, and I might have been freed from my most dangerous enemy. Now he will be able to carry on his intrigues from Jummoo without interruption. Since the death of Runjeet his hands have been tied to a certain extent, first by his brother Dhyan, and then by Heera being prime minister, and he had to take care that no movement of his endangered their popularity or position. Now that his two brothers and his nephew have gone, he need consult only what he thinks is his own interest, and it is distinctly his interest that his son should be governor of this district, which is flourishing and capable of being squeezed to a large extent, and which lies so close to his own territories."

" Is it only on account of this that he is your enemy, uncle? " "No, the matter is of much longer standing. It began at one of the battles against the Afghans. The sirdars and their troops commanded by Ghoolab did very badly, and had it not been for the courage and obstinacy of my three regiments and those of Portalis we should have been defeated. Runjeet always managed to keep himself thoroughly well acquainted with what was going on, and Ghoolab was for a time in considerable disgrace, while very handsome presents were made to Portalis and myself, and three months' pay given to each of our officers and soldiers. I warned Portalis that Ghoolab would not forgive us, but he was a little headstrong and scoffed at the danger. Three months after, he fell by the knife of an assassin. He was a good comrade and friend of mine, and was indeed the only man among the European officers I really cared for, and I did not hesitate to denounce Ghoolab to Runjeet in open durbar as the author of his assassination. Of course I could not prove it, but the maharajah was certainly of my opinion, and Ghoolab was ordered to go

and live on his estates, and was for some months in great disgrace.

"All my acquaintances warned me that I was throwing away my life by thus venturing to denounce one of the all-powerful trio of brothers. But, as you see, I have lived through it thus far. Still, it has only been by the most unceasing caution and wariness. I have had at least a dozen narrow escapes from assassination, and during the lifetime of Runjeet Singh the intrigues against me were incessant; but the Old Lion knew when he was well served, and stuck to me staunchly. He was, in the last year of his life, compelled by the pressure brought upon him to sign my dismissal, but he sent me a private note by the hands of a trusty messenger. It contained only a few words. '/ am obliged to yield, but there is no reason why you should do so. The sword should always protect the head.' I was aware of what was going on at court, and had already resolved to hold my governorship till the last. But I was very glad to get the old man's note; he had been a kind and good master to me, and I should not have liked to take action that might appear rebellion against him. What others said or thought I did not care. Now I had the Old Lion's approval, my conscience was perfectly easy.

" Ghoolab himself commanded the force that came to put his son in possession, and the fact that he had to retire after losing some hundreds of men, without accomplishing his object, did not, as you may suppose, in any way diminish his feeling of unfriendliness towards me. I get constant and accurate intelligence of what takes place at Jummoo, and I know that I am constantly in his thoughts, and that denunciations of me form one of his staple subjects of conversation among his intimates. I need hardly tell you how great is the terror among the inhabitants of my districts at the thoughts of falling into Ghoolab's hands. The cruelty which he displayed in his conquest of Cashmere was appalling, thousands of people being put to death by all forms of torture.

The trade of this district would be destroyed, the merchants plundered, and under one excuse or other all private property would be confiscated by him. Therefore I am well served. The traders have naturally agents and correspondents all over the Punjaub, who inform them of every rumour current, and these accounts are promptly transmitted to me, so that I get the earliest possible intelligence of every movement or intrigue as soon as it is set on foot, and no body of men can be set in motion within a couple of hundred miles of this fortress without my receiving news of it in the course of a day or two."

A few days later the colonel said when they met at breakfast: "There is trouble coming, Percy. I have had a letter from my agents at Lahore, saying that several of the punches —as the leaders of the soldiers are called—have for the last day or two been loudly denouncing me, saying that it is a disgrace to the Sikh nation that an insolent foreigner should not only remain among them, but, in the teeth of his dismissal by the ruler of Lahore, maintain himself by force of arms as the governor of a district of the Punjaub. As the ranee has no vizier, and is entirely helpless in the hands of the soldiers, there can be no doubt that she will authorize an expedition against me, and will indeed be glad to agree to a project which will remove a number of her insolent soldiery from the city. The clamour for a war against the British grows daily in strength, and most of the leading sirdars are in this matter in agreement with the troops, and the ranee cannot but think that it is very much better that they should occupy themselves in an expedition against a man in whom she has, of course, no interest, than embark in a great war which may end by costing her infant son his kingdom."

" What are you going to do, uncle ? "

The colonel shrugged his shoulders. " Sharpen my sword, see that the guns are in good order, and overhaul our stock of ammunition. I feel quite convinced that we can repel all attacks by a mutinous horde like this, provided only that

there is no treachery at work. That is our one weak point."

"You have never found out yet, uncle, who it was sent Ghoolab the news of my coming here? "

" No, I have no ground for suspicion against anyone. Nand Chund, and two or three of the officers of whose fidelity I feel absolutely sure, have been quietly trying to find out ever since you came here, but without success. Azim Bund, my steward, has also been trying in other quarters, but he too has altogether failed. Of course the traitor may be a member of my household and not one of my officers; in that case his treachery would be of little importance. Although by getting news of your coming he might have struck me a heavy blow, in other respects he can tell them nothing beyond the fact that I am alive and well, and very much on my guard. He may give them the number of cannons I have got, the amount of ammunition in stock, and the state of the food magazines, but the news can give them no satisfaction and can do me no harm.

"It is altogether different if it is an officer. In every considerable body of men there are a certain number who think they have a grievance of some kind; they have either been punished unjustly, or think they have been overlooked in promotion and that their services have not been sufficiently recognized. In some it is merely the desire for a change of any sort; and when the men know, as of course they do know, that the soldiers of the army are enriching themselves both at the expense of the government and of the population, they may feel dissatisfied with their dull life and regular pay here. At any rate there must be many who could be worked up by an astute rascal, and a gate thrown open, or a rope-ladder lowered over the wall, might lay the place at the mercy of our enemies. I have no fear whatever of this section being numerous enough to get up anything like a formidable mutiny, but a party of only twenty determined men might any night

break their way in here and cut all our throats long before the troops could come to our assistance, might seize my wife's jewels and valuables, and make their escape by means of a rope-ladder over the wall. That, I think, is the most dangerous contingency. I always sleep with three brace of pistols within reach of my hand, and you know I have warned you to keep arms by your bedside; still, though we might sell our lives dearly, you may be sure that the attack would not be made except by a force sufficient for the purpose."

"Why don't you keep a strong guard in the house, uncle?"

"Because, my boy, I don't know who the traitors are. The officer in command might be the very man himself, and he might so contrive it that the guard was composed of men whom he had corrupted. Where should we be then? "

" But you might appoint Nand Chund to be always officer of the guard? "

"Constable of the palace—eh, Percy?"

" Well, you might call him what you like, uncle, but surely he would be able to pick out a dozen men of whose fidelity he was assured. The duty would not be severe, they would only have to furnish the two sentries at the door, instead of these being sent from one or other of the regiments."

" I will think of it, Percy. Just at present there is less ground for fear than usual, for if an expedition is on foot to attack us openly, such a plot as this would most certainly be delayed until there was a force outside where the conspirators could betake themselves after carrying their designs into execution. The fact that, even were they successful, they would certainly be pursued, and for the most part hunted down and slaughtered by the cavalry, has, 'no doubt, been one of the reasons why no such attempt as that we are talking of has been made long ago."

" Well, I do hope that when an army approaches you will do what Percy suggests," Mahtab, who had been listening silently to the conversation, said to her husband. " You have escaped so many times, Roland, that you have come to think that no attempt against your life will ever succeed, and certainly it is likely that Ghoolab, while organizing an open assault upon you, will take measures to secure his aim being carried out in other ways if possible."

"Very well, wife; you may consider it settled that on the day when an attacking force crosses the boundary of the province, Nand Chund shall be installed as chief of a special bodyguard here."

CHAPTER VI

A SIEGE

NOT a day passed now without messengers coming in with warnings of approaching danger, and one morning early the officer on guard reported that a large number of persons could be seen approachng by the road from the south.

"Do they look like troops?" the colonel asked.

" No, sahib; they are on horseback and on foot, and there are many carts among them."

" I have no doubt then, Kur Aloof, that they are merchants of the towns coming in here for refuge. The enemy cannot be far off, and they know how the soldiers would squeeze them if they had a chance."

" Will you let all those people in here, uncle ? They will eat up our provisions and drink up our water."

"As I told you, Percy, we have sufficient of both for a number double that at present within the walls. Did four times the total now here arrive the supplies would still hold out six months, and two months is the utmost that the siege is likely to last. One need never be afraid of a long siege by men commanded by leaders having no authority over them. A powerful prince might send troops on a siege and order them to maintain it until they captured the place, even if it took them ten years to do so, but at present the Punjaub is without a master, and the troops have only been induced   103

to come here by the prospect of plunder. But as soon as they find that they make but little impression upon us, and that the siege, with its labours, and hardships, and dangers, may continue for many months, they will soon get tired of it, and in the absence of a controlling power will march away.

"They have a good many deserters from our service among them, and little as they love Europeans they will utilize their services, and I anticipate that for a while at least it will be made very hot for us. There are a score of points on that hillside half a mile away where guns can be posted to play on us, while we could make but a feeble return, and there is nothing like a plunging fire kept up night and day to weaken the spirits and lower the confidence of a garrison. That will be the time when the traitors, if there are any, will be busy among the men, and it will need unceasing care and vigilance to prevent trouble."

In a short time the people seen in the valley below began to enter the fortress. They were, as the colonel had anticipated, merchants and other people having something to lose, from the various towns in the district. Most of them brought with them carts laden with their choicest merchandise, and all had their portable valuables and money with them. They reported that news had come in the evening before, that a very large force had arrived at a point within fifteen miles of the frontier of the province, and that the soldiers had been promised the sack of all the towns and villages as an inducement for them to undertake the siege of the fortress.

"But how am I to feed so many mouths?" the colonel asked one of the leading merchants, with a smile.

"We know that our lord has great stores laid up in his magazines," the merchant answered, "and we are, of course, ready to pay for all that he will let us have."

" I have no doubt that the magazines will hold out as long as it is necessary," the colonel replied, "and as I regard all who enter here as my guests, each man, woman, and child shall draw rations of what food we have as long as it lasts. It has been bought out of the revenues of the province, and as each of you contributed, so shall you now share. But you know you will fare worse if the place is taken and you are found here than you would have done had you remained quietly ,at home."

The merchant shook his head. "There could be no worse, sahib. The soldiers plunder, kill, burn, and destroy as they did in Cashmere; they can do no more if they find us here. But we are not afraid of their taking the fortress. It is strong, and everyone knows my lord's valour and experience. The army will never be able to win their way in here."

"I hope not, my friends; I will certainly do my best to prevent them from doing so. And now about yourselves. The stream of fugitives grows broader and thicker every hour, and if it goes on like this, by nightfall we shall have over five thousand persons here in addition to the strength of the garrison. Against that I say nothing, a thousand at least will be able-bodied men capable of bearing arms, and 1 shall expect each to do his best; but where am I to stow so great a number? The barracks are already full, and but few indeed will be able to find lodging in the houses of the traders. I have tents and straw for two thousand people, but how can they be pitched? The ground is solid rock. There is no way of driving tent-pegs, and I see not how they can be erected."

" We might spread them over the carts, and so obtain a protection from the night air and a shelter for the women and children, and they might even erect poles in the carts themselves and stay them by ropes to the sides."

"That is a very good idea, and I will order the officer in charge of the stores to issue a tent to each owner of a cart, the others must manage as best they can. I daresay five hundred can be stowed away m the lofts of the stables and in other places not in use, while some with poles leaned against a wall and canvas spread over them can make shelters good enough

THROUGH THE SIKH WAR

on a pinch. The oxen must be given over to one of my officers, who will see that they are fed from the granaries and will kill them for food."

The colonel had not over-estimated the number of those likely to arrive, and before nightfall over five thousand had entered the fortress. Stringent orders were laid down that none save the regular troops should be allowed to approach the walls, and each party as it arrived was conducted to the spot allotted to it. Every open space was covered with shelters of one kind or another, the larger constructed of tents, the smaller of shawls and blankets. The principal street was left clear of such erections in order to admit of a free passage for the troops, but it was ordered that all cooking operations should be performed there, as fires would be dangerous in the extreme among the crowded tents. When night came, strong guards were placed on the walls, especially on that facing the shoulder of the hill, upon which any open attack must fall, Percy's idea was carried out, and a body-guard composed of six men from each of the two infantry regiments, and an equal number from the cavalry, marched into the governor's house under the command of Nand Chund. Their instructions were that no one was to be allowed to enter the house, whatever he might allege to be the nature of his business, unless furnished with a written order to do so from the governor.

Percy had been busy all day seeing that the new-comers fell into their places, and in aiding them to shake down in some sort of comfort, and he was thoroughly tired out when he joined the colonel and his wife in their room that evening.

"Well, uncle, I am glad it is coming at last. It is much better to know the worst than to go on wondering when it was going to begin."

"I don't know, Percy. I have been in so many troubles and frays and battles since I came out here, that the thought that we might have to stand a siege was no very great trouble to me; besides, there was alway*s the possibility that something might occur to postpone it altogether. The soldiers and most of the sirdars seem bent upon having a fight with the English, and I greatly hoped that it would begin before Ghoolab's intrigues against me had come to a head. However, now it has come we must make the best of it, and I have no great fear of the result. While you have been busy with these people this afternoon I have been superintending the mounting of two heavy howitzers as mortars, and if they erect batteries on the hill, as I expect they will, we will see if we cannot drop a few shell among them. Nothing un-steadies artillerymen more than finding that the earthworks in front of them do not as they expect protect them, and that by no ingenuity can they defend themselves from missiles that seem to drop down from the sky upon them."

" But how do you do that, uncle? "

" Simply by the amount of powder you put in. A mortar is always fixed at a certain angle, and of course you fix a howitzer the same way when you use it for that purpose. With a mortar the amount of powder of a given strength required to send a shell to a given distance is known to every artilleryman, but with a howitzer one must get it by experiment. You first put in the amount of powder you think sufficient. The ball is fired up into the air, and you watch where it drops. If it is short you add an ounce or two of powder, as the case may be. If it is too far you decrease the charge until you find that the shell drops just behind the enemy's earthworks among the artillerymen serving a gun. Having once got the exact charge of course you stick to it. This sort of thing annoys the Sikhs, who are not much accustomed to shell. A few of them were sent up to Lahore, and I managed to get hold of one and had several hundred cast here to fit those two howitzers, and had a large number of fuses made and stored away for future use. If they try to climb the rocks, a few shells rolled down from the walls are likely to be very effective."

"What are to be my duties principally, uncle ?"

"Your chief duty will be to watch, Percy, especially at night. The officers will, of course, go their rounds frequently, but as there may be a traitor among them, I can place no absolute reliance on their vigilance. I shall myself be about as much as possible, but as I shall have to look after everything in the daytime I must take some rest at night; one cannot do two or three months without sleep. I shall release you from all duty during the day, although in case of a serious attack you will take your place on the wall; otherwise I wish you to sleep in the day and to keep a sharp look-out on everything at night, being constantly upon the walls seeing that the sentries are vigilant, and listening intently for anything that might indicate a movement from below. I shall tell off four of Nand Chund's party to accompany you, for if treachery is intended there would be no hesitation in planting a dagger in your heart and then getting rid of your body over the wall. You are nearly sixteen now, and strong and active, but on a dark night that would avail nothing against a lurking assassin."

"Shall I begin to-night, uncle?"

"There is no occasion for that. The enemy have not arrived yet, and indeed no one would dream of attempting to ascend the craig unaided. I fancy they will try an open assault to begin with. When they find that fails they may try surprise."

About midnight an officer reported that a dull confused sound could be heard down the valley. The colonel took a couple of signal rockets, with which one of the boxes brought by Percy from England was filled, and proceeded, accompanied by his nephew, Nand Chund, and four of his guard, to the wall at the lower end of the rock. Lanterns placed on the ground were burning here, and a party of artillerymen were standing by the four guns looking down the valley.

"How far do you think they are away? " the colonel asked the officer in command there.

"A party of them have just crossed the wooden bridge over the stream, sahib. I heard the trampling of their horses upon it distinctly."

"That is fourteen hundred and thirteen yards from the foot of the rock. Drive those wedges a little farther. That is right. I cut those nicks upon them the other day when we had got the exact depression I required to lay the guns on the bridge. Now let us wait until another body of them are crossing."

Three or four minutes later the sound in the distance became suddenly louder.

"Now, Nand Chund, fire that rocket. I think you have got it about the right angle."

The rocket flew up in the air, and burst some distance away throwing out a dozen fire-balls. Their light enabled the governor to see right down the valley. Some slight alteration in the direction of the guns was made, and then one after another they were fired. Another rocket was now thrown up, and by its light the dark mass of men on or behind the bridge could be seen to be broken up and retreating. Almost at the same moment four guns were fired from an upper bastion.

"That is grape, Percy," the colonel said. The officer there was told to wait till the men could see a body of troops advancing up the valley. " Listen, there go the cavalry scampering back as hard as the horses can lay their feet to the ground. I doubt whether we shall hear anything more of them to-night."

"They could hardly hope to have passed without our noticing them. They must have been sure that we should have warning of their coming."

" No doubt, lad, but they may not have calculated on our opening fire upon them in the dark. They will not have reckoned upon the rockets, and hoped, I have no doubt, to push a part of their force past the place and up on to the brow before morning, for they would know well enough that they

could not pass under the fire of our guns when the sun was once up."

"But how will they get there, uncle? now we have shown them that it is almost as dangerous by night as by day."

" Probably they will march round among the hills, and come down upon us. There will be no difficulty in infantry doing it, and they may manage to drag a few light guns with them, but they can't get anything like heavy artillery up there except by bringing them along below, and taking them up the regular road. That is the first of the difficulties they have to encounter, and as I have a large stock of blue lights I don't see how they are going to get up the hill, which is commanded by a dozen of our guns. They will be safe enough from our fire as they pass along under the craig, for there is not a gun that can be depressed sufficiently to bear upon them there, though we can annoy them by pitching shell and hand-grenades down upon them. Still, determined men might manage that, and might even make their way up the hill in face of our fire, but they could never drag heavy guns up a road which we can sweep with grape. So you see they have got a stiff problem to solve before they can get a battering-gun to play on our northern wall."

For another hour they kept watch. There was still a confused sound from the lower end of the valley, but nothing to indicate any renewed advance. They therefore returned to the house.

Percy was aroused at daybreak, and at once made his way to the battery, where they had been the night before. The colonel and several of his officers were already there. The lower end of the valley was occupied by a great mass of men, horses, and waggons. Tents had been erected here and there, and the banners of their occupants were flying before them.

"How strong do you think they are, uncle?" Percy asked.

"It is difficult to say, mixed up as all arms are in such confusion just as they reached the ground last night, but we

guess them at about fifteen thousand. They have four batteries of field guns. There they are away to the right. They evidently came up together, and have kept something like order. We can make out several heavy guns mixed up with the waggons, but whether there are ten or twenty of them I could give no opinion. Do you see that large tent with the red and white flag? Those are the colours of Ghoolab Singh, and the tent no doubt is occupied by his son, the gentleman who was named my successor a week after the death of the Old Lion. He has been waiting some time, and is likely to wait longer. He is no doubt the nominal leader of the expedition; but I believe that he has none of the talent of his father or uncles, and matters will be directed really by the chiefs of the army. I have no doubt a council has been going on all night as to what the next move shall be, and the decision they have probably arrived at is to wait until they can get a better idea of the fortress and its surroundings."

A considerable movement was now going on in the enemy's camp, and the wind bore the sound of trumpets to the fortress.

"They are trying to get into something like "order," Nand Chund remarked. "The waggons are drawing out of the mass to take up their positions in the rear, and the assembly calls of the different regiments are sounding. Ah! there is a party going out to reconnoitre."

As he spoke a party of horsemen rode out to the left of the camp. Several bright banners streamed in the air, and an escort of some fifty cavalry followed them. They mounted the hill on the opposite side of the valley until they reached a spot two or three hundred feet higher than the summit of the fortress, and just opposite to it. As soon as their object had been made out the colonel had sent word to the gunners at the batteries along that face ordering them not to fire.

" I do not wish to make any more bitter enemies," he said to his officers in reply to their look of surprise when he issued the order. "At present they are only fighting against me as

instruments of Ghoolab Singh, and except on the ground that I am a foreigner, the soldiers have no animosity against me. If we wjere now to kill two or three of their favourite leaders, and perhaps some of the sirdars who have been bribed into entering upon this business, it would create an active animosity against me. Of course, when fighting begins they must all take their chance, but I don't wish to slay anyone before a single shot has been fired on their side."

The group of officers, who were but half a mile away, remained for ten minutes closely examining the fortress. They then slowly returned to camp.

" Our guns would carry easily enough into the midst of the camp, sahib," one of the officers remarked.

"I know they would, but I won't begin, for the same reason that I would not fire at the group of officers. We will let them open the ball."

An hour later a body of men which they estimated at five thousand marched away with two of the batteries of field guns, and soon were lost to sight as they wound round the hills skirting the valley.

"We shall see them at daylight to-morrow established on the hillside above us," the colonel said. "I have thought several times of establishing a fort near the crest there; but I should not be able to give it much support by my guns, and its garrison would not make any prolonged resistance when they once found themselves cut off altogether from us. With troops one could rely upon thoroughly, such a fort would immensely Binder the operations, and indeed they could do nothing until it was captured.

"It is a standard rule with us out here, Percy," he said afterwards, " never to count upon the natives unless you are with them yourself. The Sikhs are brave, but they want good leaders, and are not to be relied upon unless under the eye of an officer they respect. They may hate us as Europeans, but in the wars of Runjeet Singh they fought like lions under our

command. You will see that that will be their weak point if they come to blows with the British. They will fight, and fight pluckily, but without Europeans to lead them they will fall into disorder, and there will be no one to rally and control them, to take advantage of any temporary success, or to retrieve a temporary failure. They don't know it themselves, but they will speedily learn it. Given English officers, the natives of India fight as well as our own men. The Sepoy regiments in Clive's days, and ever since, have shown themselves worthy of fighting by the side of their white comrades; but they would be worth very little if deprived of their European officers. Another thing against them is the slowness with which they work their guns. A battery of British artillery would fire five shots while they fire one, and their infantry are proportionately slow in their movements. We have all tried, but tried in vain, to get them to work with smartness. It does not seem, however, to be in them."

That night a vigilant watch was kept along the northern wall, but nothing was heard; and it was not till an hour after sunrise that a column was seen coming along the side of the hill above them. The guns were all manned and ready for action, but the colonel delayed giving the order until the enemy breached a sort of terrace on the face of the hill half a mile away, and three hundred feet higher than the level of the fortress. "Now," he said, "we will give them a hint to come no further. We could not prevent their establishing themselves on that terrace, but they must learn that they can come no nearer. Two or three shots will be a sufficient hint."

The guns opened fire, and the enemy, who were just commencing a further descent, retired hastily, and a few minutes later their field guns opened fire. They were no match, however, for the much heavier pieces on the walls; and after half an hour's exchange of shots they drew back their guns, two of which had been dismounted by well-aimed shots from the wall. Some of the party established themselves well back on the

terrace, where they were out of sight of the fortress, but the main body ascended the hill again and encamped on the crest. Occasionally a gun was run forward, discharged, and withdrawn; and to this fire the garrison made no reply, the guns being very badly aimed, some of the shot flying right over the fortress, while others struck the ground outside the wall.

"Now we shall have quiet for a time, sahib," Nand Chund said to Percy, who was standing next to him. "They have done so much, and will want to settle what the next movement is to be."

"I think it will be our turn to move next, Nand Chund," the colonel, who had overheard his remark, observed. "Tonight when it gets dark we will sally out, and see if we cannot take those gentlemen with the guns by surprise."

" It may be, colonel, that they will expect a sally, and will move their whole force down again on to the terrace after nightfall."

"It all depends who their leader is. If he is an enterprising fellow, that is what he would do."

" Do you know, uncle, I have been thinking that their camp down in the valley is smaller to-day than it was yesterday."

"Do you think so, Percy? I will go to the battery at the other end and have a look at it. It is possible that they may have sent off another party to join those fellows up there. If they have done that, they intend to try the effect of a coup de main, and to attack us in earnest some time before morning."

After a close examination of the enemy's camp, the colonel and his officers were all of opinion that although it occupied as much space as before, there were fewer men moving about than upon the preceding day.

" You have sharp eyes, Percy, and it is well that you noticed it. Had you not done so we might have run our heads into a trap, and instead of surprising them been surprised ourselves, and that by greatly superior numbers. I shall abandon the idea now and prepare to resist a serious assault to-night,

and we will have every man capable of bearing arms in readiness. We will keep only a few men on the walls, and let the rest lie down at once with orders that they are to sleep if they can, as there will be no sleep for them to-night. Nand Chund, do you post half a dozen of your men at different points on the walls; let them keep a vigilant watch down upon the town itself, and see that no flag or other signal is waved from a roof or window. It may well be that there has been some arrangement made with a traitor here to give notice by signal of any intended sortie on our part."

Following his uncle's advice, Percy lay down for some hours; but he could not sleep, being too excited at the thought of the conflict that would probably take place during the night. When he went in to dinner the colonel was absent, being engaged in mustering and assigning to their various posts the able-bodied men among the fugitives. These were posted round the circuit of the walls, which were all, with the exception of the northern face, entrusted to their charge.

"It is probable," he told them, "that the enemy will make a diversion on this side when they attack on the other. It will not, however, be serious, for they can do nothing unless with the assistance of friends on the wall."

Among the servants of the traders were a good many who had served in the army. These were stationed at the guns, and enjoined to open fire upon the enemy's camp if they brought the heavy artillery they had there into play. To each battery and section of the wall a number of blue lights and fire-balls were served out—one or more of the former was to be lighted every few minutes, and the fire-balls occasionally thrown into the valley, so that no considerable body of the enemy could escape observation. The traders were appointed as commanders at the various points. Of the garrison a thousand men were placed on the north wall; the rest were stationed close at hand in readiness to support them, or to move to any point threatened.

"Percy," the Ranee—as she was usually called in the fortress—said, as they sat waiting the colonel's return, "I want you to devote yourself to the protection of my husband to-night. I have no fear of the wall being carried by assault, it is too strong and will be too well defended for that, but I <io fear for his life. That we have one or more traitors here we are sure, and an occasion like this with its confusion and excitement will afford them just the opportunity they desire. When all are engaged in repulsing the attack of an enemy it would be easy for an assassin to use knife or pistol without fear of the action being noticed, and the colonel will be thinking of nothing but directing his men and repulsing the attack. Therefore, I pray you station yourself near him. Leave the fighting to others, and keep your eye closely upon those about him, and your pistol in your hand in readiness for action."

" I will do so, aunt. If there is anyone here who wants to assassinate him, it is just the time he would choose for the attempt, I think it would be as well to ask Nand Chund to pick me out four of his best men, and to hand them over to my orders. However sharply I might look out in the darkness and confusion, someone might spring suddenly forward upon uncle from the side opposite that on which I was standing; but with five of us on the watch, we ought to be able to prevent anyone getting near him. I will tell no one the purpose for which I require the men, and will bid Nand Chund be equally silent. There is no saying who the traitor may be, perhaps someone we have never thought of suspecting; and if he knew we were on the watch he might drop it altogether. I only hope he will try it, it would be the best thing that could happen, as it would relieve us from the uncertainty we have been feeling. Nand Chund himself with the rest of his men will, I know, be on duty here; for I heard uncle give him his orders, which were that he was to suffer nothing, not even the entry of the enemy into the town, to induce him to leave the house, as traitors would be very likely to take advan-

tage of the confusion to rush in and perhaps to kill you, and plunder and fire the place. There will be one advantage of my having these men with me. Uncle might send me round with a message to some other part of the wall, and I should be obliged for a time to be absent; but with them round him, I could leave him for a few minutes without fear."

"Do not do it if you can help it, Percy; the night will be dark, and if you keep well behind him he may not notice you, for he will have other things to think about. Should he send you on a message, take it yourself if it is of great importance; if not, send one of the men in your place. I rely upon you more than on anyone else. Ah, here is Roland at last."

By ten o'clock everyone was at his appointed post. The colonel took Percy with him on a circuit round the walls, where he exhorted everyone to be watchful and vigilant and to preserve absolute silence until they could hear the enemy in motion down the valley.

"I have no fear there whatever," he said, as he returned to the northern wall. " Even were there a score of men among our troops who have been bought over to play a treacherous part, they could do nothing where there are so many around them on the watch. Treachery strikes when least expected. It is powerless among a multitude, and all the traders and others from the towns know that their lives are at stake, and are just as well aware as I am that the place on that side is all but impregnable unless the assailants were aided from within. They can be trusted, therefore, to keep their eyes well open. I shall not assign you any special duty, Percy. I have told Ram Bund, your commander, that I shall keep you near myself, but there is no occasion for you to stay close to me. If you see any point specially threatened you can go-there and encourage the men by your voice and presence, but I have no fear whatever that they will gain a footing on the wall.

" I shall take my post over the gateway, that is where I fancy

the brunt of the attack will fall. They will either try to fill up the cut there with faggots or bundles of grass, or throw planks over and then blow in the gate. At least that is how we should act under the same circumstances, and as, if they make the attack, they must have some fellow of uncommon enterprise in command, it is likely he will proceed in the same course. As for the wall, it is fifty feet from the parapet to the bottom of the cut, and there are no native Indian troops who would try to scale such a wall on ladders in the face of a strong and determined garrison. Of course, if they could have brought their heavy guns up here, made a breach in the wall, and half filled up the cut with its ruins, it would have been a different affair altogether, though even then I feel sure that we could beat them off. As it is they can only reckon on finding us quite unprepared for an attack, and on carrying the place by a sudden rush. I believe myself that a quarter of an hour will see the end of it, and that as soon as they understand we are fully prepared they will give up the idea as hopeless. Now we have nothing to do but to wait. I expect the attack about an hour before daybreak, which is the hour at which they will think they are most likely to find the sentinels drowsy."

CHAPTER VII

STARTLING NEWS

THE hours passed slowly as the garrison awaited the attack of the enemy. The men had been told that they could all lie down where they stood, leaving only the officers and sentries on watch; and the top of the wall and the yard behind were crowded with sleeping figures wrapt in their mantles. About two o'clock those on watch were sensible of a low confused sound in the air.

"They are moving, 1 ' the colonel said to Percy, who was sitting on the parapet, against which he was leaning. " It is probable that they have been ordered to leave their shoes behind them; and in any case the walk of a Sikh in his soft leather shoes is almost noiseless, besides they are as yet a long distance away. They are coming down the hill," he continued a quarter of an hour later; "the noise is certainly more distinct. But I give them credit for the manner of their approach. We should scarce notice the noise if we were not prepared for it, and a drowsy sentry would take it for the wind rising among the hills. One can hardly imagine that ten thousand men are moving down towards us."

Two or three of the officers came up to report that they were sure the enemy were stirring, and the colonel ordered them to get all the men quietly under arms. Another half-hour passed.

"They are a long time in coming, uncle," Percy said in a low voice.

"They are; they might have been here long before this. If I did not want to give them a lesson I would send up a rocket in order to find out what they are doing. I believe they are only a short distance away now, but we will wait for them to begin."

In a short time they were convinced that the enemy were within a hundred yards at most from the wall. Quiet as their movements were, a low hum as of orders being given in suppressed tones could be heard. On the walls all were in readiness. At a distance of a few yards apart men stood with port-fires in one hand and matches in the other, while between them lines of muskets rested on the parapet. Several times the watchers thought they could make out dim figures on the opposite side of the deep cut at the foot of the wall. Suddenly a bright light burst out exactly opposite the gate, and a moment later twenty guns opened, sending their balls crashing through the drawbridge and gate. At the same instant a rocket soared into the air from over the gateway, and a moment later a line of blue lights flashed out along the wall. A mass of men were rushing forward towards the gate, all carrying great bundles on their heads, while a tremendous yell burst from thousands of throats. It was answered by one of defiance from the wall.

The assailants paused for a moment in astonishment at the line of lights, and the proof that the garrison were prepared; out the pause was momentary, and they rushed forward again. The leaders were but a few yards from the edge of the cut when the colonel shouted " Fire!" A flash of flame ran along the wall, and twenty guns loaded to the muzzle with grape poured their contents among the enemy. Like a field of wheat levelled by the blast of a tornado the rnob of men were swept to the earth, the few that remained erect throwing down their bundles and flying for their lives. Percy, mind-

PERCY SHOOTS THE ASSASSIN PURING THE ATTACK ON THE FORTRESS.

ful of his special work, had, the moment the light flashed out opposite the gate, summoned the four men, who were standing a short distance away, and stood on the watch near his uncle.

For a few minutes there was a duel between the guns of the fortress and the Sikh cannon, which had been drawn down by hand, the wheels thickly wrapped with cotton cloths to prevent the slightest sound being made. The infantry kept up a storm of fire, which was replied to by volleys of musketry from the defenders. The din was tremendous, and presently another body of men carrying long beams and planks again rushed forward. Many of them reached the edge of the moat and tried to push the poles across, but the destruction was so great from the musketry fire from the walls, and from six guns which had been kept in reserve loaded with grape, that the survivors again fell back followed by the exultant shouts of the garrison.

At the moment that they had advanced the two port-fires over the gate went out simultaneously, and before others could be lighted Percy saw a figure that had been crouching under the parapet a short distance off spring forward. The guard nearest to him also observed the movement, and threw himself in the man's way. A knife flashed in the air and he fell. His assailant then sprung towards the colonel, whose back was turned to him, when a ball from Percy's pistol struck him in the head and he fell dead in his tracks. The pistol-shot attracted no attention amid the roar of firearms, and Percy, without paying further attention to the fallen man, ordered the remaining three guards to redouble their vigilance.

"The scoundrel may not be alone," he said. "The attempt may be repeated."

With the retirement of the second body of men charged to bridge the fosse the enemy lost heart. It was evident even to the most determined that success was impossible, now that the garrison were prepared. The guns, too, suffered so terri-

bly from the heavier metal of those on the wall, that half of them lay dismounted, and the gunners would no longer work the others in the face of the heavy fire that mowed them down. The yells subsided and the fire ceased, and as noiselessly as they had come the assailants glided away into the darkness, pursued, however, for some time by the bullets and shot of the defenders. Convinced that there was no fear of a repetition of the assault, the colonel ordered the greater part of the troops back to their quarters.

Now that the din near at hand had ceased, the rattle of musketry and the boom of guns could be heard from the other walls. The colonel hurried away to see what was going on there. He found that the moment the firing began on the north face of the fortress it broke out from the valleys on either side, where large numbers of men had stolen up in the darkness, while at the same time the heavy guns in the camp had also opened fire. The defenders had at once replied, and the fire had been continued on both sides, but it had begun to die away on the side of the assailants as soon as it ceased on the northern face. The colonel sent for a party of artillerymen to aid the men working the guns, and ordered a steady fire to be kept up on the camp, and then dismissed his allies to their tents and returned himself to his house, to which Percy had gone as soon as the fighting was over to tell his aunt that the attack had been repulsed and that all was well.

"Then my fears were groundless, Percy?"

"No, aunt, they were the means of saving my uncle's life," and he then related the attempt at assassination and its result.

" Heaven be praised ! " she said, bursting into tears. " I had a presentiment of evil, as I have more than once had before when his life has been threatened. Thank God the danger has come and gone and that he is still unharmed. Did you know who the man was?"

" I did not notice, aunt, or think of looking at him after he had fallen. There was such a tremendous roar going on that I

felt quite confused, and thought of nothing but that the attack might be repeated. I will go and see who it is as soon as it is light."

By this time some hot coffee had been prepared, and Percy had already partaken of it when the colonel returned. As he entered his wife threw herself into his arms.

"Thank God you have returned safe, Roland, and have once more escaped the dangers that threatened you."

"The dangers were not great this time, love, being only from a stray bullet; for the artillery confined their fire to the gate, in hopes no doubt that a lucky shot might bring the drawbridge down. Not that this was likely, for I had it fastened up by half a dozen chains, anyone of which would have held it."

"It was not the bullets of the enemy, but the knife of an assassin that I feared," she said.

"Pooh, pooh, my love! you are always dreaming of assassins."

"And not without reason, Roland; had it not been for Percy's pistol you would not be alive now."

The colonel looked surprised at Percy. "What does this mean, lad? I did not hear you fire, and, indeed, did not notice you from the time when the attack began to the time when it was over. Do you mean to say that my life was attempted, and that you saved me?"

"It was aunt's doing, not mine, uncle." Percy then related the injunctions his aunt had given him and the results.

"You have saved my life again, Mahtab," he said embracing his wife tenderly. "At least this time you and Percy have done it between you. And who is the traitor?"

"That Percy does not know; he did not think of examining the body."

"Then we will do so at once," the colonel said, putting on his cap again. "Daylight will soon be breaking, and as soon as it does the soldiers will be at work removing from the wall the bodies of those who fell in the fight. I heard just now that there were twenty-five men killed by the enemy's musket-fire, and another twenty or thirty hit in the hand or arm as they fired over the wall. Come along, Percy, you will know exactly where the man fell."

Calling a couple of his guards and bidding one bring a lantern with him, the colonel, accompanied by Percy, went to the wall, where the latter at once pointed out the body of the man he had shot, lying close to that of the guard who had fallen by his knife.

"Throw the light on his face," the colonel said, and as the soldier did so he uttered an exclamation of surprise and disgust.

"It is Azim Bund—the scoundrel! He was the last man I should have suspected. He was penniless when I picked him up years ago. He professed the greatest attachment for me, and being clever and shrewd I raised him step by step until at last he became my confidential steward. He was bound to me by every tie of gratitude, and I certainly thought him absolutely devoted to my interests. Ever since the attempt to seize you on your way here showed that there was a traitor in the fortress, he has appeared most earnest in his attempts to discover him; and to think that all this time it was the scoundrel himself! Mahtab has never liked the man, though she never suspected his fidelity. I suppose he had been heavily bribed, and had the promise of some good place from Ghoolab Singh. Well, he richly deserved the fate that has befallen him. I am glad that it was not a soldier, for I like to think that all my men are faithful to me to the last.

"That was a good shot of yours, Percy, your ball struck him just in the centre of the forehead. Well, there is one thing, there need be no fear at present of another attempt of this kind. This fellow would never have dared to make a confidant. An officer might enlist some of his men in such a plot, but a man in Azim's position would not venture to do so. A steward is not often popular with the men he looks after, and I don't think this fellow was any exception to the rule. Do you two men remain with the body until the morning, and see that no one touches it. You can search his pockets now, but it is not likely that such a cunning knave would be carrying any documents that would incriminate him, about on his person."

"There is nothing in his pockets, sahib," one of the soldiers said, "but I can feel he has a heavy belt round his body."

"Take it off and examine it."

It was found that a hundred gold mohurs were sewn up in the belt. "The first instalment of the price of my life," the colonel said. "Here is one apiece for you, men; the rest shall be laid out in charity. There must be scores of people who have been made homeless in the last day or two.

" In the morning make a thorough search of the fellow's clothes, he may have some paper sewn up in them. Now, Percy, we will go back to the house."

The Ranee was greatly agitated when she heard who was the author of the attack upon the colonel's life.

"It is terrible, Roland, to think that we can trust no one, and that for months your life has been endangered by that man. I cannot think why he waited so long."

"He was waiting for a safe opportunity, as he thought," the colonel replied. " Our private apartments are always locked at night, and during the day the opportunities for putting a knife into me without suspicion falling upon him were not frequent. No doubt he knew that Ghoolab was going to send an army here, and it was probably arranged that the affair should not take place until it arrived, as with me out of the way the garrison would probably surrender, and Ghoolab's son would only have to enter and take possession; and would, moreover, gain a certain amount of credit for what would be regarded as his capture of the olace. He might, perhaps,

have done it at night, but your idea of putting Nand Chund and the guard here would altogether upset that plan, and drive him to choose some other opportunity. At any rate we can sleep in peace now. It is morally certain that Azim would not run the risk of having an accomplice, especially as he would regard it as certain that he would be able to carry out his design without aid."

The morning light showed how terrible had been the effect of the fire of the besieged upon the assailants. The ground for two hundred yards back from the fosse was thickly strewn with dead, and around the spot where the cannon stood the men who had served them lay in heaps. After sending out a party to make sure that the enemy had all retired right, a force was sent out to collect and bring in the deserted guns and the wounded. There were over three hundred of the latter, and eight hundred dead were counted. Shortly afterwards two men with a white flag were seen coming down the hill.

The colonel and an officer went out to meet them, and it was found that they were the bearers of a request to be permitted to carry away the dead. This the colonel readily granted, being well pleased indeed at being saved the trouble of burying them, which would have been a work of great trouble and labour, owing to the shallowness of the soil. A large body of men came down for the purpose, but it was nightfall before the last of the bodies were carried away. The enemy's camp in the valley had, at daybreak, been removed out on to the plain, a mile and a half farther away, so as to be beyond the range of the guns.

Late in the afternoon a large force was seen to march in there, and the garrison had no doubt that this was the main body of the troops who had attacked them in the night.

A week passed without any further movement, and then it was noticed one morning that the tents had been struck, and shortly afterwards the whole army was seen to march away to

STARTLING NEWS

the south. Some of the merchants at once sent off messengers to gather news, and by nightfall the colonel learnt that it

reported that the mother of the maharajah had consented to

the demands of the army to make war against the British. An ** >

officer who had passed through the nearest town had stated that he was the bearer of despatches, ordering the force who were besieging the fortress to return at once to Lahore.

"That must have been very welcome news for every man in camp," the colonel said. "The soldiers must be already sick of the business, which must have cost them at least a thousand men, counting those that died after the fight from their wounds; and they must have seen well enough that this was nothing to what the loss would be before the place was captured. The leaders must be even more glad; the fact that no movement has been made since the repulse shows that they are at their wits' end as to what their next move should be. They must have known that another repulse might cause a mutiny among the troops, and might even cost them their lives. They must have been glad indeed at the news of their recall.

"And now, Percy, we must lose no time in warning our friends of what is intended. They may have got news already from Lahore; but we cannot risk that—their agents there may be imprisoned or killed, therefore you had better prepare to start for Loodiana in an hour's time. Nand Chund shall go with you again with fifty men. There will no doubt be many sirdars moving with their followers towards Lahore, and you will therefore excite little attention; and if questioned, Nand Chund will say that he is on his way to join the army. No, it will not be quite true; but that is a matter that will not rest at all heavily on his conscience. Lying is not considered a great moral offence at any time by the Sikhs, or indeed by any natives of India; and to deceive an enemy in time of war, is considered absolutely meritorious. There will be no occasion for you to say anything one way or another; he will

appear as the head of the expedition, and you will pass unnoticed and unquestioned. Nand Chund is perfectly capable of talking for himself and half a dozen others. Fondness for using his tongue at all times is one of his principal failings.'"

"Am I to come straight back again, uncle? "

The colonel thought for a minute or two. " I will leave that entirely in your hands, Percy; you are old enough now to act on your own account. If you can be useful—and it is probable that you may be very useful owing to your acquaintance with the language and the knowledge that you have gained of the people—to the Resident at Loodiana, I should say that it would be best for you to put yourself at his service. It would be a very useful beginning for you, and would give you a claim that might be of great advantage to you in the future. Besides, I should think you would wish to see what is going on, and there are likely to be some stirring events in the next few months. Here we shall have a quiet time of it, for with a war with England on their hands no one will think of troubling about us, and they will need every man for the work they have cut out for themselves. Do you agree with me, Mahtab? "

"Yes, I shall be sorry, very sorry for him to go; but I think it would be best for him. You always tell me that if my people go to war with yours it is sure to end in the Punjaub being annexed. There will then be no career for him here, and it will be better so since his life would be, as yours has been, one of constant danger. Thus then, it will be much better for him to make friends with officers in the Company's service, so that he may, as you have pointed out many times, become an officer of theirs when they are masters of the Punjaub."

"You will want a servant; indeed you had better have two. They must be trusty men above all things, and shrewd fellows too, whom you can, if necessary, despatch on difficult errands. I should say you had better let Nand Chund pick you out two of his men, unless you have any fancy yourself."

" He spoke very highly to me of those he chose for me last night, uncle. However, I will speak to him."

"Do so, Percy; a man may be faithful and an excellent guard, and yet not be the one you would choose as a servant. You want two cheery good-tempered fellows, who will always do what they are told without grumbling. I should say that you had better have Pathans, for a Sikh's sympathies would certainly be with his countrymen. I will walk down with you myself and have a chat with Nand Chund; next to a good horse and good arms, a good servant is the most important point on entering on a campaign; a handy fellow will make you comfortable under almost all circumstances, while with one who has not a knack of cooking, or of managing things for your comfort, you will be in all sorts of straits,"

When the matter was explained to the officer he said: " You could not do better than take Akram Chunder, he is a Pathan, and one of the men you had last night He was Sohan Verdi's own man for a time; but the major is hot-tempered, and spoke sharply to him one day, and he chose to go back into the ranks again. Sohan has told me more than once that he was one of the best men he ever had. He is a good soldier, he has been in your service for ten years, and he has a high character for coi:rage. I do not think that the young sahib can do better than take him. As to the other he shall have my own man, Bhop Lai. He is an invaluable man in the field, merry, good-tempered, eager to please, ready to do anything for his master's comfort. Here, however, he has been too long inactive, and is getting idle. Were I going on a campaign I should be sorry indeed to part with him; but as it is I can find a roan who will suit me just as well, and he is the very man for the young sahib; he is intelligent and trustworthy, a good groom and cook."

"Then Percy cannot do better than try them. Send for them to come to my house at once, I will myself speak to them and see how they like the proposal; a man who goes

unwillingly had much better stop behind. I am obliged to you, Nand Chund, for giving up your man to my nephew."

Ten minutes later the servant announced that the two men were at the door, and they were at once brought in.

"My nephew is going to Loodiana," the colonel began, "and it maybe that he will remain with his friends. You have, of course, both heard the news that the maharanee has yielded to the wishes of the army, and that they are going to war with the English. My nephew is going to join his own people, and will, I daresay, remain with them until the war is over. He wants two servants, good fellows who can be thoroughly relied upon, who can look after his comfort in the field, carry messages if necessary from, one end of the country to the other, and who can be relied upon to be thoroughly faithful and devoted to him. I have consulted Nand Chund, and he has strongly recommended you both. I do not wish you to go unless you are perfectly willing to do so. While you are with him, you will receive double pay, and a present will not be wanting when he returns here if he gives a good report on your services. Now, what do you say? "

Both men expressed their willingness to follow Percy, and it was evident by their manner that they considered it no small honour to have been selected to attend upon the colonel's nephew.

"That is settled then," the colonel said. "I need tell you nothing about your duties, for you are both accustomed to the work. I will see that you are well mounted. Have you each good arms and a brace of pistols?" Both replied in the affirmative. " Make your preparations at once. Nand Chund will start in half an hour with fifty men to escort my nephew to Loodiana."

The men saluted and retired, and the colonel gave orders that two good horses should be picked out for them. Three quarters of an hour later Percy rode out from the gate of the fortress with his escort, his two followers falling in in the rear.

STARTLING NEWS

Being this time unencumbered by baggage animals, the march was more rapid than it had been on the way up. As the country was full of armed parties making their way to Lahore, their passage attracted no attention until they turned off from the road to that city. After that they avoided towns, and riding without a halt for twelve hours they crossed the Sutlej on the evening of the fifth day, and on the following morning rode into Loodiana. A considerable change had taken place since Percy had left it six months before. Then there were but two or three battalions of troops stationed there, now the long line of tents showed that this force was largely augmented, and that six or seven thousand men were collected in the camp. It was evident that the British authorities were alive to the coming danger, and that they would not be surprised by the unprovoked invasion of the Sikhs.

Sir Henry Hardinge had arrived in July as governor-general, and being warned by the Residents at Loodiana and other frontier stations of the probability that the Sikh army would insist upon war, and overcome any opposition on the part of the maharanee, he had quietly made preparations for the event by moving up considerable bodies of troops to the north-west. It had indeed for some time been evident, that unless Ghoolab Singh accepted the office of prime minister troubles must come. He was the one man in the country whose personal power and influence would enable him to control the mutinous army, and his refusal to accept the post rendered it certain that the struggle would come sooner or later.

Ghoolab possessed talent and astuteness equal to that of his brother Dhyan, and was, like him, convinced that the power of England was too great-for that of the Sikhs; he was, therefore, strongly against war. On the other hand his position was a difficult one. Had he attempted to stem the tide of popular clamour his own army would have turned against him, and he might have lost both his possessions and his life. He

was therefore obliged to temporize, and believed that he would gain advantages whichever way the struggle went.

To the Sikhs, then, he professed a complete agreement with their views, but at the same time under one excuse or another he remained at Jummoo, replying to their repeated requests that he would advance with his army to Lahore, by saying that he was perfectly ready to do so, but that he thought it would be in all respects better to keep his army as a separate force and so co-operate with the main body. On the other hand he sent secret messages to the British, assuring them of his friendship, and promising them that whenever he saw the opportunity he would throw the whole weight of his influence and power into the scale on their side.

Nand Chund and his detachment of cavalry did not enter Loodiana, but took leave of Percy when they came within sight of the place, and started at once on their return.

"I shall travel by another road," he said, "and if we should be questioned hereafter we can strongly deny any report that we have paid a visit to Loodiana, for were it known it would excite a feeling against our lord, who would be accused of being in communication with the English. There is, it is true, no cause whatever to fear another attack upon the fortress while the war continues, but it might prejudice him afterwards, and if things go badly with the Sikhs some fanatic might endeavour to take vengeance upon him."

" Give my love to my uncle and aunt, and tell them I hope to see them again before long."

Percy's two followers closed up behind him, and as soon as the troops had started he rode with them into Loodiana.

The Resident was alighting from his horse at the door of his bungalow when Percy rode up.

"Ah, Groves, is it you?" he said. "I was wondering whether I should see you soon. I heard that an army had marched to attack your uncle's place, and a few days ago my agent at Lahore wrote me there were rumours that they had

been repulsed with very heavy loss, which I was glad to hear, not only for your sake, but because a reverse of that sort would not raise the spirits of their army. How did it all end, and what are you here for? But you can tell me that while we are having tiffen; you know it is about my hour. You have become a regular young Sikh. I did not recognize you at the first glance in that finery."

"I have worn it ever since I have been there," Percy said. "I did not like it at first, but I soon got accustomed to it, and it is certainly cooler than my own clothes. But there is such a prejudice against Europeans that my uncle thought that I had much better follow his example and dress in the fashion of the country. I brought a couple of English suits down with me in my valise, but I was obliged to ride down in this dress in order to escape notice. Shall I change before tiffen, sir?"

"No, you look very well as you are, Groves. Have you come far this morning? "

"Only about ten miles. I came down with an escort of fifty men, and crossed the Sutlej yesterday evening. They left me a couple of miles outside the town."

"Well, you had better go in to your old room and have a wash while I take my bath. Tiffen will be ready in a quarter of an hour."

Two or three officers were present at tiffen, and these had difficulty at first in crediting Mr. Fullarton's assurance that the young Sikh to whom he introduced them was really an English lad. At tiffen Percy related the events of the siege of the fortress at his host's request.

"It must be a strong place by your description," Mr. Fullarton said when Percy concluded his narration, "and would puzzle even British troops to carry it by assault. Still I have no doubt our engineers would manage somehow to get heavy guns on to the hill commanding it, and once there it could not hold out long."

"My uncle was quite aware of that, sir; but the Sikhs are very clumsy with their cannon, and he calculated that the troops would soon be tired of the siege. But it would certainly be a very difficult matter to get heavy guns up there. There is some sort of road round behind through the hills, but I believe it is a mere track, and uncle thought it hardly possible at any rate for the Sikhs to bring heavy artillery along it. The only other road is that commanded by the guns of the fortress, and runs but a little more than a quarter of a mile away from it. The guns could not be taken up without very heavy loss."

After the officers had left, Mr. Fullarton asked, " And how about yourself, Groves? What are you thinking of doing, and what can I do for you? "

"My uncle thought I might be of use, sir. I can speak Punjaubi well enough to pass as a native, and he thought that you might accept my services as a volunteer, and might find me useful in obtaining information, communicating with any of the Sikh nobles who might be friendly, or in any other way. I have two men with me, both of whom can be trusted thoroughly, either as messengers or to go into the Sikh camp if necessary to gather information. I started the moment the Sikhs moved away from before the fortress, and we had news that they were summoned to join the main army at Lahore as the maharanee had given way to the wishes of the war-party. The news was so important that my uncle sent me off at once, thinking that probably your agent at Lahore might be unable to send you news, as anyone known to be in communication with you would probably be arrested at once when war was finally determined on."

"You are the first bearer of the news," Mr. Fullarton said. "It is ten days since I had a message from Lahore. It was in that letter my agent sent me the news that the first assault on the fortress had failed. He said then that the war-party had completely gained the ascendency, and that he thought

the final decision would shortly be taken. He warned me that he might be unable to send me further news at present as he was in very bad odour, it being known he was in communication with me, and that he was sure to be watched if not imprisoned.

" Not having heard, I felt no doubt whatever that war had been decided upon and wrote accordingly to the authorities, but I have had no absolute certainty until now, as other causes may have prevented my agent from writing. Take a seat out in the verandah for a few minutes. I must send off a despatch at once with the news, and also inform Brigadier Wheeler, who is in command here, that the reports that the Sikhs have determined on war are now confirmed. After I have sent the despatches off I will join you again and talk over what you were saying about volunteering."

CHAPTER VIII
IN THE SERVICE

PERCY was not kept waiting long, for in twenty minutes Mr. Fullarton joined him in the verandah.

" Now about yourself, Groves. I have no doubt that you will be able to make yourself very useful, and I at once accept your services as a volunteer in the civil service. I do not know yet whether I myself shall accompany the troops if they march from here. If I do I will take you with me, if not I will introduce you to General Wheeler, and transfer your services to him. There is a great dearth of men who speak Punjaubi, and I am quite sure he will be very glad to have someone with him so well acquainted with the language as you are. I expect him here shortly; he is sure to come across to talk matters over with me as soon as he receives my note. I will introduce you to him then. Before he comes you had better change and get into English dress. He is a soldier of the old school, and might regard your present attire as a sort of masquerading, and receive an unpleasant impression of you."

Half an hour later General Wheeler and three or four officers of his staff rode up to the door and had a long interview with the Resident. At its conclusion a servant brought a message to Percy that Mr. Fullarton desired to see him. He had by this time changed his clothes,

"This is the young gentleman of whom I have been speaking to you, general," the Resident said as Percy entered. " He is the nephew of the Colonel Groves who has been many years in the Sikh service. His father was an officer in our own army. He speaks Punjaubi like a native. He has volunteered, and will, I am sure, be very useful to us. I came out with him in the same ship from England, and formed a high idea of his intelligence. It is, I believe, his wish to enter the service of the Company later on. He is not without some little experience in war, for but a week ago he took part in the defence of his uncle's fortress when attacked by fifteen thousand Sikhs, whom they beat off handsomely. I have been telling General Wheeler, Groves, that you might be very useful in obtaining information or in communications with the natives, and that the fact that there might be some little peril in the work would not be any obstacle to your undertaking it. I said that I was going to keep you by me as a sort of civilian aide-de-camp, but the general has been good enough to say that he will attach you to his staff nominally as interpreter, but in fact as an extra aide-de-camp: and as my assistant and myself both speak the language well, while the general is short of officers who know it, I feel that you will be of more service to him than to me. But I consider you as lent only, and I shall be glad at any time if

General Wheeler no longer requires your services to take you on in the capacity of an extra assistant."

" Can you ride ? " General Wheeler asked. " But I suppose I need hardly ask that, as you have been living among the Sikhs."

"Yes, I can ride, sir, in the Sikh fashion or the English." "Mr. Fullarton tells me that you could pass as a native." "In anything like an ordinary conversation I could, sir; and as I have worn the native dress for the last ten months I am perfectly at home in it."

"Very well, then, you can consider yourself as from the

present time attached to my staff. Major Clissold, v/ill you see after him? I should think that you, as adjutant-general of the division, will find him even more useful than I should do as an aide-de-camp."

"You can leave us now, Groves," Mr. Fullarton said, "but wait outside and Major Clissold will speak to you presently."

Percy bowed and withdrew. The conversation still continued to turn upon him.

" I should think one might put him in general orders, Clissold, either as an extra aide-de-camp or as attached to your department. I don't know what the rules of the service are with regard to the uniform of volunteers attached to the army. It is so seldom done now that I really do not know, but in the old days they were dressed, I believe, as officers."

"No, that won't do," Mr. Fullarton laughed. "I am going to make a civilian of him. If he does well in the campaign he might perhaps get gazetted as an ensign, but it would be very much better for him to have a claim on the civil side. Therefore, I shall take upon myself to appoint him as my deputy-assistant. I shall write to Sir Henry Hardinge asking that the temporary appointment may be confirmed, seeing the urgent necessity for more officers up in the language and with a knowledge of the country. So we may consider the appointment made. Now I lend him to you, and you can put it in general orders that the temporary services of Deputy-assistant Groves have been placed by me at your disposal as interpreter, and that he is henceforth attached to the headquarter staff of the division. That will give him an established position, and he can wear his civilian clothes, a white helmet, and so on."

"I think that will be a very good plan," the general said.

" He has two servants with him. They are Pathans, both first-rate fellows, whom he will employ when necessary to obtain information,. I would suggest that they be put on rations as a matter of convenience to Groves, and they could

be entered either as civilian servants or guides. It is no question of money, for although the lad's uncle has a reputation for moderation, very rare among the adventurers who served Runjeet Singh, he must be a rich man."

"I will make a note of it," Major Clissold said, and the conversation then turned to other matters.

Half an hour later the officers came out and rode away. Mr. Fullarton said as they did so, " I will myself ride over with Groves later on," and he then came into the verandah, where Percy was waiting. "I think I have done a good stroke of business for you, Groves."

"You have indeed, sir. I am awfully obliged to you, although I would rather have stayed with you."

"And I should have been glad to have had you, but it is better as we have arranged it. You will have much greater opportunities for seeing service with the brigadier, and a report in your favour would come much better from him than it would from me, as I appointed you. It is probable that I shall remain at my post, and in that case there would be little for you to do here. While acting as an interpreter on the staff you will have abundant work, making bargains for the quartermaster's department, for waggons and transport, finding out about roads and fords for Major Clissold, and in general interpreting work. You must change your head-gear. That pithtopee you have got is really better, but we generally wear either the helmet or a cap like a forage cap, with a pugaree wrapt round it, and the ends falling down behind to keep the sun off the back of the neck and spine. I should advise you to adopt that, for there is no getting a helmet here. When you ride about always take one or both of your mounted servants behind you. They are soldierly-looking fellows, and it will give you weight with the natives. I need not tell you that now you will hardly be free to go about quite as you like, and that even when there is nothing for you to do you will be expected to be at hand if required. Major Clissold is a capi-

tal fellow to serve under. He may work you hard, for there will be an immense deal of work to be done, but he is always pleasant and agreeable to his subordinates, and is very much liked in the force. I have some writing to finish, but in about an hour I shall be ready to start with you, so you may as well warn your two fellows to be ready. I have a forage cap that I have only worn once or twice, for it is too small for me. I will tell Ram Singh to put a pugaree on, and if necessary put some folded cotton inside the lining to make it fit you."

An hour later they rode into the head-quarter camp.

"I have brought you your interpreter, Clissold," Mr. Fullar-ton said as he entered that officer's tent, followed by Percy, their horses being held by the latter's men. " Where are you going to stow him? As there is no getting tent furniture here, I have told my man to send over what is necessary; but as I did not know whether Groves would have a tent to himself or not I told him to wait till I returned before he started."

" No, I have put him in a tent with Hunt. We can't afford a tent each for subalterns, so they are doubled up two together. But Hunt happens to be an odd man, which is lucky. Orderly," he called out, and as the soldier entered, "tell Mr. Hunt I shall be glad if he will step here."

A minute later a young officer entered. "Hunt, here is the young gentleman who, as I told you, will have to share your tent. He is a volunteer in the civil service. Mr. Ful-larton has kindly lent him to us for a time as interpreter, which I am sure we want badly enough on the staff, for none of you young fellows are of the slightest use with the natives. He is the son of an officer late of our service and has been for the last six months with his uncle, who was one of Runjeet Singh's colonels, and still holds the fortress he was appointed to some time ago, although ordered by the Sikhs to leave. I am sure you will get on well together, and I hope that you will make him as comfortable as you can, and introduce him to the other aides. He will mess with you for the present."

The young officer shook hands with Percy. " If you will come with me I will show you our tent."

"If you don't mind, Hunt, I will come with you," Mr. Fullarton said; " then I can see what is wanted in the way of furniture."

The tent was a square one with double canvas, the two walls being four feet apart, thus making a passage round it, one side being utilized as a bath-room and receptacle for luggage, the other being used by the servants as their living and sleeping apartment. There was a carpet spread over the floor, a native camp-bed, two folding chairs, a table, and a portable bath.

"All you want, as far as I can see," Mr. Fullarton said, "is another charpoy -and a couple more chairs."

"That is all," Hunt agreed; "this is all the furniture one is allowed, which we think rather hard. Do you think the Sikhs are going to cross the Sutlej, sir?"

"Of course, they may do so, but the general impression is that it will not be in force; they may begin by making raids, but probably the real fighting will take place when we get across.

Well, now, I shall leave you, Groves; I think you will get on very well, and I daresay we shall meet pretty nearly every day."

"Are those two fellows yours?" Hunt asked, as, going out of the tent with Mr. Fullarton, he saw the two natives sitting like statues on their horses in front of the tent, while one of them held the bridle of Percy's horse.

"Yes, they are my two servants; they are two of my uncle's soldiers. Both have been officers' servants, they are extremely useful fellows, and I can trust them thoroughly. One is a Pathan from the hill frontier of Afghanistan, the other is from Cashmere, therefore neither of them have any special leanings towards the Sikhs."

"That is a capital horse of yours?"

"Yes, he is very fast, and has much more endurance than the horses of the plains. My uncle bred him. He has a

European sire, and his dam is considered as having some of the best blood in the Punjaub. What shall I tell my men to do with the horses? "

" They can picket yours over there; that line of horses all belong to the staff. Their own they can put with that line behind, those are the horses of the orderlies. I will go across with you and see about it, or some of the soldiers will be interfering."

The horses were soon picketed, and the men brought Percy's saddle and valises to his tent. By night he felt quite at home. The aides-de-camp were pleasant young men, and having already been spoken to by Major Clissold, received the newcomer cordially. Percy had inquired of Hunt as to the messing arrangements. " I am well supplied with money," he said, "and wish, of course, to pay my share of all expenses."

"That can easily be managed," Hunt replied. "The way it is arranged is this. There were five of us: Long and myself are the general's aides-de-camp; Humphreys and Lascelles, who are deputy-assistant-quartermaster-generals; and Egerton, who is an assistant-adjutant-general. They are all lieutenants. We brought up with us a certain amount of mess stores, principally liquor, which are all common property. I will see to-morrow what stock is left, and you can hand me over a sixth of the value, which will go to the fund for general expenses. However, these are not heavy, for being under canvas we draw rations—meat and bread—and I buy what I can get in the way of vegetables, game, and so on, from the country people. Of course, if you leave us before our store of liquor is exhausted, I shall, as it were, buy your share back again."

Percy found the society very agreeable. His experience of the junior officers' mess on board a ship had prepared him for the tone of light chaff and fun that prevailed. Although by some four years the youngest of the party, the fact that he was acquainted with the country they expected shortly to invade gave him a certain weight with the others, none of whom had

been in that part of India before. He was asked innumerable questions as to the Sikhs, and what he thought of their righting powers; and had to recount in full detail the story of the attempt to storm the fortress.

"That uncle of yours must be an uncommonly plucky fellow to hold on there in the face of the whole of the Sikhs, and he must be amazingly liked by his troops for them to stick to him against their own countrymen."

"That is not so wonderful," Percy said, "for the Sikhs are constantly fighting against each other. Most of his men have served under him for eight or ten years. The rest were recruited in his district, which was only conquered by the Sikhs in Runjeet's time, so they are still considered as interlopers by the natives. Still, of course, there is always the fear of treachery; and my uncle nearly lost his life while the attack was going on; the man who attempted it was one of those he trusted most thoroughly, being his steward and the head of his household."

"You did not tell us about that," Hunt said. "How was it? " and Percy had to tell the story.

" And you shot him ? Well, I have never shot a man yet, and I don't know how I should feel. Were you very uncomfortable afterwards? "

"Not in the slightest. . He was going to kill my uncle, and I fired and he went down, and I thought nothing more about it till I mentioned it to my uncle after it was all over."

" I suppose you are a good shot? "

"I am a fair shot," Percy said. "I have practised nearly every day since I left England, except when I was travelling up country. Mr. Fullarton advised me to do so on board ship, and my uncle kept me regularly at that and riding and sword exercise every day, partly because he said these things would De most useful to me, and partly because the Sikhs look up to anyone who can do things better than they can."

" It must be awfully jolly to be able to speak the language, Groves?" Lieutenant Egerton said, "and I hear you speak it like a native. You must have a wonderful knack of picking up languages to have learnt it so completely in six months."

" It was not exactly in six months. I had studied Hindustani before I left England; and luckily Mr. Fullarton had a Punjaubi servant with him, and I worked with him regularly five or six hours a day throughout the voyage, so that I was able to get on pretty fairly with the language by the time I got out here."

"I wish I had spent my voyage as well," Egerton laughed, "instead of spending it spooning with a young woman who was on her way out to be married, and who did marry the man a week after she landed."

"These things are very sad, Egerton," Lieutenant Lascelles laughed. "I suppose you were heart-broken for a time."

"Not quite. I will do her justice to say that she made no secret of her engagement, and never flattered me with the hope that she intended to break it. At the same time she had no objection to flirt with me, it being an understood thing on both sides that it was to end with the voyage. It was very pleasant while it lasted; but it would have been very much wiser to have done as Groves did, and spent the hot hours of the day in getting up a language. I should be a hundred a year better off if I had passed in one of the dialects, and besides, I should have had much better chance of getting a ^good appointment."

" Ah, well, you can console yourself, Egerton, by thinking that if you had you would now be in some small cantonment down in Bengal, instead of having a chance of seeing whatever fun may be going on here."

"That is a consolation certainly, Hunt; but I don't care how soon the fun begins, for I own that I am getting sick of bargaining for bullocks and working like a horse eight or tern hours a day. It is all very well for you aides-de-camp, whose work consists in writing a few letters for the chief and can-

tering across with some message; but for us hard-worked quartermasters it is no holiday here. 1 do hope most heartily that the Sikhs will not be long before they begin their raids, and give us a decent excuse for fighting them."

" How strong do you think they are likely to turn out, Groves? They tell us a hundred thousand."

"I should say a good deal more than that," Percy replied. "There will be over a hundred thousand troops, for ;,11 who have passed through the ranks will be certain to rt join them. Then the great sirdars can put almost as many fignting men into the field."

"That sounds serious, and I suppose there is no doubt they will fight bravely."

"lhat they are sure to do," Percy said. "What force do you think we shall be able to put in the field? "

"There are over ten thousand men at Ferozepore, with twenty-four guns. Here we have, by the field state to-day, seven thousand two hundred and thirty-five, and twelve guns. At Umballa there are about thirteen thousand men, with thirty-two guns. You see, ever since Hardinge came out he has seen this thing brewing, and has been quietly preparing for it. When he landed in India last year there were at these three stations only between thirteen and fourteen thousand men and forty-eight guns, and in the last eighteen months he has increased the force by seventeen thousand men and twenty guns.

"At Meerut there are about ten thousand men and twenty-six guns, but as that place is two hundred and fifty miles away, we can't count upon any assistance from there at first, if the Sikhs should take it into their head to cross the Sutlej. Of course if we invade we shall wait until the Meerut force is brought up before we advance. Sir Henry arrived at Urn- | balla on the second, and was to leave yesterday. Ostensibly he is not here for any warlike purpose whatever, but is occupied in making an inspection of the protected district, inter-

viewing the chiefs, and ascertaining what their feeling is towards us. These states voluntarily put themselves under our protection some five-and-thirty years ago, having no desire to fall under the sway of Lahore; and they have greatly benefited, for Runjeet Singh would assuredly have annexed the whole territory between the Sutlej and the Jumma, if he had not been warned that if he attacked these petty princes he would bring us into the field against him. It has always been a sore point with the Sikhs beyond the Sutlej that we prevented them from obtaining what they considered their natural boundaries. The protected states are indeed to a great extent Sikh, and even now, although they owe the continuance of their existence as separate states to our protection, and the chiefs are all with us, the sympathies of the great body of the people are entirely with the Sikhs across the Sutlej.

"Runjeet Singh was wise enough to know that he would have risked losing all he had were he to try to wrest them from us. Had he thought himself strong enough he would have risked a war for it, for the country south of the Sutlej is far more fertile than it is to the north, and it would largely increase the revenues of the Punjaub did it form part of it. This is the real cause of their hostility to us, and of their present threatening attitude. Sir Henry is going, as I said, among the chiefs here. Some of these are really friendly, others only pretend to be so. But there is one thing certain, if any misfortune happened to our arms the whole country would be up against us; and in any case we shall have to take every possible precaution to guard our depots and communications, for directly fighting begins it would be unsafe for small parties to travel about the country."

Percy's stay in camp was of very short duration, for on the following evening Major Clissold sent for him.

"The general has just received a despatch from headquarters, Groves; the news from the north is to the effect that

the Sikhs are making great preparations there, and Major Broadfoot, the chief political agent at head-quarters, requests that you will at once proceed there to join him, as he wishes to question you as to your own personal observations of the state of feeling as you came down. I think it probable he will keep you with him for the present; and as you may have more important work to do there than buying bullocks and so on, I hope for your sake he will do so, though I shall be sorry to lose you, for I have already found by your work today that you would be a very valuable assistant. Still there is nothing like being at head-quarters and having the eye of the chief of your department upon you. You had better start this evening late."

"Very well, sir, I will be off in half an hour. I suppose I can ride round and say good-bye to Mr. Fullarton."

"Certainly. There is no absolute occasion to start until morning, but it is always well to show zeal, and it will no doubt please Broadfoot if you arrive there by daybreak. You needn't start till two o'clock; it is only a three hours' ride. The head-quarter camp is close to Basseean."

" I am sorry you are going," Hunt said when Percy returned to his tent and told him the news, " and I hope you will be back again in a day or two. If not, it will save me the trouble of taking stock of our liquors, which I was going to do to-morrow morning. We shall be glad at any rate to have had you as our guest for a day, and shall all be sorry at your leaving."

Percy at once rode over to the Residency.

"You are in luck, Groves," Mr. Fullarton said when he told him of the order he had received. "There is nothing like getting to head-quarters; it is there that honours and rewards fall thickest; and if Broadfoot keeps you with him you may be sure that any recommendation he makes in your favour will be attended to. I have heard this afternoon that the Sikhs are certainly marching down towards Ferozepore, and are within a few miles of the river. Of course they may not cross

148 THROUGH THE SIKH WAR

Once or twice before they have come down, but without crossing. Still, if they are in earnest there is no doubt it means serious fighting, for the force at Ferozepore is quite isolated and will at once be cut off if the Sikhs cross near the town, and there will be no chance of relieving it until we get together a force sufficient to give battle. Sit down a moment and I will write a letter of introduction for you to Broadfoot; it will put you on a pleasanter footing with him."

The next morning before sunrise Percy with his two followers rode into the head-quarters camp. He had at Mr. Fullarton's recommendation bought a pony, or "tat" as it is called, to carry his valises and his dress as a young Sikh sirdar.

"I should stick to that, Groves; it may be of use to you. There is no saying what work Broadfoot may give you."

Percy was, on his arrival, directed to the tent of the political agent. When the orderly took in his name he was at once called in. "I did not expect you so soon, Mr. Groves," Major Broadfoot said looking up; "nor did I expect," he added smiling, "to see quite so young a man."

"I daresay not, sir," Percy replied. "This is a letter Mr. Fullarton has given me for you."

"Sit down while I read it," the major said as he opened it. He read it through. "Mr. Fullarton speaks of you in extremely high terms, Groves, and as I know him well I am sure he would not praise unduly. Now tell me what is the opinion of your uncle and the people about him as to the state of affairs. Does he think that the Sikhs will be mad enough to cross the Sutlej ? "

"He has no doubt whatever about it, sir; he is convinced that the troops have for a long time made up their minds to conquer the protected states, and as they are completely masters of the situation in Lahore there is nothing to prevent them doing so. Such was also the opinion of all his native officers, and although we did not have much communication with the people on the way down, all whom we did speak to seemed to think that war was certain."

"The news we received from Lahore has always been the other way," Major Broadfoot said. "I have received a message this morning to the same effect, but Captain Nicholson reported yesterday from Ferozepore that a considerable Sikh force had arrived within three miles of the river. Orders have been sent for a general forward movement of the troops. Sir Henry is going to ride over to Loodiana this morning to inspect the force there."

" I have two followers, sir, who can be trusted to obtain any news you may desire to get. If you like, one of them will cross the river and make his way to the Sikh force opposite

Ferozepore and find out its strength and whether there is any intention of crossing; or if you prefer it, I will go myself. I have always been accustomed to wear the Sikh dress since I came out, and could, I think, pass without suspicion."

" It is most important that we should obtain some definite news," Major Broadfoot said, "and I am much obliged to you for your offer, but I do not think I can entertain it. It is too great a risk for you to run to go yourself, and the importance of the question is so great I should not dare to forward information, which would perhaps involve the movements of the whole army, merely upon the report of a native, however trustworthy he may be."

"I do not believe there is any danger whatever in my going, sir. I might take my two men with me, and should disguise myself in a dress similar to theirs. My own, which is that of a young sirdar, might so far attract attention that I might be questioned, while three of us in ordinary soldiers' dress could move about without being noticed in any way. That is just the sort of work that I came here to do, and my uncle thought that as a boy I could pass unquestioned where a man could not do so. One of my men is five- or six-and-thirty, so I could pass well enough as his son if any questions were asked, which I don't think would be the case."

" Well, Groves, if you are ready to go I do not think myself

justified in refusing your offer, as it is of such extreme importance to find out the intentions of the Sikhs. When will you start? "

"I would give the horses an hour's rest, sir, and then I will be off, if I can get a disguise by that time."

" That I can manage for you. I have numbers of natives in my pay, and can get what you require, a native dress with shield, tulwar, and matchlock, in a quarter of an hour. Fer-ozepore is twenty miles from here, and the Sikh force some four miles farther; but, of course, you won't be able to cross the river there, and must do it ten or twelve miles higher up and then ride round. Are you well mounted? "

"Very well mounted, sir."

"Then I will get you a strong native 'tat.' Your being mounted on a good horse would attract attention. Here," he went on, pointing to a map, " is a point where the river is almost if not quite fordable for cavalry; at any rate you will not have to swim your horses far. I should advise you to make for that. It is as you see about ten miles above Feroze-pore. It is not at all likely to be guarded; and should it be so, you could of course give out that you are natives of one of the protected states, say of Putiala, making your way to join the Sikh army that you hear is going to free you from the dominion of the English. As you have at present no tent of your own, you had better come across here in half an hour to make your change of clothes. I am myself going over to Sir Henry's, and may be detained there some time, but I will tell my servants to get breakfast ready for you. We must not send you off fasting."

Three hours later Percy and his two followers arrived at the bank of the Sutlej. They had been directed to the ford by a peasant in a village near, and crossed without difficulty, being only obliged to swim their horses for twenty or thirty yards in the middle of the stream. When they reached the opposite bank they rode up to a small party of armed Sikhs

who were watching them. Percy had asked Bhop Lai to act as spokesman.

" We hear that the army is going to cToss the river and to sweep the English away," he said, "and we have come over to join them. Our rajah is all in favour of the Feringhees, but most of us are the other way, and we were not going to stop quietly at home without taking a share in the good work, so my brother and son have come off with me without waiting to ask for leave. There are thousands of others who will do the same as soon as they are sure that the army is really in the field; but there has been so much talk about it for the last two years without anything coming of it, that they are waiting to see if it is true this time."

"It is quite true," one of the men replied. "There are ten thousand men now opposite Ferozepore, and the rest are on their way down from Lahore. There will be fifty thousand of them at least, with, they say, over a hundred and fifty guns. What can the English do against them? They have not ten thousand men they can put in the field, and these are scattered over the country, and will be crushed before they can assemble."

"That they assuredly will," Bhop Lai agreed confidently. " Fifty thousand men could sweep away every white soldier this side of the Jumna, and there will be nothing to prevent them marching on to Delhi if they choose."

"We shall see about that," the man replied. "Fifty thousand is only a beginning, and there will be another fifty after them in a very short time; and I for one don't see why we should not drive the Feringhees altogether out of India."

"That is the way to talk," Bhop Lai said cordially. "We shall always have trouble till the last of them have gone, and who so fit as the Sikhs to be masters in their place! How far is it to this camp you speak of? "

"About twelve miles. Ride two miles farther and you will come upon a broad road. Turn to the left, and it will bring you there."

"What are you doing here? "

"We have been sent here to see that none of the English horsemen cross the river to gather news. There are two hundred of our cavalry a quarter of a mile behind, and if we saw any of the Feringhee cavalry coming they would be here to defend the ford before they could cross."

With a nod of farewell Bhop Lai and his two companions rode on. They passed within a couple of hundred yards of the body of Sikh horsemen, encamped in a grove. But there was no sign of movement among them, a few figures sat talking together here and there, the rest had evidently lain down to sleep the hours away in the shade.

CHAPTER IX

MOODKEE AND FEROZESHAH

TWO hours after crossing the river, Percy with his two companions saw on the plain the camp of the Sikhs. As they did not wish to enter until evening, they turned off from the road and rode into a clump of thick bush a quarter of a mile away, and there waited until sunset. Then they mounted again and rode boldly into camp. With the exception of the tents of a few of the military chiefs and sirdars, the troops were not under canvas, although many had erected shelters of bushes or blankets. Here and there some attempt at regularity marked the places where regiments of the regular troops had established themselves. Here the horses were picketed in line, but among the followers of the sirdars every man had fastened up his horse just where it pleased him, without the smallest attempt at order.

The new-comers chose a vacant spot at the edge of the encampment, picketing their three horses together, and raised in front of them a rough tent consisting of a couple of blankets supported by some sticks they had cut in the bush. Here they lighted a fire and cooked a meal. One or two of the Sikhs strolled across to question them, and Bhop Lai and his comrades repeated the story that had been told at the ford, which was accepted as perfectly satisfactory. They in turn asked a questions as to the various sirdars present, and as

to which body they had better attach themselves. When they had finished their meal they sauntered off into the camp.

There was but one topic of conversation among the troops. They were to cross the Sutlej, if not on the next day, on the one following. A portion of the army was to besiege Feroze-pore, while the rest marched forward to sweep away the British forces at Loodiana and Umballa. It was evident from their conversation that they greatly under-estimated the British strength at each of these cantonments, and that the gradual arrival of reinforcements had passed entirely unnoticed by the Sikhs on the northern side of the Sutlej. They anticipated no difficulty whatever in destroying the British forces at the first onset. Their statement as to the number of troops who would take the field at once, agreed with those of the soldiers at the ford, and they deemed that this fifty thousand men would amply suffice to conquer the whole country north of the Jumna, and that with their full fighting power they should be able to overrun the whole of India.

"We have heard all that we want," Percy said to the men after they had strolled for an hour in the Sikh camp. "We had best move quietly off at once before the camp begins to get quiet. Our fire will have burnt out by this time, and even if they should notice us moving, the men near will suppose that we are merely shifting our quarters, and are moving over to the sirdar we have decided to follow."

They had some difficulty in finding their tent again in the darkness, and as soon as they did so the blankets were taken down, rolled up, and strapped behind the saddles. The picket pegs were pulled up, and leading their horses they moved off, skirting for a time the line of the camp, but gradually increasing their distance until two hundred yards away from it, when they thought it quite safe to mount and ride off in the darkness. They had some trouble in striking the road again; when they did so they halted for a consultation. It was decided to turn off and encamp again for three or four

hours in order to rest the horses, and then to make for the river bank and wait there until the first light of morning showed them a point where they could swim their horses across, for the presence of the guard at the ford rendered it impossible for them to use that passage again. This plan was carried out, and they arrived at the bank, some three or four miles below the ford, just as daylight began to appear. The bed of the river was wide, and the stream, broken by sand-banks, flowed in several channels.

"There will be no great difficulty in crossing anywhere here," Percy said; "the channels are nowhere very wide, and even if we are swept down the stream it will not matter, as we can rest after each swim. We had better start at once. Should there be any Sikhs about they will hardly make us out till it gets lighter, and we may hope to be pretty well beyond musket-shot before they can come down to the water's edge. They will not be likely to try to follow us across, and if they do so, with the start of a quarter of an hour we ought to be able to throw them off our track."

They were not disturbed while making the passage. This was, however, more difficult than Percy had anticipated, for the current in two of the channels was very strong and swept them down some distance before they could obtain a footing on the sand-bank. Apparently no watch whatever was kept by the Sikhs excepting at the fords, and nothing was seen of the enemy. On reaching the opposite bank they gave the horses a short rest to recover their breath, and then rode on to Basseean.

"What! are you back already? " Major Broadfoot said when Percy was shown into his tent. " I did not expect you back until to-morrow at the earliest. Have you really been in the Sikh camp?"

"Yes, sir; we were there about three hours, which was quite sufficient to learn everything that we required; " and he then gave the officer the news that they had gathered.

JN^

"This is most important," Major Broadfoot said. "Sir Henry returned half an hour ago from Loodiana. I will take you with me to his tent. He may want to ask you further questions."

The commander-in-chief after hearing Percy's report asked him several questions in order to find out whether the statements had been made by one native only; but Percy replied that they had spoken to a score of soldiers, and that all were in perfect agreement as to the force that would cross the river, and the division that would be made of the forces and their object in so doing.

"I thank you, sir," Sir Henry said when he had finished. "Your information is most important, and you have carried out your mission with great ability and intelligence. Major Broadfoot will take notice and bring it to my attention later on."

Half an hour later despatches were sent off to the commander-in-chief at Umballa, ordering him to move forward at once with his whole force; and to Loodiana, ordering General Wheeler to carry out the measures that had been agreed on between him and the governor-general on the preceding day, namely, to abandon the cantonments, to place all stores in the fort, to move there all the sick and others unfit to take the field, with a force sufficient to hold the place for a time against any attack that might be made upon it, and to march with his main body to Basseean so as to protect the vast amount of stores accumulated there, from any sudden dash by the enemy. In the evening a messenger came in from Feroze-pore, saying that a large body of Sikhs had during the day crossed the river.

The next morning, the i3th of December, the governor-general issued a proclamation to the chiefs and people of the protected states, pointing out that since 1809 the British government had scrupulously fulfilled the terms made with Runjeet Singh, and that notwithstanding the disorganized state of the

THE COMMANDER-IN-CHIEF THANKS PERCY FOR HIS REPORT.

Lahore government during the last two years, and several most unfriendly proceedings on the part of the durbar, the governor-general had continued to evince his desire to maintain the relations of amity and concord which had so long existed between the two states.

The attitude of the Sikhs, however, had continued to be more and more unfriendly, and the army had now, without a shadow of provocation, invaded British territory. The governor-general therefore declared the possessions of Maharajah Dhuleep Singh, on the left or British bank of the Sutlej, confiscated and annexed to the British territory. The ranks of all sirdars, zemindars, and tenants in the said possessions who should evince their fidelity to the British government should be respected. The governor-general called upon all chiefs and sirdars to co-operate cordially with the British government. Those who did so would find their interest promoted thereby, while those who took the opposite course would be considered as enemies and treated accordingly. The inhabitants of all the territories on the left bank of the Sutlej were requested to abide peacefully in their respective villages, and all parties of men found in arms would be treated as disturbers of the public peace.

Fortunately the Sikhs after crossing on the i2th, instead of marching at once upon Basseean, halted until their heavy guns were taken across on the i6th. On the afternoon of the i4th General Wheeler, who had marched at daybreak, arrived in front of Basseean: and on the i6th General Gough, the com-mander-in-chief, arrived there with the force from Umballa. Had the Sikhs pushed forward at once after crossing, Basseean with its great stores of provisions must have fallen into their hands, and a week or ten days must have elapsed before arrangements for provisioning the Umballa force could have been made. In that case the whole Sikh army would have been able to concentrate its efforts upon the capture of Feroze-pore, which, in the absence of any fortifications capable of

withstanding powerful artillery, could scarcely have been defended successfully.

Percy had been kept actively employed during the three days that intervened between his return to Basseean and the arrival of the column from Umballa, in the work of carrying copies of the general's proclamation over the country, and delivering them to the head men of the villages. He acted as interpreter to the officers who, attended by small escorts of cavalry, performed this work, and was on horseback from daylight to dark each day. After the arrival of General Wheeler's division he spent his evenings with his acquaintances there. The troops were all in high spirits because the long uncertainty was at an end, and that at last they were to meet the men who had so insolently been threatening an invasion. The fact that the odds would be enormously against them was considered a matter of no importance whatever, for the British troops had so long been accustomed to victory in India that the idea of a reverse was not entertained for a moment among the soldiers, although among the officers, who were aware of the bravery and fighting power of the Sikhs, the prospect was regarded with a good deal of anxiety.

All the accounts received bore out the correctness of the information that Percy had obtained. Twenty-five thousand Sikhs, all regular soldiers, had taken possession of the wells round the village of Ferozeshah, half-way between Basseean and Ferozepore, and entirely cut the communication between the two places; for owing to scarcity of water no other road could be used for the advance of an army except that passing through Ferozeshah. The Sikhs were well aware of this fact, and on their arrival they had at once begun to throw up strong intrenchments. Another Sikh army of twenty-three thousand, and sixty-seven guns, under Tej Singh, remained watching the British force at Ferozepore.

The British force at Basseean consisted of three thousand eight hundred and fifty Europeans and eight thousand natives,

MOODKER AND FEROZESHAH 159

with forty-two guns, and on the morning of the i8th of December marched for Ferozepore. They reached their camping ground round the village of Moodkee at one o'clock in the day, and as soon as arms were piled began to cook their dinner. A few Sikh horsemen had retired from the village on their approach, and some scouts were sent out to ascertain if there was any considerable body of the enemy near at hand; these returned in a short time, saying that a large force had taken up a position three miles away. There were, indeed, twelve thousand of them, principally cavalry, with twenty guns. From friends at Basseean they had learnt that an advance was to be made by the British, and thinking that it would be but an advance-guard, Lai Singh had with this body of troops left the camp at Ferozeshah early in the morning and had taken up his position before the arrival of the British army at Moodkee. As soon as the news was received the troops got under arms and moved forward, the artillery and cavalry leading the way and the infantry following in support. When they had gone two miles the enemy was seen ahead of them.

The country was a dead flat, covered at short intervals with a low thick jungle and dotted with sandy hillocks. It was difficult to judge of the strength of the Sikh force, but in order to oblige them to display it, the cavalry, with five troops of horse-artillery, moved forward, and as the infantry formed into line opened fire. This was answered by a very heavy cannonade on the part of the enemy; but in a very short time the rapid fire of the horse-artillery, aided by two field batteries, so discomfited the enemy's gunners that their fire gradually subsided.

In order to allow the infantry to advance without the artillery in front of them being pushed forward too closely to the jungle, Sir Hugh Gough ordered a portion of the cavalry to make a movement on the enemy's flanks. The 3d Light Dragoons, the Governor-general's Body-guard, the 5th Light Cavalry, and a portion of the 4th Lancers dashed round the

left of the Sikh array, and sweeping along the whole of its rear, forced the artillerymen to leave their guns, and put their cavalry to flight. At the same time the remainder of the 4th Lancers and the gth Irregular Cavalry, with the Light Field Battery, performed a brilliant charge round the enemy's right. Successful as these operations were, they would have been much more so had not the enemy been so hidden in the jungle that their position could scarcely be made out.

The British guns again opened fire and the infantry advanced. Evening was now falling, and the increasing darkness added to the difficulty of the attack through the thick jungle.

The Sikhs fought stoutly, and several times clung to their positions until driven from them at the point of the bayonet; but they were not able to withstand the steady pressure of the British advance, and, astounded and discomfited at the unexpected valour of a foe whom they professed to despise, they fell back from point to point, and finally made off in the darkness. Had the battle commenced at an early hour the cavalry would have converted the defeat of the enemy into a rout. As it was, seventeen of their twenty guns were captured, and their losses in killed and wounded were very severe. Lai Singh himself was wounded, and had a narrow escape of being taken prisoner.

The British loss was sixteen officers and two hundred men killed, and forty-eight officers and six hundred and nine men wounded. Sir Robert Sale, the hero of Jellalabad, was among those mortally wounded. The defeated Sikhs made their way back to Ferozeshah, while the British returned to Moodkee, which they reached at midnight. The next morning two heavy guns, escorted by the 6th Light Infantry, and the 4ist, reached Moodkee. Their march had been a long and fatiguing one, as they had made twenty-seven miles through an arid desert, and were overcome with thirst and fatigue, when some elephants sent out with water to meet them brought them

\&

relief. It was late in the evening before the column came in, and in order to give the men time to recover from their fatigue it was decided to halt for another day.

It was settled that the sick, wounded, and baggage should be left in the little fort at Moodkee, with a regiment and a half of infantry to protect them should the enemy's cavalry work round to the rear of the army. Messengers were sent off to Ferozepore to inform Sir John Littler, who commanded there, of the victory at Moodkee, and to order him to leave five thousand men to hold the town and watch 1'ej Singh, and to march with his five thousand remaining men and twenty-one guns to join the commander-in-chief, both forces to march at three o'clock on the morning of the 2ist. Sir Henry Hardinge offered to serve as a military man under Sir Hugh

Gough, and was appointed second in command of the army.

The marches were well timed, and the junction with Sir John Littler's force was effected at the village of Alisriwala, within sight of the Sikh camp, at one o'clock.

The British force after the junction had been effected consisted of five thousand six hundred and seventy-four Europeans and twelve thousand and fifty-three natives, with sixty-five guns; the Sikhs numbered twenty-five thousand regular troops and ten thousand irregulars, with eighty-eight guns; while Tej Singh with his twenty-three thousand regulars and twenty-seven guns was only ten miles distant. The country was a dead flat studded with trees and jungle, and the clouds of dust that rose beneath the feet of the troops rendered it extremely difficult to direct their movements in such a country. Skirmishers were sent forward to ascertain the exact position of the enemy, but the troops were allowed to rest for some time after their hot and dusty march. The commander-in-chief would gladly have waited until next morning before calling upon them for the efforts that would be necessary to carry a position so strong as that occupied by the Sikhs. It was, however, impossible to wait, for there was no water, and

moreover Tej Singh with his army would certainly be up before morning.

At Moodkee Percy had seen but little of the fighting, although for some hours he had been under fire. His place was behind Major Broadfoot, who was with the commander-in-chief's staff. The jungle at first and the darkness afterwards shut out the absolute conflict from view; and as the enemy's cannon-balls flew overhead or ploughed up the sand, and the air resounded with the sharp short ping of their musket-balls, his feeling as he sat inactive on horseback was one of far greater discomfort than he had felt when exposed to an even heavier fire at the attack on his uncle's fortress. That the British were winning he knew by the advance that was from time to time made by the party, and by the fact that the firing gradually receded.

"You have been under fire before, Groves," Major Broad-foot said to him, "so I suppose you don't mind it."

"I certainly don't like it, sir. Before, I had something to do and did not think much of the danger, and I should not at all mind if you were to send me with a message into the thick of it, but to sit here doing nothing with balls buzzing about is certainly very unpleasant."

"It is unpleasant; I find it so myself," the major said; "but as my post is here with the commander-in-chief, and there is no errand on which I can send you, we must sit it out. If the general wants to send a message and his aides-decamp are all away, I will tell him that you will carry it for him."

There was, however, no message to be sent. Beyond the fact that the troops were steadily advancing, the commander-in-chief himself knew but little of what was going on. It was a soldier's battle. Except for the flank movements of the cavalry there was no manoeuvring. Each regiment pressed straight forward, pushing the enemy back wherever it found him.

"We shall see more of it to-day, Groves," the major said as they were waiting for the orders for the troops to advance against the Sikh intrenchments. "There is daylight, and as the task of carrying that position will certainly be a severe one, Sir Hugh will move forward with the men, and is likely to be in the thick of it."

The Sikh intrenchment was about a mile in length and half a mile in breadth, including within its area the strong village of Ferozeshah. The Sikhs had the advantage of being thoroughly acquainted with the country, and as they were prepared for an attack upon either side of their position, it was decided that the effort should be made against the long front. The British were formed in three divisions, commanded respectively by Major-general Gilbert, Sir John Littler, and Brigadier-general Wallace. They were formed in line, with the whole of the artillery in the centre, with the exception of a troop of horse-artillery on each flank and one in support. The second line was composed of the cavalry and the reserve under Sir Harry Smith. The artillery were first moved to the front, and the battle began by a discharge from a mortar battery. The Sikhs did not reply, and the whole of the artillery then opened fire to ascertain the position of the enemy's batteries, when the Sikhs at once responded.

The whole line then advanced and again the artillery opened fire. This movement was repeated until the guns were within three hundred yards of the enemy's intrenchments. In spite of the much more rapid fire of their guns, our artillery were unable to silence that of the enemy, whose pieces were protected to a great extent by the earthworks. Seeing this, the general gave the order for the infantry to advance to storm the intrenchments. General Littler's division directed its march against the village, and by so doing caused an opening in the line between it and Brigadier Wallace's division.

In spite of the terrible storm of grape from the enemy's batteries and the heavy Sikh musketry fire, Littler's men held

on their way until close up to the works. Then they were unable longer to withstand the storm of fire, and fell back.

The left brigade of the reserve under Sir Harry Smith was at once ordered forward to fill up the opening left in the line, and advanced against the village with splendid bravery. Wallace's and Gilbert's divisions on the right and centre were more successful than that of Littler, and gallantly stormed the intrenchments in front of them in spite of the desperate bravery of the Sikhs; but just as they had achieved this feat night fell suddenly, as it does in India. The air was obscured by dust and smoke; none knew the position of the troops to the right or left of them. Great piles of dry forage were alight in the Sikh camp, and frequent explosions of loose powder took place.

Sir Harry Smith's brigade had stormed the village and held it, but were in complete ignorance of what was taking place elsewhere; while Littler's division, which had suffered terribly in its advance, had retired, but no one knew in which direction. Just before dark the 3d Dragoons, on the extreme right, were ordered to charge, and dashed headlong into the Sikh camp, adding to the utter confusion that prevailed there, and cutting down numbers of the enemy, but losing themselves ten officers and a hundred and twenty men out of four hundred.

To advance further was hopeless. There was no saying what obstacles might be encountered in the darkness—friends might fire into each other, regiments lose their way and be destroyed, and all order and regularity be lost. Consequently Sir Hugh Gough, fearing to keep his men in a position in which they would be exposed to be overthrown piecemeal by rushes of the enemy, told the officers about him to ride off and order all the troops to abandon the positions they had won, and retire outside the intrenchments, and there to lie down in readiness for a renewed attack in the early morning. Wallace's and Gilbert's divisions obeyed the orders, Sir Harry Smith's received none, but after holding the village until about ten

o'clock at night, and knowing nothing of the position of the troops on his right, he abandoned it and also fell back.

The position of the British was most serious; the whereabouts of the divisions of Sir Harry Smith and General Littler could not be discovered, and the other two divisions, thinned by their losses, might be attacked in the morning by a vastly superior force, for it was probable that Tej Singh with his army would arrive during the night. The Sikhs had withdrawn their guns as the British rushed forward to the assault, so that their artillery was still intact, and as soon as they found that their intrenchments were evacuated they advanced and kept up a continuous fire of cannon and musketry at the unseen foe, who were lying but a hundred and fifty yards away. The fire of one of the batteries was so destructive that Sir Henry Hardinge mounted his horse and called to the 80th Regiment:

"My lads, we shall have no sleep until we take those guns." The regiment leapt to its feet and at once advanced, and, supported by the ist Bengal Europeans, again stormed the intrenchments, drove the Sikhs from their guns, spiked them, and retired.

Percy had had nothing to do during the advance, but when the orders were given for the troops to retire he had assisted to carry them to the different regiments, as the whole of Sir Henry Hardinge's staff, with the exception of his son, had been killed or wounded, as had most of those of Sir Hugh Gough. Major Broadfoot had fallen. Captain Nicholson, assistant political agent, was also killed, and indeed all the political agents with one exception were either killed or wounded. Percy had felt almost bewildered with the roar and din of the battle; but the feeling of excitement was so great, that although officer after officer fell round him the thought of danger to himself scarcely entered his mind. He mechanically followed with the rest of the staff as the general had ridden hither and thither along the line, but he felt almost as one

in a dream until he was called upon with all the rest of the officers round the general to carry orders to the troops to retire.

On his return from this duty, Sir Henry Hardinge begged of him to ride off and to try and discover the whereabouts of the missing divisions; and, accompanied by his two men, who had kept a short distance behind him during the fight, and had both escaped unwounded, he rode about for some hours in the jungle, but without success. He was, indeed, himself lost, and at last threw himself off his horse to wait till morning should show him the bearings of the enemy's camp. But few words had been exchanged between him and his followers during the ride, for he was still dazed by the battle, and was parched with thirst and exhausted by fatigue and emotion.

"It has been a terrible day," he said, as he threw himself down on the ground after flinging the bridle over a bough of a low tree to prevent the horse from straying.

"It has, indeed, sahib," Akram Chunder replied. "Never did I hear so terrible a roar of fire. I thought that my time had come, for it seemed as if every man must be swept away. It looked like madness to attack such a position. I did not think that men could do it."

"It was wonderful," Bhop Lai joined in; "truly the British are marvellous fighters. The Sikhs are no cowards, and yet though they must have been two to one, and had strong intrenchments behind which their guns were sheltered, they could not withstand them. I have wondered often how it was that so many kingdoms have been conquered, so many armies defeated, by your countrymen. Now I wonder no longer. When you said that the English would certainly beat the Sikhs I thought you were wrong, thought it was not for me to contradict you. Now I see that you were right. The Sikhs have found their masters, and after all their boasting have been defeated on their own ground, and with numbers, position, and everything in their favour."

"They are not defeated yet," Percy said; "they have again

entered their intrenchments, and if Tej Singh comes up during the night their numbers will be overwhelming."

"The English will win," Bhop Lai said carelessly; "they are not to be conquered. Besides, the Sikhs move slowly, and Tej Singh will not be up till morning."

They had some bread and cold meat in their valises. Percy had a flask of brandy and water, and his two followers' water-skins hung from their horses' saddles. Percy was only able to eat a few mouthfuls, and then fell asleep; but his followers ate a hearty meal, and remained smoking and talking until, when day began to break, they aroused their master. Bhop Lai climbed up into the highest tree he could find, and exclaimed:

"There are the intrenchments, sahib, two miles away at least."

They mounted and rode off with all speed, and found the troops already forming up. The commander-in-chief and Sir Henry Hardinge placed themselves in front of the troops in order to prevent them from firing. Moving round to the right, they entered the intrenchments with but slight opposition. The enemy's guns were taken in reverse, and wheeling round, past the village of Ferozeshah, the British line swept down through the Sikh encampment, and did not halt until they reached the works on the opposite side. Scarcely had they won the Sikh position and captured his guns, seventy-four in number, when the army of Tej Singh appeared in view, marching towards them.

The divisions of Smith and Littler, which had passed the night in the jungle, had joined the force just as they entered the enemy's works, and the troops now prepared to defend the position they had won.

No attack, however, was made. The crowd of Sikh fugitives made for the army they saw advancing to their assistance, and rushing down in confusion disordered its front line and communicated their panic to the newly-arrived troops.

After opening fire for some time at a distance that rendered it perfectly innocuous, Tej Singh's troops turned and marched away to the river, which they crossed without a halt.

The British were too weak in cavalry to follow up the enemy. Several regiments had been sent off at daybreak to Ferozepore in order to water their horses, as they would have been useless against the Sikh intrenchments, while those that remained were unfit for active work, the animals having been twenty-four hours without food or water.

The delight of the army was immense at this unexpectedly easy termination of a fight that at one time had looked well-nigh lost, and as Sir Hugh Gough and the governor-general rode down their lines they saluted them with outbursts of cheers.

The loss, however, had been heavy, and had fallen chiefly upon the Europeans, who had four hundred and eighty-eight killed and eleven hundred and three wounded out of a total of six hundred and ninety-four killed and one thousand seven hundred and twenty-one wounded, of whom five hundred and ninety-five died subsequently or were permanently disabled.

As soon as the Sikhs retreated, every effort was made to succour the wounded, and by noon all were in quarters at Ferozepore and provided with cots and blankets.

Among the killed were Major Somerset, military secretary to the governor-general; Colonel Wallace; Major Baldwin, an old Peninsular officer; and many other officers distinguished for their bravery. The 62d, which went into the battle weak in numbers, had seven officers killed and ten wounded, and seventy-six rank and file killed, and one hundred and fifty-four wounded. This regiment belonged to General Littler's division, which had advanced against the strongest part of the Sikh position.

After the engagement was over Percy reported himself to Captain Mills, the only one of the political officers who had escaped unwounded.

MOODKEE AND FEROZESHAH

"I am glad that lad went through it uninjured," Sir Henry Hardinge said when Captain Mills reported that he was the only assistant available for service. " He is a very plucky young fellow, and I noticed him several times during the fight. He was always cool and collected even under the heaviest fire, and Major Broadfoot reported to me very strongly upon his conduct in going into the Sikh camp and obtaining for us a trustworthy report of their strength and intentions. He mentioned that he was only a volunteer serving without pay, and appointed temporarily by the Resident at Loodiana on the civil staff. I shall be glad if, when you send in a written report to me, you will specially mention his name."

Although the Sikh invasion had been repelled with such heavy loss of guns and men, the British were in no condition to follow up their advantage. Were they to cross the river they might expect to meet forces far larger than those they had defeated. They were without heavy guns with which to attack fortified towns, and their numbers were altogether insufficient for such an enterprise as the conquest of the Pun-jaub. They were therefore forced for a time to remain inactive, pending the arrival of reinforcements and siege-guns.

CHAPTER X

ALIWAL AND SOBRAON

"PINDING that the British army did not follow up its success at Ferozeshah, the Sikhs determined to maintain their position on the left bank, and proceeded to construct a bridge of boats at Sobraon, not far from the spot where they had crossed the river in their flight. In front of the head of this bridge an exceedingly strong work was thrown up. The position was very well chosen, the bridge being placed in a curve of the river, and the artillery posted on the bank, which on their side was high, was therefore able to sweep the ground across which a force must advance to attack the work. Ten thousand men under the Sirdar Runjoor Singh were also thrown across the river near Loodiana, in order -not only to menace the place with its small garrison, but to cut off the passage of supplies for Ferozepore and to interrupt the communications between the two posts.

As soon as the force at Meerut, consisting of the gth and 16th Lancers, the loth and 53d Foot, and the 43d and 5gth Native Regiments, arrived with the battering-train, steps were taken to reinforce Loodiana and Basseean with some heavy guns; additional troops were sent to each of these posts, and the sick, with the women and children, were removed thence and sent to Umballa.

Sir Harry Smith's division was increased to seven thousand

ALIWAL AND SOBRAON . 171

men and twenty-four guns, and he was despatched to drive the force that threatened Loodiana across the river and to cover the line of the British communications.

The whole country in that quarter was in a state of disorder. The advance of Runjoor Singh had caused great excitement among the peasantry, while it created something like a panic among the European residents of Umballa and Simla, either of which places could have been reached and plundered by the Sikhs, who from the crossing point near Loodiana were two days' march nearer to them than was the army of the com-mander-in-chief. It was all-important to Sir Harry Smith to reach Loodiana, where, being on the flank of the Sikh army should they advance, it would be necessary for them to meet and defeat him before they ventured upon a raiding expedition. But to do this it was necessary to pass within a short distance of Runjoor Singh's position, and as the column passed along the Sikhs sallied out, opened a heavy fire, and cut off a considerable portion of the baggage of the force, taking several officers prisoners. Sir Harry Smith did not suffer himself to be diverted from his object or to be forced to fight a battle save on ground of his own choosing. Without returning the fire he pressed forward until he reached Loodiana, the troops being completely exhausted with the efforts they had made.

Some more political officers having come up with the force from Meerut, Sir Henry Hardinge had placed Percy's services at the disposal of Sir Harry Smith. "He is a mere lad," he said to the latter, "but you will find him quite as valuable for most purposes as any older man would be. He speaks the language like a native, can go in disguise and obtain any information you may require, and has plenty of pluck. He was close behind the commander-in-chief and myself all through the fight here, and was one of the few of the staff who escaped uninjured. He is a volunteer serving without pay, no doubt in the hope of obtaining civil employment under the government in the future. This he has already richly earned, not only by his service in the battle of Ferozeshah, but by obtaining most valuable news by going in disguise to the Sikh camp before they crossed the river. Poor Broadfoot reported on his conduct very warmly indeed, in almost the last official document he sent me in, and having seen the young fellow under fire I shall certainly, at the proper time, take advantage of Broadfoot's report to recommend him to the Board of Directors for an appointment in the Civil Service, and for special employment upon this frontier."

Being recommended to him in such a manner, Sir Harry Smith had 'at once taken Percy upon his staff, and more than once sent for him and questioned him as to the country, the width of the river, and other points; and as Percy had on his way down crossed the Sutlej not far from Aliwal, he was able to give some valuable information on the subject. As soon as they reached Loodiana he went to see his friend Mr. Fullar-ton.

" Back again, Groves ? You were fortunate in getting through that fight at Ferozeshah, where poor Broadfoot and several other politicals were killed or wounded. I had a note from him written the day before, saying how useful he had found you. You have come up with Sir Harry Smith, I suppose? "

"Yes, sir, they are very short of officers who speak the language, and so sent me on with him."

"It shows they think well of you; I am glad you are doing credit to my recommendation. You see it was very much better for you to go with the army than to remain here with me. Now you have been through two battles, and have fairly earned your right to a permanent post in the service. But, mind, don't let them put you on the uncovenanted branch; you will get very few chances of real promotion there. Should an offer be made to you, you had better decline respectfully and say that you would rather wait in the hope of entering the Company's service in the regular way. Three or four years'

waiting would do you no harm, though I do not suppose you will have to wait anything like that time before you get appointed to our service."

" I am quite content to wait, sir, for at my age it would be absurd to think of getting such an important appointment; but I am very glad, indeed, to have found the opportunity of seeing so much."

" We shall have another battle here in a day or two," Mr. Fullarton said. "I have just seen Sir Harry. He says he must give the troops a couple of days' rest before he advances to attack Runjoor Singh. Indeed there is no hurry; now that he is here the Sikhs dare not advance, and he is therefore master of the situation. It was a bad affair losing so much of the baggage at Buddeewal, but the general was right in not bringing on a battle. The troops were worn out with their long march, and would have fought at a great disadvantage. It would not have made much difference to the white soldiers, who are always ready to fight however tired they may be; but it is not so with the natives. Fatigue, hunger, or thirst always depress their spirits, and a native who, in the morning, would have fought stoutly by the side of our own men, would be worth nothing if taken into the field tired and hungry on the evening of the same day. I hear that some of the native regiments did not do at all well at Ferozeshah, and I have no doubt that this was the reason of it. They will have a very short march before they fight this time."

After a day's rest the force moved out again to Buddeewal. Runjoor Singh's force had just received a reinforcement of four thousand regular troops, with twelve guns, and his army now amounted to nineteen thousand men and sixty guns. Early in the morning of the 28th of January Sir Harry Smith marched from Buddeewal towards the enemy. The Sikhs were so inspirited by the success that had attended their attack on the column during its passage—a success which they attributed to fear on the part of the British—that, instead of

waiting to be attacked in the intrenchments they had formed, they moved forward, and took up their post in the open, the village of Aliwal being the key of the position.

The troops were already advancing in order of battle, and a column was at once directed to attack and carry the village, the artillery preparing the way by a heavy fire. The Sikh guns opened all along their line, but their fire was very wild; most of the shot went far overhead, and the attacking force suffered but little. They did not fire a shot in return, but when within a short distance of the village went at it with a rush, carrying it at the point of the bayonet, and driving the Sikh infantry headlong before them. The guns defending it fell into their hands, and as soon as they established themselves in the village, the rest of the force moved forward with admirable regularity, and the whole Sikh line was driven backwards, leaving their guns behind them.

The i6th Lancers charged the enemy, who were falling back sullenly and in order. The Sikhs threw themselves down on the ground and slashed at the horses with their swords as they passed over them, or discharged their muskets at their riders, and the regiment lost upwards of a hundred men killed and wounded. As they fell back the horse-artillery opened upon the dense masses of Sikhs, the infantry continued their steady advance, and the cavalry again and again charged. Instead of retiring towards their intrenchments, which having been denuded of their guns were now untenable, the enemy retreated direct upon the river, which they crossed at the ford. Their loss was comparatively small to that which they had suffered at Ferozeshah, but the whole of their guns fell into the hands of the British.

Only one had been carried across the river. This was captured and spiked by the irregular horse and horse-artillery, who crossed the river in pursuit. The total loss of the British in killed and wounded in the battle of Aliwal was only four hundred—an astonishingly small amount when it is considered

that they attacked a brave enemy of double their strength both in men and guns. The victory was a most important one. It relieved the north-west of all fear of invasion, and enabled the commander-in-chief to direct his whole attention to concentrating his force against the main body of the Sikh army at Sobraon.

Percy had watched the conflict from a distance. He had, as usual, taken his place among the staff when the general mounted his horse to advance against the Sikh intrenchments: but when Sir Harry Smith's eye fell upon him he said, "You will not ride with me to-day, Mr. Groves. I can have no occasion for your services as a political officer, and will not have you risk your life uselessly by your exposing yourself to fire. You will, therefore, please follow at considerable distance, and will, when we get within the enemy's range, take up any position you like that will enable you to see what is going on and at the same time keep you out of fire."

Percy looked a little downcast, and Sir Harry added kindly: "It is no reflection on your courage, lad, that I send you back. The governor-general himself told me how fearlessly you had exposed yourself at Ferozeshah; but as I do not require you on duty I have no justification for taking you with me under a heavy fire."

Percy brightened up as he rode off. Sir Harry Smith's staff were for the most part strangers to him, as he had not been connected with it until it marched, and he had feared at first that it might be thought the general had ordered him to the rear because he doubted his steadiness under fire.

" I am only to look on to-day," he said to his two followers as they joined him when he reined up his horse on a little knoll affording a view of the enemy's position half a mile away.

"And a very good thing too, sahib," Bhop Lai said bluntly. " I had quite enough of being shot at the other day, and have no stomach for sitting on horseback again doing nothing while they are pelting us with shot and bullets. If the sahib said 'Charge!' I would follow into the middle of the Sikh in-campment, but as for sitting doing nothing I want no more of it."

"Besides," Akram Chunder put in, "we know all about it now; for if what people say is true as to Runjoor Singh's strength, the odds are not so great as they were at Ferozeshah, even though they have seventy guns to our thirty. But what is that? The British are not to be stopped by guns; they will do as they did the other day, go right at the Sikhs and beat them. The Sikhs have thrown away their only chance by coming out from their intrenchments. Besides, they will not fight so well as they did last time. Then they thought they were invincible, now they know that the British are better fighters than they are, and that makes all the difference."

"We may as well dismount," Percy said, "and picket the horses down behind. We can see well enough over the jungle on foot, and if the Sikh gunners should notice three mounted men they might take us for officers of importance and send a few shot in this direction."

The Sikh gunners, however, were too occupied with the foes marching against them to notice the detached figures, and no shot came in their direction during the battle. Percy and his two followers watched the capture of Aliwal, and then saw the whole British force advance, and with scarce a pause push back the Sikhs all along the line.

"Truly it is wonderful," Bhop Lai said, stroking his beard. "These men in red coats make no more of the fire of sixty guns than if they were children's playthings. As for the Sikh infantry, though more than twice their numbers, they seem to sweep them before them like chaff. I thought I knew something of fighting, but I feel to-day that I know nothing, for I have seen nothing like this from the day when I first handled a sword."

ALIWAL AND SOBRAON 177

"The loss cannot have been very heavy," Percy said, "it has been done too quickly."

"That is the way, sahib," Akram Chunder remarked. "If men have but the courage to go on in the face of a heavy fire they suffer much less than if they hesitate and delay; but it is only lions who rush forward with sixty cannon firing at them, to say nothing of thousands of men with muskets. That is what takes the life out of the Sikh fighting. They are brave, but they are accustomed to victory, and when they see men rushing on against them in spite of the fire which they thought would have swept them all away, they lose their confidence in themselves, and say, what use is it to fight against men like these? "

" Bring up the horses, Bhop Lai; we may as well ride forward now that the battle is nearly over, for I believe the roll of musketry and the discharge of guns still going on are caused by our troops firing at the Sikhs as they recross the river."

Great was the satisfaction that prevailed among the troops at the splendid victory they had gained over an enemy of nearly thrice their force in men and guns, and that with a loss which, considering the numbers engaged and the strength of the intrenchments, was trifling. As after so crushing a defeat as this there was little chance of Loodiana being again threatened, or of any large force endeavouring to intercept our communications, Sir Harry Smith marched back with his army and rejoined the commander-in-chief on the 8th of February.

On the following day the heavy guns from Delhi arrived, and orders were given for the whole force to prepare for the attack on Sobraon. During the fortnight that Sir Harry Smith had been absent the Sikhs had continued to labour unceasingly at their intrenchments, which were erected under the superintendence of two or three of the foreign officers who had been in Runjeet Singh's service. These were not regarded

by the Sikhs with the same hostility with which they viewed Colonel Groves and two or three other English-speaking officers. They had, indeed, been deprived of their commands at the demand of the army, who objected to the European discipline and to the severe methods by which it was enforced; but several of them had been allowed to remain in the country, and the Sikhs, when the war began, gladly availed themselves of their scientific knowledge in the erection of intrench-ments.

The enemy had surrounded their position with works of great strength, which could only be surmounted by the aid of scaling-ladders. The works were so arranged that they afforded complete protection to three lines of infantry, one above another, who could thus pour a tremendous fire upon an advancing foe. These works were held by 34,000 men with seventy guns. They were connected by a well-built bridge, and also by a ford, with another camp of 20,000 men across the river, and the guns of this force, placed on the high bank, were in a position to play upon the flanks of an army advancing against Sobraon.

To attack this formidable position Sir Hugh Gough had but 16,224 men, of whom 6533 were Europeans and 9691 natives. His force, therefore, was numerically inferior by 1500 men to that with which he attacked the Sikhs at Ferozeshah. His artillery force had, however, been augmented to ninety-nine guns by the addition of thirty-four heavy guns and mortars, and the commander-in-chief relied upon his artillery to clear the way for the assault of his infantry. The army was to be in motion at half-past three in the morning, in order that darkness should not, as at Moodkee and Ferozeshah, intervene to prevent the full results of victory being obtained.

The troops were under arms punctually, and at precisely the hour named marched in silence against the Sikh position. The battering guns and most of the field batteries took up their post in an extended semicircle, so as to open fire against

every point of the Sikh intrenchments. It was intended that they should commence the attack as soon as it was light enough for the men to point their guns. A heavy mist, however, hung over the country, and it was not until half-past six that this lifted sufficiently to allow a view to be obtained of the enemy's works. Then the cannon opened along the whole line, and a storm of shot and shell was poured in by the gun and mortar batteries, while rockets were discharged in numbers against the intrenchments.

The Sikhs replied with equal vigour, and for a time the roar of artillery was unbroken. It had been intended that the cannonade should be continued for four hours before the infantry were called upon to make their advance, but so rapidly did the gunners work their pieces that the ammunition carried with them was becoming exhausted long before that time had elapsed, and the elephants who should have brought up reserves had become unmanageable from their terror at the tremendous din. But even had the fire continued during the whole day, it could not have made any serious impression upon such strong and extended earthworks, and its object was rather to shake the courage of the defenders than to produce any material damage. The loss of the Sikhs was afterwards found to have been heavy, but they and their general were confidant that they could repulse any attack upon the tremendous works they had erected, Tej Singh having been assured by his chief engineer, a French officer named Mouton, that the position was absolutely impregnable.

While the artillery duel was in progress the British infantry had remained inactive in the rear of the guns, longing for the time when they should be called upon to take their share in the action; and there was a general feeling of satisfaction when the fire began to slacken, and orders were given for the advance to begin. On the left were two brigades of General Sir Robert Dick's division; these were to commence the engagement The seventh brigade, commanded by General Stacey, was to lead the attack, headed by the icth Foot reinforced by the 53d, and supported by the other brigade.

General Gilbert's division was in the centre, Sir Harry Smith's on the right, while Brigadier-general Campbell's command was thrown back between Gilbert's right and Sir Harry Smith's left. A part of the cavalry threatened to cross a ford and attack the enemy's horse on the opposite bank, the rest of the cavalry were-in reserve. At nine o'clock Stacey's brigade, supported by three batteries, moved to the attack. The former marched steadily on in line, the latter took up successive positions at a gallop, until within three hundred yards of the heavy batteries of the enemy. The fire of cannon, camel guns, and musketry was so tremendous, that it seemed to the lookers-on impossible that any troops could advance successfully under it.

The two British regiments, and the 43d and 5pth Native Infantry brigaded with them, advanced, however, with splendid bravery. This brigade had not been present at the previous battles, and had been specially selected for the desperate service of effecting the first breach in the enemy's lines because their ranks were still intact, and they had not gone through the terrible ordeal at Ferozeshah which had, in spite of their eventual success, greatly impressed those engaged in it with the courage and obstinacy of the Sikhs in defending a strong position. Well did the seventh brigade deserve the confidence the commander-in-chief placed in it. With scarcely a pause the troops pressed steadily forward, surmounted every obstacle until they reached the crest of the intrenchments, and drove the Sikhs from their guns.

The moment the success of the attack was apparent General Gilbert and Sir Harry Smith were ordered to advance with their divisions, and Brigadier Ashburnham began to move forward his brigade to support Stacey. Gilbert's advance took him in front of the centre and strongest portion of the enemy's line, and although unsupported by artillery, the 291)1 and the ist Light Infantry dashed forward under a withering fire and crossed a dry nullah in front of the intrenchments, but they then found themselves in front of a high wall too steep for them to climb and exposed to a terrible fire from above. To remain there would have been to be annihilated, and the regiments were withdrawn, but only to charge again at a fresh point.

Thrice they reached the walls, thrice they had to fall back, each time followed by the Sikhs, who cut the wounded to pieces. The second division, however, managed at several points to effect a lodgment within the intrenchments, while Stacey's and Ashburnham's brigade maintained themselves in the position the former had captured, in spite of the desperate efforts of the Sikhs, who in vast numbers swarmed down upon them and tried to recapture it. Thus for a while the battle raged, nor were the British able to advance beyond the points wnere they had gained a footing, until the sappers cut a narrow opening through the works, by which the cavalry were able to pass in single file. As soon as the 3d Dragoons had entered the work they formed up, and charging along in the rear of the intrenchment, cut down the Sikh gunners in their batteries and captured their field-guns.

As their fire ceased the rest of the infantry poured into the works, and advancing along the whole line, while the field batteries which had entered joined their fire to that of the musketry, they pressed the Sikhs before them in masses across the river. The bridge was an excellent one, but one of the Sikh commanders had caused two of the boats forming it to be removed, in order that his men, seeing there was no mode of retreat should defend their works the more desperately. The river had risen during the night, and the ford, which had the day before been but breast-deep, was now scarcely passable.

The scene was a terrible one; the crowded masses of the enemy threw themselves into the river, and strove to cross by wading and swimming, while the guns of the British horse-

artillery, which had come up, played upon them unceasingly, and the infantry poured volleys of musketry into them, all feeling of pity being for the time dissipated by the fury with which the murder of our wounded by the Sikhs during the «arly portion of the fight had inspired the troops.

Hundreds of the enemy fell under the cannonade; very many hundreds were drowned. The battle terminated at noon, the infantry having been engaged without intermission for three hours. Sixty-seven cannon were captured, and upwards of two hundred camel guns. This great and decisive victory cost those engaged in it dearly. The 2gth Foot had 13 officers, 8 sergeants, and 167 men killed and wounded; the ist European Light Infantry, 12 officers, 12 sergeants, and 173 men; the 3ist, 7 officers and 147 men; the 5oth, 12 officers and 227 men; the 53d, 9 officers and in men.

These were the heaviest losses, but all the regiments engaged suffered severely, as the total loss was 2383 in killed and wounded. The losses among the staff of officers were small compared to those which they had suffered at Ferozeshah, as it was not necessary at Sobraon for the governor-general and commander-in-chief to expose themselves close to the enemy's intrenchments as they had done on that occasion. General Sir Robert Dick, who had gone through the Peninsular War, and led the 42d Highlanders at Waterloo, was killed as he led his men forward against the Sikh intrenchments; and Brigadier-generals M'Laren and Taylor also fell. The loss of the Sikhs was never known; but the carnage was, in proportion to the numbers engaged, enormous, and many of their leading sirdars were among the slain.

At Ferozeshah, the greater proportion of the loss among the assailants was caused by the grape-shot from the enemy's guns. At Sobraon, on the other hand, in spite of the number and weight of the enemy's guns, and of their very numerous camel pieces, it was the musket that inflicted the great proportion of loss. This was due, in the first place, to the fact that a

ALIWAL AND SOBRAON

large number of the skilled Sikh gunners had fallen in the previous battles, and that the artillery fire was in consequence very wild and ill-directed. In the next place, the artillerymen were unable to depress their pieces sufficiently to play upon the British when they reached the foot of the intrenchments, while the infantry, well sheltered behind their earthworks, were able to keep up a murderous fire upon their helpless foes. These facts account for the unusually large number of men wounded in proportion to the killed.

As the division of Sir Harry Smith had only reached the camp two days before the battle, Percy remained attached to his staff and rode behind him in the engagement. He had wished his two men to remain in camp, but they resolutely declined to do so.

" If you were killed, sahib, how could we face the colonel, and tell him that while you were killed we were cooking our dinners four miles away ? No, sahib, whatever comes, we must ride behind the general's escort. Had we not seen Feroze-shah, we should say that success to-morrow is impossible, for the intrenchments there were but dirt-heaps in comparison to the great works opposite. We can see with our own eyes how-big and high they are. They say there are three lines of parapets for the infantry to fire over, besides all their guns. But now we know that nothing is impossible to the white troops, and believe that somehow, though we cannot say how, they will capture it, and drive the Sikhs across the river. If we live through it, it will be a thing to talk of for the rest of our lives; and if we die, you will tell the colonel, sahib, that we did our duty. He told us to watch over you, and though no watching can turn the course of shot or bullet, we can at least be near to carry you off should you fall wounded."

However, Percy escaped without being hit, as did most of the staff, though he did his share in carrying orders to the officers commanding the different regiments in the division. As they rode back from the field after the engagement was over the general called him up to his side.

"I ought to have kept you out of the battle, lad," he said kindly; "but I did not like to baulk you again. You have done very well, and I shall mention your name in my report as among the members of my staff who did good service."

The battle of Sobraon completely broke the power of the Sikhs. In these and the preceding fights all the picked regiments of the regular infantry had been destroyed or dispersed, and two hundred and twenty of their guns captured. No time was lost by the commander-in-chief in following up his success. A bridge of boats had been already thrown across the river half-way between Ferozepore and Sobraon, and messages were sent to Sir John Grey,'who commanded a force there, and to Sir John Littler at Ferozepore, to cross at once. At daybreak next morning six regiments crossed the Sutlej from Ferozepore, while Sir John Grey, with two regiments of cavalry, three of infantry, and a battery, crossed by the new bridge, both forces thus placing themselves on the road by which the defeated Sikhs would retire upon Lahore. This speedy movement completed their discomfiture. Cut off from the capital, and deprived of the leadership of all the principal sirdars, they dispersed to their homes, and the bridge at Sobraon having been repaired on the day following the battle, the British crossed without opposition.

Ghoolab Singh, who had all this time been negotiating secretly with the British, while promising the Sikhs that he was on the eve of advancing to join them with his whole force, now endeavoured to figure as mediator, and came secretly into the British camp with the object of persuading the governor-general to abstain from making an advance against Lahore. Sir Henry Hardinge refused to receive him, and sent a message to him by his political officers that terms of peace would be dictated at the capital. The crafty sirdar was not to be defeated; riding back to Lahore, he took the young maharajah and rode with him to the British camp. Sir Henry received the young prince kindly, but was not to be diverted from his

purpose of moving forward to Lahore, where the army arrived without a shot being fired.

Here terms of peace were dictated to the humble Sikhs-The expenses of the war, estimated at a million and a half, were to be paid, all the guns taken were to be retained, and all others that had been used against us during the war were to be handed over; the troops were to be disbanded, and the fertile province known as the Jalindar Doab, situated between the Beas and Sutlej rivers, was to be handed over to the British. Many of the officers considered that it would have been better to have annexed the whole of the Punjaub, but even with the army that was marching from Scinde under Sir Charles Napier the force was insufficient for the work. The Sikhs had strongly fortified cities, that could scarcely have been taken without a regular battering train, and the hot season was coming on. Besides, although the army trained with so much care by Runjeet Singh had been broken up and scattered, the Sikh nation had as yet taken but little part in the struggle. It was, however, certain that they would, under their great chiefs, fight desperately to preserve their independence, and the whole of the dispersed soldiery would speedily be reunited under the banners of the leaders.

The crafty Ghoolab Singh gained the advantages he had hoped, for the treasury of Lahore was empty, and with the greatest difficulty half a million was raised to pay the first instalment of the indemnity. Ghoolab Singh, therefore, out of his vast resources paid another half million, on condition that Cashmere should be handed over to him, and that from being merely the governor of that province, he should become its independent ruler. The price paid by him for this rich province was absurdly inadequate, but so far as the British were concerned the bargain was a politic one. There was little doubt that a second war would, sooner or later, have to be undertaken; Ghoolab Singh could put a very large army into the field, and by making him ruler of Cashmere his inter-

ests were at once separated from those of the Sikhs, and his neutrality, if not his active alliance, ,were secured in any future struggle. It was arranged that a British force should remain in Lahore for a year, nominally to insure the payment of the rest of the indemnity, but really to maintain the authority of the maharanee and the boy maharajah, who were in no way responsible for the war against us, and who doubtless would have been overthrown by some ambitious sirdar, aided by the disbanded troops, had they been left unsupported by British bayonets.

CHAPTER XI
AN AMBUSH

MR. FULLARTON had accompanied the army to Lahore, his knowledge of the country and people being so valuable that the governor-general sent over on the evening after the Sikh intrenchments at Sobraon had been stormed, to request him to join the army at once, as Loodiana had for the present ceased to be a station of importance. He had, as soon as he joined the camp, claimed Percy Groves' services, and in the negotiations that followed, and as interpreter between the British and Sikh authorities, he was found of great use, especially after they reached Lahore, where many of the Sikh sirdars, especially those whose possessions lay in the Jalindar Doab, considered it prudent to come in and to assume an appearance of friendship with the British.

"Now, Qroves, what are your wishes as to entering the service?" Mr. Fullarton said to him one day, when the various court ceremonials were over, and preparations were beginning for the withdrawal of the main body of the army. " The governor-general mentioned your name to me to-day, and said that you had rendered very valuable services during the campaign. Mr. Broadfoot had reported most favourably of you; you had acted as aide-de-camp to the commander-in-chief at Ferozeshah and to Sir Harry Smith at Sobraon; the latter had mentioned you in his report, as Sir Hugh Gough and himself

had both observed your coolness and readiness to carry messages under the heaviest fire at Ferozeshah; and that since then your services as interpreter have been very valuable.

" He said that you had earned an appointment, and that he should be glad to write to the Board of Directors to request one for you, but that he feared the board would consider you too young. He said, however, if you strongly desired to enter the service at once, he would put the matter in such a light that they could hardly refuse; for as you had been doing man's work throughout this campaign, you could do it during peace time. I think his own opinion was that it would be better for you to wait for another two or three years, for that, if you received an appointment now, you might be sent down to an office in Calcutta. You see that at your age you could hardly occupy a post that would not only place you in communication with native chiefs, as the British representative, but might place you in a position where, as political officer, you might have to requisition the assistance of troops and of officers old enough to be your father."

"I quite think so," Percy said, "and would much rather not enter the service for another three years, sir; even then I shall only be nineteen."

"That is about the right age to enter," Mr. Fullarton said, "and you will have great advantages over other young fellows just out. There would be your record in your favour, and your knowledge of the language and people, and you would be certain to obtain an appointment in this province such as a man direct from England could hardly hope for until after at least ten years' service. I think if I were you, I should turn my attention for the next two years to acquiring as thorough a knowledge of the Pathan language as you now have of Punjaubi. When we have annexed the Punjaub, which is a question of a few years, we shall be in direct contact with the hill tribes, who are nominally subject to Afghanistan, but are practically independent, and if you happened to be stationed in any of

AN AMBUSH

the northern districts you would find the knowledge of that language invaluable. You have evidently a knack of picking up languages, and your knowledge of Punjaubi will, of course, help you considerably in learning Pathan."

As Percy was anxious, now that everything was settled, to return as speedily as possible to his uncle's, he at once wrote a formal request that his services as a volunteer might be dispensed with.

The next day Mr. Fullarton said to him : " I informed Sir Henry Hardinge yesterday evening that you had sent in your resignation, and he requests me to bring you to him this morning that he might say good-bye to you, and thank you for your services."

The commander-in-chief was with the governor-general when Mr. Fullarton called at the palace, where he had taken up his quarters, but on his name being taken in he was requested to enter at once, which he did with Percy.

"I should have been sorry had you gone without saying good-bye to me, Mr. Groves," Sir Henry said. "Both the commander-in-chief and myself have noted your conduct very favourably, and reports to the same effect have been made by Mr. Broadfoot and Sir Harry Smith. I think you are wise to decide to wait another three years before entering the service. I shall write to the Board of Directors requesting them to appoint you to their civil service at once. But I shall ask them to date the appointment three years on, and at the same time to send instructions to the officer who will remain as Resident here to the effect that should there be any signs of fresh trouble before that time, he can at once ante-date the appointment and employ you in any way in which your knowledge of the country and language, and your zeal and activity, can be utilized. Should I still be in India, I shall make it a point to see that you have an appointment in this province; and should I return to England before that time, your name will be placed in the list I leave behind for my successor of

promising and intelligent officers. Sir Hugh Gough will also, he tells me, keep an eye on your interests, and doubtless you will receive a notification from the Court in due time as to your appointment. You will do well, after you receive it, to write to the Resident here, telling him that although you do not wish for employment until the date of your appointment, your services are at his disposal should they be required. I have no doubt Mr. Fullarton will, before leaving, speak to him personally on the matter."

The commander-in-chief added a few words, and Percy on returning to the house began preparations for his departure.

"We shall have to be careful as we ride back, sahib," Bhop Lai said. "Things are quiet enough about here, but from what I learn the country is overrun with disbanded soldiers. They have gone back for the most part to their own villages; but what will they do there? They have lived an idle life for years, and quite considered themselves masters of the country. They will never set to at steady work to plough the fields, they will soon tire out their friends, and then they will wander away and gather in bands, and become dacoits. I hear in the bazaar that the country is everywhere unsafe for travel; that merchants dare not send their goods except in strong parties guarded by a force of disbanded soldiers they pay to act as guards. The peasants are robbed and plundered, and things are even worse than they were before the war began. After getting through the battles without so much as a scratch, it would be unfortunate, indeed, should ill befall us now that the war is all over."

"There is one thing, Bhop Lai. We shall have no dangers except from an accidental encounter with robbers. Now that Ghoolab Singh is ruler of Cashmere, he will have too many other matters to think of to trouble further about my imcle and his little district."

"Nothing is too small, as nothing is too large, sahib," Akram Chunder said, "for the greed of Ghoolab Singh. He

may now have a kingdom, but that will not prevent him from fleecing a trader if he has an opportunity. See how he has filled his coffers at the expense of the people. Has he not paid half a crore of rupees to your people for Cashmere, and I doubt not he would have paid three times as much if it had been needed. There are many other sirdars could have paid the half crore, but they say that Ghoolab could buy up any four of them. It is true there is no fear that he will now try to seize the colonel sahib's government by force, at least until fresh troubles begin; but if he can have him quietly removed you may be sure he will do so, as he could then easily enough get the maharanee and the Lahore durbar to confirm the former appointment of his son as governor.

"The colonel need no longer fear force, but he must be more than ever on his guard against treachery. Still, sahib, I agree with you that just at present Ghoolab must have too many things to think of to be giving attention to your matter, and that we can travel without fear of him. As for the bud-mashes, we shall have to be careful of them, as my comrade says; and we must mind that no one suspects for a moment that you are English; for although the people here are respectful enough, you may be sure that outside the range of your guns there is not a Sikh, save perhaps the humblest cultivators, who is not full of rage and hatred against the English. Have you not defeated them in four battles, humbled their national pride, and taken their richest province? To be suspected of Toeing an Englishman would be your death-warrant in the smallest village of the Punjaub. The sahib would do well to-morrow not to wear his dress of a sirdar, but to dress as he did when we visited the camp of Tej Singh. Then, if we are questioned, it is we who will do the talking; while, if you are dressed as a chief, it is to you the questions will be put. Besides, most of the sirdars are known by name, at least to the bulk of the people, and it would be difficult for you to reply to close questioning; whereas, passing as disbanded

soldiers, who are tired of doing nothing in our native village, and are going north to take service with Ghoolab Singh, our story is simple and natural enough."

" But Ghoolab himself cannot be popular in the country at present," Percy said; " they must all see now that he has been playing a double part; and that he has, moreover, wrenched from the Punjaub a territory as valuable as that which we took after such hard fighting."

"That is so, but Ghoolab is everywhere feared; no man offends him or his without paying for it; and besides, they may hope that if there is again trouble, Ghoolab may join them against the British. They may not like him, but there must be many disbanded soldiers who have been going to take service under him, and the people will bear us no ill-will for that: it is the most likely story for us to tell, and the one that will be least questioned."

" I think you are right, Akram Chunder; at any rate I will ride to-morrow dressed as you are."

The next morning they started from Lahore at daybreak, and rode north. They had agreed to travel by the main road, as they would there attract no attention; whereas passing through villages on unfrequented roads, their passage would excite comment. After riding for fifteen miles they came upon a party of ten men, evidently disbanded soldiers, seated in the shade of a clump of trees by the roadside, cooking their breakfast.

"Better stop and talk with them," Bhop Lai said; "it will look strange if we ride on."

They reined in their horses, and Bhop Lai gave the usual salutation. After the customary return of greetings, one of the men said, "Will you not dismount and share our breakfast?"

"We took food before we started from Lahore," Bhop Lai replied.

"Ah, you came from Lahore: what is the last news there?"

"There is nothing new, everything is quiet, and they say that most of the English will soon march away."

" We will make short work of the maharanee and her son as soon as they go," the man said savagely. "They are but puppets now in the hands of the English, and have signed away the best doab in the Punjaub so as to buy protection for Dhuleep Singh. He is no longer a Sikh prince, and we will speedily place one of our own sirdars on the throne."

"That is what we all mean to do," Bhop Lai agreed; "we want no boy as our ruler now, but a sirdar who can lead us to battle. It will be different next time; last time we despised the English, and so they beat us; next time it will be they who will make too sure, and we shall beat them."

"Where are you going? "

"We are thinking of taking service under Ghoolab Singh."

"The old fox is a traitor," the man said angrily, while a general murmur broke from his comrades.

"There is no doubt that he played us false," Bhop Lai agreed; "but now that he is master of Cashmere he may think it his interest to go with us next time; and besides, at present his gold is as good as another's, and none of the other sirdars will increase their forces until the English have retired; so there is just the choice of taking service with Ghoolab or of starving."

"There is no occasion to starve for those who have got arms," the man said; "and we find it easier to help ourselves and to be our own masters than to serve anyone else. You had better join us, comrades."

"Thank you; we have thought it over, you may be sure; but we have had enough of marching about and sleeping in the air for the present, and we are likely at any rate to sleep and eat our meals in peace with Ghoolab. There is little chance of any rising for a long time yet, and till then, at any rate, there will be peace in Cashmere. When fighting begins again here, we have made up our minds to come back, if we

find that Ghoolab has forgotten that he is a Sikh. And now, with your permission, we will be riding on," and Bhop Lai turned his horse, and with his companions trotted off.

"We got through that well enough," Percy remarked.

"They did not think we were worth robbing, sahib; and as we are well armed, it would not have been worth their while to meddle with us. Besides, you see their horses are on the other side of the grove, and they must have noticed that we were well mounted, and could have got a long start before they were off. It is as likely as not that they did not believe my story, but thought we were on our way to join some other band we knew of. I have no fear of these fellows if we meet them openly in the daytime. The danger will be if we come upon them suddenly, and they attack us before they see what we are."

In the course of the day they passed several parties of threes and fours, sometimes mounted and sometimes on foot; but they did not draw rein, and contented themselves with the exchange of passing salutations. Only once they came upon a large party. It consisted of twenty carts laden with merchandise, and escorted by some thirty men armed to the teeth.

"You see they get employment both ways, sahib," Akram Chunder remarked; " some of them make money by turning robbers, others make money by selling their services to merchants to protect their goods from robbers. No doubt those carts are on their way down from Serinagur and Jummoo, and are laden with shawls and embroidery, and such other goods as the merchants think the English officers at Lahore will be glad to buy to send home to their friends."

" I should think they will make a good venture," Percy said, " for the bazaars at Lahore are very poorly stocked. Trade has been bad there for a long time, owing to the troubles and disturbances, and I hear that many of the traders who had remained fled when the news came of the defeat at Sobraon, fearing that the English army would act as the Sikhs would

have done under the circumstances, and would march straight to Lahore and plunder the city. What part of Cashmere do you come from, Akram?"

" From the hills ftfty miles north of Serinagur. Cashmere has no authority there, and the hill tribes have their wars with each other without interference. I was fifteen when our village was attacked and destroyed by a tribe we had raided a few months before. Most of the people were killed, but I was fleet-footed and got away. I worked for a time at Serinagur, but got tired of carrying burdens from morning to night, so I went on to Jummoo, and stopped there for three or four years; and then, when I was about one-and-twenty, went down to Lahore, and finding it hard work to get a living in any other way, I took service in Runjeet Singh's army, and had the good luck to enlist in the regiment of my lord your uncle, and there I have remained ever since. It was a lucky day when I chose his regiment, and I did so because I heard two soldiers in the street speak well of him. Had I been in one of the others, I should most likely have fallen at Ferozeshah or Sobraon, even if I hadn't been killed before."

That night they slept at a khan in the town. There were but few other guests, and the keeper of the place bitterly bemoaned the change of times.

"In the days of Runjeet," he said, "there were seldom less than a hundred travellers stopping here nightly; after his death the number fell to about twenty, for who would go to Lahore if he could help it, when, for aught he knew, he might find fighting going on in the streets, or the city being sacked when he arrived there ? Now it is rare for more than three or four to pass the night here; no one will travel for trade or for pleasure; no one will go to Lahore as long as the English are there. Sometimes, it is true, a caravan comes down, such as that which stayed here last night; but there are few of these, and were it not for the passage of those who, like yourselves, are on their way to their homes, or to take service in Cashmere,

I might as well close and lock the gates, and go away to earn my bread at some other business. The country is being ruined fast. There are even those who say that it would be better the English should come and be our masters; there would be peace then, and they would soon put a stop to robbery and dacoitism, as they have done wherever they have established their rule, and the peasants would be able to plough their fields, and the traders to carry on their business without fear of any man so long as they paid their taxes and kept the law. I do not say that those are my opinions," he added hastily, "but I know that such is the talk among the peasants, who have had, it must be owned, a rough time since Runjeet Singh died. Heavily taxed they were in his time, but beyond that they had nought to complain of; but of late, what with one trouble and another, their lot has been hard."

"There is no doubt about that," Bhop Lai agreed heartily. " I have been a soldier, but I have been a peasant too, and know where the shoe pinches. Perhaps things will be better now."

The man shrugged his shoulders. " I see not how this is to be," he said; "the Lahore durbar is under the protection of foreigners, and no one heeds it, as it has no power save in the city. Better a thousand times a prince who can make himself obeyed, even were it Ghoolab Singh, or else a strong foreign rule. I would rather have a native prince, but far better than the nominal rule of a boy, protected by foreign bayonets, would be the rule of the foreigners themselves, for they, at least, can make the law respected, punish ill-doers, and preserve peace and order."

" I fancy there are a great many who think as you do," Bhop Lai said; "but these for the most part keep their thoughts to themselves. Well, we shall see what we shall see. Things will never go on long as they are at present; and, as you say, the Punjaub will either be ruled by a strong native prince, or it will, like Scinde, become a possession of the English. I have had enough of fighting, and mean to remain quiet until one or other of these things comes about."

"There are many like you; but some of the soldiers who come through say they would like to fight the English again."

"Then take my word for it," a soldier sitting by said, "the men who said that were not among those who fought on the Sutlej. There were brave men there, and plenty of them, but I do not believe one of those that fought there will ever wish to fight the white troops again. There was no withstanding them. They came on as if they minded the rain of iron and lead no more than if it had been a thunder-shower. It was that which beat us; we were told by our chiefs that it was impossible, absolutely impossible, for men to force their way into our lines, and when we saw them do it, we said to ourselves it is hopeless to fight against such men: and we who, under Runjeet, have won victory after victory, and that against stout fighters like the Afghans, lost heart for the first time in our lives, when we felt that we, though two to one, were no match for these terrible soldiers."

" Is it true," the keeper of the khan asked, " as all have told me, that they neither plunder nor rob; and though really masters of Lahore, the English go about quietly, ill-treating none?"

"It is quite true; they have discipline; brave as these men are, they are quiet and orderly, as our troops never were even in the days when Runjeet was strong and firm. Not a man has been robbed, nor a woman insulted, since they crossed the Sutlej. They are our enemies, but they are a great people."

"If you have aught to lose, gentlemen," the other said, "be careful how you ride to-morrow; scarce one has arrived from the north for the last week who does not complain bitterly of being robbed on the way. Some were wounded sorely, having ventured on resistance. They say there are as many as two hundred disbanded soldiers lurking among the woods and bushes between this and the next town. The Sirdar Lai Miz-rah, moved by the complaints of the country people, cleared the road of them a few days since, breaking up their parties, and killing many; therefore, at present they are more cautious. That is how the convoy got through safely yesterday. I should advise you, therefore, to travel by country roads, though even these are not safe, for the robbers, finding that people have deserted the main road and have taken to these paths, have beset them also."

"We have nothing to lose but our lives," Bhop Lai said, "but as these are somewhat precious to us, we will take all the care we can to avoid these gentry you speak of."

After a consultation with Percy, it was agreed that, as time was no particular object, they would strike off at once to the west, travel for a day in that direction, and then make north, thereby getting well out of the line followed by travellers from Lahore.

"After having been through three battles," Percy said, "it would be folly to risk getting our throats cut merely for the sake of saving a day's journey."

Accordingly the next morning they took this route. They passed several villages in the course of the day; as they were seen approaching, men and women ran into their houses and closed the doors, and not a soul was to be seen in the streets as they passed through.

"We need not have been afraid of being questioned," Percy said; "it is evident that the whole population of the country is scared by the exactions of these disbanded soldiers, and that they are only too glad to see us pass by without interfering with them. It would have been well for the country if the Sutlej had risen another foot on the day of the storming of Sobraon, it would have relieved the country of some thousands more of these plunderers."

They met with no adventure whatever until they arrived within a few miles of the fortress. Then, as they were riding along through a wood, a party of men on foot suddenly sprang

PERCY AND HIS FOLLOWERS ARE ATTACKED UY DACOITS,.

out from among the trees. Before they had time to draw their swords Akram Chunder and Percy were struck from their horses. Bhop Lai, who happened to be a horse's length behind his comrades, snatched his pistol from his belt, and shot two of the assailants; then a ball from a matchlock struck him, and he fell from his horse. As he lay he was gashed with a dozen severe wounds, and was speedily stripped of his arms and clothes; the party then gathered round the two prisoners.

"I know this man," one of them said, stooping over Akram Chunder; "he is one of the men at the white colonel's fortress. I know him because he was servant to one of the officers, and when I went in there with ghee, he bought some of me and came back accusing me of having sold him false weight. He fetched his master, who examined my scales, and found that somehow a bit of lead had got stuck under one of them, and the villain had me flogged, and told me if ever I entered the place again he would cut off my ears. I swore I would pay this fellow out some day, and having changed my appearance somewhat went back some time ago to find him and pay him with a knife stab if I got a chance, but I heard from a friend I had there that he had gone away; he had ridden off with a party that went with the colonels' nephew. The rest had returned all but this fellow and another; and as it was just when the war broke out, it was supposed they had gone with the young sahib to act as his servants, for both were accustomed to that sort of work."

"Well, there are three of them here," the other said; " maybe it is a lucky day for us, and that the third of them is the white lad."

"Sure enough it's the governor's nephew," one of the men exclaimed as he walked across to Percy, who was lying a little apart. "I have seen him a dozen times at the fortress."

"Then this is a fortunate day for us indeed," the leader of the party exclaimed; "put them both on their horses again and mount without delay; we will settle what to do with them afterwards. We have two strings to our bow: it is certain that we can get a handsome ransom from the colonel, but I fancy Ghoolab Singh would give us still more. You remember the talk there was of a party of his men lying in ambush here to capture this lad as he came up two years ago; and everyone knows it was his doing that the place was besieged three months since."

"Would it not be as well to give this fellow a stab and leave him here?" the man who had recognized Akram Chunder asked.

"Not at all," the leader said harshly; "at any rate not at present. We may find him useful if we want to send a messenger in to the white colonel. Besides, if we ransom the boy to his uncle it is no use setting him against us by killing his servant. Even if the colonel agreed to leave us unmolested, some of his men might take the matter up and make the country too hot for us. I am always against killing unless there is something to be gained by it, and I see nothing to be gained by this fellow's death."

Percy had been stunned by the blow from the heavy cudgel that struck him off his horse, but he heard the latter part of the conversation. He knew that resistance would be fatal, and submitted quietly to be placed on his horse. His hands were first bound in front of him, the reins were then cut and two horsemen, one on either side of him, took the ends. Akram Chunder was similarly treated, and, surrounded by the whole party, numbering about twenty, they rode off. By their dress and attire he judged the men into whose hands they had fallen were not discharged soldiers but regular dacoits, and when he heard one of them address the leader by the name of Goolam Tej, he recognized it as that of a dacoit who had for years been a scourge to that part of the country, although he had seldom ventured to molest the villages in the colonel's district, knowing how speedy and relentless would be the pursuit. He had heard numberless stories of the atrocities committed by

this band; how they had tortured men and women to force them to reveal the hiding-places of their money; how they had slaughtered not only those who ventured to offer resistance, but their wives and families. However, he had no fear as to his own safety; there was nothing to be made by killing hin:, while there might be a large sum to be obtained as a ransom from his uncle or by his sale to Ghoolab Singh.

The band were all mounted on wiry little ponies, and for some hours they rode at a rapid pace. They halted in a wood at the foot of the hills. Here the leader, upon asking the question whether any of them had ascertained beyond the possibility of doubt that the man they had left behind was dead, was furious at finding that none of them had done so. The men who had stripped him declared they felt quite certain of it: " He had half a dozen wounds any one of which must have killed him," one of them said; "and that being so, I did not think of putting my hand on his heart to feel if it beat. Make yourself easy, Goolam Tej, the fellow is dead beyond all doubt."

"There is never any saying," his leader replied; "some men are so tough that they get over wounds which should have been sufficient to kill them a dozen times. It is always well to make sure, either by a stroke with a dagger through the heart, or by cutting off the head. There is no great trouble about either job, and it prevents mistakes occurring. If I determine on sending to Ghoolab Singh first, I don't want the colonel to know what has happened till we are at the other end of the country. If that fellow should be found on the road, and his wounds bound up, he may recover so far as to tell them what has happened, and then we shall have the colonel scouring the whole country with his force. Besides, he may send to Lahore and lay a complaint before the durbar, and as he and the boy are English they would get up a hue and cry after us through the whole of the Punjaub. I daresay the man is dead, still there ought not to be a possibility of a doubt about it, and I blame myself as much as I do you for not having given a thought to the matter."

On dismounting, Percy's legs were firmly bound, and he was laid down on the ground at a short distance from his follower, a dacoit with a gun and sword taking his seat by each of them, so that even conversation was impossible. The next morning they started up the hills, and after some hours' riding crossed the crest, and then, leaving the bridle-path by which they had travelled, dismounted and led their horses along the steep face of the hill until they reached a perpendicular crag standing out from it, upon the summit of which stood a castellated building. A long shed had been erected upon a comparatively flat piece of ground among the trees at its foot; into this the dacoits led their ponies, and then mounted a path a few inches wide cut in the rock, and leading up to a strong door which gave access to the building. A watchman on the wall had seen them coming, and as they entered they were greeted with cries of joy by a number of women.

Percy saw at once that the building was ancient, but that it had recently been roughly repaired, and doubted not that it was a deserted fortalice that the band had occupied and made their head-quarters. During that day's ride the dacoits had taken the precaution of bandaging the eyes of their prisoners, and only unloosened the wraps when, on nearing the place, the ground had become so steep and difficult that it was necessary for them to have the use of their eyes. The prisoners were taken to a small room in a little tower at one of the angles of the building, their cords were then unloosened, and they were left alone together.

"This is a nice fix that we are in, Akram Chunder," Percy said.

" It is, indeed, sahib. I care not so much for myself, but to think that you, after going through those battles, should be seized by these robbers within a few miles of home, cuts me to the heart."

AN AMBUSH

203

"I am awfully sorry for Bhop Lai," Percy said. "Do you think he was killed? "

"That I cannot say, not having seen his wounds, but if they were not in a vital place he may live through them, for he is as hard as a piece of iron, and was not given to drink. Men who drink have but little chance of making a good recovery. He would have the sense, I know, to lie still and sham dead; but I hope ere this he may have carried the news to your uncle. He would obtain help and assistance from the first passer-by when he told his story, for there is not a peasant in the district who does not love the colonel."

CHAPTER XII
A PRISONER

PERCY went to the window and looked out. There were J- three of these, mere arrow slits, and from each of them he had a view of the wood stretching away down the hillside into a narrow valley, which a short distance down took a turn and the hills cut off further view.

"Where are we, think you, Akram Chunder? " " I have no idea, sahib, beyond the fact that by the position of the sun we are looking eastward. I should say the place where we halted yesterday was some thirty miles to the northeast of the fortress; it may have been more, but it certainly was not less, or I would have known the country. To-day we were mounting all the time till the last hour, and then I could feel that we descended sharply. I should say that we were some six hours on horseback; we travelled part of the way at a trot, but more often walked, so at five miles an hour we should be thirty from our camp of last night. If we travelled straight to the east all the time we may have crossed the main crest of the hills; if not, we may be anywhere among them, for they tied the bandages so carefully over my eyes that I could see nothing, not even the road under the horse's feet."

"It would not have helped you much had you done so," Percy said with a laugh; "one road is a good deal like another."

"The shadows would have shown me the direction in which we were travelling, sahib, more accurately than I could tell by the heat of the sun."

" So they would, Akram. I did not think of that. At any rate we may take it that we are in some very out-of-the-way spot, where it would be difficult for anyone to find us without a guide."

"That is so, sahib. I can see nothing but trees, and no signs of human handiwork. This place could not be seen at a great distance, for it does not rise very much above the tops of the trees. The rock was about thirty feet high where we mounted it, though it must be well-nigh double that on the lower face. The building itself is not any great height; though it could be seen well enough from that valley down there, it could not be made out from above, and even from the hillside was scarcely visible. It would be a difficult place to capture except by a force provided with cannon, for it occupies the whole of the top of this crag, and, as far as I could see, that is quite unclimbable except by the path up which we mounted. Above the gate there was a projecting turret, and the loopholes of those at the corners both commanded it. A dozen men with muskets ought to be able to hold that path against any number; for even if they got up to the gate, I noticed as I entered that there are holes in the floor of the turret above by which they could fire down or pour hot lead on the heads of any trying to break open the gate."

"You heard what they said about the ransom? "

"I heard them, sahib, and only hope that they will go direct to the colonel; but I am afraid they will try Ghoolab Singh first. They know that he has plenty of money in his treasure-chests."

" I am afraid so too, Akram. The fact that Ghoolab tried to catch me before shows that he thinks he could work upon my uncle through me; and as he seems to have set his mind upon obtaining possession of the fortress, I should think he would pay any sum these scoundrels elected to ask."

The man nodded. "He will pay anything, sahib; it is not only that he wants the place, but that he owes the colonel a grudge for having held it so stoutly in spite of him, and Ghoolab never forgets an injury or forgives one he hates."

"I see no chance of making our escape," Percy said, again examining the windows.

"None, sahib; a rat could hardly creep through these loopholes, and had we means to cut away the stone we should be no nearer escape, unless we had also a rope, and that a long one, for we are at the lower angle of the rock, and I should say these loopholes must be eighty feet above the ground. We have nothing to make a rope of, as you see they have stripped me to my Cumberland, and have taken away your coat; so our clothes, if torn up and twisted together, would scarce make a rope eighty feet long that would support its own weight. I see no shadow of a chance of escape that way, nor in any way if the guard is vigilant. We may have a better chance if we are taken to Ghoolab; he would not have us at Jummoo, for should any complaint be laid against him on your account, he would, of course, deny that he knows aught about you; but wherever we are taken, we shall probably find better chances of escape than there are here. Once free, we might manage; it is not likely that any of these dacoits can know that I'm from Cashmere, and you may be sure I shall not let them find out that I speak the language. If we could get out, then, I could pass as a peasant, and however hot the pursuit, we ought to be able to evade it."

Five days passed; the prisoners had nothing to complain of in their treatment, being kept well supplied with food. This was always brought in by two armed men, while two others stood at the door, partly, Percy guessed, to prevent any attempt to escape, partly to see that they held no conversation with those who brought in the food.

"They can't trust each other," Akram Chunder said; "they know well enough that the bribe you could offer for assistance

to escape would be too much for any single dacoit to resist, and their leader is wise not to trust them."

"The sooner we are out of this the better," Percy said. "I am heartily tired of looking out of these loopholes, and don't care how soon I am on my way to Cashmere. How long will it be, do you think, before a message can come from Ghoolab Singh?" '

" If he is at Jummoo a messenger should be able to go and come in five or six days, sahib; but it will probably be some little time before he can get an interview with Ghoolab. This is the fifth day since we were brought here; if we hear nothing to-morrow it will be either that he is not there, or that the dacoit has demanded so large a sum for you that he is unwilling to give it. Ghoolab is too fond of money to pay if he can help it; and it is quite possible that when the messenger gets there he will seize and torture him until he reveals the position of this place, and will then send a force to capture you without the necessity of paying for you. I wonder whether the dacoits have foreseen that possibility. It is just the sort of thing that Ghoolab would delight in."

" I hope he won't attempt anything of the sort," Percy said; " if the dacoits find themselves surrounded and attacked here, they would likely enough avenge themselves upon him by cutting our throats before his men could force their way in."

"That is just what they would do, sahib; but as Ghoolab would foresee the risk, it will, I hope, prevent him from carrying out that plan. He will learn from the messenger that the place can hardly be taken by a sudden surprise, and, therefore, he may think it better to pay the sum demanded, provided it is net too large, to running the risk of losing you altogether. He would not be ill-pleased to hear of your death, for he would reckon that were you out of the way, sooner or later the fortress and district would fall into his hands; but doubtless he would rather have you, in order that he may drive

a good bargain with the colonel and get him to hand the place over in exchange for you."

"I hope my uncle will do nothing of the sort," Percy said.

Akarm Chunder shook his head. "You are his son by adoption," he said, "and to save your life he will give up the fortress."

" Well, I hope at any rate he will negotiate for some time, Akram, in which case it will be hard if we don't manage to slip away somehow. I wish we had our knives with us."

"What for, sahib? The stonework of the windows is solid, and it would take us an immense time to enlarge one of the loopholes so that we could slip through."

"I was not thinking of that; but if we had our knives we could get off one of the back legs of the charpoy, so that its loss would not be noticed, and cut it up into wedges, which we could drive in all round the door if we heard a row going on outside. The door is a very strong one, and if we could fasten it like that inside they might not be able to break it open before Ghoolab's men could fight their way in."

"That is a good idea, sahib, and if we had knives we would carry it out, but without them I don't see that we could do anything. We might move the two charpoys against the door, but half a dozen men pushing on the other side would soon drive them out of the way."

"No, there is nothing to be done," Percy agreed; "and I do hope that Ghoolab will quite see that in the event of his trying to take the place, the dacoits will be pretty sure to finish me before his men can get in."

That evening they unlashed the thin binding that held one of the beds together, and each one armed himself with one of the legs.

"It is not much of a weapon," Percy said, "but it is something anyhow, and it would be a thousand times better to make a fight of it than to stand still and have one's throat cut. We will take it by turns to keep awake to-night, so as to hear if there is anything stirring."

The night, however, passed without any unusual sound being heard. Just after daybreak they heard a shout.

"That is likely to be the messenger returning," Akram Chunder said. " If it had been an enemy, they would have come in the dark."

"But they would not be able to find their way," Percy objected.

"They would make the messenger act as their guide, sahib; there would be no difficulty about that. Besides if it had been an enemy, we should have heard other shouts; the whole place would be in a turmoil. I have no doubt that it is the messenger, and we shall presently hear what Ghoolab says."

An hour passed, and then the door opened and the men brought in food. "You are to eat this quickly," one said, speaking for the first time since they had been imprisoned; "you have to mount and ride in a quarter of an hour; and Goolam Tej bade me tell you that you had best eat a good meal, for you have a long ride before you, and may not get another before nightfall."

When, after eating a hearty meal, Percy and his follower mounted and made off, escorted by twelve of the dacoits, they congratulated themselves that they had escaped the danger they feared.

" I think that your life is quite safe now, sahib," Akram said. "Whatever Ghoolab Singh may threaten, he will scarcely venture to do you harm. He was always opposed to war with the English, knowing that they would assuredly defeat the soldiers, and he is far-sighted enough to see that ere long the Punjaub will belong to them. It is true that another time the Sikhs might put a larger force in the field than that with which they last fought; but so can the English, for had the war lasted two weeks longer, the army that was coming up from Scinde would have joined that which fought at Sobraon and would have well-nigh doubled its strength. This being so, Ghoolab Singh, who has received the kingdom of Cashmere at the hands of

the English, would fear that, did he murder one of your race, troubles would arise when the English became masters of the Punjaub. In the case of your uncle he would have no scruples, for, as all know, Englishmen who take service with native princes do so without the consent of their government, and forfeit all right to their protection. Besides, it will be represented that the colonel was in fact a rebel against the durbar, since he held by force the government of which he had been deprived by the orders of Runjeet Singh and his ministers, and that his life was thereby forfeited. He may not know that you have been serving as an officer in the English army; but you must let him hear that, and that the governor-general himself has promised you an appointment in the Company's service, and has taken great interest in you, and that, should anything befall you, he will assuredly punish whoever may be the author of the deed. I think that if Ghoolab had known that, he would not have accepted the dacoits' offer. Before, you were only a relative of a man with no friends save his own soldiers, and had he executed you publicly as a rebel in the market-place of Jummoo there would have been no one to gainsay him. But now that you are known to the governor-general and the commander-in-chief, he will see that he cannot act as he will without drawing upon himself the anger of the English authorities, when the colonel reports the fact to them."

"There is something in that, Akram, but not much. Were he asked to explain why he had put one of English blood to death, he would simply reply that he was the nephew of a man who had set the government of Lahore at defiance, had maintained himself by arms, had inflicted heavy losses on the force sent to place the lawful governor appointed by the durbar in power; that the person executed had taken part in this act of rebellion, and that his life was justly forfeited. As all this would be in a way true, there could really be no answer to it, and the English would certainly not embroil themselves with

a powerful prince, with whom they were anxious to keep on good terms, on such a matter. Still, if I do see Ghoolab himself, I shall certainly make the most of the kind expressions of Sir Henry Hardinge and the commander-in-chief when I left them at Lahore. I should hardly think, however, that he will see me. He would prefer being able to deny, without chance of contradiction, that he knew anything at all about me."

" But in that case, sahib, how could he use you as the means of forcing the colonel to give up the fortress and his governorship of the district? "

" I should think that most likely he will send word to my uncle that he has learned I have fallen into the hands of some dacoits, and that if my uncle will surrender the fortress he will take measures to rescue me from these men, who will otherwise put me to death."

"The colonel will never believe that," Akram said decidedly; "he will guess at once that you are in the hands of Ghoolab."

"Very likely he will, Akram, but he won't be able to prove it, and Ghoolab will know well enough that if he were to put me out of the way my uncle could not accuse him of my death, as he would have no evidence of my death to produce in support; and indeed, if Bhop Lai recovered and took him the news of our being carried off, all he could say would be a confirmation of Ghoolab's story, and would show that I had indeed been carried off by a band of dacoits. It will most likely be known that Goolam Tej's band were in the neighbourhood, and were doubtless the party who attacked us."

Akram Chunder was silent. He could not gainsay Percy's argument, and it seemed to him that Ghoolab Singh had indeed the game completely in his hands.

"I am afraid it is as you say, sahib," he remarked after a while, "and that we shall have, as we agreed, to slip out of their hands somehow. I see no chance at present."

"Certainly not," Percy agreed; "we have no arms, and though they have not tied us this time, they must be sure that we dare not try to escape, surrounded as we are by them, for they would be able to shoot us down before we had ridden ten yards. Moreover, the wood is too dense for us to force our way through, and even if we got away at first, we should be overtaken."

The road they were traversing was a mere track cut through the dense forest, and it was with difficulty that they rode two abreast. Six of the dacoits rode ahead of them, six behind, those immediately following them having, as they observed when they mounted, their pistols in their hands, in readiness to shoot at the first indication of an attempt to escape.

"Do you think we are going towards Jummoo?" Percy asked after they had ridden for some three hours.

" I cannot say for certain, sahib, but I think not. I feel sure that Jummoo lies much to the right, and I believe that we shall come down into the valley of Cashmere somewhere between that and Serinagur. Winding about as we have been doing in the bottom of valleys, it is very difficult to judge which way we are really going."

" I agree with you, Akram. I have been watching the way in which the sun falls upon us, and as you say, though we have wound and turned a good deal, I do not think we have ridden to the right as we should have done had we been making for Jummoo. It does not make much difference whether we are taken there or to Serinagur," Percy said; "the end of the journey will be a prison in any case."

" There is no doubt about that, but I would rather they took us to Serinagur, sahib. Ghoolab Singh has been years at Jummoo, and you may be sure that in that time he has built new and strong prisons, from which it would be very hard to escape. Serinagur is an old place, and its prisons would not be like those of Jummoo, and ought to be much easier to get out of; besides, being so much farther from the frontier, they might

PERCY AWAKES, TO FIND THAT THE GUARDS ARE VIGILANT.

not watch us so closely, thinking we should know it would be next to impossible for men ignorant of the language to make their way down the valley, however disguised."

Half an hour later they passed through a village, and as the forest thinned as they approached it, and the path became broader, the dacoits closed in on both sides of the prisoners and completely surrounded them. The inhabitants fled into their houses as the troop rode through. No halt was made, and they presently came upon a broad road, and following this again began to mount. All day they travelled among very lofty hills, but towards evening made a long and steep descent.

"I think I know that last pass we went through," Akram Chunder said; "I believe we are now descending into the valley of Cashmere. If I am right, this road will fall into it ten miles below Serinagur."

Shortly afterwards a halt was called, the dacoits turned their horses loose to graze, and proceeded to light a fire to cook the food they had brought with them. They gave the prisoners a share, but when the meal was concluded tied them securely hand and foot and placed two guards over them. These were relieved at short intervals, and one of the men kept the fire burning briskly. Percy woke several times in the night, and each time found the guard vigilant; and being convinced that there was no possibility of an escape while in their charge, he at once went off to sleep again.

In the morning their bonds were loosed, and they resumed their journey. About mid-day they came down into a wide flat valley. A large river meandered with many turns and windings down it, and smaller streams fell into it at many points.

"Are those small rivers for the most part navigable? " Percy asked, pointing to the silver threads among the bright green expanse of vegetation.

" Yes, sahib, the rivers are the roads throughout the valley; it is by them that the peasants take in their products to

Serinagur. I do not say they would carry a large barge, but small boats can make their way along them right up to the foot of the hills."

" It must be a very rich country judging from the numbers of villages scattered about."

"It is, sahib; with good government Cashmere would be a paradise. It is never very hot or very cold; the air is soft and balmy, the soil is so rich that everything grows in abundance with but little trouble to the cultivator; he has but to gather his crops and pitch them into his boat, and he can make his way to market without the necessity for horse or bullock. But the government is bad, and has been so for long. Ghoolab is a hard master, but no harder than its former rulers have been. The people would be rich and contented indeed under such a rule as that of the English, firm and just, for in addition to agriculture they have many other means of earning their living. There are the shawl-weavers and silver workers, and those who paint on lacquer, and every member of the family can help to earn something.

"The mountains abound with game, and there is pasturage for countless flocks and herds. The poets of India have always sung of Cashmere as the fairest and most blest by nature of any spot south of the Hindoo Koosh; and they have not spoken a bit too strongly. With good rulers it would be that and much more. The fault is that the country is so fair, the climate so balmy, and life so easy, that the people are too soft in their habits to make good soldiers, and the country has therefore been overrun countless times by more warlike races. At present the Sikhs are masters, but their rule is likely to be even shorter than that of others who have conquered it. When the English are lords of the Punjaub, they will see how fair and how rich is this valley of Cashmere, and that they have but to stretch out their hand to take it. It will be a blessed day indeed for the people when they do so."

"I don't think they want further conquests, Akram; they would gladly have left the Punjaub alone, but they were forced against their will into annexing first the provinces beyond the Sutlej, now Jalindar, and next time perhaps the rest of the country, but there can be no aggressions from Cashmere."

" No, sahib, but the same necessity may arise here as elsewhere. The English hate oppression, and if Ghoolab or his successors grind down the people beyond a certain point, they will interfere. Moreover, Cashmere is necessary to them. Through it runs the best road over the great northern chain of mountains. It is, quite as much as Afghanistan, the door of India, and round the valley at its northern end are troublesome tribes, whom the rulers of Cashmere have never been able to keep in order; the boundaries of China are not far away. A generation or two at the outside and the English will be rulers at Serinagur I think, sahib. What a blessing it would be to the country! In the first place, there would be neither over-taxation nor oppression. All would live and till their lands and work their loom, secure of enjoying their earnings in peace. Money would flow into the country, for the sahibs would come in great numbers from the plains, for health and for sport, and would spend their money freely, and would buy our manufactures from the weavers and silversmiths at first hand, while now they have to be sent down to market at great expense, and in troublous times at great risk. There, you see, sahib, we are taking the northern road; in two hours we shall be at Serinagur."

"All the better, Akram; this is a lovely view, and I should be a long time before I was tired of looking at it; but I am eager to see what kind of a place we are going to be shut up in, so as to judge our chance of escape. I wish we could get hold of a couple of long knives and hide them somewhere about us, before we reach the town;" for the clothes they had worn when they were captured had been restored to them before starting.

"One might persuade one of these fellows riding by us to part with his knife, sahib; but our pockets are empty; at least mine are, and I don't suppose they have left you any better provided."

" No, Akram, but I have twenty gold pieces wrapped up in flannel and stowed away in a flap-pocket at the bottom of my holster. My uncle had it made on the day I left him. He said that it might be useful to have a small store of money there in case I ever fell among thieves; and it is so contrived that even if anyone put his hand right down to the bottom of the holster he would not suspect that there was a pocket there, for the flap exactly fits it, and makes a sort of false bottom. The money was stowed away there, and I have never thought of it since."

"It must be well hidden, sahib," Akram Chunder said with a laugh, "for I have put the saddle on and off a hundred times, and put your pistols and sometimes food into the holster, and never for a moment suspected that there was money lying there. Are you sure that it hasn't been taken? "

Percy put his hand down into the holster.

"It is all right, Akram, I can feel the roll of flannel under the flap."

"Well, sahib, if you can get out four pieces it is hard if I don't manage to get a couple of knives from this fellow next to me; as for the rest, if we can but hide them about us they may prove the means of our getting free from prison. Thinking it over, it seemed to me that our greatest difficulty was that we had no means of bribing anyone."

Percy managed to get out four gold pieces, and passed them quietly to his follower.

"Comrade," the latter said in a low voice to the dacoit riding beside him, " you have two knives in your girdle, at what do you value them? "

The man looked keenly at his prisoner. Their clothing had been searched with scrupulous care, and he felt sure that no hiding-place could have been overlooked.

" It depends on who wanted to buy," he said cautiously.

"Suppose I wanted to buy."

"Then they would be worth two gold pieces each."

"That is beyond my means. I would not mind giving a gold piece for each of them."

"Where are the pieces to come from?"

"That is my business; perhaps I have them hidden in my mouth, or my ears, or my hair."

"I dare not do it," the man said; "it might be noticed."

"'Not if you managed it well," Akram said. "You might ride close up to me when the road happens to be narrow, and pass them in a moment; besides we are not thinking of escape now; but they may be useful to us afterwards."

"It is too great a risk," the man repeated irresolutely.

" Well, I will give you three pieces for the two, though it is hard that you should beggar me."

The man nodded, and presently Akram saw him shift the two knives to the side of his girdle next to him. A short distance farther on he glanced round at the two men riding behind. They were laughing and talking together, and evidently paying but little attention to the prisoners. A moment later he touched his horse's rein, and his knee rubbed against Akram's. The latter passed three gold pieces into his hand, snatched the knives from his girdle, and thrust them under his coat, and the dacoit at once drew off to his former position. Riding close together, Akram had no difficulty in passing one of the knives to Percy, who then again opened the flap in the holster and took the money from its flannel inclosure and handed seven pieces to Akram.

" Where do you mean to hide them ? " he asked.

"In the folds of my waist-sash; that is the only place to put them at present. Of course if they search us they will discover the money and the knives, but they will be so sure that the dacoits have taken everything from us that they may not think it worth while to do so. If they once leave us in a

room alone we can hide them away so that nothing but a careful search will find them; but at present we must trust to chance."

They were now approaching the town, which extends some two miles on either side of the river Jelum, across which several bridges are thrown. Percy was disappointed at the appearance of the place, which contained no buildings of sufficient importance to tower above the rest. He was most struck with the green appearance of the roofs. On remarking this to Akram, the latter replied:

"They are gardens, sahib; the roofs are for the most part flat, and they are overlaid with a deep covering of earth, which keeps the houses warm in winter and cool in summer. The soil is planted with flowers, and forms a terrace, where the family sit in the cool of the evening."

"That explains it. It is a pity the same thing is not done in other towns; it looks wonderfully pretty."

The people they passed on the road were dressed somewhat differently to those of India; the men wore large turbans and a great woollen vest with wide sleeves; while the women were for the most part dressed in red gowns, also with large loose sleeves. Round the head was a red twisted handkerchief, over which was thrown a white veil, which did not, however, cover the face.

"Is the language at all like Punjaubi? " Percy asked.

"No, sahib, it differs altogether from all the Indian tongues, so far as I have heard, and is therefore very difficult to be learned by the natives of other parts."

Before reaching the town the horsemen turned off from the main road, and making a wide detour so as to avoid it altogether, continued their course along the foot of the hills on the left of the valley, and after proceeding some two miles above the upper end of the city, mounted the hill, and in half an hour reached a building standing at considerable height above the valley.

"That is just as we expected, sahib. You see we have avoided the town, and Ghoolab will, if questioned, be able to affirm that we have never been brought there. None of the people we met on the road will have noticed us, dressed as we are, in the middle of this band, whom they will take to be the following of some sirdar."

" If that is to be our prison, Akram, it does not look anything like such a difficult place to get out of as the dacoit's castle; but of course it all depends on where they put us."

They stopped at the entrance to the building. They were evidently expected, for an officer came out at once, followed by six armed men. He addressed no questions to the dacoits, but simply nodded as they led the two prisoners forward. Two of the men took the bridles of the horses and led them inside the gates, which were then closed.

Percy and Akram dismounted, and the officer, entering a door from the court-yard, ordered them in Punjaubi to follow him. To Percy's great satisfaction he led the way up a staircase, instead of, as the lad had feared might be the case, down one leading into some subterranean chamber. After ascending some twenty steps they went along a narrow passage, at the end of which was a strong door studded with nails. One of the men produced a key and opened it, and on entering Percy found himself in a chamber some fifteen feet square. It was not uncomfortably furnished, and had two native bedsteads. The floor was covered with rugs. A low table stood in the centre, and there were two low wooden stools near it. Percy's first glance, however, was towards the window. It was of good size, and reached to within a foot from the floor. It was, however, closed by a double grating of strong iron bars, with openings of but four or five inches square.

"Do not fear, no harm is intended you," the officer said. " For a time you must make yourselves as comfortable as you can here. Your servant will be allowed to be with you. If there is anything you require it will be supplied to you."

So saying he left the room, and the door was then locked.

"Thank goodness you are left with me, Akram," Percy exclaimed. "The thing I have been dreading most of all is that we should be separated; and if that had been so, I should have lost all hope of escape."

" I have feared that too, sahib, though I did not speak of it; but before we think of anything farther, let us hide one of the knives and half the money in the beds."

"Why not hide them both? " Percy asked.

" Because we might be moved suddenly, sahib. Ghoolab might order us to be taken to another prison, or might send for us down to Jummoo; there is never any saying; so it is well to keep some of the money about us. Of course we may be searched, but in that case we should loose but half. However, I do not think they will do that nowl They will make quite sure that the dacoits will have taken everything there was to take."

CHAPTER XIII
ESCAPE

HAVING carefully hidden one of the knives and nine pieces of gold in the beds, they divided the remaining eight pieces between them. Akram took off his turban, unrolled his hair, and hid his four pieces in it. He then, with the point of a knife, unripped two or three stitches in the lining of Percy's coat and dropped his money into the hole.

"How about the knife, Akram? That is a much harder thing to hide."

" It must be hidden on you, sahib, so that if we are separated you will be able to use it if you see an opportunity."

He took the knife, and with it cut off a strip an inch wide from his cloak; then he pulled up one of the legs of Percy's long Sikh trousers, and with the strip of cloth strapped the knife tightly against the side of the shin-bone; the handle came close up to the knee, the point extended nearly to the ankle-bone.

"There is no fear of that shifting," he said when he had fastened the bandage and pulled the leg of the trouser down again. "And even if they felt you all over they might well omit to pass their hands over the leg below the knee."

"It is certainly a capital hiding-place, Akram; I should never have thought of putting it there, and it is the last place they would think of searching for anything. Now, we can have a look at the window; it is very strongly grated."

Akram shook his head. "There is no getting through there, sahib; these bars have not been up many years. The stonework is perfect, and with only our knives it would be absolutely impossible to cut through that double grating. The room has doubtless been meant for someone whom they wanted to hold fast and yet to treat respectfully. We may give up all idea of escaping through the window. That stonework was evidently put up at the same time as the gratings. You see the rest of the wall is of brick."

"I don't see it, Akram; it is all covered with this white plaster."

"Yes, sahib; but all the houses here are built of brick, that is to say of brick and woodwork, and I noticed this one is also; besides, if you look at the plaster carefully you can make out the lines of the courses of brick underneath it; it is a thin coat, and badly laid on."

"It is a nuisance it is there," Percy remarked. "If it hadn't been for that it might have been possible with our knives to have cut away the mortar between the bricks, and so have got them out one by one, till we made a hole big enough to get through. Of course it would be a long job, but by replacing the bricks carefully in their places and working at night it might have been managed. But this white plaster renders it quite impossible unless the whole thing could be done in one night, which would be out of the question. There is the floor; we must examine that presently. I have read of escapes from prison by men who managed to raise a flooring stone, made a hole underneath big enough to work in, and so made their way either into another room or through the outside wall. It would need time, patience, and hard work; but unless we are able to bribe the man who brings us in food, that is how it must be done."

He pushed aside one of the rugs. The floor was composed of smooth slabs of stone about a foot square. " It could not be better," he said. "There should be no great difficulty in getting up a couple of these slabs. They are fitted pretty closely, but we ought to be able to find one where there is room for the blade of a knife to get in between it and those next to it."

"That is good, sahib; I should never have thought of getting out that way. However, if you tell me what to do I will do it;" and Akram went to the place where he had hidden his knife.

"There is no hurry, Akram. We can fix on a stone while there is daylight, but we can't begin until we are sure that everyone is asleep. They may bring us in some food at any moment; and before we begin in earnest we shall have to find out the hours at which they visit us, and how late they come in at night."

At this moment they heard steps coming along the passage.

"Sit down on that stool," Percy said, while he threw himself down on one of the charpoys. "We must look as dull and stupid as we can."

A man brought in a dish of boiled rice and meat. Akram addressed him in Punjaubi, but he shook his head and went out without a word.

"If none of these fellows speak anything but their own language, sahib, it will be difficult to try and get them to help us, for it will not do to let out that I can talk the language; for if we once get free, that will be our best hope of getting through the country."

"We will try the other way first at any rate, Akram. The money we have is not sufficient to induce a man to risk his life in assisting us, and he might possibly think he could do better by betraying us; in which case we might be separated and put in a much worse place than this."

"That is true enough, sahib; at the same time the money we have is a very large amount here. He would not get above three or four rupees a month, so that it would be four or five years' pay. Still there is the danger of his betraying us.

As you say, we had better try in the first place to get out as you propose."

"It is nothing to what men have done sometimes, Akram. They have escaped through walls of solid stone. They don't build like that here. The bricks are not generally well baked, and are often only sun-dried. As soon as we have finished this food we will examine the stones. We will begin near the outside wall—we might get into an inhabited room if we went the other way—and working towards the outside we know we have only to get through it to be free, for these rugs will make ropes by which we can slide down without difficulty."

Examining the flags along the side of the outer wall they found two or three where, without much difficulty, they could insert a knife in the interstices.

"Let us set to work at once, Akram; we can hear the man's footstep right along the passage, and shall have plenty of time to drop the stone in and throw the rug over it before he reaches the door. I want to see what is underneath, and I specially want to have a place to hide the two knives in case they should take it into their heads to search us."

The cement in which the flat slabs were laid was by no means hard, and in half an hour they had cut it all round one of the stones. This was, however, still firmly attached to the cement below it. " I am afraid to use any pressure, Akram, for we might break the knives."

"That is so, sahib; if we had an iron bar we might break the stone, but I see no other way of loosening it. Perhaps if we were to jump upon it we might shake it."

"I don't think there would be much chance of that, and if there is anyone in the room below they might come up to see what we are doing. We might fill the cracks with water all round and by pouring in more water from time to time it might soak in and soften the cement, but of course that depends entirely upon its quality; however we might as well do that at once."

They filled the cracks with water, drew the rug over the place, and then returned to their seats. Presently Akram said:

"We might try wedges, sahib."

"So we might, I did not think of that; and there are the beds, of course."

"Yes; I could cut away some pieces from the under part of the framework of one of the beds."

"That will do capitally."

It was slow work cutting out a piece of bamboo sufficiently large to make a couple of dozen of wedges, and it was dark long before Akram had finished. It took another three hours to split it up and make it into wedges. As soon as these were completed, they drove them in close to each other along one side of the stone, pressing them in with the haft of a knife with their united weight. When all were wedged in Akram tried the stone.

" It is as firm as ever, sahib."

"Yes; I did not expect that we should be able to move it, especially as we have not hammered in the wedges. If it does not move by morning we must tap them in, giving a tap every four or five minutes; that would not be noticed; but I hope we shall find it is loose then. You see the crack is full of water, and so the wedges will swell and exercise a tremendous pressure. In some places they split stone like that."

They threw themselves down on the beds and slept till morning broke. Percy was the first to open his eyes, and at once leapt up, ran across the room, moved the rug, and examined the stone.

" It has moved, Akram. The side opposite the wedges is jammed hard up against the next stone."

"It is as firm as ever, sahib," Akram said, trying it with his knife.

"Yes, because it is held by the pressure of the wedges. When we get them out we shall find that it is loose from the cement."

They found, however, that there was no possibility of getting out the strips of wood.

"We have only to wait," Percy said. "As soon as they are dry they will be loose." It was, however, two days before the moisture had evaporated sufficiently for them to be able to draw out the wedges.

" Now, let us both put our knives in on this side and try and lift it."

Repeated trials showed them that this could not be done. In the evening, however, when the lamp was brought them, they heated the point of one of the knives in the flame until it had so far lost its temper that they were able to bend the point over by pressing it on one of the flags. Again heating it they dipped it in water to harden. They then ground the point down on one of the stones until they were able to pass it down the joint that the action of the wedges had widened. The bent point caught under the stone, and they had no difficulty in raising it.

"There is the first step done," Percy exclaimed in delight. "You had better warm the knife and straighten the point again."

They experienced no great difficulty in getting up the next stone, which they had loosened in a similar way to the first while waiting for the wedges to dry. As soon as this was up they began cutting into the cement. The surface was hard, and the knives at first did little more than scratch it; but below they found it much softer and got on more rapidly. As they removed the cement they placed the powder a handful at a time on the window-sill, and blew it gradually out through the grating. After three nights of continuous work they had made a hole a foot deep and come down upon wooden planking.

"This is doubtless the ceiling of the room underneath," Percy said. "There can be no one sleeping there or they would have heard the scratching overhead." By lifting up

PERCY AND AKRAM ATTEMPT TO ESCAPE FROM PRISON.

ESCAPE 227

the stones, which they always replaced at daybreak, they could hear voices, and did not recommence their work at night till they were well assured that no one was stirring below. As the stones they had taken out were next to the wall, they now commenced operations on the brickwork. This they found much easier, as the mortar was nothing like so hard as the cement, and on cutting it out between the bricks they had no great difficulty in moving these. After two nights' work they had taken them all out with the exception of the outside layer, as they were able to calculate by the thickness of the wall at the window. During the daytime the bricks that had been removed were stowed away in the hole.

"We shall be out to-night," Percy said exultantly, as they replaced the flags for the last time. "This last layer will be easy work, for as soon as we have cut round one brick we shall be able to pull it in, and can then get a hand through the hole, and the others will come quite easily as soon as we cut away the mortar a bit. There will be no occasion to tear up the rugs to make a rope. We are not more than eighteen or twenty feet from the ground, and two or three of them knotted together will be enough. We will set one of the beds over the hole and tie the end to that."

Percy felt nervous all day, being in fear every time he heard a footstep in the passage that something might occur which would upset all their plans. They had now been ten days in their prison, so there was time for a messenger to have gone to Jummoo, and thence to the fortress and back. Still he hoped that his uncle would at any rate refuse to accept Ghoolab Singh's first offer, whatever it might be, and that lengthy negotiations would go on. Nothing out of the ordinary routine happened; their guard came three times a day as usual with their food; and after his last visit Percy sprang from the couch.

" Hurrah! Next time he comes he will find the place empty, Akram. Now let us set to work at once."

Four hours of hard work sufficed to make a hole large enough for them to crawl through. The charpoy was brought over the hole, the money stowed away in their clothes, and the rugs knotted. Then, feet foremost, Percy wriggled out through the hole, holding the rope tightly, and slid down to the ground, while two minutes later Akram stood beside him. They had already taken off their turbans and rewound them much more loosely, so as to resemble closely those worn in Cashmere. They started at once up the hill, and continued their course until they reached a wood high up on the mountain side. They had already determined upon their course. It was of the greatest importance that they should obtain dresses of the country, for though they might have made their way along the hills they would have difficulty in buying food, and might find horsemen already posted at the various passes by which the mountain ranges were traversed. At daybreak Akram took off his long coat, arranged his clothes in the fashion of Cashmere peasants, and started boldly for the town.

"The shops will soon be open," he said, "and unless anyone happens to go round to the back of our prison, which is not likely, they will not find out that we are gone until the man enters at nine o'clock with our food, and long before that I shall be here again. You need not be uneasy about me, sahib. Being really a native of the valley, no one can suspect me of being anything else."

Soon after eight o'clock he returned with two complete suits, in which they were soon attired. As the natives of Cashmere are fairer than those of the plains of India, it needed but a slight wash of some dye Akram had brought up with him to convert Percy's bronzed face to the proper tint, and as soon as this was done they descended the hill and came upon the main road below the city. Soon afterwards some horsemen passed them, galloping at a furious rate. These did not even glance at the supposed peasants, but continued their course down the valley. Other and much larger bodies of horsemen

ESCAPE

afterwards passed them, but, like the first, without asking a question.

"Doubtless they think we have at least twenty miles start," Akram said. " I expect the first party were going right down to the mouth of the valley, warning all the towns and villages to be on the look-out for us. The others, when they think they must have passed us, will scatter and occupy all the roads and passes. Some of them will push on until almost within sight of the fortress, so as to catch us there if we manage to get through the woods and pass the lines of watchers."

At a leisurely pace they proceeded down the valley, Akram sometimes entering into conversation with peasants they met, and going into shops and buying provisions; he learnt in the villages that strict orders had been given to watch for a Sikh with a young Englishman who had escaped from a prison at Serinagur. Akram joined in their expressions of wonder as to how an Englishman could have got there, and how the escape had been managed, and mentioned that he was on his way to visit some relations at Jummoo.

When near the mouth of the valley he purchased some cotton cloths, such as peasants working in the fields would wear, and presently they put on these and left those behind them that had proved so useful, Percy's skin being stained brown wherever exposed by this more scanty costume. Thus attired they issued out from the mouth of the valley and went forward into Ghoolab Singh's country, as they agreed that this was the place where they were the least likely to be looked for. They had been four days on their way down from Serinagur, and decided to travel still farther west, so as to return to the fortress from the side opposite to that where a watch was likely to be kept up for them.

Three days' more walking, and, having made the detour, they approached the fortress on the west. They met with no suspicious party on their way, and as they ascended the zigzag road from the valley felt with delight that they were now per-

fectly safe. As usual the drawbridge was down and the gates open, and they passed in without question from the men on guard there. As they went down the street they saw a figure they recognized, and Percy ran forward and exclaimed:

" Bhop Lai, I am indeed glad to see you! So those rascally dacoits did not kill you after all? "

" Blessed be the day, sahib!" Bhop Lai exclaimed with delight. "There has been sore grief over you. The colonel has been in a terrible state since I was carried in here and told him how you had been seized by dacoits, and still more has he been troubled since, ten days ago, he learned from a messenger of Ghoolab Singh that you had fallen into the clutches of that notorious scamp Goolam Tej. The Ranee is ill and keeps her bed.

"Ah, Akram Chunder! truly I am rejoiced to see you also. I was glad indeed that you were with the young sahib, for I knew you to be a man of resources."

" It was the young sahib himself who devised the plan by which we escaped, Bhop Lai; and how are your wounds? "

"They are very sore yet, and the hakim says that it will be many weeks before I am fit to sit in the saddle again; but now that our sahib is back safely I shall have no more to fret about, and shall mend rapidly."

By this time they had arrived at the door of the colonel's residence, and Percy ran in.

"You cannot enter here, fellow," a servant said, as he was about to push aside the hangings of the entrance to the private apartments.

Percy laughed, and without waiting to explain pushed the man aside and ran in.

"Well, uncle, here I am," he exclaimed, as he entered the room where his uncle was sitting writing. The latter leapt to his feet with a cry of joy.

"Why, Percy, is it you in this disguise? Welcome back, my boy, a thousand times! But before you tell me anything,

come in to see Mahtab, who has been downright ill from grief since Bhop Lai brought in the news of your being carried off by dacoits."

The Ranee's delight at seeing Percy was unbounded, and it was some time before she and her husband could sit down quietly and listen to his story.

"All is well that ends well," the colonel said when he had brought it to a conclusion. "You have had a bad time of it, Percy; but I doubt if your aunt and I have not had a worse. Of course, I was a good deal troubled when I heard that you were carried off; but as to that Bhop Lai could tell us nothing, having been shot down at once, and so hacked that he knew nothing of what took place until he was revived by water being poured down his throat. Three traders coming along the road on their way here had found him, and as soon as they learned from him who he was and what had occurred, they bandaged his wounds and had him carried here in a dhoolie. They reported that they had seen nothing of you, and one of them at once rode back with me with a troop of horse to the spot where they had found your man, and as, after a most careful search, we could find no trace of blood, we concluded that you had been carried off.

" We followed the traces of the band for some distance, but then lost them just as it was becoming dark. As they had had some eight hours' start of us, and were making for the mountains, we gave up the pursuit and returned here. I made sure that in the morning I should receive a message from the rascal demanding a ransom for you, but as the day went on I became more uneasy, as the idea struck me that they might not be dacoits, but fellows in the pay of Ghoolab. It certainly did not seem likely that he could have heard that you would be on your way back; but his men might have been there for weeks, for he would gue*ss that when the war was over you would be making your way back here again.

" For the next six days I sent out parties of horsemen all

over the country, but could obtain no news whatever, and was getting in a terrible state of mind when a man rode in with a letter from Ghoolab Singh. He stated that he had learned that you were in the power of dacoits somewhere among the mountains. He said that it would be a long and difficult task to find them, but that he would use every effort to do so, and would either by force or bribery obtain you and restore you if I, on my part, would undertake to resign the government that I held in defiance of the orders of the durbar. As a rebel, he felt that he should not be justified in exerting himself on my behalf, but if I would submit to the orders of the durbar he would guarantee that my past conduct should be overlooked and that you should be restored to me. I had very little doubt that you were already in the scoundrel's hands when he sent the message, but in any case I saw that he had me on the hip. I don't suppose he expected a direct answer to his proposal, and he did not get one. I sent an answer back that I was ready to pay any reasonable sum for your ransom; but as for resigning my governorship and handing over the fortress, I wished to know what guarantee he could offer that I should be permitted to retire from the Punjaub in safety with my family and treasures. To that I received an answer that he was ready to take the most solemn pledge for my safety, and that he was sending off to Lahore to obtain a free pardon for me from the durbar, and a permission for me to retire with all my family and as many of my followers as might wish to accompany me across the Sutlej. I then wrote back that this would be perfectly satisfactory, but that, naturally, I should require that you should be handed over to me prior to my evacuating the fortress. To this I received no answer. I thought perhaps he was waiting for a reply from Lahore, but I now understand that before the messenger returned with my second letter you had already slipped through his fingers. I should have liked to have seen him when he received the news of your escape. Now, Percy,

tell us all about your adventures since you left us. There was no believing any of the reports that reached us about the various battles. I know, of course, that the Sikhs must have been thoroughly thrashed, or we should never have had a British occupation of Lahore. Beyond that I really know nothing for certain."

It took some time for Percy to describe all the military operations.

"I knew that it would be so," the colonel said gleefully when he concluded. " I told them over and over again that if they thought, because they had won victories over the Afghans and other tribes, that they were a match for the English they were completely mistaken.

"They scoffed at the idea of defeat; but now they find that I was right, and so was old Runjeet Singh. These fellows have plenty of courage and plenty of dash, but though a good many thousand have been drilled in our fashion they cannot be called soldiers. They have no generals and no officers to speak of, and when it came to fighting they would be nothing better than a mob. Still our fellows must have fought well to turn them out of their strong intrenchments. In the open field I had no doubt whatever as to the result, but behind earthworks discipline does not go for much, and a brave fellow who is a good shot counts for nearly as much as a trained soldier. Now you may as well get yourself into decent clothes again, Percy, and while you are doing that I will go out and see your man, and tell him that I am well pleased with his conduct, and that he and his comrade shall both be well rewarded for the dangers they have passed through."

In the evening Percy went more into details, and the colonel was highly pleased to hear that he had attracted the attention of the heads of the army, and that the governor-general himself had promised to apply at once for a civil appointment for him.

"What are you thinking of doing, uncle? "

" I shall hold on, Percy. You say there is to be a British Resident at Lahore, and that probably troops will remain there permanently, in which I agree with you, for it is morally certain that if the maharanee and her son are making peace with us and surrendering the Jalindar Doab, they would be turned out and probably massacred the moment the troops retired. Well, with an English Resident there, and being to a great extent under British protection, and having besides no regular army, Lahore will be glad enough to let me alone. So there is only Ghoolab. He is not very certain of his position yet, and I have no doubt he knows as well as we do that before long there will be another war, which will end in our people annexing the whole of the Punjaub. I think," therefore, that there is no chance of his trying again to take this place by force. He may, of course, and I daresay he will, try assassination again, but I shall be on my guard."

" I think, uncle, there ought to be more care at the gate. We came in without being questioned, and we might, for aught the guard knew, have been two men sent by Ghoolab to assassinate you. I think that every man coming into the place ought to be questioned as to his busines."

" But they would lie, my boy. What is the use of questioning?"

"Ah! but I would not let them in, uncle, unless they could prove that they had business with some person living in the fort. You are not recruiting now, and if you were you could get plenty of men well known in the district. I don't say that you could keep assassins out, whatever the means you adopt; but I do think that if it were known in the district that no one is admitted within the walls until after he has given a satisfactory account.of himself, Ghoolab would find it more difficult to get men to undertake so hazardous a business."

As the Ranee thoroughly agreed with Percy the colonel consented to make more rigid rules, although still maintain-

ing his opinion that no precautions of the sort would be of the slightest avail in keeping a determined man from entering the place.

The next morning another horseman came in from Ghoolab.

The colonel laughed as he read the letter he had brought.

"The old fox still hopes to catch you again, Percy; he simply continues negotiations, and asks what guarantee I can offer on my part that I will retire from the fortress if you are, as I demand, given up to me before I surrender. I will put him out of his agony."

So the colonel wrote a short note to the effect that his nephew had returned, and having informed him who was the brigand into whose hands he had fallen, there was no longer any need for any further negotiations on the subject.

"You must be doubly careful now, Roland," the Ranee said when her husband told her what he had written to Ghoolab. " He has always been your bitter enemy, but he will be more so than ever now. I do beg that you will again have that guard you had during the siege, and that you will have the two men who have proved so faithful to Percy to sleep always at the entrance to our apartments."

"I hate being guarded," the colonel said; "still, if it will make you more comfortable, of course it shall be as you wish."

When the officers of the garrison understood that Ghoolab had again been foiled, there was a general opinion that too great precautions for the colonel's safety could hardly be taken.

The watch at the gate was carried out most vigilantly, for the colonel was so much beloved by his men that each considered himself personally responsible for his safety, and whatever might be the story told by strangers arriving at the gate, they were not allowed to pass until the trader or other person they wished to see was brought down to the gate to vouch for the truth of the statement.

During the next three months seven or eight men whose story proved to be false were seized and imprisoned. The officers were all in favour of applying torture to them to extract the truth, but the colonel would not hear of it.

" I will have no one tortured in my district. Such a thing has never been done to my knowledge since I was appointed governor ten years ago, and I won't have it begun now. In the second place, you cannot depend in the slightest upon anything that may be told under torture. And lastly, if I knew it for certain, as I think it probable, that they were agents of Ghoolab, I should really be none the wiser. They came here with a false story, and, therefore, for no good purpose. Consequently they should be punished. Therefore, let each man who is convicted of lying be kept for a week in the cells; then give him a sound flogging, shave off his hair, moustache, and beard, and turn him out. That will be quite enough to deter other people from following his example."

This decision met with general approval, and was in each case carried into effect, the shaven men being turned out from the gates amid the gibes and jeers of the soldiers, with many threats of what would happen if they were again found in the neighbourhood.

Six months after his return to the fortress Percy received a letter (forwarded to him by Mr. Henry Lawrence, the Resident at Lahore, from the Court of Directors), saying that in accordance with the very strong recommendation of the governor-general he had been appointed to the Civil Service of the Company on the date of his attaining his nineteenth birthday, that a note had also been made of his willingness to serve at an earlier period if required, and that instructions had been given to that effect to the Resident at Lahore, who was authorized to employ him if required, in which case his appointment would date from the day of his commencing service.

The time passed pleasantly to Percy. He rode, practised shooting and sword exercise, and worked for several hours a day at the Pathan language, in which, by the end of eighteen months, he had become almost as efficient as in Punjaubi, for, there being several Afghans among the officers, he was enabled to learn it colloquially. At the end of that time he wrote to the Resident at Lahore saying that he was now well up in Pathan, and thought it right to inform him of this in case any occasion should arise for the use of his services on the northern frontier.

Six months later he received a letter from Sir Philip Currie, who had just succeeded Mr. Lawrence as Resident, stating that he had been requested by Mr. Agnew, who was going as political officer to Mooltan, to furnish him with an assistant capable of speaking both Punjaubi and Pathan fluently. The Resident added that from what he had heard of Mr. Groves' conduct during the campaign, and from the strong manner in which the governor-general had personally recommended him to the Court of Directors, and the very favourable terms in which his friend Mr. Fullarton had more than once spoken of him, he would be well fitted to undertake the duties of assistant to Mr. Agnew. Having been authorized by the Court of Directors to appoint him at any time to a post where his services might be useful, he had therefore much pleasure in now nominating him Mr. Agnew's assistant.

CHAPTER XIV

TREACHERY

BHOP LAL and his comrade were delighted when they heard that Percy was again going off, and that, as before, they were to accompany him as his servants.

"There will be no fighting or adventures this time," Percy said. " I expect your life will be just as quiet there as it is here. Still it will be a change, and I suppose that sometimes I shall have to ride out from Mooltan to see people in the district. Your being a Pathan will be a great advantage, Bhop Lai, on this occasion, just as Akram Chunder's being a native of Cashmere got me out of a bad scrape last time. As a Pathan you will be able to gather intelligence, as the population is largely composed of your countrymen. Of course, on your journey you will take your arms with you, but you will have no occasion for them there as the followers of a peaceable civil servant."

"Arms are always useful," Akram Chunder said. "The Pathans are quarrelsome fellows, though Bhop Lai is an exception. The population of Mooltan are said to be the most turbulent of those of any town in the Punjaub. You will miss your horse, sahib. I suppose it is in Ghoolab Singh's stables. The one you ride now is a good one, but not so good as Sultan."

" My uncle has just given me Sheik. He says it will be more useful to me than to him.."

"Then, sahib, you need never fear being caught when you are once on his back. Even with the colonel's weight there is not a horse in the district can touch him, and with you in the saddle he will go like the wind."

Before starting Colonel Groves presented the two men with horses of his own breeding.

" Without being comparable with Sheik, they are powerful and well-bred horses, fast, and capable of accomplishing long journeys. As I know you will serve my nephew as well and faithfully as you did last time, I shall never regret having parted with the horses," he said to them. "One or other of you will always be with him, and it is useless for a master to be well mounted if his followers cannot keep pace with him. I do not say that either of these horses could keep up with Sheik if he were pressed, but at least you will find few that can go faster."

The men were overjoyed with the present. The Sikhs, like the Indian irregular cavalry, provided their own horses and equipments, and it was a matter of personal pride to be well mounted. To be the possessors of animals like these, uniting the hardiness of the native horse with the power and speed of their English sire, was an unhoped-for pleasure, and they expressed their thanks in the warmest terms.

As it was evident that Mr. Agnew would very shortly be leaving for Mooltan, and that therefore speed was necessary, Percy and his two men started at daylight next morning and rode by long stages down to Lahore.

Until the last halt before reaching the city Percy had ridden in native dress, as, although things had now settled down a good deal, the feeling was as strong as ever against the British, who still, at the earnest request of the maharanee and the durbar, maintained a force at Lahore to support the young maharajah's authority. It was, therefore, advisable to avoid attention until they reached the capital. As soon as they arrived there Percy rode to the Residency.

"I am glad you have come, Mr. Groves," the Resident said as he was ushered into the study. " You must have come down fast indeed. I told my messenger to carry my note as quickly as he could, but I hardly fancied that you could have been down for another three days; and Mr. Agnew starts to-morrow, so you are just in time."

"You did not mention in your letter, sir, the day on which he would set out; but I came down as rapidly as I could in order to catch him here if possible." At this moment a gentleman in civilian dress, with a young officer, entered the room. They hesitated on seeing that the Resident was engaged.

"Come in, Mr. Agnew," Sir Frederick Currie said. "This is Mr. Groves. He has come down post-haste to take up his appointment as your assistant."

" I am very glad that you have arrived in time, Mr. Groves. I have learnt a good deal about you from the memorandum handed over to Sir Frederick by his predecessor, and shall be very glad to have your assistance. This is Lieutenant Anderson of the ist Bombay Fusiliers, who also accompanies me. We will leave Sir Frederick to his work at present and talk over matters. I need not ask if you are well mounted," he went on when they were seated in another room; "the speed with which you have come down shows that. Are there any preparations you want to make in the way of hiring servants? "

" I have two excellent men, sir. They were with my uncle for many years, and accompanied me through the last campaign. They are thoroughly trustworthy, are up to their work in every way, and have plenty of courage."

"You are fortunate, Mr. Groves, in getting two such men. Sikh servants as a rule are not to be depended upon, especially in any trouble with their countrymen; while servants from other parts of India are of little use here from their ignorance of the language; Do you know anything in reference to the situation at Mooltan?"

"Nothing, sir. I know, of course, that Moolraj's conduct was very doubtful during the last campaign, and that it was considered probable he would have attacked General Napier's force coming from Scinde had it not been too strong to be meddled with. I do not know anything more than that."

"As you know he succeeded his father as Dewan of Mooltan, and in fact of all the country beyond the Jhelum, in 1844. He nominally remained neutral, but there was very little doubt that he would have taken part in the war had he seen his opportunity, and would have joined the Sikhs with every man he could put in the field on the condition that when we were crushed his government should be altogether independent of that of Lahore. The passage of General Napier's army overawed him at that time. He had promised to pay to Lahore a large sum of money in return for the confirmation by the durbar of his succession to his father's office; but when once firmly established in it he declined to pay the stipulated amount, and with the army in a state of mutiny the durbar was unable to compel him to do so; nor had he paid the regular revenue of the province.

" Accordingly one of the first measures of the durbar after things had settled down at the end of our campaign was to send a force against him. Moolraj, however, completely defeated it. Henry Lawrence then acted as mediator, and matters were arranged on the basis that Moolraj should pay up a considerable amount of arrears, and should, for three years from last autumn, pay a fixed sum annually. Last November he paid a visit here, and expressed to John Lawrence, who had succeeded his brother Henry as Resident, that he wished to give up his position as Dewan of Mooltan and its province, his reason being that by the new arrangement the people under his government had the right of appeal to Lahore, which interfered greatly with his power of taxation.

" Lawrence recommended him not to carry out his determination; but he insisted on sending in his resignation to the

durbar. They at first refused it, but after some negotiations it was accepted on the understanding that it should, for a time, remain secret. When, six months later, in the beginning of March, 1848, Mr. Lawrence was about to give up his post to Sir Frederick Currie, the former wrote to Moolraj saying that if he wished to reconsider his resignation he had now the opportunity of withdrawing it. Upon his reply that he had not changed his mind, Sir Frederick took the matter up and laid it before the durbar, who had hitherto, in accordance with the agreement between Lawrence and Moolraj, remained in ignorance that the latter had persisted in giving in his resignation. The durbar, who I have no doubt were glad enough to be rid of a governor whose power and ambition rendered him very formidable, accepted the resignation, and have appointed Khan Singh in his place. He sets out to-morrow with us for his new government. We take with us as our escort a regiment composed of Ghoorkas in the Sikh pay six hundred strong, about the same number of Lahore Sikh cavalry, and a battery of native artillery.

"Such a force as this is not, of course, required for our protection on the road, but is intended as a garrison for Mooltan, where, for aught we know, the people may view the change of governors with disapprobation. You know yourself, Mr. Groves," he added with a smile, "that governors are not always amenable to orders from Lahore."

Percy laughed. "That is true, sir; I believe it is often the case. My uncle often said he would give up the governorship as soon as a maharajah with power to keep order was firmly seated on the throne; but to have given it over when there was neither law nor order would have been to have given up his life as well as the fortress. He has always recognized the authority of the durbar in all other matters, and has sent the revenues in regularly, deducting only the actual amount of pay given to his troops and his own pay as governor, according to the terms of his appointment by Runjeet Singh."

"Yes; I am aware that he has done so," Mr. Agnew said. "The matter was brought up at the first durbar I attended, by one of Ghoolab Singh's party, and I was asked whether I would give my approval to a force being sent against your uncle; but as both the I^awrences strongly protested against civil war when the matter was brought before them one after the other, I threw my weight altogether against such a project, especially at the present time when there will be trouble at Mooltan. But, indeed, the majority of the durbar were equally opposed to any action being taken, first upon the ground that the revenue was punctually paid by Colonel Groves, which was much more than could be said for most of the other sirdars; and in the second place, because the fort had already repulsed an attack by fifteen thousand of the regulars, or as they call them Khalsa troops, with great loss, and that another attempt might prove equally disastrous. But at bottom I think the real reason for the opposition to the proposal was that, were your uncle to be succeeded by Ghoolab Singh's son, the district would virtually become part of Cashmere, and Ghoolab's power is already much too great and threatening. From the instructions left by the two Lawrences for the guidance of their successors, I know that upon this ground alone, if upon no other, they opposed any operation that would tend to increase Ghoolab Singh's dangerous authority."

"At what time do we mount to-morrow, Mr. Agnew?"

"We do not mount at all. Our party, with our servants and baggage, will go down the river in boats. The troops will march, and we shall join each other at the Eedgah, a mile or so from the fort of Mooltan. There will be a boat for ourselves, one for our servants and baggage, and a flat for our horses."

"That will be much more pleasant, sir, than a march through the heat. I enjoyed my journey up from Calcutta by water very much indeed."

The journey was performed by easy stages, as the rate of travel by the boats had to be timed by that of the troops; but on the 18th of April they arrived at the Eedgah, a spacious Mohammedan building, round which the troops had already pitched their camp. Upon the journey Percy had been able to be of considerable service to the party in their communications with the natives at the various points at which they stopped. Mr. Agnew and Lieutenant Anderson had both some knowledge of the language, but were unable to converse with anything like the facility that he had attained. Mr. Agnew had with him several moons his to translate for him and to act as clerks. The conversation in the boat had naturally turned upon the subject of Moolraj's probable course.

"I am wholly unable to understand," Mr. Agnew said, the first time the matter was discussed, "what the man's object is in resigning the governorship. It is, of course, less profitable than it was, owing in the first place to certain districts being taken from his jurisdiction, and in the second, because the right of appeal to Lahore by persons who consider themselves oppressed renders it impossible for him to carry his exactions to so great an extent as before. Had Moolraj been a peace-loving man I should understand his resigning an office he considered no longer profitable; but he is an ambitious one, and has always been credited with the desire and intention of one day making himself independent of Lahore, just as Ghoolab has done. His natural course would have been to announce that he could not afford to pay so heavy a sum annually, and to declare that if pressed he should defend himself; especially as, on the last occasion, he defeated the troops sent from Lahore. Resignation means the annihilation of his hopes, and a descent from the rank of dewan to that of a sirdar of no great consideration. His conduct is an entire mystery to me. It is the very last thing one would have expected from a man of his character. If it had only been decided in a moment of irritation I could have understood

it; but it is six months since he first sent in his resignation; he has again and again had opportunities of withdrawing, but has persisted in resigning. What do you think, Khan Singh?"

"I can understand it no more than you can, sahib," the new dewan replied. "I do not see what design he could have in thus maintaining his resignation if he did not intend to carry it out."

"That is the point," Mr. Agnew said thoughtfully. "If he wanted to raise the flag of rebellion he could have done so at any time, for they say that his troops are well paid and devoted to him."

" If he never meant all along to resign," Lieutenant Anderson remarked, " it seems to me that he could only have pretended to do so in the hope that the durbar would send a considerable force with his successor, and yet something less than an army, in which case he might have surprised and destroyed it, and thus have scored a material and moral success to begin with. He would scarcely have calculated upon his successor being accompanied by three British officers."

"That does seem a feasible explanation, Anderson. No doubt in that case our coming up with twelve hundred troops and a battery will have altogether destroyed his calculations, for although he might feel himself strong enough to defy Lahore, now that the resources of the government are so diminished, he would never be mad enough to think that he could oppose with the remotest hope of success the power of England."

Upon the morning after their arrival at Eedgah, Moolraj rode in with a small party of his officers and had an interview with Mr. Agnew. He expressed his satisfaction that his successor had arrived, and that he should now be relieved of a government that was burdensome to him. He said that he would return in the afternoon, when he would inform them of

the arrangements he had made for handing over the fort on the following morning. This promise he fulfilled, and the arrangements were then completed for the fort to be transferred to Khan Singh early the next morning, Moolraj saying that he himself would be present to see that matters went off smoothly.

That evening when Percy went to his room he found his two men waiting for him there.

"What are you sitting up for?" he asked. "You know I never want you after dinner."

"We wanted to speak to you, sahib," Bhop Lai said. "Is it true that the fort is to be handed over to-morrow morning to Khan Singh?"

" It is quite true, Bhop Lai; the arrangements have all been made with Moolraj this afternoon."

"And will you go into the fort with Khan Singh, sahib? "

" No. Mr. Agnew and Lieutenant Anderson are going with him; and as there are arrangements to be made for the purchase of provisions for the troops, and other matters, Mr. Agnew asked me to remain here."

"That is a comfort indeed, sahib."

"Why so? Do you think there is going to be trouble? "

"I don't know that there will be trouble to-morrow, sahib; I cannot say what the plans of Moolraj are; but there is going to be trouble. You told me this morning to try and find out the sentiments of the people, so I dressed myself as a peasant and went boldly into the town. Everyone there thinks there will be fighting. They say the troops will never accept Khan Singh as their dewan instead of Moolraj, and the budmashes ^ of the city all seem to be of the same opinion.

"They are not, they say, going to submit, like the people of Lahore, to be governed by a man who is but a servant of the Feringhees. What they will do I don't know, but the place is all in an uproar, and I greatly fear there will be trouble. Now that we know you are going to remain here, we

shall no longer be anxious. The Ghoorkas and the guns can defend the place if the Sikh cavalry go over, and at any rate we will have Sheik and our own horses saddled and in readiness either for fighting or flight."

The next morning, as soon as Mr. Agnew was up, Percy went to him and told him what he had learned from Bhop Lai. The officer, however, made light of it. " All that was, of course, to be expected, Mr. Groves. Soldiers may grumble when a leader who has paid and fed them well is removed; but one must not take their grumbling in earnest. As soon as they learn that they will not be disbanded, but that their new dewan will take them all into his service and will treat them well and liberally, they will soon be contented enough. As to the rabble of the town, no doubt they would be ready enough for any mischief, providing the troops were with them; but as soon as they learn that the fort has been handed over and that the troops have accepted Khan Singh as their dewan, they will know better than to give trouble. Moolraj is going with us to the fort, and his influence will easily bring the troops to a better frame of mind."

Percy had so much confidence in Bhop Lai, and the latter was so evidently convinced there was danger of serious trouble, that he by no means shared Mr. Agnew's sanguine anticipation that all would pass off well. He felt, however, that it would be altogether out of place for him, a newly-joined assistant, to urge his opinion against that of Mr. Agnew, and he therefore merely bowed and said:

"Very well, sir, I hope that it will .all go off well, and that your anticipations as to the troops accepting Khan Singh will be realized."

An hour later Moolraj, with a number of officers, rode up to the Eedgah. Mr. Agnew, Lieutenant Anderson, and Khan Singh mounted, and started with the two companies of Ghoorkas who were to be placed in possession of the fort. Still feeling extremely uneasy, Percy first looked to the prim-

ing of his pistols, placed them and his sword in readiness near the table at which he was sitting, and then proceeded to interview the natives who came in offering to furnish supplies of grain, forage, and other provisions. An hour and half elapsed, and then Akram Chunder came in.

"Is anything the matter, Akram?"

" I don't know, sahib. I have been on the roof of the house looking towards the fort, and it seemed to me half an hour since that there was a sudden confusion at the bridge over the ditch. There were a number of men gathered round there, and directly afterwards I saw a group of horsemen, I think Moolraj and his officers, gallop away towards the city. Then presently I saw an elephant with a few footmen coming this way, but no signs of the white sahibs. The elephant is coming hither, and I can see by the trappings that it belongs to a person of importance. Will you call the troops under arms, sahib? "

"No; I can't do that until I know something definite. As likely as not they will refuse to take orders from me. Besides, there can be no danger from this elephant and a handful of footmen, and if all is well Mr. Agnew would naturally be very indignant at my interference."

Putting his pistols in his coat pockets and taking his sword in his hand, Percy went to the door. The elephant was now but two or three hundred yards distant, but a native who had run on ahead was close at hand.

"My master, Rung Ram, brother of the Dewan Moolraj, sends his greeting. The white officer is badly hurt, and he is bringing him hither; he and Khan Singh have themselves bound up his wounds as they brought him along in the howdah."

Percy at once called the servants to the door and then hurried forward to meet the coming party, anxious to discover which officer it was that had been wounded. When he came up with them he saw Mr. Agnew supported in his seat by

Rung Ram and Khan Singh. He was conscious, and leaning forward said to Percy:

"Order the troops under arms at once, Mr. Groves."

Percy hurried away to the camp, and in two minutes the trumpets were calling to arms and the men hurrying out from their tents, surprised at this sudden summons. As soon as he saw that the troops were falling in, Percy returned to the house. Mr. Agnew had been carried into his room and laid on the couch.

" You were right, Mr. Groves, and I regret that I did not treat the warning you gave me as one of importance. Sit down, please, and take pen and paper. I must send off a despatch at once to Sir Frederick Currie. I am too weak to talk much, and you will learn what has happened from the despatch I dictate to you."

Percy was about to begin when Bhop Lai entered.

"There are a party of Ghoorkas carrying a litter approaching, sahib."

"Go out at once, Mr. Groves, and see if it is Anderson they are bringing in. I did not know what had become of him, and am most anxious concerning his fate."

"Your horse is ready, sahib," Bhop Lai said as Percy hurried out.

" Bring it round at once, and mount your own and ride with me."

The party were still but half-way between the fort and the Eedgah when Percy started, and dashing forward at full gallop he was soon alongside. Lieutenant Anderson was lying motionless on the litter.

"Is he dead?" Percy asked as he reined up his horse.

"No, sahib; he is insensible from loss of blood, but his heart beats."

"How did it happen?" Percy asked the native officer in command of the party.

"I had just placed the sentries at the gate when, as the two officers rode over the bridge, one of Moolraj's soldiers who was standing on it rushed at the Sahib Agnew, knocked him off his horse with a spear, and then struck him twice with a sword. Then a trooper of the escort who was riding behind him spurred his horse forward against the sahib's assailant, and knocked him into the ditch. Lieutenant Anderson raised the Sahib Agnew. Moolraj, who was riding by him, pushed on across the bridge, and forcing his horse through the crowd rode away. A sirdar on an elephant then came forward, and the sahib was lifted into the howdah. Khan Singh got off his horse, and also mounted with the sirdar and Mr. Agnew. It seemed to me that all was over. Our men, who had piled their arms, had run to them when I cried out; but directly afterwards some of Moolraj's own party rushed at Lieutenant Anderson as he was remounting his horse and cut him down. They then rode off and the crowd dispersed, fearing no doubt that our men, who now crowded the wall, would fire on them; but this we did not do; we had no one to give orders, and feared that if we fired it might make matters worse. So when the place was clear I went out with this party, and finding that the white officer still lived, thought it best to bring him here at once."

While the native officer had been telling the story the party with the dhooly had continued their way, and Percy rode forward at full speed to acquaint Mr. Agnew with what had happened.

"Order that everything possible shall be done for him," Mr. Agnew said when he had made his report, "and go on with the despatch. Every moment is of importance. I will tell you what happened first: and you can then tell the rest as you have heard it, for I myself know nothing about it."

Mr. Agnew then dictated the first part of the despatch, saying that he had entered the fort with Moolraj and Khan Singh. The former had handed over the keys to him, the Ghoorkas had taken possession and had replaced the Mooltan sentries.

Seeing that Moolraj's soldiers looked sullen and discontented Mr. Agnew addressed them, telling them that they would not lose by the change of governors, but that their services would be retained on the same terms as before. Then, thinking by their manner that he had allayed their discontent, he had ridden out of the fort. He was conscious of receiving a heavy blow that knocked him from his seat, and remembered nothing more until he found himself in a howdah on an elephant, with Rung Ram, who had been introduced to him as Moolraj's brother-in-law, bandaging up his wounds.

When Percy had written the native officer's report of the affair, Mr. Agnew dictated an earnest appeal to the Resident to send forward troops with all possible speed, as it was likely they would be besieged in the building, which certainly could not hold out for many days against the whole force at Mooltan.

This letter was at once sent off, and another was then dictated to Lieutenant Edwardes, a young political officer who had with him a Sikh force of twelve companies of infantry, three hundred and fifty troopers, two cannon, and two camel guns. He was on the other side of the Indus, and was occupied in settling the country and collecting revenue. Lieutenant Edwardes was urged to advance immediately with all speed to his assistance.

This letter also despatched, Mr. Agnew dictated a letter to Moolraj calling upon him to prove that he was innocent of all complicity in the attacks by at once arresting the criminals and coming in in person to the Eedgah. At the time that Moolraj received this letter he was presiding over a council, while the garrison, which was composed of Afghans, Hindus, and Sikhs, were taking the oath of allegiance to him. He briefly replied to Mr. Agnew's letter, saying that he could not comply with his request, for the garrison of the fort were all in rebellion, and the British officers had better look to their own safety. On the following evening a strong body of

Moolraj's cavalry swept down and carried off the whole of the baggage animals of the force, the troops offering no active opposition. As, with the loss of the baggage animals, there was no possibility of the column retiring, the force was called into the building and ordered to prepare to repel an attack. Mr. Agnew was now so far recovered as to be able to get up and to issue the necessary instructions to the native officers.

"Things look very bad, sahib," Bhop Lai said as he and his comrade came into Percy's room when he went in with the intention of snatching a few hours' sleep, as he had been up the whole night before with Lieutenant Anderson.

"You think we shall not be able to defend ourselves until help comes? " Percy asked.

" There will be no defence at all, sahib. There have been men all day in camp moving about under pretence of selling things, but really as messengers from Moolraj and his officers, calling upon the men not to fire upon their brethren, but to join those who were resolved to fight to the death against the Feringhees and the traitor Lahore government who are their servants. All in Mooltan—Sikh, Mohammedan, and Hindu —had united for the common cause. Moreover, resistance, it was said, would be vain; no help could reach the Eedgah, and all who drew sword in defence of the Feringhees would be slain."

"And were they successful, Bhop Lai? "

"You will see, sahib, that not a shot will be fired when Moolraj advances against the place."

Percy went down again to Mr. Agnew, and told him what he had heard. "I cannot doubt what you tell me, Mr. Groves; your man's information proved right before. But in any case there is nothing to be done. Anderson can scarcely stand. I am not fit to be out of bed. You and your two men, with perhaps the moonshis, seem to be alone to be relied on; and I need not say that resistance, even by two or

three hundred men, would be hopeless, and would but entail the death of all. Escape, as far as Anderson and myself are concerned, is out of the question. We could not sit our horses half a mile, and the motion would cause our wounds to burst out bleeding again at once. It is not to be thought of. Danger for us there can be none. Moolraj can have no object in murdering two defenceless men, especially as he must know that such a crime would never be forgiven, and would involve him in a desperate war with England. At present he can assert that the attack upon us was the work of fanatics, and that he regrets the matter greatly, as, although determined to free himself from the dictation of Lahore, he had no thought of any hostility towards the British. Our lives, therefore, are perfectly safe. But I see no use in your waiting to share the captivity that we may probably have to undergo for a time, and I should recommend you to mount and ride off with your two men this evening."

"I can't do that, sir," Percy said bluntly. "I cannot desert you and Mr. Anderson, wounded as you are. It is possible, too, that the troops will, after all, prove faithful. But in any case it is impossible that I should leave you. It would be a bad beginning indeed of my service in the Company were I to run away and leave two of its wounded officers behind me."

Mr. Agnew was silent for a minute. " I cannot press the point, Mr. Groves," he said gravely, "for I feel that were I placed as you are I might myself disobey instructions. Stay, therefore, if you will; but I give you my stringent orders, and I will write them down and hand them to you in the morning, that if the troops here mutiny and surrender the place to Moolraj you are, if possible, to effect your escape and carry the news at full speed to Lieutenant Edwardes. If he marches on alone, ignorant of what has happened here, he will be met and overwhelmed by the whole of Moolraj's forces, and it is even probable that his troops, when they hear

that those here have fraternized with the enemy, may also go over in a body. But whether they do so or not, it is of the highest importance that you should warn Lieutenant Edwardes of the treachery of the troops here. I shall put that down in writing in the morning, and I rely upon you to carry out the order. You can do no possible good to us by staying, and would probably indeed do us harm, as it might excite the passions of the Mooltan men when they enter to see one of us still uninjured, and blood once shed we might all be killed."

"Very well, sir; if you give me the written order I shall, of course, obey it, and, indeed, I acknowledge that your view of the matter seems to me unanswerable. The destruction of Lieutenant Edwardes' force would be a great misfortune, for it would immensely encourage the people here, and would enable them to make all their preparations for war undisturbed, as it would be a long while before the Lahore people could get together an army capable of capturing Mooltan.

" I see that I cannot be of use to you, and I agree with you. Moolraj will naturally protect you and treat you well, as he cannot wish to bring down the vengeance of the government of India upon him."

The two men were still waiting in Percy's room when he returned to it.

"Get the horses in readiness to mount at any moment," he said. "I have Mr. Agnew's orders that if the troops here 1 join Moolraj, I am to ride ; at all speed to carry the .news to Lieutenant Edwardes, who was ordered to advance from Dera-Futteh-Khan and to cross the ferry at Leia, where I shall probably find him. It is ninety miles away, but our horses will carry us there."

" It would be better to start to-night, sahib. We shall be hotly pursued if we.go off in the daytime."

"I know that," Percy replied; "but it must be risked. Until it is certain that the troops here intend to join Moolraj I cannot go."

"Very well, sahib, whatever are your orders we shall obey them. If we get but a fair start there are not many horses in Mooltan that will be able to overtake us."

"That is so, Bhop Lai; and any that do come up with us we shall probably be able to give a good account of."

"We will watch by turns to-night, sahib; it is possible these rascals may intend to surrender the place to Moolraj before morning."

CHAPTER XV

THE NEWS OF THE MASSACRE

THE night of the ipth of April passed off quietly. In the morning the guns of the fort opened fire against the Eed-gah. A single shot only was fired in reply by the battery of the garrison, and then the whole of the artillerymen quitted their guns. The fort continued to fire for some time, but the distance was too great for any damage to be done, and the fire presently ceased. Mr. Agnew and Percy went to the gunners and exhorted them to return to their duty, but the men listened in sullen silence and gradually dispersed. In a short time they began to leave the building in parties of twos and threes, and by mid-day half the garrison had deserted.

"Here are your orders, Mr. Groves," Mr. Agnew said, placing a letter in Percy's hands. "You can use your own judgment as to going now or waiting until nightfall. My own opinion is, that it would be best for you to start at once. I do not know why Moolraj delays, for he must know that he will meet with no resistance. However, at night the place may be surrounded, and you might have more difficulty in getting off. In the next place, as you are ignorant of the country, you might miss your way and lose much precious time. And lastly, every hour is of consequence to Edwardes. Even now emissaries from Mooltan may be at work among his troops. I have mentioned in my orders that as the troops

here have refused to fire and are deserting in great numbers, it is evident that Moolraj can enter whenever he chooses; and as it is of paramount importance to warn Lieutenant Edwardes to arrest his march, I have ordered you to start immediately, as you have expressed your willingness to undertake the service, although it is undoubtedly one of great danger. I have said that your own wishes would have led you to remain here with myself and Anderson and to share our fate whatever it might be, but that you have yielded to my anxiety that Lieutenant Edwardes should be warned. I have also inclosed a note to Edwardes, saying that your services will be at his disposal until you receive orders from the Resident."

" I will start at once, sir, as you think it best," Percy said, much moved at the thoughtful kindness of the wounded officer; " and there is little doubt I shall get through safely. I am splendidly mounted, and my men have also very good horses. I trust, sir, that I shall ere long meet you again."

" I hope so, confidently, Mr. Groves. It is evidently Moolraj's interest to treat us well, even if he keeps us as hostages, and I cannot think there is any danger. Good-bye, lad, and a safe ride to you! "

Percy then went in and said good-bye to Lieutenant Anderson, and with a heavy heart went out to his men.

"I am ready to start," he said; "get the horses to the back entrance without attracting more notice than you can help. These fellows might oppose our leaving. I will follow you in a minute or two and join you at the gate."

"There are many more of them about there, sahib, than there are at the main entrance. They are slinking away by scores, and I do not think that there is even a sentry on guard at this end. If we bring the horses up here and you mount, Akram Chunder shall mount also and lead my horse. I will run forward and unbar the gate, and if any of the fellows standing about interfere with me the three of us will be able to overpower them. We will have our pistols in readiness."

"Very well, perhaps that will be the best plan. I see there are very few of them about here. Do you fetch up the horses at once; I will get a couple of bottles of wine and some bread for our joruney."

Percy was at the door of the court-yard again before the men came up with the horses. As they did so several of the soldiers standing about moved forward with scowling faces. They were, however, unarmed, having ostentatiously piled their muskets when the firing ceased. Percy drew the pistols from his holster, slipped the bottles and bread into their place, and leapt into the saddle.

"Stand back, men," he said authoritatively; "any one who interferes with us will get a bullet in his head. Keep abreast of me, Akram," he went on; "lead the other horse between us."

Bhop Lai ran forward ahead to the gate and began to undo the bars. Several of the men loitering near ran to stop him, but as Percy and Akram rode up they shrank back from the four levelled pistols. Bhop Lai threw the gate open, and leaping on his horse they rode out together, regardless of the angry shouts that pursued them.

"We will ride quietly for a while," Percy said, reining his horse into a canter when they had gone a few hundred yards. "We shall be within sight of the walls of Mooltan as we ride along between it and the river, and if we are galloping hard they may suspect something. The great point is to get to the ferry at Beelun before they are close to us. Once across we can laugh at them."

When they had gone half a mile Akram Chunder looked back.

"They are after us, sahib. There are fifty horsemen at least just coming out from behind the Eedgah, and," he added, " there are four men away to our right galloping at the top of their speed towards Mooltan."

"Then we will quicken our pace," Percy said, touching his

horse with his heel. "We have six miles to ride to the ferry. We will gain another quarter of a mile on them if we can."

The horses were now put to their full speed and went along at almost racing pace. When abreast of the fort of Mooltan, which lay a mile away on their right, they could perceive that they had sensibly increased their lead. They had gone a quarter of a mile further when there was the boom of a heavy cannon, and a ball ploughed up the field a short distance behind them.

"I expected that," Percy said. "Those fellows from Eedgah have taken them the news of our escape. They are only wasting their shot. The betting is a thousand to one against their hitting us at this distance, going the pace we are."

Six guns were fired, but none of the shots came as near them as the first had done, and in twenty minutes they drew up their horses at the ferry. The boat was not there but was coming across and was within a couple of hundred yards of the shore.

"Do you dismount, sahib, and stand by your horse," Akram Chunder said; "they will take us for natives. But if they see you they may refuse to bring their boat up, for the sound of the cannon will have told them that something is wrong."

Percy did as his follower suggested.

"How slowly they come ! " he said impatiently.

"There is time, sahib; it would not do to shout to them to hurry. We will dismount and lead our horses d (own to the water's edge; if you keep close to their heels you will not be noticed."

Some twenty country people got out of the boat when it touched the shore. Percy's men at once led their horses on board and he followed. The four boatmen looked surprised at seeing an Englishman, but made no remark.

"Push off at once," Bhop Lai said.

"We are going ashore to get our meal," one of the men replied; "we shall not start till we have got a boat-load."

"You will go at once," Bhop Lai said, drawing a pistol. " I will pay you as much as a whole boat-load would do, but I have no time to spare."

As the others also drew their pistols the men sullenly thrust their poles into the water and pushed off. They had gone less than a hundred yards when a body of horsemen rode furiously down to the water's edge and shouted to them to return.

"Go on," Percy said authoritatively; "if one of you hesitates for a moment, he is a dead man."

Seeing that the boat continued its way the sowars opened fire with their pistols, but though the balls fell round the boat the distance was too great for accurate shooting, and in two or three minutes they were altogether beyond range, the men poling lustily now so as to place themselves out of danger. The Indus is of great width at this point, but the waters are comparatively shallow and the stream gentle, and in an hour they gained the opposite shore. Percy had directed them to make for a point half a mile below the town of Kote, instead of the ordinary landing-place, where they might have encountered a number of people waiting for the boat to return, as the traffic was considerable and they had on their way across met two laden boats. As the water was shallow they had to get the horses over the side fifty yards from shore, and then, having well paid the boatmen, they rode to the bank. Cutting across the fields they avoided the town altogether, and struck the road a mile beyond it. Before leaving the river bank they saw that there were seven or eight loaded boats half-way over, the troopers having doubtless seized some of the country craft to convey them across.

"We shall be three or four miles on our way before they have all landed and mounted," Akram Chunder said. "We shall see no more of them."

The road was a good one, and for some time they rode fast; then they reined in their horses and proceeded at a slower pace.

"We have ninety miles in all to do," Percy said, "and we must not risk foundering the horses. They have had no exercise since they left Lahore and we must husband their strength. The troopers are not likely to pursue more than thirty miles from the ferry at the outside, perhaps not half that. When they learn that we are keeping our distance ahead of them they will see that they have little chance of overtaking us and will not care about killing their horses in a hopeless pursuit."

Whenever they passed through a village they went through at a regular pace as if in no way pressed for time. The natives were doubtless aware of the attack on the two English officers, but could hardly know that the Sikh troops had proved faithless, and would imagine that the white officer and his two men were riding ahead of that force on its way to join Lieutenant Edwardes. Before leading the horses out from the stable the men had filled their bags with grain, and after riding twenty miles from the ferry they stopped for two hours under some trees on elevated ground, where they could command a view down the long straight road two or three miles. As there were no signs of their pursuers at the end of that time they felt sure that these had given the chase up as hopeless, and therefore continued their journey at the pace the horses could best keep up. Soon after they started night fell, and the riding was much more pleasant than it had been during the heat.

They halted again for three hours at midnight, finished their bread and wine, and gave the horses another good feed. At eight o'clock in the morning they approached Leia, but hearing from some peasants that no force had arrived there up to the previous evening, they made a circuit of the town and crossed the river at the ferry, two or three miles distant

from it. As they rode into the next village they saw that the street was crowded with Sikh soldiers, who were engaged in cooking their food.

"Are you from Mooltan?" a young officer asked, running out as they drew rein at the house where they had been told Lieutenant Edwardes had taken up his quarters.

"We are," Percy said, as he threw himself off his horse. "We left the Eedgah at one o'clock yesterday."

"How are Agnew and Anderson? Doing well, I hope?"

"They were both doing well when I left them, as far as their wounds went; but they are in a desperate positon."

"Why, the place is a strong one; I know it well," Lieutenant Edwardes said. "Twelve hundred men with a battery of artillery ought to be able to hold it at least some days against all the troops in Mooltan."

"They might have done so if the troops had fought," Percy said; " but they have gone over to Moolraj. Half of them had left when I came away, and the others were leaving fast. I do not think there would be a score of men left them by sunset yesterday. I have a note for you, and I shall be glad if you will read Mr. Agnew's written orders to me. You will see that I did not leave the two wounded officers willingly."

By this time they had entered the house.

"Sit down and take something to eat while I glance through these papers. Mr. Agnew does you full justice," he went on, more warmly than he had before spoken, after reading the two documents. "You were, of course, obliged to obey orders, and could have been of no use to them under the circumstances. Agnew was evidently thinking much more of me than of himself. What do you think will happen to them?"

" Mr. Agnew was perfectly confident that as it was clearly to the interest of Moolraj not to draw the English into the quarrel between him and Lahore, he would protect and take good care of them."

"I sincerely hope so," Lieutenant Edwardes replied; "but Moolraj showed a very hostile front to us when Napier passed through with his force to join Sir Hugh Gough. He professed to stand neutral, but there was no doubt he would not have been neutral had he dared fight. Besides, there are the Mooltan rabble to deal with. Agnew would have done better to surrender at once to Moolraj directly he saw that the Sikhs had turned traitors. If he puts it off till night the budmashes of Mooltan, knowing that the Eedgah is no longer defended, may take the matter in hand, in which case I would not give a rupee for the lives of the two Englishmen."

"When did the messenger reach you with the news?" Percy asked.

"At eight o'clock last night. So you have gained some fourteen hours upon him, as the despatch is dated half-past eleven."

"I was well mounted," Percy said. "I might have been here some hours earlier, but my horse is a very valuable one, and I knew that an hour or two could make little difference."

" I sent off a messenger as soon as I got Agnew's despatch, to Lieutenant Taylor, who is with General Van Cortlandt, who is, as I daresay you know, an officer in the Sikh service at Bunnoo, begging him to send me a regiment of cavalry and four guns at once. I then issued orders for my force to start at daylight, and we have marched twelve miles. I intended to go on to Leia and halt there for the night and to move forward quietly till Van Cortlandt's detachment joined me, and then push forward with all speed. What you have told me now, of course, changes the situation altogether. I shall go forward to Leia as I intended, but shall halt there and intrench myself, and wait to be attacked. I may be able to raise my force considerably from the Pathan portion of the population, between whom and the Sikhs there is a longstanding enmity. I see Mr. Agnew has placed your services

at my disposal, Mr. Groves. I shall be glad indeed to have an Englishman with me. It is a great relief to have someone to chat with and discuss matters in one's own language. Of course you are quite new to this district. I suppose you have only just come up country. You have dropped, indeed, into a very hot corner for a young civilian."

Percy laughed. " I daresay you think I look very young even for a young civilian, Mr. Edwardes."

Lieutenant Edwardes joined in the laugh.

" Well, I was thinking so. Of course you must be twenty or you would not have been sent up from Calcutta, but you do not look more than eighteen."

"I am a month or two under that age," Percy said; "but I do know the country pretty well, though not on this side of the Punjaub; and in fact I speak both Punjaubi and Pathan almost as well as I do English." He then gave Lieutenant Edwardes a sketch of his life since his arrival in India.

"I congratulate myself very heartily," Lieutenant Edwardes said cordially. " You will indeed be of assistance to me. I can quite understand now your being in the service so young and your being appointed as assistant to Agnew. It will be an immense comfort to me having with me one who understands the people so thoroughly, and can speak both with the Sikhs and Afghans. But it is time for me to be moving forward, or I shall not get my men across in time to occupy Leia before nightfall. I will leave a party of fifty men here, so you and your two followers can rest yourselves and your horses and join me to-morrow."

"Thank you. I feel quite capable of going on with you, but I certainly should be glad to let the horses have twenty-four hours' rest after doing something like a hundred miles since they started yesterday."

"You may as well take possession of these quarters. I think it is the best house in the place, and as the owners are Afghans they are ready to do anything they can for us."

A quarter of an hour later the Sikhs started on their forward march. Percy found his men had been told that they were to have a halt till the following morning, and so, after seeing they had comfortable quarters and paying a visit to his horse, he lay down and slept until evening. Then he got up and had a meal, walked round the village and had a talk with the Sikh officer of the detachment, and then turned in again until the next morning, when, as soon as the sun was up, he started with the detachment, and presently joined Lieutenant Ed-wardes at Leia. The latter had occupied the town without opposition, Moolraj's governor, with the small body of troops he had with him, having retired at his approach.

The next few days were occupied in throwing up intrench-ments round the town. They heard that Moolraj was about to cross the Chenab with five thousand men on his way to attack them, but as he hoped that Van Cortlandt's regiment with the four guns would join him before Moolraj could arrive, Lieutenant Edwardes determined to maintain his position. One morning, however, he came with a serious face into Percy's room.

"I have terrible news," he said; "a messenger has just returned—the one I sent with a letter to Mr. Agnew telling him that I would be with him as soon as possible. On the way he met Moolraj's force, and, mingling with them, learned what had happened at Mooltan after you left. By nightfall there remained at the Eedgah only some twelve men, the native clerks, and the officers' servants. Mr. Agnew had already sent to Moolraj to say that he was ready to surrender, and begging him to come in person to take over the place. Whether Moolraj delayed purposely in order that the work should be finished before he arrived was a matter of doubt, but at any rate he did not come. Soon after dark a mob of the ruffians of the town with some soldiers, among whom were many of the Sikh mutineers, proceeded to the Eedgah, burst in the doors, and with shouts of ' Death to the Feringhees!'

rushed in. Mr. Agnew was sitting by the bedside of Anderson. They had heard the tumult of the approaching mob, and doubtless felt that their fate was at hand. Agnew rose as they entered, and was cut down at once and despatched by two or three blows. They then rushed at Anderson and hacked him to pieces."

"This is terrible indeed," Percy said, much moved at the news of the death of the two gentlemen with whom he had spent the last fortnight. " Do you think that Moolraj was a party to this atrocity? "

"They say that Agnew's head was taken to him, and, in his presence and with his apparent approval, treated with every indignity. Certainly he rewarded his murderer with a large present and a robe of honour, and also gave presents to the man who had taken the principal part in the murder of Anderson. From my own knowledge of Moolraj, although he is doubtless ambitious, I should say that he is a weak man, without courage or resolution. I do not think he had anything to do with the first attack on the two officers, but seeing that the harm was done, knowing that he would be blamed for it, and-being really in the hands of his turbulent soldiery, he resolved to throw in his lot with them, and from that moment he was, like many other timid men when driven to the wall, in favour of desperate measures. He would, no doubt, consider that by allowing, if he did not direct, the murder of the two officers, he bound the soldiers all the more closely to his interests, as the deed would put an end to all possibility of a reconciliation.

" Of course this sad affair altogether alters my position. I was ready to push forward at all hazards until I heard from you that the Sikhs had mutinied; then the necessity for speed was at an end, for it was evident that the Eedgah would be captured the day you left. Another serious circumstance has occurred that renders it more than doubtful whether I can maintain myself here. One of the native officers has just

brought me a document that has fallen into his hands. It is an address from the Sikhs who deserted at the Eedgah to the men here, calling upon them to join their countrymen and make common cause against the English, for that all the Pun-jaub was about to take up arms against the Feringhees. The worst of it is, the officer says that from what he learns this document has been here for the last two days, and has been read by all the soldiers; and if that is the case I can no longer place the sightest reliance upon them.

" I am desirous of holding on here until the last moment for two reasons. I hear that Moolraj has sent men all over the country to enlist the Pathans. They are by far the most warlike people here, and will certainly take service with him unless they take sendee with me. For choice perhaps they would join me, because they have no love of the Sikhs, who conquered their country. So long, then, as I remain here they will believe that the success of Moolraj is not assured, and not only shall we get a large number of valuable recruits, but prevent their going to Mooltan. In the next place, I have to pay the men I enlist, and to do so I must collect, as far as possible, the revenues of the districts in this neighbourhood, for the money, like the recruits, will go to Mooltan if it does not come to me. So you see it is of the greatest importance that I should hold on here as long as possible in spite of this ugly business of the Sikhs. I wish I could get rid of them altogether, but that, until I can get together a strong force of Pathans, is impossible."

Percy was greatly struck with the energy and firmness of the young officer. Edwardes had for the past year been acting as political agent in the greater part of the district between the Indus and the foot of the mountains, and had also completely pacified Bunnoo, a most turbulent district, inhabited by tribes of the Afghan race who had for five-and-twenty years successfully resisted the efforts of the Sikhs to conquer them, while he had so completely gained their confidence that at his

bidding they levelled the four hundred forts that constituted the strength of their country, and many of them had already sent in offers of service.

For the next two or three days there was no outward change in the position. A good many Afghans were recruited, and messengers had arrived, saying that the whole of Van Cort-landt's force were on the march to join him; but as these had not arrived, while Moolraj's force, which was provided with eighty guns, had approached within a day's march, Edwardes deemed that it would be imprudent to remain longer when he was more than doubtful of the fidelity of two-thirds of his men. He accordingly evacuated Leia and recrossed the Indus. He had hardly done so when he received news that the bulk of the enemy's army had suddenly changed their course and marched north; and he therefore directed a body of some two hundred Pathans who had not yet crossed the river to remain there. Four hundred of the enemy occupied Leia, and the Pathans were ordered to retire across the river if they advanced. Thinking it probable that they would not do so, as a retreat is of all things the most distasteful to men of this race, he sent over fifty more men to reinforce them. The enemy did advance; the Pathans defended the bank of a nullah, and after a time took the offensive, rushed across the nullah and fell furiously upon the enemy, whom they utterly routed, pursuing them a long distance and retaking possession of Leia. The town, however, was not retained, for Edwardes had just received orders to undertake no operations on the eastern side of the Indus, but to confine himself to preventing the passage of the river by the enemy and to maintaining order in his district. He therefore marched his whole force a few miles up the river to the fort of Girang, where he awaited the arrival of General Cortlandt with his command.

That officer joined him there on the 4th of May, with the Mohammedan regiment of Loobdan Khan and a battery of six guns. Moolraj did not attempt to cross the river, and by the

igth further reinforcements had arrived, bringing up Ed-wardes' force to about four thousand eight hundred men, of whom four thousand were believed to be faithful, while the eight hundred Sikhs were known to be disaffected. More than this, he had heard from Bhawul Khan, the Rajah of Bhawulpoor, a state on the southern side of the river Ghara, that he was ready to move in a short time against Mooltan from the south, and with this assistance Lieutenant Edwardes felt strong enough to offer to undertake the blockade of Mooltan for the rest of the hot season and through the rains, if commissioned to do. The first step taken, however, was the capture of Dera-Ghazee-Khan, a strong place on the western bank of the Indus, interrupting his communication with Bhawulpoor and forming a strong outlying post to Mooltan. The governorship of this place and the country round had been given by Moolraj to one of his followers named Julal Khan, belonging to the Lugharee tribe, to the great anger of a powerful chief, Kowrah Khan, a personal enemy of Julal.

Kowrah at once made his submission to the British, and sent his son Gholam Hyder with a contingent of men to join General Cortlandt, who was moving with a part of the force to besiege the town. On the 2oth of May Gholam Hyder told General Cortlandt that he was ready to go on in advance, to raise the whole of his father's clan, and with them alone to drive Julal Khan and the troops with him across the river. General Cortlandt accepted the offer, though doubting much Gholam Hyder's ability to carry it out. However, the young man at once left the column with his contingent and rode rapidly on ahead to his father's place.

Having obtained the latter's consent, messengers were sent off in all directions to call upon the tribe to assemble, and the same night a desperate attack was made upon the town. The men of the Lugharee tribe, who formed the principal part of the garrison, fought stoutly, and the combat continued without

success on either side; but when morning broke Gholam Hyder Khan led his men forward with such bravery that after a severe hand-to-hand contest he gained a complete victory, killing numbers of the Lugharees, among whom was one of their chiefs, and making another prisoner. Some of the garrison shut themselves in the fort, but capitulated in a few hours on condition of being allowed to cross the river unmolested. Moolraj's force moved to Koreyshee with the intention of crossing by boat and retaking the town, and, failing in doing this, of opposing any attempt on the part of Edwardes to cross.

They found that the boats had been removed, and the two armies remained for over a week watching each other across the wide river. Kowrah Khan and his son received the thanks of Sir Frederick Currie, and the durbar bestowed an additional rank upon them. They shortly afterwards joined the army with four hundred horsemen of their tribe, who fought gallantly through the whole campaign. They received no pay for their services, but at the end of the war were rewarded by the grant of an estate and pension.

By this time, although communications were still uncertain, Lieutenant Edwardes learnt that, for the present, no British force would advance against Mooltan. The commander-in-chief felt that, in the first place, no confidence whatever could be placed upon the Sikhs, who would be a source of danger rather than of aid. In the second, it would take a considerable time to collect an army sufficiently large for the purpose. Lastly, it was considered extremely unadvisable to engage a large British force upon arduous operations during the hot season. The rebellion of Moolraj was against the Sikh government, and the durbar at Lahore was called upon to take active steps to repress it. Later on Moolraj would be called to account by the British for the murder of the two officers.

THE NEWS OF THE MASSACRE ZiL

The Lahore government had accordingly despatched three columns, who were to converge upon Mooltan and blockade the town. These were commanded respectively by the Rajah Sher Singh, Sheik Emamoodeen, and Jowahir Mull Dutt. The Nawab of Bhawulpoor's troops were to form a fourth column and to meet the others before Mooltan. The three Sikh columns, however, made very little progress, the commanders being each doubtful what the others would do, and uncertain as to the fidelity of their troops. The Nawab of Bhawulpoor was perfectly ready to do his share of the business, but he altogether declined to march upon Mooltan until he saw the other columns making fair progress in that direction.

Lieutenant Edwardes, on learning of the hesitation of the three Sikh commanders, again wrote offering to undertake the blockade of Mooltan with his own force in conjunction with that of the Nawab of Bhawulpoor. He had now got rid of his Sikh regiment, which he had just sent off accompanied by two hundred and fifty Pathan horsemen, and under the general command of a Pathan chief, to garrison the fort of Mithun Kote, where they were out of the way of doing mischief, and far removed from the influence of their co-religionists at Mooltan.

The passage of trie Indus at this time was difficult and hazardous. Augmented by the melting snow on the hills it was rushing down in a mighty river fifteen miles wide, and it was impossible for either army to cross in the face of the other. At the beginning of June, however, the nawab crossed the river and advanced towards Soojabad; and having sent a pressing request to Sir Frederick Currie that Edwardes should have permission to co-operate with him, the injunction against that officer crossing the Indus was removed, to his immense satisfaction and that of Percy.

By this time the Pathan force had increased to three thou-
THROUGH THE SIKH WAR

sand men, while two thousand of the same race had joined General Cortlandt, so that it was possible to leave a force sufficient to ensure order in the district west of the Indus, and yet to carry a considerable number to reinforce the nawab. The prospect was all the brighter since a Pathan officer who had come to Leia when Edwardes occupied that town, under the pretence of negotiating on the part of Mool-raj, now sent him information that the Pathan officers at Mooltan, who had from the first taken no part in the attack on the Eedgah, and were altogether opposed to the war, would desert as soon as an opportunity offered, and with their men join the British.

Slow as the nawab's advance was, it alarmed Moolraj, and his army was ordered to fall back from the Indus and take post at Soojabad. Edwardes was well informed by his spies of the movements of the enemy. They broke up their camp by the river before daylight on the loth of June, and before nightfall he had conveyed a portion of his army across the wide river in the great fleet of boats he had collected. General Cortlandt was to follow with the rest the next morning, for they had been joined by so many of the chiefs from Bunnoo and by zemindars of the dstrict, that he had no fear of disturbance breaking out in his rear, so long at any rate as all went well at the front.

Percy had been very busy during the halt at Dera-Ghazee-Khan in marshalling the native levies as they arrived, acting as Lieutenant Edwardes' mouthpiece, and paying complimentary visits to the chiefs and thanking them for their loyalty. Bhop Lai had acted as drill-instructor to the Pathan recruits, who were formed into companies as they arrived; and Edwardes would have appointed him to the command of one of these bodies, but he declined the offer, saying that although ready to aid at other times, in the day of battle his place was by his master's side, and nothing would induce him

to leave it. Akram Chunder, not being able to speak the Pathan language, could not be utilized in the same way as his comrade, and indeed the Pathans would hardly have obeyed anyone not of their own nationality save an Englishman; and he therefore continued his usual work as Percy's attendant, looking after his horse and cooking for him and Lieutenant Edwardes, who took their meals together.

Percy was delighted when forward move was at last made. Lieutenant Edwardes had at first thought of attaching him to General Cortlandt's column, but he afterwards decided to take him with him, feeling how great was the comfort of having someone with him to whom he could talk over all his plans and difficulties, and whose opinion, however modestly given, he came, as time went on, to regard as valuable.

When the force reached the opposite bank of the river, Edwardes learned from coolies who had been forced to assist in carrying the enemy's baggage and were now returning to their homes, that they had halted at Khangurh. This was a disappointment, as it showed that they were making for Soo-jabad instead of, as he had hoped, for Mooltan; and a few hours later he received a letter saying that two thousand men with four guns had already been sent from Mooltan to Sooja-bad, and orders had been issued for another two thousand men to march there. Had the nawab shown a little more activity he could easily have possessed himself of Soojabad, in which case the army of the Indus must have fallen back to Mooltan, against which town the allies could then have marched without opposition; whereas Moolraj was now concentrating his whole force at Soojabad, and it was evident that a battle would have to be fought there before advancing against Mooltan.

The next day Edwardes' anxieties were greatly increased by the news that the column of Jowahir Mull Dutt, which was at last approaching Leia, was in a state of disorganization,

and that one of the cavalry regiments had deserted and joined Moolraj. This fresh proof of the general disaffection of the Sikhs was alarming, especially as the Sikh force at Bunnoo was composed almost entirely of old soldiers who had fought against us on the Sutlej. Fearing for the safety of his assistant, Lieutenant Taylor, at that place, he sent him orders to leave Bunnoo and establish himself at Dera-Ismail-Khan.

CHAPTER XVI

SEVEN HOURS OF SUSPENSE

T IEUTENANT EDWARDES pressed forward with all speed, -L' in hopes of effecting a junction with the Bhawulpoor force before the Mooltan army could fall upon them. Unfortunately the River Jelum intervened between the allies, and had the rebel army used expedition they could have annihilated the Bhawulpoor contingent before Edwardes joined them. The latter had already made every preparation for his advance, having sent on messengers ahead to collect boats at Koreyshee, with instructions that his ally should avoid battle if possible and retire before the enemy until joined by him.

On reaching the Jelum late in the evening he heard that the Mooltan force had just arrived at a point three miles from the camp of his ally, but had established themselves and evidently did not intend to attack until the next morning. " You had better start at once across the river, Groves, and see that the nawab's force is in a position to defend itself if the enemy attack before I can get across. Its commander is an old man, and, as I hear from our agent, Peer Ibraheem Khan, hopelessly muddle-headed and inefficient. You will find Ibraheem himself a thoroughly good and reliable officer, and he will aid you in every way. It is he who has got all these boats collected in readiness for us. Two or three of the nawab's regiments are commanded by Englishmen. If you find that

the general will do nothing, I authorize you to take the command out of his hands, and to make the best dispositions you can under the advice of Ibraheem. The boats are coming up fast, and I shall begin to cross at daylight with the infantry to aid the Bhawulpoor men in keeping the enemy at bay until Cortlandt can get the guns across. Until we have them to help us we shall be at a terrible disadvantage, for the enemy have at least twelve pieces. Remember to-morrow is the i8th of June, the anniversary of Waterloo; it is a good omen for us."

As Percy was about to ride down to the river bank a boat came across, and he stood chatting with Lieutenant Edwardes until it arrived. It contained a messenger from Peer Ibraheem, saying that the force would march down to a point opposite the ferry during the night and so cover the crossing.

"Could you guide this officer," Lieutenant Edwardes said, "so that he can meet the army on the march?"

The messenger said that he could do so, and Percy with his two men and horses took his place in the boat. After two hours' ride from the other side of the river they met the head of the approaching column, and Percy, hearing that Peer Ibraheem was with "the regiment that followed, waited till he came along and then handed him a pencil note that Edwardes had given him, repeating to Peer Ibraheem the instructions he had already given Percy.

"I am very glad that you have come, sahib," the officer said. " Futteh Muhommud pays no attention to what is going on, and is in fact no better than an idiot. I received authority from Edwardes sahib yesterday to supersede him if .it were absolutely necessary, but it might possibly cause discontent among the troops, and it were better to leave him in nominal command."

The morning was breaking when they approached the river. When half a mile distant they met three thousand of the Pathans, who with fifty mounted chiefs had effected their

passage during the night under the command of Foujdar Khan, a capable and energetic native officer who acted as Edwardes' adjutant-general. A halt was ordered, and Percy and Peer Ibraheem tried to get the men into line and to remedy the tremendous confusion that prevailed, baggage animals, waggons, elephants, and guns being all mixed up in the column. There was the more occasion for haste, as the rising sun showed the enemy marching towards them. Their object had evidently been to take possession of the ferry and thus separate the two allied forces; but the night march of the Bhawulpoor men and the passage of the Pathans had forestalled them, and they at once took up their position on the salt hills of the village of Noonar and their guns in a few minutes opened.

Two or three of the nawab's guns were with the greatest difficulty extricated from the confused mass and returned the fire of the enemy, and the Bhawulpoor men, uttering, as was their custom before fighting, the name of the rajah in a sonorous shout, rushed headlong without order or regularity against the enemy. In vain Percy and Peer Ibraheem and their own officers shouted to them to stand their ground. They went forward at a run until they were checked by volleys of musketry from the traitorous Sikh troops, while the guns swept them with grape. Though accustomed to irregular warfare, the nawab's troops were new to fighting disciplined soldiers, and, confounded at the storm of lead and shot to which they were exposed, they fell back in disorder.

At this time Lieutenant Edwardes, who had crossed the river in a small boat, arrived upon the spot. He found the most utter confusion prevailing; the excitement had apparently dissipated the remains of sense in Futteh Muhommud's brain, and the old man was sitting under a tree counting his beads apathetically, while a group of officers were standing round vainly endeavouring to recall his shattered senses and to get him to issue orders. Lieutenant Edwardes at once took

the command. He saw at once that after the severe check the Bhawulpoor men had received, and amid the confusion that prevailed, the battle was lost if the enemy at once advanced. Turning to Peer Ibraheem, who had just arrived, and the chief officers, he pointed out that the enemy had taken up a strong position and evidently expected to be attacked, and that therefore they had time to get the men in order and to retrieve the day.

The guns of the nawab were old pieces of various sizes, quite unfit for service, and there was no hope of successfully contending against the far better guns and experienced artillerymen of the enemy. Nothing could therefore be done until General Cortlandt arrived with his artillery, which was a match for that of the Sikhs. He therefore ordered that the troops, after being got into order, should all lie down, and that the guns should keep up an incessant even if an ineffectual fire. Feeling confidant now that they had a commander on whom they could rely, the officers hurried away to carry out their instructions, and similar orders were sent to the Pathans, who had with the greatest difficulty been restrained from following the example of the Bhawulpoor men and rushing against the enemy's position. A messenger was instantly sent off to Cortlandt, urging him to get his guns across the river with the greatest possible despatch and to bring them forward to the field of battle.

Lieutenant Edwardes then rode along the line, and was loudly cheered both by the allies and his own men. The latter had stuck their standards upright in the turf and were lying down in a line behind them. When he had made an inspection of the line and seen that his orders had been carried out, Edwardes despatched another messenger to Cortlandt lest the first should have gone astray, telling him that he thought it possible to hold the position until three o'clock in the afternoon, but that if he did not arrive with the guns by that time the battle would be lost.

It was now but eight o'clock in the morning, and for several hours this body of undisciplined troops would have to support in patience the fire of the enemy, a situation most trying even for the most disciplined soldiers. For six hours it continued without slackening. The enemy's guns were directed principally to the right, where the Bhawulpoor artillery continued to fire steadily, but sufficient shot fell among the Pathans to work them up into a state of desperation, so that numbers kept leaping to their feet and demanding to be led against the enemy instead of lying there to be killed without even firing a shot.

At two o'clock Futteh Muhommud recovered his senses sufficiently to issue an order for his army to retire, and as it was supposed that the order was authorized by Edwardes it was obeyed, and without the latter being aware of what was taking place the Bhawulpoor force gradually fell back. From his position on the opposite hill Rung Ram, who was in command of the enemy, observed the movement and at once prepared to take advantage of it. He sent forward his cavalry to reconnoitre, and moved his infantry and artillery slowly down the hill. Hitherto ten camel guns that the Pathans had brought across the river with them had been silent, as the men were partly concealed in the jungle, and Lieutenant Edwardes was anxious to avoid betraying their position and drawing the fire of the enemy upon them by the use of these small pieces, which could do but little execution at that distance.

It was now necessary to run the risk, and the camel guns opened upon the enemy's cavalry, who cantered back to their lines in disorder. Their guns, however, at once began to play, and their shot tore into the jungle, rendering it more difficult than ever for Lieutenant Edwardes to restrain the impetuosity of his men. The enemy's cavalry soon rallied and again advanced. As nothing had been heard of the guns, and the moment was most critical, Edwardes ordered Foujdar and all the chiefs and mounted officers to form into a compact body and charge the enemy's cavalry. Delighted at being at last employed on service however dangerous, the brave fellows mounted and with a shout charged down upon the enemy, and, in spite of their inferior numbers, drove them back in headlong flight upon their infantry. They rallied quickly, however, and the whole line again advanced.

"I cannot longer delay," Lieutenant Edwardes said to Percy; "our only chance is in a general charge. If we remain here we must be beaten, whereas if we go at them and escape annihilation by the artillery and musketry as we advance it is just possible we may be successful."

He rose from his seat under a tree to give the order, when a bugle sound was heard in the rear. As if by magic the sound of excited and angry talk along the Pathan line ceased, until a minute later the bugle-call was again heard. .

There was no mistaking it. Van Cortlandt's guns had passed the river and would soon be at hand, the long and terrible time of waiting was over, and at last the tables would be turned. Messengers were sent off to the guns to tell their commander how urgent was the need of their arrival, while officers were despatched all along the line of Pathans to bid the men stand up, and, when the word was given, to advance in good order and in regular line, company by company, against the enemy. With shouts of delight the Pathans sprang to their feet, standards were plucked up and waved enthusiastically in the air, and then the long line stood panting, eager as greyhounds in the slips, for the order to advance. Soon the rumble of guns was heard, and then amid wild cheers the six guns passed through a space opened for their passage, unlimbered, and opened fire upon the advancing enemy.

The effect was instantaneous. The Sikhs, believing that the day was won, were advancing in good order through the intervening fields of sugar-cane, breast-high; but as the balls sung overhead they disappeared from sight, dropping among the canes as suddenly as if each had been mortally struck. They had believed that the only guns opposed to them, those on the right, had left the field, and at the discharge in regular order of guns of equal weight and calibre, the truth broke upon them that the force under the white officer who had so long withstood them had crossed the river and was ranged on the field before them. Not only had the guns arrived, but Van Cortlandt had managed to send two of his Mussulman infantry regiments with them, and these, breathless with the speed at which they had hurried after the guns, now came clattering up. They were ordered to lie down to the right and left of the guns, while the Pathans took post behind them.

For a few minutes the guns of the contending forces discharged volleys of grape at each other, but Cortlandt's gunners were better trained and cooler. Two of the enemy's pieces were silenced and as the men serving the others were in confusion, Edwardes gave the word for the Mussulman regiments to charge. With a cheer the brave fellows dashed forward at full speed, but not so swiftly but that a little party of seven or eight of the Pathans' mounted officers dashed past them, and charging the guns captured two of them while the gunners were in the act of hastily withdrawing them before the approach of the charging infantry. The infantry captured the only other gun which awaited the assault. During the charge Cortlandt's guns poured grape into the canes where the enemy's infantry were lying. Hearing their own artillery retiring, the infantry abandoned their cover and retreated at full speed, rallying, however, at the point where their guns halted, when the artillery on both sides renewed their duel. The Pathans were now ordered to charge, and with a yell expressive of their delight at the prospect of avenging their losses during the long hours of the day, they rushed forward through the smoke.

The enemy were unable to withstand the onset of the brave irregulars and the two newly arrived regiments, but hastily retired, falling more and more into confusion, and pressed in their retreat by the eager Pathans, while the nawab's troops, anxious to retrieve their first retreat, now hotly pressed on the enemy's left. Something like order was maintained by the Sikhs until they reached the crest of ^the hill on which they had been posted during the early hours of the day. Then they threw away their arms and fled in utter disorder towards Mooltan, pursued by the nawab's cavalry, and mowed down by the guns that opened upon them as soon as they could be got into position on the hill.

Eight out of the ten guns that they had brought from Mooltan were captured by the victors. Some twelve hundred were slain, and great numbers of the fugitives at once made for their homes. Their Pathan cavalry had, for the most part, remained inactive during the day, and the heaviest loss fell upon the revolted Sikh regiments, the Goorkhas who had so basely deserted Agnew suffering very severely. The loss upon the part of the allies mounted to three hundred killed or wounded. The enemy's tents, ammunition, and stores at Noonar all fell into the hands of the victors.

Percy had remained with Lieutenant Edwardes but a short time, having been despatched by him to aid Peer Ibraheem in keeping the Bhawulpoor men in their position. When the order had come for them to retreat he had made his way as rapidly as possible through the jungle to inform Edwardes of what had taken place, but arrived only in time to see the charge of the mounted officers.

"You must get them back into their places again, Groves. Here is an order to Peer Ibraheem; " and he scribbled a line on the page of a note-book and tore it out. " He is to bring them back into position again, and to disregard any orders that Futteh Muhommud may give."

Percy hurried away again, and by his exertions and those

of Peer Ibraheem the Bhawulpoor men were brought up in time to join in the final charge and pursuit of the enemy. He accompanied the native cavalry as they chased the fugitives across the country, and it was almost dark before he returned to the scene of battle. Edwardes shook him warmly by the hand as he dismounted.

" It has been a great day, Groves, but I would not go through those seven hours' waiting again for any money that could be offered me; it was an awful time."

"It was, indeed," Percy agreed. "I thought at one time that it was all up with us."

"So did I. It was well indeed that you were able to bring up the nawab's men in time. They were not wanted for the righting, but if it had not been for their horse the rebels would have got away in some sort of order, and their leaders might have taken them in a body into Mooltan. As it is, I expect the great proportion of them will scatter to their homes. I have just sent off a messenger with my report of the engagement to the Resident. It will be a relief to him, for although he gave way at last to my entreaties, I know he thought I ought never to have crossed the Indus. Now, if they will but give us leave, I think that we can take Mooltan."

A few days later Lieutenant Lake, who had been appointed political agent to the nawab, arrived at the camp, thereby relieving Edwardes of the anxiety caused by the inefficiency of Futteh Muhommud, as Lake's auhority completely overrode that of the general. He was, too, an intimate friend of Edwardes, and being full of life and animation, he was a great addition to the pleasure of the little mess. Marching forward, they were joined by Sheikh Emamoodeen with the remains of his division. His Sikh troops had all deserted him, and he had with him but a few Mussulman infantry and a strong body of cavalry.

On the ist of July the force started for its last march towards Mooltan. They had received news that the Sikh gooroo —a

man regarded with the greatest veneration — had, after consulting the stars, declared that day to be a most auspicious one, and that Moolraj had decided, therefore, upon again giving battle. He came out in great force, and took up his position at a bridge across a wide and deep canal. As this could not be forced without heavy loss, Edwardes moved along the west of the canal towards Mooltan.

Moolraj followed on the other side of the canal, crossed by a bridge near Mooltan, and at one o'clock moved forward against Edwardes in order of battle. The Bhawulpoor men, commanded by Lieutenant Lake, were on the right; General Cortlandt's two regiments and ten guns were on the right centre; the Pathan levies were next to these, having on their left Sheikh Emamoodeen's troops. The battle began on the right, Lieutenant Lake seizing some mounds in front of him, and placing his guns there opened a heavy fire on the enemy's left. This was returned by the Sikh guns, and in a short time the battle became general along the whole line. The village of Suddoosam was in the centre of the enemy's position. His troops lay for the most part concealed in jungle, the guns occupying two or three small villages. The allies were superior in artillery, and the rebel guns were presently obliged to withdraw from their position.

The order was then given for an advance, and the whole line pressed forward. Village after village was captured at the point of the bayonet, the Sikhs, inflamed with religious ardour, offering most determined resistance, favoured by the nature of the ground, which was largely covered with jungle and date groves and intersected by irrigation canals. There was, however, no check in the advance A brilliant charge was made by one of Cortlandt's regiments led by Mr. Quin, a young man who had a few days before come up as clerk or writer to Lieutenant Edwardes. The guns were captured, the whole line then went forward with a rush, and the enemy broke and fled in complete disorder.

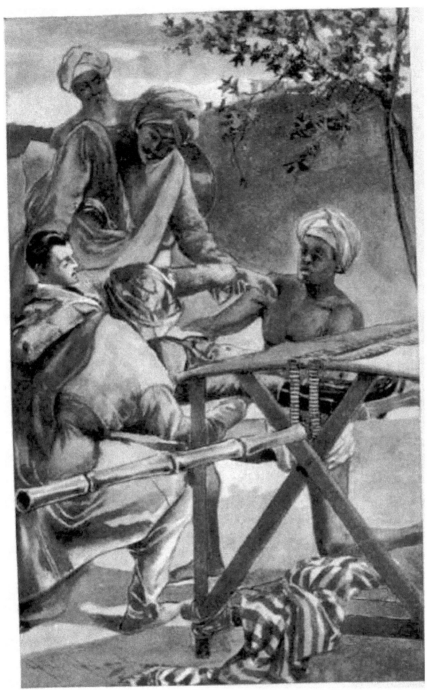

PERCY IS CARRIED OUT OF THE FIGHT WOUNDED.

The loss on the part of the allies in killed and wounded was under three hundred; that of the enemy was vastly greater, being the result to a large extent of the cowardice of Moolraj, who was the first to leave the field, and who, in order to check pursuit, planted guns at the bridge over the canal, with orders to allow no one to pass. The Sikh fugitives on their arrival were fired at by the artillery; the greater part of the crowd, pressed hard by their pursuers, forced a passage, but hundreds were drowned in trying to cross the canal. At the close of the day the allied force halted for the night within range of the guns of the fortress.

Percy saw but little of the fight, as early in the advance he was struck by a matchlock ball while riding forward with the Pathan cavalry. He for a moment lost sensibility and fell. When he recovered himself his two followers were beside him.

"Where am I hit?" he asked.

" In the left shoulder, sahib; it is a bad wound, and will be troublesome, but thanks be to Allah, it might have been much worse. Now that you have recovered I will fetch up a dhooly with its bearers and carry you on after the others. The white sahibs will know best what should be done with your wound."

A few minutes later Percy was placed in a dhooly, and was borne in the rear of the advancing troops, and as soon as these halted for the night he was brought forward to the house which had been chosen by Edwardes as his head-quarters.

" Not badly hurt, I hope, Groves? " that officer said, running out from the house as soon as he heard that Percy was outside. " I have been wondering what has become of you, but had no idea you had been hit."

"I do not think that it is serious," Percy said. "My left shoulder-bone is smashed, I think, by a ball, but my men were close behind me, and bandaged it up; then one of them fetched a dhooly for me, and we have been following pretty close behind you all the afternoon."

" Lake and I will bandage it up properly, and will soon have you comfortable. It is a nuisance that we haven't an English surgeon with us. These native doctors are quite useless. If it is nothing worse than a smashed shoulder I think we can manage well enough, and you may hope to be about again with your arm in a sling before long. The only thing we have to be afraid of in this hot place is fever. Still, I hope that we shall avoid that."

During the weeks that followed Percy lay on a charpoy. • The heat was terrible, although everything possible was done by putting tatties in front of all the windows and keeping them soaked with water; Bhop Lai and his comrade sat by turns night and day fanning him, while a punka made of a door taken off its hinges, was kept constantly going overhead. He was not alone in his misfortunes, for Lieutenant Edwardes was lying, also wounded, in a bed in the same room. Two days after the battle he had, on the news that the enemy were again sallying out, hastily thrust his pistols into his belt, but being engaged in giving orders he paid little heed to what he was doing. The hammer of one of the pistols caught in his scarf, and without looking down he seized the barrel in his right hand to pull it down, when the pistol exploded. The ball went through the palm of his hand, shattering the bones and inflicting a wound that deprived him of the use of his right hand for life.

Fortunately, twelve days later, an English surgeon arrived from Lahore, and at once afforded him some relief from the intense pain he was suffering from the unskillful treatment of a native surgeon. Percy, too, gained great benefit from the arrival of the doctor, and was in a few days able to be about with his arm strapped tightly to his side. Immediately after the battle of Suddoosam Edwardes had written off to Lahore begging that a few heavy guns might be sent to him, in order that he might undertake the siege of the place, which he, Lieutenant Lake, and General Cortlandt were convinced could

be successfully carried out, Moolraj's garrison being greatly weakened by desertions after the two battles, and disheartened by the failure of the gooroo's prophecies. The request had been refused by the governor-general and the commander-in-chief, whose opinion was that no operations should be undertaken by English troops until the hot season was over.

He pointed out that Lieutenant Edwardes, who had now received the rank of brevet-major as a reward for his great services, had carried out all that he had proposed to do. The districts to the west and south of Mooltan had been wrested from Moolraj, and the collection of revenue was going on quietly and regularly. Moolraj was couped up in Mooltan, and was practically powerless for mischief, therefore all that was necessary was that Edwardes should carry out the plan he himself had originally proposed, namely, to drive Moolraj into his fortress and blockade him there through the hot season.

A few days later, however, Sir Frederick Currie, influenced by a letter Edwardes had sent him before the decision of the government had been arrived at, determined to take upon himself the responsibility of ordering General Whish, with two regiments of European and two of native infantry, three regiments of native cavalry, three companies of European and one of native artillery, and two troops of native horse-artillery to march from Lahore. They left on the 24th of July, were taken down by water to Bhawulpoor, and reached Mooltan on the i8th of August. The heavy guns, however, did not arrive until the 4th of September.

In addition to the pain Edwardes had been suffering from his wounds he had been going through a period of great anxiety. The whole Sikh nation was in a ferment. The disasters that had befallen Moolraj had in no way checked their ardour. Chuttur Singh, the father of Sher Singh, was in open rebellion, and had, it was known, been urging his son in the name alike of patriotism, religion, and family honour to join

in a great national effort to wipe out the defeats of the last campaign and to restore to the Punjaub its lost territory.

So far Sher Singh had resisted these entreaties, and had given every evidence of ,his desire to remain faithful to the government of Lahore. But from the first he had been almost powerless in the hands of his troops. Numbers of them had deserted and made their way to Mooltan. Constant communications were kept up with the rebels, and it was certain that at the first opportunity that offered the whole force would go over in a body to Moolraj. While the battles of Korey-shee and Suddoosam were being fought, the divisions remained inactive at a little more than a day's march from Mooltan, and Moolraj showed, by sending out every available man to attack the force of Edwardes, that he had no fear whatever of hostility on the part of the Sikhs. When, therefore, a few days after Suddoosam, Sher Singh's army advanced and encamped within half a mile of the allies, a heavy burden was added to the various anxieties of the wounded English commander. Sher Singh himself visited him frequently, and was profuse in his declarations of loyalty, as were the two officers next in command, Uttur and Shumsher Singh; but while the former hoped that his troops would remain faithful, his two lieutenants were absolutely convinced that they would all go over to the enemy.

Edwardes felt that should the understanding between the Sikhs and Moolraj be complete, and the former fall upon his flank while the whole Mooltan force attacked him in front, his position would be one of the greatest difficulty. It was a great relief to him when two or three more English officers came up, and he was at last certain that the orders he issued from his bed of sickness would be thoroughly carried out by them. It was a still heavier load off his mind when General Whish arrived with his force, and assumed the command of the siege operations.

By this time he himself was able to get about, and Percy's

wound was almost completely healed. On the 7th of September the plans for the siege were arranged at a council of the chief political and military officers. The trenches were opened, but at a much greater distance than usual, as the ground outside the walls was largely occupied with houses and gardens and cut up by small canals. This was all in the hands of the enemy, and it would be necessary to advance gradually step by step. On the gth the fighting began, an attempt being made to carry some houses and ruins occupied by the rebels. The latter, however, defended themselves stoutly, and but little ground was gained.

The Sikhs, who were skilled in defensive warfare, had thrown up numerous intrenchments and stockades in front of our lines, but on the i2th they were attacked and a large village was carried, but only after desperate fighting, some two hundred and fifty men being killed or wounded on the British side. A point was gained, however, close enough to the walls for the establishment of the battering guns, and a few days at most would have seen the British flag waving over the walls of Mooltan, when suddenly Sher Singh with his whole army went over to the enemy.

This defection entirely changed the situation. The addition of the Sikh force of disciplined soldiers to the army of Moolraj raised it to a strength far exceeding that of the besiegers. Even without this addition it had only been by very hard fighting that the British had won their way forward. These difficulties had now been enormously increased. The communications might be threatened and cut off, and even the officers most sanguine of the success of the siege now felt that it was no longer feasible with so small a force.

But their decision to abandon the siege was arrived at chiefly upon other grounds. Until now, although Moolraj had been joined by a great many Sikh deserters, the Sikh nation still stood irresolute, and it was hoped that the capture of Mooltan would have decided them to abstain from engaging in a con-

test which was nominally one between the maharajah and his advisers at Lahore, and Moolraj their rebellious servant. The defection of Sher Singh and the Lahore army, of which he was commander, changed the whole situation. It was certain now that the Sikhs would everywhere rise, and that the whole of the Punjaub would soon be in arms. The capture of Mooltan, therefore, became a matter of secondary importance, and it behoved General Whish to keep his force intact in view of the campaign that must ensue.

Moreover, he could now no longer rely upon his communications being kept open or supplies forwarded, for the Sikh sirdars with their followers might throw themselves on his rear. Lahore itself might fall into the hands of the Sikhs, for since the despatch of General Whish's force to Mooltan it was very weakly garrisoned. It was, therefore, unanimously decided that for the present the siege must be raised, and the army, abandoning its new works, fell back a couple of miles and took up a strong defensive position, expecting to be attacked by the allied forces of Moolraj and Sher Singh.

No such attack was, however, made. Sher Singh had up to the last moment so strongly opposed the wishes of his troops to go over, that when at last he gave way, Moolraj suspected the movement to be a snare and refused to open the gates of Mooltan to the Sikhs. His suspicions were heightened by a letter that Edwardes sent to Sher Singh by the hand of a messenger whose fidelity he strongly suspected. As he anticipated, the letter was carried to Moolraj, and was of a nature to increase very greatly his suspicions of the good faith of Sher Singh. The latter, however, at once issued proclamations, which were signed and sealed by himself, Moolraj, and the principal officers and sirdars, calling upon the whole Sikh nation to rise.

Moolraj still declared that the only thing to satisfy his mind would be for Sher Singh to issue out and attack the British

position. This he did, but as soon as the English artillery began to play upon him his troops retired hastily, their conduct increasing the suspicion felt by Moolraj of their intentions. The ill feeling between the allies increased until on the 9th of October Sher Singh marched away with his army to join the Sikh force already in arms, plundering and burning all the Mahomedan villages through which he passed.

The news of his defection was followed immediately by the revolt of the Sikh troops at Bunnoo and other places, and in the course of two or three weeks the whole Sikh nation was under arms; and the work that had been done, and as was hoped completed, at Moodkee,

Ferozeshah, Aliwal, and So-braon, had to be begun afresh.

Percy Groves was not with the British force that fell back from its position four or five hundred yards from the walls of Mooltan. Three or four days before Sher Singh's defection Major Edwardes had said to him:

" Mr. Groves, I think it would be best for you to take up your quarters with Sher Singh's force. His position is a difficult one; he is weak and vacillating, and it would be well that he should have someone by his side to whom he could appeal frequently; the presence too of a British officer would strengthen his authority with his troops. I have no doubt he is well disposed, but the influence brought to bear on him is tremendous. As a son it would be contrary to Sikh notions of honour to oppose his father, however much he might differ from him. Then there are the appeals to his patriotism and to his religion. He knows that the whole of his men are in favour of revolt, and there are but two or three of his officers who are not of the same way of thinking. I do not say that there is not some danger in your taking up your abode among them, for if he goes over he will go over suddenly; but, even if he does, I cannot think that he would suffer you to be injured. He is not a fanatic, and would see that did any harm come to you he would have no hope whatever of pardon.

You will, of course, ride in here at once should you discover that there is any change in his attitude towards us."

Percy accordingly moved across to Sher Singh's camp, a tent being erected there for him. He liked the rajah, of whom he had seen a good deal since his arrival, and, like Edwardes, was convinced that his assurances of loyalty were made in good faith, and believed he would be perfectly safe whatever might happen, and that he was sure to have warning of any change in Sher Singh's intentions.

CHAPTER XVII
WITH SHER SINGH

SHER SINGH had at once acceded to the proposal of Major Edwardes that Percy Groves should establish himself in his camp. "Let him come," he said; "he will see that all I say to you is true, and that I am a faithful servant of the maharajah. There is nothing I wish to hide from him or from you. I have sworn to you over and over again, that I am faithful; and did he live in my tent, he would see how true I am to my oath."

The rajah, indeed, was sore that his fidelity should be suspected, and in his conversations with Percy, after the latter had established himself in a tent close to him, he frequently complained that after having so long withstood the entreaties of his father and the wishes of his troops, he should be suspected. Percy did his best to assure him that personally Major Edwardes had no doubt- of his loyalty, and that he feared only that he might not be able to control the troops.

"But I have so far controlled them," Sher Singh said; " have I not brought them here instead of allowing them to march into Mooltan. Why, then, should I be doubted now? If I had wished to go, would it not have been better that I should have done so before these white troops arrived? You had hard work in beating Moolraj alone; if I had joined him before, Edwardes and the Bhawulpoor troops would have been destroyed."

"Had you joined Moolraj, rajah, we should never have crossed the Indus, nor would the troops of the nawab have been here. Major Edwardes knows well that you have done your best, and believes that did your troops revolt you would ride into our camp. It is not your good-will that he doubts, but your power over your soldiers. We know that they are in hourly communication with the enemy, that they go freely in and out of the town, that messengers pass between them and their countrymen who have gone over; and it is easy to understand that, placed as we are here, and carrying on a siege with but scant forces for such an operation, he cannot but be most anxious regarding a force like yours lying so close to him. But he has still strong hopes that you will be able to keep them firm. Were it otherwise, he would not have sent me here. It is anxiety, and not suspicion, that causes him so earnestly to beg yeu to stand firm."

Bhop Lai and Akram Chunder were both charged to learn as much as they could from the soldiers as to their intentions. Their reports were favourable to the rajah.

"The soldiers are all for Moolraj," Bhop Lai said. "They speak of. the rajah by the nickname of 'the Mahomedan.' It is he alone who keeps them here, for though Uttur Singh and Shumsher both support him, they are almost alone among his officers. Sher Singh is a powerful rajah, and his family one of the first among the sirdars of the Punjaub. That is the reason why he has been able to keep them from going over, for they fear that if they did so in the face of his opposition, they would afterwards suffer at the hands of himself and his family, even if their cause were victorious. All seem agreed that there is no chance of the rajah's throwing in his lot with his father, and they curse him as one who is false to his family, his country, and his religion."

It was then a complete surprise to Percy when, after retiring to bed on the night of the i3th of September, he was suddenly aroused by the entrance of a body of armed men into his tent.

They belonged, as he saw at once, to the rajah's own bodyguard, and were commanded by one of his most trusted officers.

"No harm is intended," the latter said; "the rajah's orders are that you are to be honourably treated, but I must beg you to rise and dress at once, as we are going to move our camp."

Seeing that resistance would be altogether useless, Percy at once rose. After putting on his clothes he saw that his arms had been taken possession of by the soldiers, and that he was in fact a prisoner. Without making a remark, he passed out of the tent, and saw his two men standing there with very crestfallen faces, holding his horse, and surrounded by a body of Sikhs. He mounted, and the Sikh cavalry at once closed in round them. The tents had been struck already, the baggage packed, and the troops formed up. Uttur and Shumsher Singh had, as he afterwards learned, done their utmost to carry off the men under their command to the British lines, but they had been surrounded by officers entreating, abusing, and threatening them and stirring up their soldiers till they were forced to abstain from opposing the popular demand.

Uttur Singh had then mounted his horse, and with great difficulty made his way through the crowd, riding off to carry the intelligence to Major Edwardes, followed by two other officers. Shumsher Singh had been carried off as a prisoner, and was confined in his tent; but the next night he managed to crawl out under the bottom of the tent, and made his way in common clothes and bare-footed several miles to the British camp, killing on the road one of Sher Singh's vedettes, who tried to arrest him. Two, therefore, out of the three Sikh leaders justified Major Edwardes' belief in their fidelity.

On arriving at the new place of encampment under the walls of the fort, Percy remained for an hour in the centre of

his guard, and was then conducted to his tent, which had again been pitched. Half an hour later his two servants came in; both were deeply humiliated that they should have given their master no warning of what was coming, and poured out their apologies and expressions of regret.

"It is not your fault in any way," Percy said; "it was but yesterday afternoon that the rajah was even warmer than usual in his protestations of loyalty, and yet at that time he must have fully made up his mind as to his course. Had the troops known it yesterday you would certainly have noticed a difference in their bearing. He cannot have issued any orders until late in the evening, and you see he took measures for my protection by sending his own bodyguard to protect me; and has probably carried me off partly as a hostage and partly perhaps with the thought that I may be useful should circumstances make it necessary for him again to enter into negotiations with our people. How is it we have not entered the fort?"

" The Sikhs intended to go in, sahib, but Moolraj kept the gates closed, and sent orders that they were to encamp here under the guns of the fort. I suppose that he is afraid of treachery. The Sikhs are very angry."

"I suppose they have taken your arms," Percy said.

"Yes, sahib; we were sleeping at the door of your tent, they pounced upon us suddenly, twisting scarfs round our mouths to prevent our calling out. They carried us a short distance away, and then released us. They ordered us to saddle our horses and yours, and warned us that if we made the least outcry it would be the signal for your death as well as our own."

In the morning Sher Singh came into the tent. "I am sorry that I have been compelled to make you prisoner, Sahib Groves, but I had no choice. Had I not done so, the stir among the troops would have awoke you, and you might have carried the news to your camp in time for horsemen and guns

to interfere with our movements. I did it, too, as much for your protection as my own, for some of the troops might have rushed in and killed you had you not been in the hands of my own guard."

"I thank you for that, rajah," Percy said quietly; "but my life is of little consequence in comparison to other matters. Until now it has only been a question of the overthrow of a dewan who refused to render obedience to his government, and whom you and your army were despatched to conquer. Instead of this, your army has gone over and joined his. You know, even better than I do, what that means: that all the Punjaub will be up, and that tens of thousands of lives will be lost. I can only hope that you, like myself, are here against your will."

"No," the rajah said passionately. "I was faithful, and I was doubted. I withstood the entreaties of my father, the adjurations of the chief men of my religion, and the wishes of my army; but when I found that in spite of all this, I was suspected, it was useless for me to strive longer. I am no longer a general of the durbar of Lahore, but a Sikh prince."

"I am truly sorry to hear it," Percy said gravely, "for your own sake, and for that of the Punjaub. There can be but one end to it. If, when the whole Khalsa army was intact, the Sikhs could not withstand the advance of a weak British force to Lahore, what chance have they against such an army as will be collected now? The last time England astonished the Sikhs by her clemency, and by taking so little when all was in her power. She thought that her strength and her clemency would alike have made such an impression that the Sikhs would henceforth be content and remain in peace. This time she will assuredly make no such mistake, and I consider that your highness' defection will lead to the destruction of the independence of the Punjaub."

"That we shall see," the rajah said. "Last time but a small portion of our sirdars took up arms. You had but to

fight against troops who had long lost their discipline; now you will have the whole of the Sikh nation against you."

"Were the Sikh nation ten times as numerous as they are," Percy said quietly, " the end would be the same. However, as your highness has now taken your course, it is useless for me to endeavour to dissuade you. I have to thank you for having taken means to secure my safety, but I should have thanked you still more had you ordered your bodyguard to conduct me to our camp instead of- bringing me here."

"That I could not do," Sher Singh replied; " it would have caused my own men to suspect me; but, be assured that you will be well and honourably treated. I told you I regarded you as a guest in my camp, and as a guest you will always be treated; save in the matter of your liberty, every wish you may express will be granted; and if at any time you have any complaint to make, send me a message and I will come and see you and set matters right."

In the morning, when Sher Singh's men were about to march against the British camp, Bhop Lai said to Percy: "There will be no fighting, sahib. The Sikhs are very angry at the refusal of Moolraj to admit them into the town, and they say they have not revolted in order to fight for Moolraj, but for their country. They may advance, because the guns of Mooltan look down into their camp, and they dare not therefore refuse; but they will soon be back here again. They are eager to march away, and will do so ere long. Mooltan is nothing to them, and they know well enough that Moolraj is fighting for himself alone, and that were the British expelled, there would be another war to decide whether Moolraj or the Sikhs were to be masters of the Punjaub."

Until the Sikhs marched away on the gih of October Percy did not again see Sher Singh. The rajah, indeed, sent him a message that contained the most bitter complaints against Major Edwardes for having, by the letter that was intercepted, increased the doubts of Moolraj as to his loyalty.

Percy replied that he, of course, knew nothing of the letter; but that a general like Sher Singh must know well that in war it was always a matter of policy on the part of a leader to cause disunion, if possible, between allies opposed to him, and that doubtless he himself would, under similar circumstances, have acted in precisely the same manner.

There was no actual prohibition against Percy leaving his tent, but the officer in command of the guard, who kept a vigilant watch round it, strongly advised him not to do so.

"The rajah has given you into my charge," he said, "and holds me responsible for your safety. But how can I guarantee that, if you go about in the camp? I might surround you with a guard, and yet a musket or pistol ball fired by a fanatic might hit you. It is far better that you should remain in your tent, where you are out of sight of all, and out of their thoughts. If they once see you about, the fanatics might stir up the men to demand your life, and to insist that Sher Singh should give us some stronger proof of his hostility to the English, as Moolraj did when he permitted the murder of the two English officers; and although the rajah wishes you well, he may be unable to resist the demands of the troops, who are rather his masters than he theirs."

Percy felt the justice of the argument, and remained quietly in his tent, where he learned from his two followers all that was passing, as these in their native costume were able to move about freely among the Sikhs, of whom indeed but few were aware that the servants of the British officer, who had been carried off with them, had also been taken. Both the men, being Mahomedans, burned with indignation at the atrocities committed by the Sikhs upon the Mussulman villages on the line of march, where they burned the houses, robbed the people, defiled the mosques, and murdered the priests.

"Is that the way to fight for the independence of their country, sahib? Are there not great numbers of Mahomedans in the Punjaub, and is it not enough to have to fight the

English without making every Mahomedan hostile to them? It was not so before. Mahomedans and Sikhs were of one mind as to the independence of the Punjaub. Now the

Mahomedans will be as one man in their hopes that the British will win. They know that under the British masters every man can worship in his own way without interference; and they must see now that if the Sikhs conquer, they will root out the Mahomedans from among them. Akram and I followed you, sahib, and stood the fire of the Sikh guns because our lord had bidden us guard you, but except for that our hearts were rather with the Sikhs than with your countrymen, for have we not taken Sikh pay and fought under Sikh standards? Henceforth it is different. The Sikhs have showed themselves our bitter enemies, and all our hopes must now be with the English."

"You see no chance of my escape? "

"None at all at present; four guards watch day and night near your tent. We are forced to picket our horses in the lines of the Sikh troopers, and your horse is placed among those of the rajah, whence we have to fetch it every morning for the march. A party of sowars always ride with us to fetch it, and accompany us back. Of course we both have knives, which we have stolen at night from sleeping men; and we could get other arms, but we do not see that at present we could do anything with them."

"No, there is no possibility of escaping in the daytime," Percy agreed. "The men who ride beside me always have chains between their horses' bits and mine, so there is no possibility of my making a sudden dash for it, as I otherwise would have done. If I once got beyond the range of their pistols I should have little fear of being overtaken, for there can be few horses in the camp that are a match for Sheik."

Day after day passed; the officer in charge of Percy in no way relaxed his vigilance; the orders of Sher Singh being most emphatic as to the care to be exercised in guarding his prisoner. He learned from his followers the rumours current in the camp that the Sikh troops at Bunnoo and Rhotas had also mutinied, and were upon the point of effecting a junction with Sher Singh's force. They were considered the flower of the Sikh army, being composed entirely of old soldiers with trained cavalry and artillery. Sher Singh was marching to Lahore, and although the people there were for the time powerless in face of the force that had been hurried up to hold the city as soon as the defection of Sher Singh was known, they were reported as ready to rise at the first appearance of the army before their walls.

Some of the Sikh cavalry had been pushed on ahead of the army, with orders to destroy the bridge of boats across the Ravee, a mile and a half from Lahore. They succeeded in burning some of the boats, but were then driven off by the 14th Light Dragoons under Colonel Havelock. So far no large force of the British had arrived. A brigade with one English regiment had been pushed forward, and one of cavalry had assembled at Ferozepore, and native reports stated that large reinforcements were going forward tc General Whish and others advancing towards Ferozepore. Sher Singh's army moved but slowly, and it was still the opinion of many British officers that, although constrained to desert us at Mooltan, he would be glad to make his peace as soon as a strong British army approached him.

At the end of the first week in November the first British division under General Thackwell crossed the Sutlej and advanced towards Lahore, and two days later the commander-in-chief, with General Gilbert's division, followed it. The heavy guns had not yet come up, but were only a short distance behind, and the general was anxious to interpose his force between Lahore and the Sikh army, which might any day advance to its attack. He remained for two days at Lahore, Thackwell's division having already advanced.

"They will be here in two or three days, sahib," Akram

Chunder said one morning to Percy. " We have a strong position here on the right bank of the Chenab, and how the English are going to cross I don't know; still they will do it somehow, that is quite certain. Now, sahib, is the time. You must look to yourself; so long as the Sikhs are confident of victory no doubt you will be as well treated as you are at present; but if they are defeated, as we very well know they will be, who could answer for your life? Sher Singh will have enough to do to look after his own safety, and even if the soldiers did not rush in and kill you, these men of your guard will not want to be encumbered with a prisoner, and they would know that, after a defeat, no one is likely to inquire much about you. So you must try to escape. The worst of it is, that with your friends so close, they will be more watchful than ever, for this is the time that you would be naturally trying to get away to join them. The officer looks so sharp after the guard, that I fear there is no chance of giving them liquor and making them drunk or of drugging them. They are forbidden even to speak to us as we go in and out. We are allowed to attend on you by the rajah's orders, but I have no doubt the officer is afraid we might try to bribe his men. Bhop Lai and I have talked it over in every way, but we can see no means of getting you out."

" I can see no way myself, Akram; the sentries are very vigilant, they keep constantly on the move, and they challenge anyone who approaches within twenty yards. If they were to march during the night I would take my chance of slipping off my horse, for it is impossible, chained as it is to the others, to dash through with it. That is the only possibility of escape that I can see at present."

"I can see no other, sahib, but unfortunately they never have marched at night; still they may do so, and the first time they do we might try it. The worst of it is, that we shall not be near you, sahib. You see, on the march we always have to keep with the cavalry, among whom our horses are picketed."

"Well, at any rate, Akram, let it be a distinct understanding that if we are suddenly ordered to make a night-march, and I have no opportunity of speaking to you before we move, I mean to make my escape; and if by any possibility you can do the same you are to do so."

"As we have told you often, sahib, there is no difficulty about us. They have got pretty well accustomed to us now, and believe that we are all in favour of their cause, though we remain with you, because, in the first place, we are attached to you, and in the second, because we have wives and families who are in the hands of your uncle the colonel, and we dare not therefore leave you. So they have come to believe that we have no wish to escape at all, and pay no attention to us on the line of march. Of course we ride at the rear of the regiment, and the last four men were always told off to ride behind us; but they have given that up long ago, and we could easily drop behind without being observed, on a night-march. The difficulty would be to find you after your escape."

"That can't be helped, Akram. If I do escape, I will make my way back to the last place at which we halted; and if you get away, do the same. If we find each other there, all the better; if not, we must make our way separately as best we can to the British lines, wherever they may be. I will, if I can, come to the spot where this tent was pitched; we shall all know the position pretty well, and ought to be able to get somewhere near it, even on a dark night. Now, remember that these are final orders, if I have no opportunity to give you others. The first night there is a march—whether before a battle has been fought or aftenvards—I shall try to escape. If I do not appear at our last halting-place during the night, you are to go straight on to our lines; and if I do not turn up there in the course of a couple of days, you will know that I have either failed to make my escape, or been killed in attempting it."

" I understand, sahib; and you may be sure Bhop Lai and 1 will act according to your orders."

Two days later there was a great hubbub heard in the camp. Bhop Lai, looking out from the door of the tent, said:

" The army has come, sahib. The Sikhs on the other bank are retiring."

Percy went to the entrance of the tent, which faced the river, and stood there looking out. Numbers of horse and foot could be seen crossing. A cloud of dust rose a mile and a half away, while in camp there was the deep rumble of guns as these were brought up to the river to command the passage.

"They are cavalry, sahib," Bhop Lai said, as amid the cloud of dust there was a sparkle of steel, and a body of horse came dashing forward. Almost at the same instant the crack of guns was heard and shells burst over and among the Sikhs on the other side of the river, greatly hastening their movements. The bed of the river was of great width, but was now for the most part dry. On the other side the bank was high, and from its foot a very wide bed of sand extended to what, in the wet season, was a green island in the middle of the river. The stream itself ran on the Sikh side of the island.

Before the British cavalry and guns came up, the last of the Sikh force on the other side were well on their way across the river, but the guns were at once unlimbered and sent shot after shot into them, until they were almost across and out of range, for the width from bank to bank was nearly two miles.

Not content with this, two British batteries moved down from the bank, and charged across the sand, from time to time firing at the Sikhs retreating across the ford; but when they came near the edge of the river the Sikh batteries on the high bank opened upon them.

"They will have to fall back," Percy said; "the guns here are much heavier than theirs, and they can never remain there in the open exposed to this fire."

It was not long before the officers commanding the British

batteries discovered this, and gave the order for the guns to limber up. Some confusion was visible among them. The horses were taken from two of the guns and attached to another.

"That gun has got into a quicksand or something of that sort," Percy said, "and they can't move it."

The Sikhs were not long in seeing this. The fire of their guns was redoubled, and the infantry at once paused in their passage of the ford and returned in great numbers to the left bank and opened a heavy musketry fire.

"They will have to leave the guns behind them," Percy said, as the artillery mounted and rode off. The guns, indeed, dragged so heavily through the deep sand that a squadron of the 3d Light Dragoons galloped forward to cover their retreat. Dashing over the sand they swept round the island where some hundreds of the enemy were drawn up, cut their way through them, sabring numbers, and then r in spite of the fire of six guns on the opposite bank, cantered back again. They had only one man wounded and two horses killed. Other charges were made by the 3d Dragoons and 8th Light Cavalry, but the Sikhs took refuge in nullahs, and kept up such a galling musketry fire that the cavalry drew off. The Sikhs now exultingly advanced to the abandoned gun, and as from the river bed the British force could no longer be seen, numbers of them made their way across the sand, ascended the high bank, and opened fire at the troops halted within rifle-shot.

"They won't be there long," Percy said to his men. "You will see them coming back quicker than they went in a minute or two: look at that body of cavalry sweeping down upon them."

The Sikhs, too, saw the danger, and came rushing in a confused mass down the bank. The cavalry, as he learned afterwards, consisted of the i4th Dragoons under Colonel Havelock, supported by the 5th Light Cavalry. The impetu' osity of the gallant leader of the i4th carried him away, and followed by his men he dashed down the bank in pursuit, with the intention of driving the Sikhs back again over the river. But great numbers had now crossed the ford; some guns had been placed near the islands, and these and the batteries on the other bank opened a heavy fire upon the cavalry.

Encouraged by the fire of their guns and by their numerical strength, the fugitives now made a stand. The horses of the dragoons were already blown, and with difficulty made their way through the deep sand; but Havelock charged into the middle of the enemy well in advance of his men, and disappeared from their sight. They tried to urge their horses after him, but could not break through the infantry, while the Sikh guns still continued their heavy fire. Colonel Cureton, who commanded the cavalry, rode forward to recall them from their dangerous position. He himself fell, shot through the heart. For a time the unequal contest was continued, many desperate single combats taking place between Englishman and Sikh; but at last the i4th were called off, having had upwards of fifty men killed and wounded.

" It seems to me," Percy said, as the last of the cavalry rode up the opposite bank, " that was a very foolish charge. Suppose they had driven the Sikhs across the river, they could not have stayed to guard the ford with all these guns playing upon them, and the Sikhs could have recrossed directly they had retired. It seems a pure waste of life."

So thought many others. The charge was as rash and ill-considered as that of Balaclava. Colonel Havelock paid for his mistake by his life, just as did Nolan, who gave the order that led to the charge of the Light Cavalry at Balaclava.

The Sikhs were in high spirits at the advantage they had gained, and complete confidence in themselves took the place of the doubt, that a good many of them had felt, of their power of resisting the British. This increased, as day after day passed, and no forward movement was made from the opposite

bank. It could be seen, however, that the force there had been largely augmented, and that batteries were in course of erection at several points. The Sikh guns fired at times at the working parties, but the distance was too great for the fire to be effective. Bodies of Sikh cavalry crossed the river at other points, and often rode round the rear of the British lines, occasionally cutting off men who had straggled too far out of camp, and then riding off before the English cavalry could mount and pursue them. A few soldiers who were taken alive were carried to the camp, where they were well treated by Sher Singh, and were sent back to the British lines bearing a communication from the rajah expressive of a desire for peace.

But the time had passed for negotiations. It was necessary for the peace of India that the Sikh strength should be broken once and for all, and the answer sent to the rajah was that the commander-in-chief could not treat with men in arms against him. A week passed after the cavalry fight, and then it became known in the Sikh camp that the heavy guns for which the British had been waiting had arrived.

" I do not see the use of those batteries they are erecting on the opposite bank," Akram Chunder remarked, as, standing at the door of the tent, they watched what was going on. The Sikhs too had been working hard; strong works had been erected commanding the ford, and a number of guns placed there in position.

" I do not see any good in it either, Akram; the guns are too far off to be of any use whatever in covering the advance of a column trying to cross. I do not think it is possible to ford the river in the face of such a fire as will be concentrated upon them if they attempt it."

"Then what will they do, sahib? "

" I should say they would send a force either up or down the river to cross at some other point ten or twenty miles away. When they have got across they will either intrench themselves there and defend the ford until the whole army can cross, or they will march this way and attack the camp while the army opposite tries to cross the river."

"There would be great risk in that, sahib, for the Sikhs could throw their whole force on those that have crossed and destroy it before they could get any aid from their friends on the other side."

" Yes, it would be very dangerous, too dangerous to try, I should say, against another European force; but you see, Akram, we have been so accustomed to win battles in India that we feel quite confident of victory even when the odds are three or four to one against us."

Early in the morning of the ist of December Percy heard an unusual stir in the Sikh camp.

"What is the matter?" he asked the officer of the guard when the latter as usual came in for a talk with him.

" A peasant came across before daylight with the news that a large force of your people have marched somewhere down the river. We had thought that they might try to cross at the ford of Ghuree-kee Puttum, and were ready to receive them, but they have not gone there. It is supposed they have gone to Wuzeerabad."

"How far is that away? "

"Twenty-four miles."

" Have you any force there ? "

" No, it is a very bad ford, and unless they get some boats they can hardly cross there; but we would not stop them if we could. How the British, who know so much of the art of war, can throw themselves like this into our hands is more than we can tell. We shall let them march up some miles, so that they can no longer retreat to the ford, then we shall fall upon them and exterminate them. We know their force, for the peasant, who was awakened by the noise made by the camp-followers and the growling of the camels and the rumbling of guns, crept up and counted them as they passed.

There were five batteries, two of them native; five regiments of cavalry, four of them native; two white regiments of foot, and five regiments and a half of Sepoys. If you put them at five hundred men to each regiment, there are less than four thousand foot. What is that against the force we can bring against them? They will get to Wuzeerabad to-day, but it is a long march. The white troops will not be ready for much at the end of it, and few will get across to-night. It will be mid-day to-morrow before they are all over, even if they have boats, so that at most they will not arrive nearer than twelve miles by to-morrow night. The next day we shall finish with them."

Percy thought it was as well to keep to himself his conviction that the Sikhs would not find it so easy a business as they anticipated; yet he saw that unless our main army moved across to the attack, and so occupied a large portion of the Sikh force, or else considerably reinforced that advancing up the river bank, the position of the latter was indeed a perilous one. But he still felt confident in their power to resist an attack made upon them.

"I should be glad," he said to his two followers, as he talked the matter over during the day, " if they would move this tent of ours somewhere farther back from the bank. That battery below us is sure to come in for its share of the fire from the guns on the other side, and any ball that goes too high is as likely as not to pass through this tent."

"You may be sure that our guard won't wait here when that happens, sahib; they may leave the tent standing, but they will certainly march themselves and you off out of range."

Late in the afternoon a heavy fire was opened by the batteries on the opposite bank, and as the shells exploded, some over the Sikh batteries, some farther back over the bank, a great hubbub arose. The artillerymen ran down to their guns and replied to the fire. Drums and bugles called the troops under arms, orders were shouted in all directions, and the noises of the horses and baggage animals added to the uproar. The guard at once ran up and surrounded the tent.

"Come out, sahib," the officer said, "we are going to pull it down at once."

"All the better," Percy replied; "I have no desire to be shot by my friends."

The tent was speedily lowered, and it and its contents carried by the men half a mile from the bank and there re-erdcted. All the other tents along the bank were similarly removed.

As Percy had foreseen, the fire from the distant guns inflicted but little damage upon the Sikh batteries, so these, after replying for a short time, ceased to waste their ammunition, and the men retired behind the. shelter of the bank, where they remained until the British fire ceased.

Upon the following morning Percy learned from the officer of his guard that a Sikh horseman, who had been sent down the river, had reported that only a battery of artillery, two regiments of cavalry, and a brigade of infantry had crossed on the previous night, some wading the ford and others being brought over in boats, by which the guns had been conveyed across.

At night he heard that it was two o'clock before all had crossed and the march began, and they would probably halt at Doorewal, which was twelve miles on the way, somewhere about nightfall. The Sikhs reported that the cavalry were scouting in their front and on their left flank, and that the troops were marching in several columns, so that they could at once open out into order of battle if attacked. The guards were in high spirits that night, and sat round a fire laughing and talking until morning. The vigilance of the sentries, however, was in no way relaxed, and the officer several times peeped into the tent to see that all was right.

Before daybreak there was a hum of movement in the camp, and Percy knew that the Sikhs were mustering for the attack.

CHAPTER XVIII

REJOINING

AS Percy went to the door of his tent he saw the Sikhs moving off in solid bodies.

"Those are the Bunnoo regiments," the officer of his guard said, "they are our best. Some of Sher Singh's regiments are good, but they are not equal to those from Bunnoo. They have been drilled by Van Cortlandt, and march as truly and well as the best regiments of the Feringhees. They are going to take their revenge to-day. Every man of them fought at Ferozeshah or Sobraon, many at both, and they will wipe out those defeats to-day. A very strong force is going, nearly the whole indeed. What do we want men here for? They will never venture to cross from the opposite side while our guns sweep the ford. Besides, there is a regiment left to guard it, and the Feringhees cannot tell that Sher Singh has marched with his whole force to exterminate their comrades on this bank. You will not be lonely any more, for to-night there will be many prisoners here, for those who throw down their arms may be spared; I know not the orders Sher Singh has issued, still mercy is sure to be shown to a few. By the way, I have just seen a man who has come from the river bank, and he says that during the night your people have thrown up two batteries about midway between their bank and the river, so as to command the ford. Doubtless they feared that, know-

ing they would be so weakened, we should march across and destroy them. That was indeed the plan advocated by many of our leaders, but it was thought best to destroy this army first; for you see we can fall upon them when entangled in rice-fields and jungle, whereas here we should suffer from the batteries on their bank before we came to close quarters."

As the officer had been very civil to him throughout the march, Percy abstained from dashing his confidence by the expression of a doubt.

"You are going to fall upon them during the march? "

" Yes, and'all the regular horse are to ride round and capture their baggage and then charge down on their rear. The river is on their right, and not a man ought to escape if the affair is well managed."

Throughout the day the guns of the British batteries across the river again maintained their fire, the Sikhs making no reply. Percy from time to time listened attentively, hoping to hear the rattle of musketry that would tell him that Lord Gough was making a vigorous attempt to cross the river in order to give aid to the little column that was cut off from him. He heard that the British were constructing two batteries close to the river, and was astonished that they should be permitted to do this without interruption.

"I was mistaken," the officer said to him at eight o'clock. "I thought that the batteries were still manned, and that a regiment was there. I find that the guns have been withdrawn, and that every man has gone to the fight. It is very strange that, seeing everything is silent, the English do not send a party across the river to reconnoitre. Their commander must be asleep," the Sikh said contemptuously.

" But why has the passage been left open to them? "

"What do we care if they do cross? Your tent is almost the only one left standing. If we saw them appear on the river bank we should mount and ride at once; there are the horses all standing ready. Almost all the baggage is moved

away. I think Sher Singh would be glad if they did cross to-day, then we should come back and attack them in the morning. With the river in their rear, how many would escape?"

It was past mid-day when an exclamation burst from Percy's guard, as the boom of a gun some six or seven miles away was heard.

"The battle has begun," the Sikhs exclaimed.

There was an animated discussion among them as to the distance, but it was agreed at last that it must be somewhere in the neighbourhood of the village of Sadoolapore, which was situated close to a ford, and the British had probably halted there in order to have a loophole for retreat. The halt had indeed been made at this point in order that the infantry brigade of General Godby, which the commander-in-chief had sent to reinforce them, might cross the ford; they had not, however, as yet arrived. The column having halted, prepared to take their breakfast. While so engaged a cannon-shot fell close by, and Nicholson's irregular Pathan horse at once went out in the direction from which the shot was fired, and were soon in contact with the enemy, whose artillery opened a heavy fire.

The troops at once formed up for battle. In front of them were three small villages surrounded by plantations, which afforded an admirable cover for the enemy, and would have enabled them to mass unperceived and to pour down upon our line. Seeing the disadvantage of the position, General Thack-well, who was in command of the force, ordered them to fall back so as to have clear ground in front of them. The movement caused shouts of exultation among the unseen enemy, who construed it into a movement of retreat. Some time, however, elapsed before the Sikh forces had all assembled, but as soon as they had done so their batteries opened fire, while yells of defiance, mingled with the blowing of horns and the beating of drums, added to the tumult of cannon and musketry.

The British infantry lay down on the ground, and the storm of iron and lead swept over them almost harmlessly. Great bodies of the Sikh cavalry now showed on both flanks, with the evident intention of penetrating to the rear, but the cavalry, aided by the horse-artillery, met and checked them on both flanks; while three other batteries, placed in the intervals of the infantry regiments, replied to those of the enemy, and their accurate fire caused considerable confusion among the Sikh gunners, whose fire gradually slackened and at last ceased, though the infantry still maintained their position in front.

The extreme rapidity with which for two hours the British artillery worked their guns had almost exhausted the supply of ammunition they had brought with them, and when General Thackwell consulted his officers whether he should now take the offensive and attack the Sikhs, the reply was an almost unanimous negative. It was about four o'clqck in the afternoon, and there were but two hours' daylight left. The enemy's infantry were intact, and were in full force to the front. The three villages constituted a very strong position. The nature of the ground beyond was altogether unknown, but it was believed that sugar-cane fields extended to the Sikh intrenchments; the troops were already exhausted with the long day's exposure to the sun. Godby's brigade had not yet crossed, and with but two white regiments it would have been perilous indeed to engage in a conflict on unknown ground against an enemy of vastly superior strength, and containing the Bunnoo regiments, the flower of the Sikh army. The force, too, was already weakened by the strong detachment covering the head of the ford, and by a larger body detached to guard the baggage in the rear. It was therefore determined to rest for the night in the position occupied, and to renew the engagement in the morning, when it was hoped that Godby's brigade would have joined. The loss had been but small, twenty-one men killed and fifty-one wounded, most of

whom belonged to the artillery, against which arm the Sikh fire had been mainly directed.

To the surprise and disappointment of the British it was discovered in the morning that the Sikhs had evacuated their position in front of them. Godby's brigade had been all night crossing the river in three or four little boats, and joined the force at nine o'clock. Upon advancing into the villages it was found that the Sikh loss had been very large, great numbers of dead being discovered here and among the sugar-canes behind. The cavalry were at once sent ahead to endeavour to discover the course taken by the Sikhs, and learned from villagers that they had passed during the night along the roads leading towards the Jhelum river; but though the cavalry pressed far in pursuit they did not succeed in coming up with them. The infantry marched twelve miles in the direction they had taken, and then halted for the night. It was not until that morning that Lord Gough sent a small force across the river and discovered that the Sikhs had left thirty-six hours before.

For four hours Percy had listened anxiously to the continuous roll of artillery. When it ceased at four o'clock the men round him shouted triumphantly that all was over, and the Feringhees annihilated; but no news had been received, when Percy, feeling worn out with the excitement and the worry of the day, threw himself down on his bed. At ten o'clock he heard a horse approaching at a gallop. A few words were said, of which he could not gather the import, but as they were followed by a volley of execrations his heart gave a bound of delight, for he felt that the Sikhs had failed in their attack.

Two minutes later the officer entered his tent. "You are to mount and ride with us at once, sahib," he said shortly.

Percy asked no questions, feeling that silence was at present the safest policy. His first thought was for his men, who always slept in the camp of the sowars, where his horse was picketed. He had not seen them all day, and had no doubt

that they had been obliged to accompany the cavalry when they moved off at daybreak. He mounted his horse, which was as usual linked to those of the troopers on either side of it, and the party moved off silently, leaving the tent standing. For an hour but few words were spoken beyond occasional muttered execrations among the Sikhs. Then the officer rode up beside him, taking the chain from the trooper on his right hand side.

"I was wrong, sahib; we have not eaten up the Feringhees as I expected. It has been a drawn battle. Your guns fired at us, and we fired at them; many were killed on both sides. Our infantry never attacked, nor did yours; but we suffered most, for your infantry lay down on the ground like cowards, while ours stood up like men; still they could not advance under the terrible fire of your guns. So the combat ceased, and we march to-night to take up a new position on the Jhelum, where it is all bush and jungle."

" But why should you fall back if the battle is an indecisive one?"

" Because, sahib, we felt too sure of victory. We left the ford open here, thinking, as I told you, that after we had crushed the troops we went out to fight we should march back here and destroy the force from across the river. Our calculations have been wrong; we have not won the battle; and the blind people on the other side have not crossed, though they must have seen that there was neither a man nor a gun to resist them. To-morrow they must surely discover it, and then when they cross we should find ourselves between two fires; so there was nothing to do but to fall back. The next time we will fight on our ground, in thick jungle, where the white cavalry cannot act nor the gunners discover our position; then you will see."

For three hours longer they rode on. The officer had ceased to talk, the men were all silent, and were, Percy guessed, half asleep on their horses. The night was so dark

REJOINING

that he could scarce make out the figures riding beside him. It went to his heart to leave Sheik, and he wondered whether he could- lean forward and unbuckle the chains. However, he abandoned the idea, for even could he do so the rattle of the ends of the falling chains would at once rouse the men. He knew nothing of the country on either side of the road they were following, and would assuredly come to grief did he attempt to gallop over it, therefore he fell back upon his original plan.

Taking his feet from the stirrups and letting go the reins he quietly lifted himself back out of the saddle, and then holding on by it let himself slip off noiselessly over the crupper. As he did so he stooped low on the ground. The troopers behind were riding two and two, with an interval of some feet between them. They passed along on either side of him, but the horses of the two last troopers, who were riding closer together than the others, swerved suddenly, nearly unseating their riders, and causing them to burst into angry exclamations.

"What can the brutes have shied at?" one asked the other.

"It might be anything," was the reply. "Lots of carts have been passing down the road, and I suppose something has dropped off one of them."

As soon as they had passed, Percy left the road. He found that the ground on either side was covered with low scrub bushes. Among these he made his way cautiously, and had gone but fifty yards when he heard a sudden shout, followed by a string of furious exclamations, and a minute later the troopers came galloping back along the road. He stooped among the bushes as they passed, although confident that he could not be seen. He had almost expected they would rein in their horses as they came to the point where he had left the road, and indeed they would certainly have done so if the troopers had told the officer of the sudden start their horses had given them. As they rode on without a check he con-

eluded that the men had said nothing of the incident, thinking that if they did so they would certainly incur blame, and probably severe punishment, for not ascertaining what it was that the animals had shied at.

As soon as they had passed he returned to the road, for although he could have kept the general direction by means of the stars, he might have got far away from the direct track, and, moreover, might in the dark have come upon broken ground and fallen down some hole or nullah, and this possibility would necessitate very slow and careful walking. He therefore kept along the road, but was so frequently obliged to leave it, owing to the number of carts, horsemen, and peasants all flying before the expected advance of the British, that he made but slow progress. This, however, did not trouble him. The Sikh army had fallen back, and the British cavalry would soon be scouring the country. His principal reason for wishing to be back before the evening was his arrangement with his two men. It was, of course, uncertain that they would, any more than himself, return to the tent that night. Having been with the cavalry during the battle they would know nothing of what had taken place in the camp they had left, and could not have been certain that he and his guard had not started for the rear early in the day, in which case he would not have attempted to escape. However, if they reached the tent before morning they would be sure to wait unless they saw the British troops crossing the river, in which case they would probably make off, as they might be cut down before they could make it understood that they were the servants of an English officer.

As soon, therefore, as the first dawn of light appeared he moved farther away from the road and entered a patch of low trees and brushwood, and there sat watching the road. From time to time bullock-carts and pack-animals came along, generally in parti-es under the escort of small bodies of sowars, who were evidently urging them to push forward with all

haste. Sometimes the bullock-carts were provided with curtains, and no doubt contained the ladies of the zenana of some zemindar of the district, who with his retainers was with the army. The spot where Percy was hidden was at the very edge of the cultivated ground, and beyond wide fields stretched away as far as he could see. Here and there peasants were at work as usual, heeding very little the events passing round them, and confident they would suffer no molestation at the hands of the British, and that any change would be likely to benefit rather than to harm them.

As the sun gained power Percy began to feel the torture of thirst, but he well knew that there was no hope of obtaining water, as he could not quit his place of concealment until night again fell, for his dress would betray him even at a considerable distance. He had intended to watch until he saw English troops coming along, but he had been walking all night, and as the heat increased found it impossible to keep his eyes open. Besides, as he told himself, there was no certainty whatever that the British cavalry would come along that day. After having allowed themselves to be checked for a day and a half by deserted earthworks there might be still farther delay, and even after crossing a day might elapse before any farther advance was made. He was turning this over in his mind when his thoughts gradually became confused, and he was soon sound asleep.

The sun was setting when he awoke. On looking round he saw that the road was entirely deserted, and determined therefore to push forward through the fields at once in hope of discovering water, for he woke with a raging thirst. He had walked for half an hour when he saw a cloud of dust on the road, and at once leapt down into a small nullah, and there, concealed from sight, ran towards the road. When he heard the tramping of horses and the rumbling of wheels he took off his white helmet and raised his head sufficiently high to look through a tuft of grass at the edge of the nullah. A moment

later he was standing on the top of the bank waving his hat to the troops passing along the road fifty yards away. The glimpse he had caught of the white faces had been enough, it was a battery of British horse-artillery. The order was given to halt, and an officer rode up to meet him.

"Who are you, sir? "

" My name is Groves. I am in the civil service, and was assistant to Major Edwardes before Mooltan. I was attached by him to Sher Singh's force, and was carried off by it when he deserted. I effected my escape last night."

The officer held out his hand. "I am very glad to see you," he said. "Of course, we heard that Sher Singh had carried off a political officer. What are you going to do now? What can I do for you? My orders are to push forward at once. The gth Lancers are ahead of us; did you see any of them?"

"The first thing you can do for me is to give me something to drink," Percy said, "for I have had nothing since yesterday."

The officer at once pulled out his flask and handed it to him.

"Thank you very much," Percy said, after taking a drink. " No, I did not see anything of the cavalry. I was walking all last night; and when it got hot this morning I could not keep awake. I only started again half an hour ago. They must have passed before that, for I saw nothing of them."

"Are there any of the rebels along on this road? "

Percy shook his head. "There were not fifty men left in the camp on the bank of the Chenab all yesterday," he said. "I was there, and was expecting you to cross all day."

"Yes, we made a hideous mess of it," the officer said in a tone of deep disgust. " If we had crossed yesterday, as we ought to have done, we should have come on the rear of Sher Singh's army when he was engaged with Thackwell, and have smashed him into a cocked hat. It has been an astounding

blunder. There is no chance of our overtaking any body of troops?"

" Not the slightest, unless this road runs into the one by which the Sikhs are retreating. I hear they are retiring on the Jhelum, and will make a stand there."

"Well, as you have no horse," the officer said, "the best thing you can do is to get up on one of our limbers and go with us. Our force is crossing the river, and will, I suppose, to-morrow push on to join Thackwell, somewhere on the Julal-pore road."

As Percy learnt that he was still twelve miles distant from the river he accepted the invitation, climbed up on to a limber between two artillerymen, and in an hour reached Heylah, where the artillery and guns sent forward joined Thackwell's force, which had halted there. Finding that the main body of Lord Cough's force had halted after crossing the river, and that it was probable no farther movement would be made for some little time, Percy purchased from a trooper for a few shillings a horse he had picked up on the way, having found it standing by the side of its dead master, who, although terribly wounded, had managed to keep his saddle for some miles. Mounting this he started at once to return by the road by which he had arrived.

He had met no one he knew in Sir Joseph Thackwell's camp, and considered it his duty to report himself at headquarters. The chief reason for haste was his anxiety for his two men, who would, he knew, if they had managed to make their escape, rely upon his returning sooner or later to the place where he had appointed to meet them. It was ten o'clock when he was challenged by a sentry as he approached the camp. As soon as he was found to be a British officer he was permitted to proceed, and presently found his way to the tent of the principal political officer with Lord Gough. The latter was seated talking to a gentleman when Percy was shown in by an orderly.

" I have come to report myself as having escaped from Sher Singh's camp," he said.

There was a sudden exclamation, and one of the gentlemen sprang from his chair. "Why, Groves, is it you? I should hardly have known you again. Why, it is more than two years since we met."

" Some months more, Mr. Fullarton. I am indeed pleased to meet you again."

"Groves is an old friend of mine," Mr. Fullarton said, turning to the other gentleman. "You know he was carried off by Sher Singh when he deserted from Whish's camp before Mooltan. We have heard, indeed, from messages Sher Singh has from time to time sent in that he was with him and well, but I have been anxious as to what might happen if we defeated the Sikhs. I am proud of Groves, for he is, if I may say so, a protege of mine, and it was partly through me that he made his first start in the service."

"Entirely through you, sir," Percy said warmly. "I owe my position entirely to you."

"Not entirely by a long way, Groves. I accepted your services as a volunteer when we were badly off for interpreters, but it was solely to your own good conduct and bravery that you owed your permanent appointment. Sir Henry Hardinge and Lord Gough both personally recommended him in very strong terms to the Court of Directors;" he added to the other officer. " I will carry him off to my tent. I expect he has nothing but what he stands in."

"One moment, Fullarton; he may have some valuable information to give us."

"No; I am sorry I have nothing to tell you but what is known already, that Sher Singh has retreated towards the Jhelum. I was not with him in the fight yesterday. I had been left under a. guard here in camp, and I only went away with them at ten o'clock at night, and managed to escape from them four hours afterwards. I hid until I saw a battery of oui

horse-artillery coming along this afternoon, and went with them into Heylah. I picked up a Sikh horse there and started at once to report myself to you."

"Then I will not detain you, Mr. Groves. You will, of course, address a report to me as to your stay in Sher Singh's camp and your treatment by him. I shall no doubt be able to find you plenty to do in the course of a day or two."

"In the first place, Groves," Mr. Fullarton said as they reached his tent, which was close by, "I suppose you must want something to eat? "

"I shall be very glad of something, sir, for I have had nothing to-day. I found that the troops at Heylah had had nothing since they marched in the morning, and there did not seem any chance of their getting anything to-night, so it was of no use my thinking of getting food there."

"That accounts for your starting back again at once," Mr. Fullarton said with a smile as he touched a bell.

Percy's old friend, Ram Singh, entered. "Get some food directly, Ram Singh. This is Mr. Groves, your old pupil on the voyage."

The man salaamed. " I am glad to see you, sahib. You have grown since then."

"So I ought to have done." Percy laughed. "I was not fifteen when I landed here. That is more than four years ago. I owe a great deal, Ram Singh, to the lessons I had from you."

"I don't think, Mr. Fullarton," he went on when the man retired to get some food, " that hunger had much to do with my coming over to-night. I was very anxious about my two men, they are the same two I had with me when I came to you at Loodiana. They have been with me ever since, and I would not on any account that harm should come to them."

He then related the instructions he had given them as to joining him if they made their escape.

"It is quite possible that they may be in the camp now," Mr. Fullarton said. " I know that a few prisoners were taken

by the gih Lancers, who were the first to cross the ford. When they went on to join Thackwell they handed over their prisoners to one of the other corps. We have all been too busy to-day to think about them, but the first thing in the morning I will go with you and see if your men are among them. It is too late to do it to-night. Now tell me all about your sojourn with Sher Singh, and how you managed to escape from the Sikhs."

The next morning early Mr. Fullarton went out with Percy, and found that the prisoners taken by the cavalry who had first crossed had been handed over to the charge of the i4th Dragoons, and at once went over to the camp of that regiment. Mr. Fullarton was well known to the officer in command of the corps, who on learning from him the object of his visit at once ordered the prisoners to be paraded.

"There are ten of them, I think," he said. "I have not questioned them; I thought some of you political gentlemen would want to do that, and all I had to do was to take care of them."

He walked across with them to the guard-tent, from which the prisoners were just being brought out. Percy gave an exclamation of satisfaction as, in the last two who came out, he recognized his followers. They on their part would have run forward, but the habits of discipline prevailed, and giving the military salute they fell in with the others.

"Those are my two men, sir," Percy said to the officer.

" I suppose it is all right, Fullarton, for me to let them go? "

" Certainly, I can answer for them myself, for I recognize them as having been with Groves when he first joined, and I know they rode behind him in all the battles on the Sutlej. They are thoroughly good and trustworthy fellows; and indeed their presence here shows that they must have run considerable risks from our men as well as the Sikhs, in obeying his instructions to meet him here. However, I will give you a written receipt for them, and that will take all respon-

sibility off your shoulders. The others scarcely look like fighting men."

" No, I should say they are only camp-followers, who lingered behind in the hopes of picking up anything the Sikhs might have left behind them when they went off so suddenly."

" I will speak about them, and will see that their cases are inquired into at once."

" I shall be very much obliged if you would. The men have got plenty of work without looking after these fellows; and if we got orders to go forward there would be all sorts of bother in getting rid of them, and in handing them over to someone else."

"I will see about it at once; as they are not fighting men there can be no object in keeping them."

" Thank you. You will make over these two men to this gentleman, sergeant; they are released from custody."

"We have their horses in our lines, sir, and their arms; they were handed over with them; are they to take them? "

" Certainly. They are Mr. Groves' servants, and fought on our side at Sobraon. They were only awaiting their master's return when they were captured."

"Now, Groves, you may as well go back to my tent," Mr. Fullarton said as they walked away, followed by the two men leading their horses. " I will see about getting a tent for you later on, but in the meantime make yourself at home in mine. I shall be very glad to have you with me. I am first going to get authority to examine the other prisoners, and release them if proved harmless. I shall be with you at breakfast-time."

After seeing his men picket their horses with those in the political officers' lines he told them to follow him into the tent.

"Now sit down and tell me all about your escape," he said.

"There is not much to tell, sahib," Akram Chunder, who was generally the spokesman, replied. " We were ordered to mount and ride with the cavalry, just as daylight was break-

ing; and had to do so at once. On the way we agreed that if the Sikhs got the best of it we would stay with them, as in that case they would doubtless return to the camp; but that if they were beaten we would get away if we could, for you would certainly be moved. If you were moved at night we knew that you would, as agreed, try to make your escape and join us here. If you were moved in the day, and had no chance of escaping, we made up our minds to follow and to get you away if possible, for we considered your life would be in danger, and that, however great the risk, you would be willing to try to escape.

" When we got near your people we were with the body of cavalry, who were to move round their left flank and fall upon their baggage. As soon as we got out of the shelter of some sugar-cane fields a battery of the artillery opened at us, and over went men and horses. It was very uncomfortable, almost as bad as it was at Ferozeshah, for although it was but a single battery every shot told. They were firing grape and shrapnel, and many of the shell burst just in front of us and cut big gaps in the line. Then a regiment of dragoons rode at us, and though they were but a handful the Sikhs would not wait for them, but bolted back into the canes. All this was done three or four times, and Bhop Lai and I saw that the Sikh game was up. Their cavalry were beaten on the other flank just as thorough as we were, and the infantry never stirred a foot beyond their shelter. So the next time we rode back into the canes we separated from the rest. There was no difficulty whatever about it. The different troops had all got mixed up together. Half the party we were with had been killed, and the rest had enough to think of without bothering about us.

"There were plenty of others drawing off, some wounded, some who did not want any more of it. We dismounted as soon as we separated from the others, so that our heads should not show above the canes, led our horses back for a

mile, and then mounted and rode till we got to a nullah, in which we hid ourselves. The firing went on for some time, then it stopped, and we knew that the Sikhs had had enough of it. We agreed that it was best to wait where we were and find out what they were going to do. If they marched back to the camp we could slip into the ranks again and come with them; if they did not, we would come on alone and reconnoitre. We did not know how many troops had been left there, so when it got dark I made my way back again, and Bhop Lai took charge of the horses. I got in among the infantry, and found them half mad with rage that they had not been ordered to advance. They had suffered heavily, for the canes were a poor protection against shot and shell, and many hundreds had been killed there. I learned that the orders were that the whole force were to march towards the Jhelum at midnight. So I went back to Bhop Lai, and we rode till close to the old camp; then he went in on foot to see what was going on.

" It was not long before he was back again, saying that the place was entirely deserted, and that your tent had been left standing. So we rode straight in and waited there. At daybreak I went to the river and saw that some regiments of cavalry were preparing to cross. I hurried back to the tent, and we talked it over. We did not know which way you had gone, and might miss you if we went in search of you. We guessed that it would have been dark before you set out, and as we had your positive orders to wait, we made up our minds to do so. We took off our arms and laid them down on the ground, and sat quietly at the door of the tent till a white cavalry regiment rode up. We did not feel comfortable, for we were not sure that they would not cut us down at once. But as our horses were standing there and we could have ridden away had we chosen, we hoped they would see that we were not enemies.

" None of the officers could speak Punjaubi, so after trying

to question us we were handed over to a guard. The other men you saw were brought in later, and we were all transferred together to another dragoon regiment, put in a tent, and made prisoners. We did not feel uncomfortable then, for we knew that your people do not kill prisoners, and that we should presently be questioned by someone who knew the language, and would be able to explain how we came there; but we were terribly anxious about you, and when we saw you we were ready to shout with joy. Will the sahib tell us how he escaped?"

"Just as we had planned, Akram. I rode with them for three hours, by which time they were all sleepy. Then I slipped over the crupper of the horse, and as soon as they had passed on hid in the scrub. Then I walked back till morning, and lay down among some bushes till, late in the afternoon, I saw a battery of our own artillery come along. They took me on to Heylah. There I got a horse and rode back at once, hoping to find you here. It was ten o'clock when I arrived, too late to make inquiries about you then; but I heard that ten prisoners had been taken, and came over with Mr. Fullar-ton the first thing this morning to see if you were among them."

CHAPTER XIX
CHILLIANWALLA

'T'HERE was a long pause after the battle of Sadoolapore. The country between Heylah and the Sikh position, fifteen miles distant, was covered with dense jungle, and a great number of native wood-cutters were employed in cutting roads through it. Skirmishes often took place between the Sikh regular cavalry and our patrols. On the i8th of December Sher Singh moved ten thousand men to Dingee. As this movement threatened the Wuzeerabad ford, a force was despatched there to bar the passage, which if effected would have placed Sher Singh between the British force and Lahore. The Sikhs retired again, and nothing was done until the loth of January, when the British force concentrated at Lussoore. It was known that considerable reinforcements had joined Sher Singh, among these being two troops of horse-artillery from Peshawur. These batteries had been disciplined by a British officer, and had been presented to Chuttur Singh by the Resident at Lahore, to enable him to repel the attacks of the Afghans. They were in all respects exactly similar to those used in the Company's service, and were a most valuable addition to Sher Singh's strength.

During the six weeks that had elapsed since the battle, Percy had been kept busily employed; at one time buying provisions, at another questioning villagers as to routes and

the obstacles to be encountered, and gathering as much information as possible as to the Sikh position at Russool. The descriptions he obtained were vague in the extreme, but all united in describing the country as excessively difficult, being covered with jungle and abounding in deep nullahs.

"This will be a different business altogether, Groves, from our former attacks on the Sikh positions," said Mr. Fullarton.

"I should think much easier, sir. There we had to go right across the open with fifty or sixty cannon and ten or twelve thousand infantry all blazing away at us, and to storm a place difficult to climb, and where we were exposed to their fire while they were sheltered. Fighting in the jungle we have just as good a chance as they have."

"Except, Groves, that they will know every foot of the ground, and we shall know nothing of it, which makes all the difference in the world."

"It does make a difference, no doubt, Mr. Fullarton; but you see we turned them out of the jungle at Moodkee quickly enough."

"That is true; but there our cavalry got round behind them. No doubt that shook their resistance very much; nothing alarms undisciplined troops so much as the belief that their retreat is cut off. With highly disciplined troops it is just the contrary; when they know they must either conquer or be destroyed, they will fight more obstinately than on any other occasion. To-morrow morning we move forward to Dingee, and I expect that we shall fight on the following day, for it is not more than eight miles from there."

At Dingee a Pathan deserter from the Sikh camp came in, and from him further particulars than had before been learned were obtained.

The camp, he said, was round the village of Russool, a mile from the river. In front of it was a ravine some hundreds of feet deep and almost impassable. Upon the ground on the other side of this ravine the Sikhs had erected a long line of

intrenchments, to reach which they had to cross the ravine from their camp on a narrow wooden footbridge thrown over it. At a council of war held on the evening of the arrival of the army at Dingee, it was determined that an attempt should be made to outflank the Sikh intrenchments, to attack Russool on the Sikh left, and so to intercept their retreat to the river. This successful, all their guns, magazines, and stores would be captured, although doubtless the infantry would escape through the jungle.

The next morning the troops were put in motion; for a time they marched without difficulty, as the jungle had been cut for them, but after that their movements were slow. Several Pathan deserters came in as they advanced, and gave information as to the route and position. After a march of some miles a halt was made. The troops ate some of the food carried in their haversacks, and an allowance of grog was served out. The direction of the line of march, which had hitherto been direct upon the heights of Russool, where the Sikh camp was plainly visible, was now changed, and sweeping round they reached a long bare hill in front of the village of Chillianwalla, turning out some Sikhs who were stationed in a small intrenchment there. Lord Cough's intention was to encamp for the night at this spot, where plenty of water was obtainable, so that the troops could rest and prepare for the fight in the morning, when the whole day would be available for the operations.

The ground was marked out for the different regiments to occupy, and the men were in the act of falling out, when a large body of men were seen some distance in the front, and several guns opened fire. The Sikhs had left their intrenchments, and were drawn up in the jungle. Battery after battery opened fire, and the British artillery at once responded, while the troops fell into their ranks again. Lord Gough issued orders for the battle to begin. He has been blamed by many for so doing, but it is difficult to see how it could have been

avoided. The Sikh army was at hand in full force; it was out of the question to retreat, equally out of the question to remain passive under the fire of the enemy. Inaction or retreat would equally have been interpreted as evidence of fear, and would have vastly encouraged the enemy. The troops, although tired by their march through the jungle under the sun, had not had a long day's work. That the dispositions for battle were hurried, incomplete, and faulty is undeniable, but that it should have taken place was under the circumstances inevitable.

The din of the cannonade was prodigious, echoed as it was by the surrounding hills. The Sikh batteries were almost invisible, and the British artillerymen directed their fire solely at the flashes and smoke rising from the jungle. The position of the infantry was equally hidden, and it was only by the sparkle of the sun on bayonet and spearhead that any indication of its line was obtainable. But having determined upon attacking, it was necessary that some plan of operation should be decided upon, some specific object of attack assigned to each of the commanding officers of divisions and brigades. No such orders were given, and without any instructions whatever beyond the order to advance and capture the enemy's guns, the British force, numbering some eighteen thousand, of whom but a small proportion were white troops— there being but four regiments of English infantry and three of cavalry—moved forward to attack a force estimated at forty thousand, with sixty-two guns, entirely hidden in a jungle, and in an exceedingly broken and difficult ground.

The two infantry divisions of Major-general Gilbert and Brigadier-general Colin Campbell advanced boldly to the attack, and plunging into the jungle were at once engaged in a hand-to-hand struggle with the Sikhs. The cavalry on the right flank, consisting of the 9th Royal Lancers, the i4th Dragoons, and two regiments of native cavalry, were ordered to advance. They were commanded by Lieutenant-colonel Pope,

an officer of the native cavalry. He was unfortunately in such infirm health that he could not mount his horse without assistance, and had no experience whatever of the command of a brigade of cavalry. The result was that owing partly to the difficulty of keeping a straight line in the jungle, the force not only overlapped the troops of horse-artillery placed between them and Gilbert's division, but got in front of Gilbert's infantry. The guns were therefore unable to afford them any assistance.

Moving forwards at a walk, the cavalry found themselves opposed both by infantry and cavalry. Colonel Pope was wounded severely in the head. The troops, being without orders, faced about in different directions as fresh opponents appeared, and presently came to a halt. The Sikh cavalry boldly skirmished up to them, and then, under the belief that the order had been given to retreat, the cavalry turned and galloped back, hotly pursued by the Sikhs. In their retreat they rode right over the batteries of horse-artillery, disorganizing the gunners and carrying off the horses in their rush; while the Sikhs, of whom there were but a handful, following hard in the rear of the flying troopers, cut down the artillery men, captured six guns, and continued their pursuit until close to Lord Gough and the head-quarter staff. Then a couple of guns, judiciously placed, opened upon them, and they fell back, checked by the appearance of a couple of squadrons of the Lancers, which had been rallied by their officers.

Had the cavalry, when they first came in contact with the enemy, received the orders to charge, the result would probably have been altogether different. Indeed the colonel of one of the cavalry regiments requested permission from Pope to charge, but it was refused. The men who fled thus precipitately had shown an almost reckless valour at Ramnuggur, and would, under other circumstances, have distinguished themselves equally here; but cavalry at a walk are the most

defenceless of troops, and broken up as they were by the jungle, unable to see what was going on on either side, exposed to a fire from hiden foes, and feeling that they were badly handled, it is not surprising that when they came to a halt they were liable to turn and go about with alacrity at the first sound of retreating hoofs at any portion of the line.

While this was happening a battery of horse-artillery, with some squadrons of cavalry from three of the regiments engaged, had most gallantly repulsed the attack of a large body of the enemy's horse on our extreme left. Godby's brigade of infantry, which had been deprived of a chance of taking part in the battle of Sadoolapore, were the first of the infantry to come in contact with the enemy. Its advance was assisted by a well-directed fire of a horse-artillery battery which prepared the way. It plunged into the jungle with a cheer, and dashing forward through every obstacle and driving its defenders before it, came upon an open space, the opposite side of which was thickly lined by the enemy. Our troops dashed across this under a tremendous fire of musket and artillery, fired a volley, and hurled themselves upon the Sikhs, who broke and fled. Pursuit was impossible; the jungle was so thick that none could see ten yards ahead. Orders were given to collect the wounded—an imperative duty, for the Sikhs murdered every man left behind.

Suddenly, as they were engaged in the work, a tremendous fire opened upon them from the rear. A large body of Sikhs had worked their way through the jungle and cut them off, while a strong body of their cavalry issued into the open space and charged down upon them. As quick as thought the horse-artillery swept their guns round, loaded with grape, and poured in their fire, creating terrible havoc among the Sikh horse, and sending them flying back into the jungle. The infantry faced about and retired steadily, but were pressed by a crowd of the enemy. Then General Gilbert, who was with the brigade, gave the word, and the second battalion of

the Bengal Europeans turned and went at them with a cheer. The Sikhs fought desperately each for himself, but they were swept backward and bayoneted in great numbers. Three of their guns were taken and spiked, and another captured by one of the native regiments of the brigade.

The left brigade of Gilbert's division was even more severely treated. The fighting was desperate; the zgth captured and spiked several guns in.the Sikh intrenchment, but could carry off only five of them for want of horses. As it still pushed forward the brigade was swept with grape and musketry. The 5 6th Native Infantry suffered terribly, losing its colonel, seven other officers, and three hundred and twenty-two men killed and wounded. The 3oth Native Infantry suffered as heavily, losing eleven officers and two hundred and eighty-five men killed and wounded. Both the native regiments lost their colours. The brigade was at length unable to withstand the attack directed against it, and fell back.

Pennycuick's brigade of Colin Campbell's division were as roughly handled; they had, through some blunder or other, advanced unsupported by artillery, and orders were given by their commander that they were not to fire but to charge the enemy's guns. The 24th, the European regiment of the brigade, the strongest battalion of the force, advanced in magnificent order under a terrific fire of musketry and artillery, drove all opposition before them, and captured the guns opposed to them. They had commenced spiking them, when some of the Bunnoo regiments, lying concealed in the brushwood on rising ground behind the guns, opened a tremendous fire of musketry. The troops were thrown into some confusion by this sudden attack, and fell back, and as they did so they were literally mown down by the enemy's fire. General Pennycuick fell dead; his son, a young ensign, stood across his father's body and defended it until he fell dead beside it. Colonel Brooks was also killed. Eleven other officers fell,

and ten were wounded either among the guns or in the retreat that followed. The Sikh cavalry pressed hard on the retiring soldiers, while their musketry and artillery swept their ranks, and upwards of five hundred men were killed and wounded. The regiment was in fact almost annihilated. The position this brigade attacked was afterwards found to have been the strongest along the Sikh line. The two native regiments of the brigade had advanced in line with the 24th, but suffered far less severely in the retreat, the efforts of the Sikhs being concentrated against the white regiment.

The other brigade of the division, at whose head Colin Campbell had placed himself, was more fortunate. The 6ist Foot repulsed several desperate attacks, and pouring in heavy volleys swept the Sikhs before it. Wheeling round it fought its way along, and retook the guns from which the 24th had been driven. The capture of the guns was, however, but of little avail, for as soon as they were abandoned the Sikhs managed to draw the spikes, and in a few minutes they were again in action. Two native regiments fought worthily by the side of the 61 st.

The cavalry on the extreme left, under General Thackwell, did good work by checking a very large body of Sikh horsemen, a squadron of the 3d Dragoons charging and riding right through them; then gathering again with a desperate effort they cut their way back to their friends, two officers and thirty-six men having been killed or wounded in this brilliant charge.

Night was now approaching. A portion of the jungle had been for the moment cleared, but beyond this the Sikhs still swarmed, and during the battle large bodies had worked round and had only been prevented by the fire of the guns from falling on the rear. Nothing more could be done; some of the officers advised that the force should fall back to the village of Chillianwalla, in order to obtain water and to afford protection to the baggage. Lord Gough at first refused to do

so, on the ground that any wounded left behind would be massacred. The troops, especially the Sepoys, were, however, so distressed by thirst, that the wounded were as far as possible collected, and the force concentrated round Chillianwalla.

Had the enemy attacked at night the consequence would have been terrible, for the regiments were broken up and separated, and the confusion was absolute; but at eight o'clock the rain came down in torrents, and this and the fact that their own loss had been severe, especially among the gunners, checked the ardour of the Sikhs, and probably saved the British force. In the morning the enemy were seen encamped on an eminence three miles distant. The cavalry scoured the field of battle to collect any wounded that had been left, and bring in the captured guns. Twelve small cannon, however, were the only trophies of the fight. The rolls were called, and the loss ascertained: it consisted of eighty-nine officers, two thousand three hundred and fifty-seven men killed and wounded—an enormous loss in proportion to the number of men engaged. Six guns were lost, together with the ammunition that had accompanied several of the corps into the fight.

It was so far a drawn battle that the armies at night occupied the same positions they had held at the commencement of the battle, but the advantage was all with the Sikhs, for the fighting strength of the four English regiments that had formed the backbone of the force was lessened by half; while the Sikhs had proved to their delight that British troops were not always invincible, and that occasionally they were even subject to panic. The result was that their confidence was greatly increased, and their losses were far more than balanced by the great number of recruits who, at the news of the repulse of the British attack, poured into Sher Singh's camp.

The British army remained stationary at Chillianwalla from the 13th of January to February. Large numbers of the Sikhs at various times penetrated to Dingee, and cut the lines of communication through that place; there was indeed another

338 THROUGH THE SIKH WAR

line open through Hayleh, where the force that had been engaged at Sadoolapore had remained since that battle, to prevent the Sikhs from advancing towards Lahore. The regiments " that had been left behind at Ramnuggur rejoined the army, their place being taken by the 53d Regiment from Lahore.

General Whish's force which had captured Mooltan was now on its way to join that of Lord Gough. The siege of Mooltan had been renewed after the departure of Sher Singh's army, and reinforcements having reached General Whish, it was pushed on with great vigour. Two breaches were effected in the walls of the fort, and the great mosque, which was used as a magazine by the rebels, was pierced by a shell, which caused a terrific explosion, entirely destroying the building, leaving a great chasm where it had stood, levelling the Sikh works near it, and killing five hundred men. Soon after this misfortune, Moolraj, finding further resistance impossible, came out and surrendered unconditionally, just as the British columns were formed up in readiness to storm the breaches. He was taken to Calcutta and there tried; he was found guilty, but it being considered that he had acted under a pressure from his troops that he was unable to resist, he was sentenced only to imprisonment for life.

At the battle of Chillianwalla Percy Groves had been severely wounded. He was sitting on his horse with Mr. Fullarton and two or three other political officers at a distance of a hundred yards from the head-quarters staff, when Pope's cavalry issued in headlong flight from the jungle. An exclamation of dismay burst from each member of the little party.

"It is a regular stampede," Mr. Fullarton exclaimed; " there come the Sikhs after them! Why, they are comparatively a handful! What on earth possesses the men ? Why, they will be over the guns! Did you ever see such madness ? "

On came the fugitives.

"To the right there!" Mr. Fullarton shouted, "or these madmen will ride us down."

PERCY TAKES PART IN THE BATTLE OF CHILLIANWALLA.

They had but just got clear of the front when the cavalry swept past; before they could go farther half a dozen Sikh horsemen rode at them. The civilians all carried pistols, and these they used with some effect. Two of the Sikhs fell, the rest rushed on them. Percy had no sword, and thought that his end had come; when there was a shout, and his two followers rode past him, and fiercely fell upon the Sikhs.

Percy turned round in time to see two of the civilians cut down by the tulwars of the other Sikhs, while Mr. Fullarton tried with his pistol to ward off a blow aimed at him. The force of the blow struck it down and the sword fell on his shoulder. Before the Sikh had time to strike again he was shot by Bhop Lai, and the latter and his comrade then attacked the remaining two Sikhs furiously. Akram Chunder ran one through with his sword. Bhop Lai seriously wounded the other, who wheeled his horse round and fled at full speed.

A moment later there was a thunder of hoofs, and the Lancers who had rallied, came dashing down. Percy, furious at seeing Mr. Fullarton fall, exclaimed, " Give me one of those tulwars, Bhop Lai." The man sprang from his horse and handed him the one that had fallen from the hand of the Sikh he had shot.

As the Lancers came along Percy with his two companions fell in behind them. They rode over many of the Sikh horsemen; the rest fled, and were hotly pursued back to the jungle, many of them being cut down. The impetus of the charge took the Lancers well into the wood. A blaze of musketry flashed out in front of them; a fresh troop of horsemen charged down, and a moment later they were engaged in a hand-to-hand contest. A tall Sikh rode at Percy, and they at once engaged in single combat. Percy's steady training at the fortress with sword and tulwar was useful to him now. The Sikh's shield gave him an advantage, but this was counterbalanced by Percy's being accustomed to thrust as well as strike. For some time the contest was doubtful, and then,

after feinting at the Sikh's head to make him throw up his shield, Percy ran him through the body. He heard a warning shout from Bhop Lai as he did so, and the next moment another Sikh rode at him, knocking his horse off its legs, while at the same moment a crashing blow fell on his helmet. After that he remembered nothing.

When he opened his eyes it was dark. Presently he could hear talking all round him; he listened, and heard that the language was Punjaubi. He wondered to himself how he had got there, then he recalled a fight and gradually recollected his horse falling. "I must be wounded," he said to himself. "Yes, my head throbs fearfully; but how is it that I am here? the Sikhs always kill the wounded."

He made an effort to raise himself on one elbow, when he felt a hand laid on him, and a voice which he recognized as that of Akram Chunder whispered in his ear:

"Do not stir, sahib; thanks to the Great One that you have recovered. We were sure that you were not dead; the blow was a heavy one, but as you were falling when he struck, the tulwar did not catch you quite fairly, and the helmet helped to turn it, so that, instead of cleaving your skull, it has but shaved off a portion of your scalp and half your ear."

"But how is it you are here with me? "

"We were both fighting, sahib, and knew that you could hold your own against the Sikh you were engaged with. Suddenly, just as from the corner of my eye I saw that you had disposed of him, another rode at you. I gave a shout, and cut down the man I was fighting with; but before I could turn my horse you were down. I shot the Sikh, and then I and Bhop Lai, who had just rid himself of his man, leapt off our horses, intending to lift you on to one of them; but at that moment the Lancers began to fall back, and we saw that it was too late, so each seizing you under one arm, we sprang with you into a bush.

" Then, while Bhop Lai stayed with you, I ran out again,

caught up the mantle of a Sikh who had fallen within a yard of the bush, and sprang in again. We wrapped you in the mantle, then crawled on, dragging you with us into a very thick patch of bush, where you are lying now. A moment later half a dozen Sikh infantry, pushing their way through the bushes, came close. One of them caught sight of us, and cried, 'What are you doing here, comrades?' 'My brother is sorely wounded,' I said, 'and we have stopped to close his eyes before we go on to have another fight with the Fering-hees.' 'You must make haste, then,' he said, 'or there will be none of them left to fight with.'

" We heard large numbers of them pass along a short distance off, then volley after volley of grape came crashing through the jungle, and they fell back again. 'I will mix with them,' Bhop Lai said; 'you stop with our sahib. One is less likely to be seen than two. Your story is good enough to account for one if they catch sight of you, but it is not good enough for two of us.'

" For two hours the battle went on, but not near us again. The banging of cannons and muskets was as bad as at Feroze-shah. Sometimes I thought one side was winning, sometimes the other. Sometimes I could hear Sikh yells of triumph, sometimes a deep roar even above the din of the musketry, and knew that it was an English cheer, for I had heard it before. Occasionally men came along, having strayed from their parties; and each told a different story. Some said that many of their cannons had been captured by the Feringhees; others declared that the Feringhees were almost destroyed. Bhop Lai sat down only ten or twelve yards away, and I could hear him talking to them. Presently I heard him ask had anyone any water? 'I have a wounded comrade somewhere not far off in the jungle, and I want some for him.' Somebody lent him a water-gourd. He went off behind, and some minutes later worked round here with it. He would not come straight, for some of them might have followed him into the

bushes, to see if they could do anything for his comrade, but this was not likely, for there are scores of wounded men round here. However, we tore off some rags and wetted them, and laid them on your wound, and we poured a little of it into my water-flask to sprinkle your face, and drop between your lips from time to time, and then Bhop Lai went back again with the remainder."

"But how has the battle ended, Akram? "

" It has ended just as it began—the white troops have all gone up to Chillianwalla and the other villages there. The Sikhs hold the jungle. They captured six of the guns our cavalry rode over, and they have lost twelve, but all small ones. I hear that almost all their gunners are killed, for the British took several of the batteries, though they could not hold them; and you know, sahib, the Sikhs will never leave their guns, but will stand by them till they are cut down. The men about here don't know what is going to be done. Some say that they will attack to-morrow; others say that though they have shown that they are more than a match for the Feringhees, it would be too much to attack them in their own positions, especially as they have not enough gunners to work the pieces."

"Perhaps we shall attack in the morning, Akram."

"I do not think so, sahib; they say that one of the white regiments had scarcely a man left, and that the others have lost half their strength. The general, sahib, is a great man for fighting, but he must see that until he gets more troops he can never force his way through the jungle up to Russool."

There was presently a sound of someone forcing his way through the bushes, then a voice said, " I bring orders that all are to fall back. It is not that we are beaten, as everyone knows; we have won a great victory, and have taught the Feringhees that they are not invincible, but food and water cannot be brought down here, therefore all must go up and get food and drink and rest for the night. The Feringhees have had enough, and will not attack again to-morrow morning; but if they do, we will come down again and welcome them."

There was a murmur of satisfaction, for the Sikhs had taken up their position some hours before the British attacked them, and were eager for food, as although spirits had been freely served out, the supply of food in the camp was small, and many had eaten nothing that day. Bhop Lai moved off with the others, but in five minutes was back again. As in the dark he was unable to find the clump of bush in which Percy was hidden, Akram called to him in a low voice.

"How is the sahib?" Bhop Lai asked, as he pushed his way in.

"I am better," Percy answered. "You have saved my life between you. Have they all gone? "

"All that can walk, sahib; there are numbers of wounded lying about, but there is nothing to prevent our starting off now."

" I don't think that I can walk yet," Percy said. " Perhaps in a little time I may be able to do so."

"I am afraid not, sahib; but that makes no difference; we can carry you easily. Akram, do you stoop down on one side, and I will do so on the other. Now, sahib, put your arms round our necks; we will clasp our hands under you, and you can sit then as in a chair."

Percy himself was able to give but little assistance, but he felt himself lifted up and held firmly; then slowly and steadily the two men carried him through the jungle. Once or twice they were asked by a figure on the ground who they were, but the answer in their own language, that they were looking for a comrade who had fallen, sufficed, as it was too dark under the trees for it to be seen that they were already carrying a burden.

"It was well that they didn't know we had you with us, sahib. Had they done so, we should like enough have had a musket-ball after us. A wounded Sikh is as dangerous as one standing on his feet."

But Percy did not reply; he only heard the words as if spoken a long distance off. A little farther and he was con-

scious of nothing. His bearers carried him a hundred yards beyond the jungle, and then laid him down again, sprinkled some water in his face, and poured a few drops between his lips; but as he gave no sign of returning consciousness, Akram Chunder said, "We had better take him on again. It is from loss of blood he has fainted, and we must get him to camp. First, I will again try to bandage his wound."

He unwound several yards of muslin from his turban, and bound up Percy's head. Then they lifted him and went forward, this time at a faster pace than before, for there was now no fear of giving Percy pain. They had to be careful, however; the. ground they were crossing was that over which the cavalry had retreated, and it was thickly dotted with the bodies of the fallen. Once past this, they pressed rapidly up the slope to Chillianwalla. To their surprise they approached unchallenged, for they had been afraid that their reply in a native tongue would have brought a shot from a sentry; but such was the confusion, and so exhausted were the men, that while some regiments had thrown out sentries, others had not done so, and they were fortunate in having come upon an unguarded spot. A little farther and they entered the village. Numbers of men were lying asleep in the streets. Presently an officer came along.

"What have you there? "

"An officer, sahib, wounded," Akram Chunder, who had picked up a few words of English, replied.

"Where have you got him from? " the officer asked in Hindustani.

Akram could understand the question, but could not answer it in the same language, and answered him in Punjaubi.

"We brought him out from the jungle over there, sahib."

"I don't understand you," the officer muttered; and then aloud in Hindustani, " Come along with me to those lights, that is one of the hospitals."

They went with him to the door of one of the largest buildings in the village, and entered. The floor was covered

with prostrate figures. Four or five surgeons with orderlies holding torches were engaged in bandaging, probing for bullets, or, in one case, in amputating.

"Doctor," the officer said, "here are two fellows who look like Sikhs, though I suppose they are not; they have got a wounded officer, but where they found him I have no idea. Do any of you speak Punjaubi? They may be able to tell us what those fellows over there are doing."

But none of the surgeons spoke the language.

"We will just see who the man is they have brought in," the officer, who was a colonel, said; "he seems dead by his attitude. Put him down there, men."

The two men understood his gesture, and laid Percy on the floor.

"He is not dead, but he is mighty near it," the surgeon said, as he felt his pulse. "Ah, this is what it is, a cut from one of those tulwars. He is bleeding to death. Give me that brandy bottle, orderly."

He poured a spoonful or two between Percy's lips, then laid some lint over the wound, and firmly bandaged it.

" Give him another spoonful, orderly, while I go on to the next; he will come round presently."

" Is it mortal, doctor? "

"No, it is a very nasty wound, but I don't think it has cut through the skull; the sword must have been turned a little I will examine it in the morning when I get breathing time."

"I know him now," the colonel said; "it is that young civilian who came in the day we crossed the Chenab. Yes, these are the two native servants who always rode behind him. Come along with me, men; I must take you to someone who talks Punjaubi. You shall come back to your master afterwards; he is lucky in having two such faithful servants."

The men did not fully understand him, but Akram Chunder gathered the meaning, and with a look at their master they followed the officer from the hospital.

CHAPTER XX

GUJERAT

THE officer kept on nearly to the end of the village, and then opened a door and went in. "Mansfield, you understand Punjaubi. These two fellows are the servants of that young civilian—Groves, I think, is his name—the man that was with Edwardes, you know, at Mooltan, and was taken prisoner by Sher Singh, and escaped after the battle of Sadoolapore."

"Yes, I know him. What of him? "

"They have just brought him in with his head laid open badly with a tulwar. He has pretty nearly bled to death, but the surgeon who has dressed his wounds thinks he will get over it. I want you to ask these fellows where they have brought him from. I expect he is one of the party who were fallen upon by the Sikhs who came on after our cavalry. I know there were two of them killed, and Fullarton is desperately wounded. I cannot understand how it was our fellows didn't find Groves when they were collecting the wounded."

"Where did you bring your master in from? " Major Mansfield asked in Punjaubi.

"We have brought him in from the jungle over there, sahib," Akram Chunder replied.

"From the jungle?" Major Mansfield repeated.

"He joined the Lancers who came up and drove back the

Sikh horsemen; he went on with them into the jungle, and in the fight there he was cut down by a Sikh just after he had run another through."

" The dickens he was! " the officer exclaimed. " Then how on earth was it that he wasn't killed when the Lancers fell back again? They have never spared any wounded that fell into heir hands."

Akram Chunder related how he and his comrade had dismounted and concealed his master, had kept him in the midst of the Sikh infantry till they retired, and had then carried him up to the village.

"You are fine fellows," the officer said warmly, "noble fellows; " and he shook them both by the hand, to the astonishment of the colonel who had brought them in, and of the other officers who crowded the little cottage. Turning round Major Mansfield repeated the story he had heard. All broke into loud exclamations of admiration.

"Wait a moment," the colonel said, "we shall have time to talk about that afterwards. The important point is to find out from them whether they know what the Sikhs are doing to-night."

The question was then put, and when Akram Chunder repeated the order he had heard given, that the Sikhs were all to retire to Russool, there was a deep and general feeling of relief.

"That is the best news I have heard for many a day," the colonel exclaimed; "for if they had fallen upon us to-night, which I half expected they would do, it would have been a frightful business. I must take these men to Lord Gough at once. He will be even more glad than I am to hear the news, for he must feel the responsibility terribly. You might as well come along, Mansfield, to act as interpreter; he may have no one with him just at present who speaks the language."

The story was told to the commander-in-chief and Sir Henry Lawrence, who was now his chief political adviser.

"The information is most valuable if true," Sir Henry Lawrence said. " I suppose there is no doubt these two men are Mr. Groves' servants; because, as you say, he was brought in insensible. That is a very important point, for they might be two Sikhs sent in with this story to put us off our guard."

"Major Mansfield says that he recognizes their faces, Sir Henry."

" I would not say that I absolutely recognize them, but they certainly look to me like the two men whom I have seen riding with Mr. Groves."

" Do not let us make any mistake about it. The matter can be easily settled. If these men have been in camp for a month they must be well known."

"I will find one of Mr. Fullarton's men, sir. Groves was living in his tent, so any of the servants there would know them."

While the major was away Sir Henry Lawrence cross-examined Akram Chunder and Bhop Lai as to their story. In three or four minutes Major Mansfield returned, bringing with him Ram Singh.

"This is Mr. Fullarton's servant, sir."

"Do you know these two men?" Sir Henry asked.

" Yes, sahib, I know them well. They are Mr. Groves' servants. They have been with him for four or five years; they were with him at Ferozeshah and Sobraon."

"So they were," Lord Gough said, getting up from the camp-chair in which he was sitting and looking at them closely. " I remember their being with him at Ferozeshah. Mr. Groves carried messages for me several times when most of my staff were down, and I noticed then how coolly those fellows rode after him whenever he moved away from my side."

"There is no farther doubt about the story," Sir Henry Lawrence said, " and these men have clearly saved Mr. Groves in the way they have stated."

"Tell them, Sir Henry," Lord Gough said, "that I consider them to be very fine fellows, and that I thank them for their conduct in having rescued their master. As for the information they have given, that is our affair, and we can reward it. I should be glad if you could give them a hundred rupees each as a present out of your information fund."

Sir Henry repeated Lord Cough's message to the men, laying stress upon the difference between the action of saving their master's life and the information they had brought. " For the first," he said, "the commander-in-chief desires to pay you honour. Had you belonged to one of our native regiments he would have made you officers. As it is, he can only say that he honours you for your conduct, and himself thanks you for having saved the life of that very promising young officer, Mr. Groves. The information you have brought is valuable, and for that he asks me to make you a present of a hundred rupees each. You lost your horses, of course ? "

"Yes, sahib, ours and the master's."

" Come round to me in the morning. I will give you an order to receive the two hundred rupees and to take the three horses, as it is likely enough they came back with the Lancers; if not, to take three of the Sikh horses that came in with them. How is your master going on? " he asked Ram Singh.

"He is better, sahib; he can talk now, and he has asked several times whether Mr. Groves has been heard of. It will do him good to know he has been brought back."

The interview was now over, and the two men went back to the hospital, and on their arrival there, were delighted to find that Percy was conscious, and sat with him by turns through the night. He was greatly pleased to hear that Mr. Fullarton had not been killed, as he feared.

"Have you had anything to eat?" he asked towards morning.

"No, sahib, but that does not matter."

"It matters a great deal," he said. "I am sure I do not

know how you are to draw rations here, and there will be no means of buying anything."

He thought a little, and when, half an hour later, the principal surgeon stopped beside him to ask him how he felt he said, " I feel queer about the head, and weak, but that is all. I am worrying about my men, sir. I do not see how they are to draw rations."

"I can manage that," the surgeon replied. "If they are willing to help here I will put them on the list as hospital orderlies and draw rations for them with the others. I shall be very glad if they will do so, for I am short of hands, and want help terribly. We never calculated on such a crowd of wounded as we have got, and as, at present, they certainly won't be able to spare us fighting men to act as hospital orderlies, I shall be very pleased to have your fellows. Then one of them will be able to look specially after you."

Akram Chunder and his companion embraced the offer with great satisfaction when Percy translated it, and were soon at work in their new duties. As soon as the morning meal had been served Percy told Akram that he had better go at once to Sir Henry Lawrence to get the order for their horses. "There is no time to be lost about that," he said. "They are so good that they will be snapped up at once for the use of officers who have lost their own chargers."

Akram found the horses, as he had hoped, in the lines of the Lancers, but when he produced his order and claimed them he was scoffed at.

"Look here, Bill; here is a likely tale," one of the men said to another. "This chap has got an order signed Henry Lawrence, to take the horses belonging to himself and another chap wherever he may find them in camp, and I am blowed if he doesn't pitch upon these two chargers that the major and Captain Wilkins have chosen for themselves. Why, anyone can see with half an eye that they are English hunters, or have got a lot of English blood in them anyway. You get out of this, Johnny, or I may put my fist between your two eyes."

Akram quietly walked off, and held the paper out to the first officer he met.

"Are your horses here? " the latter asked after reading it.

"Yes, sahib."

The officer was as incredulous as the troopers had been, that a native, evidently of no high position, could have owned such horses; and the major, coming up and hearing the story, angrily ordered Akram out of camp as a rogue. The man went quietly back towards the political officer's house, but on the way he met Major Mansfield. He saluted and told him the story. "I will go back with you," the major said; "it is no use troubling Sir Henry Lawrence." Major Mansfield's interposition proved efficient, and as soon as the story of how the two men had sacrificed their horses and had saved their master's life was told, the major gave orders that Akram should take the two animals. " I heard there was a civilian and two men joined our squadron when they charged, though nobody noticed them fall back with it. But how on earth came two Sikh servants to have such horses as those? "

" Groves' uncle is the Colonel Groves who was in the Sikh service under Runjeet Singh, and he has held the fortress of Djarma ever since. I know he got two or three English thoroughbreds over, and bred some horses. The third horse is evidently a native, and not a particularly good one."

"Which is your master's horse, man? "

" He rides sometimes one and sometimes the other of these two, sahib. His own horse is over there," and he pointed towards Russool; " he had to leave it behind when he escaped from Sher Singh. That was a splendid horse. These are good, but nothing to Sheik. He bought this native pony when he escaped, and would have ridden it, but we could not let our master be riding on a little native horse while we were on fine horses that his uncle gave us."

"That accounts for it, you see, major."

"Well, I am sorry to give them up, but of course there is no help for it. Groves is certainly lucky in having two such servants, and it would be a shame indeed for them to lose their horses after having behaved so uncommonly well."

So the horses were taken over and picketed with those of the surgeons', and for the next three weeks the two men worked in the hospital. Percy had for a few days been very ill; fever set in from the inflammation of his wound; but as soon as that abated he gained strength rapidly, and at the end of three weeks took his discharge and reported himself to Sir Henry Lawrence as ready for service.

"You won't be fit for service for another month, Mr. Groves. But it is just as well for you to be out of hospital, for you will pick up strength faster now than you would in there."

By this time the camp extended over a large space of ground. Everything was in excellent order, and but few signs were visible of the terrible struggle that had taken place a few weeks before. Percy shared a tent with another young civilian. His head was still bandaged up, and it would be a long time before he could wear any but the softest head-gear. He consulted the doctors rather anxiously as to whether the hair would grow again on the patch, three inches wide, from the top of his head down to his ear.

"Probably it will, but there is no saying, Groves. If it does grow it will probably come white."

"I don't much care what colour it comes," Percy said, "if only it does come so as to hide my ear, or rather my half ear."

"I should not bother about that," the surgeon said. "You can let the hair at the top of the head grow long, it will hide the scar, ear and all. It will look better than a white patch there."

"I suppose it would," Percy said, regarding himself in the little hand-mirror rather ruefully. "A white patch certainly would not look well, and the people one meets would be always asking how it came, which would be a frightful nuisance. Still, if it comes white I could dye it, I suppose."

"I should not bother about it, Groves; it is an honourable scar."

"Yes, that is all very well, doctor; but it is a scar for all that."

During the fortnight that had elapsed before the camp was broken up, Percy did no work, but took a short ride morning and evening. During the heat of the day he sat in the shade at the entrance of his tent and read.

On the nth of February the Sikhs made a great demonstration, drove in a patrolling party, and seemed as if they wished to bring on another battle. A column threatened the rear of the camp, and the spies brought in news that they had determined upon attacking us. Lord Gough had no wish to bring on a battle on ground where the Sikhs, if beaten, could again retire into the jungle. The army therefore remained in their lines. It was observed that the array of tents round Russool had considerably diminished. The next day it had entirely disappeared.

Great anxiety was felt in camp as to what had become of the Sikhs, and all sorts of reports were current as to Sher Singh's intentions. Some believed that he intended to cross the Chenab at Wuzeerabad, and to march upon Lahore. The garrison there was a very weak one, and could have offered but a slight resistance if attacked by so large a force, aided as it certainly would be by a rising of the populace. Another report was to the effect that Sher Singh had stated that his intention was to make forced marches to Umritsur, to cross the Sutlej, and advance to Delhi and capture and sack the place before any force could be gathered to arrest his progress. Were not one or other of these plans intended, the only explanation why the Sikhs should desert their strongly intrenched and almost inacessible position, was that they found extreme difficulty in supplying their force with food

there; and indeed it was known from deserters that they had for some time been suffering from famine. Moreover they might consider that if successfully attacked on the flank they would be cut off by the deep ravine between their intrench-ments and Russool, and by the river still farther behind, from making their escape.

Late in the evening of the i2th some spies brought in the information that Sher Singh was marching for Gujerat. In the neighbourhood of this town the Sikhs had, in past times, gained several important victories, and they regarded the locality as being specially sacred and propitious to them. The country round was rich and fertile, and they would have no difficulty in obtaining provisions. It is true that they would have to fight in the open, but their confidence had been restored by their success at Chillianwalla. There was, too, a probability that from Gujerat the approach of General Whish's force, which was hurrying up from Mooltan, might be intercepted.

Chuttur Singh had joined his son with a force from the Peshawur district a few days after the battle, and the army with which he retired was little short of fifty thousand men. On the 13th Percy rode out with a number of other English officers to inspect the Sikh works round Russool. These were found to be extremely formidable, well placed, and constructed with great skill, and all congratulated themselves that the army had been spared the terrible loss that would certainly have befallen it in carrying the position. That evening Brigadier Cheape of the Royal Engineers, who had conducted the siege of Mooltan, arrived with a body of native cavalry, having pushed on rapidly and left the main body of General Whish's force some days in the rear.

On the morning of the i4th news came that the Sikhs had occupied Gujerat, capturing the small body of Pathan horse stationed there under the command of Lieutenant Nicholson. Major Lawrence was also a prisoner in Sher Singh's camp, hav-

ing, with his wife, been treacherously handed over to the Sikhs by an Afghan chief with whom they had taken refuge.

The next morning at four o'clock the troops marched for Lussoore. Conflicting reports came in as to the course of the Sikh army; but the balance of probability was that they were still remaining in the vicinity of Gujerat. General Whish had already sent a force to bar their passage should they try to cross at Wuzeerabad. The army moved slowly forward so as to be able to meet the Sikhs should they advance, but no engagement was desired until Whish, with the Bengal and Bombay troops who had been engaged with him in the siege of Mooltan, should join.

On the 2oth the army reached Shadeewal, effected a junction with two of General Whish's brigades, and was now ready to encounter the enemy. On the following morning it advanced towards Gujerat, across a plain cultivated in many places and dotted with clumps of trees. The drums of the Sikhs beating to arms could be heard in the distance, and the line of battle was formed. General Gilbert's division was on the right. Next to him was the division of General Whish. Separated from them by a deep nullah was Colin Campbell's division, and on the left the Bombay troops under Brigadier-general Dundas. Each of these divisions was accompanied by batteries of field and horse artillery. Part of the cavalry was on either flank, while two regiments of native cavalry and two of infantry were in rear covering the baggage.

The Sikhs opened fire while our force was still a considerable distance away, and the line was halted and the artillery and skirmishers moved to the front. Just behind the line of the infantry there was a lofty mound commanding a view of the whole plain, and on this the staff and all the political officers who were free to choose their position took up their post.

"It will be nothing to-day," Akram Chunder said to Percy. They had dismounted, Bhop Lai taking charge of the three horses while his comrade had posted himself just behind his master. "If they could not stop the English before, when they had great intrenchments and heavy guns, what chance can they have now? "

The British guns speedily opened fire, and very soon obtained the mastery over those of the Sikhs, whose fire slackened. In a short time their guns were withdrawn, the infantry falling back with them to a village in a strong position where they were almost hidden from sight. The British infantry moved forward as soon as the enemy's fire slackened, Penny's brigade of Gilbert's division advancing to storm the village. It was flanked by two Sikh batteries, and the brigade advanced under a shower of balls, dashed across a deep nullah, poured in a heavy volley, and then went at the village with the bayonet. The Sikhs in the village fought stoutly, many of them shutting themselves up in the houses and defending themselves till the last.

As soon as the British showed on the other side of the village the guns of the Sikh batteries opened upon them. The battery of horse-artillery galloped up and replied vigorously; the whole line of infantry pressed forward, and the enemy deserted their guns and fled. The 2d Bengal Europeans, that had suffered heavily at Chillianwalla, sustained a loss of six officers and one hundred and forty-three men killed or wounded, while of the two native regiments with them the 3ist lost one hundred and twenty-eight and the yoth forty-four killed or wounded.

This position carried, the whole line advanced, and although the enemy fought with dogged courage they were everywhere bfeaten back. Harvey's brigade with considerable loss carried the village of Chowta-kabrah gallantly. The Sikhs as they retired were pounded by the guns of three troops of horse-artillery, but the enemy's artillery fire was so heavy that one battery had to send to the rear for horses before it could move its guns, while another suffered such losses that they were obliged to get men from the loth Foot to work the

pieces. The Sikh cavalry made frequent efforts to work round the right flank and get into the rear, but were checked each time by a troop of horse-artillery and by the i4th Dragoons, although at one time a party penetrated so closely to the heavy guns where Lord Gough had taken up his station, that his personal escort charged and drove them back.

Steadily the whole line pressed forward, The Sikh infantry several times gathered in great numbers, supported by their cavalry, to make a rush to meet us, but were each time checked by the accurate and rapid fire of our artillery, and were pressed back until Gujerat was passed on its eastern side by Campbell's division, and by the Bombay troops on its west. The latter had met with but little resistance. On the right of the Sikh line the Afghan horse, fifteen hundred strong, with a large number of the Sikh irregulars, now threatened our left flank. They were charged by the Scinde horse and two squadrons of the 9th Lancers, driven from the field, and two of their standards taken. The whole of the enemy's right wing now fled and were pursued by the British cavalry and horse-artillery, and the rout of the Sikhs was complete.

The infantry halted to collect the guns, ammunition, and baggage of the Sikhs; but for many miles the cavalry and a troop of the Bombay horse-artillery pursued the flying foe, scattering them whenever they tried to rally, capturing many guns, and killing vast numbers of fugitives, no quarter being given by the cavalry, who remembered that every one of their own wounded comrades had been killed and mutilated by them. The cavalry did not halt until they had reached a point fourteen miles from the field of battle.

The Sikh troops who had remained in Gujerat offered a stout resistance, but were, after some hard fighting, overcome. A singular proof was given that the Bunnoo regiments retained the discipline they had learned irom British officers to the last, for when resistance fairly ceased the Sikh sentries placed round the native hospitals were found marching backward and

forward on their beats as unconcernedly as if absolutely unconscious of the events that were taking place.

Fifty-three guns were captured. They had in almost every case been defended to the last. One large gun had been the object of fire by a whole British battery. All the men had been killed but two; but as the British line advanced these two alone continued to work it. One fell with a musket-ball, but the other, unaided, fired two more rounds, and only when the British line was close at hand sought safety in flight. The Afghan horse, after leaving the field, did not draw rein until they crossed the river Jhelum, a distance of over thirty miles.

The loss of the army in this great victory was comparatively trifling, but 5 officers and 76 men were killed, 24 officers and 595 men wounded. The loss of the Sikhs was very large. They had brought sixty pieces of artillery into the field, and carried off but seven of them. General Gilbert's division followed up the enemy with such rapidity that the Sikh chieftains, despairing of successful resistance, surrendered in numbers. Chuttur Singh and Sher Singh were among the first to propose surrender, and all the other leaders, with the exception of two, came in. Forty-one guns were handed over, and 16,000 men laid down their arms. In all, the enemy lost 167 guns during the campaign. Their possession of so large an amount of ordnance was a great surprise to the British, who had believed that in the previous campaign they had captured almost the whole of the Sikh guns. The greater portion of these pieces had doubtless been hidden by the sirdars, those captured in the Sutlej campaign having for the most part been the artillery of the regular army. As a proof that this was the case, an immense number of guns were found buried in the earth at Govindghur when we took possession of that place. All the Sikhs who surrendered or were captured after the battle of Gujerat were allowed to return to their homes after being deprived of their arms. They were permitted to carry away their clothes and horses.

1'EK.CY HAS AN INTERVIEW WITH SHER SINGH.

Chuttur Singh and Sher Singh surrendered at Wuzeerabad. They came in on elephants, with a few retainers and a small escort of Bunnoo infantry. All had to lay down their arms before crossing the ford to meet Lord Gough, who with his staff and a large number of officers was on the opposite bank. Sher Singh had released Major Lawrence from his confinement, and had sent him to the British head-quarters to negotiate the terms of surrender, and that officer met him as with his father he crossed the bridge. The scene was an impressive one, as Chuttur Singh and his son, the two men who had involved their country in the struggle and had brought such terrible disasters upon it, dismounted from their elephants and paid their respects to the British general. Sher Singh was a rebel against his own government as well as against us, but at least he had not ill-treated the three or four British officers, or the two British ladies, who had fallen into his hands, and had sent back unharmed the few British soldiers who had been captured and brought into his camp. Major Edwardes' despatches too had completely established the fact that he had for a long time, under most difficult circumstances, been faithful, and that he had at last yielded to something very like force on the part of his soldiers. Although, therefore, his reception by Lord Gough was cold, it was very different to that which he would have received had his rebellion, like that of Moolraj, been sullied by the murder in cold blood of English prisoners.

As the rajah drew off from his interview with the commander-in-chief his eye fell upon Percy. He ordered his mahout to stop his elephant. Percy rode forward to him, and conversed with him for several minutes, Sher Singh expressing his satisfaction that he had met with no injury in effecting his escape.

"I liked you, and always treated you well, did I not? and you will stand my friend now?" he asked anxiously.

" I am but a young officer, and my friendship can little avail your Highness," Percy said; "but assuredly I will testify, and

360 THROUGH THE SIKH WAR

have already testified, that I was well treated. I was allowed to keep my servants and my horses, I was well fed and cared for, and, save that I had not my liberty, had everything that I could desire. I thank your Highness sincerely for the manner in which I was treated."

Percy was reining back his horse when he heard a low whinny. He turned round with a start, and saw one of the rajah's officers struggling with his horse, which was trying to turn aside out of the procession. "Why, Sheik, is it you?" Percy shouted in delight. And the horse, rearing up, all but unseated its rider, made two bounds to his side, and thrust its head against his hand.

The little stir caused Sher Singh to look around. " It is my horse, rajah," Percy said; " it knows me again."

The rajah nodded. "I had forgotten it," he said. "I knew that you had escaped, and never gave a thought to your horse. You must give it up, Aliram; it is the property of the sahib."

With an angry scowl the native alighted.

"I shall not leave you horseless," Percy said. And riding back through the officers, who were looking on in amazement at the scene, he joined his two followers, who were sitting their horses at some little distance in the rear. Both gave a loud exclamation of pleasure as Percy rode up, leading Sheik. He was himself mounted on Bhop Lai's horse. He dismounted and sprang on to Sheik. " Bhop Lai, mount your own horse and take the one you are on to the Sikh officer. You will find him standing there. He annexed Sheik, but I don't want to give him the mortification of tramping on foot after the rajah." Bhop Lai did as he was ordered, and then rejoined Percy, who was overjoyed at recovering the splendid animal his uncle had given him.

On the 30th of March the governor-general issued a proclamation declaring the Punjaub annexed to the British dominions in India. A large pension was assigned to Dhuleep

Singh, who was placed under the tuition of an English officer, and the administration of the Punjaub was intrusted to a board consisting of Sir Henry Lawrence,' his brother John, and Mr. Mansell, a civilian, to whom was assigned the financial administration of the province.

Two days after the surrender of Sher Singh, Percy obtained two months' leave of absence, and started for Djarma, which was distant about a hundred miles from Wuzeerabad. The passage of Gilbert's division north had already restored tranquillity, and he followed the main road as far as Rawal Pin-dee, where a British garrison had been left, without encountering the slightest interruption. Then he struck off along the foot of the hills on his way to the fortress thirty miles off.

At Rawal Pindee he heard that his uncle had ridden in with two hundred horsemen on the arrival of General Gilbert at the town, and had placed his troops at the general's disposal. There was, however, no occasion for their services, the Afghans having already evacuated the district of Peshawur, and there being no longer any Sikh force under arms sufficient to offer resistance to the British column.

" We need not be afraid of Ghoolab Singh this time, sahib," Akram Chunder said as they rode out of Rawal Pindee.

" No. The old fox has played his game as well now as he did in the last campaign. Throughout, he continued to promise to join Sher Singh, as we learnt when we were prisoners, while, on the other hand, he lent money to our people when they needed it for purchasing provisions. But it was not until just before Gujerat, when he saw that there was no longer the least doubt which side would prove triumphant, that he really put his troops in motion and offered to act in any way he might be required against the Sikhs. However, he knows now that there is no possibility of his ever getting a foothold across the Jhelum. It is certain that in a week or two we shall hear that the whole of the Punjaub is annexed by England, and I and my uncle might pay him a visit at Serinagur

without the least fear that he would receive us in any but a courteous and hospitable manner. Djama is as good as British territory now. I daresay my uncle has got the British flag waving over the fortress already. The Indian government have no reason either to like or trust Ghoolab, and, if he gave them cause, have only to stretch out their hand to take Cashmere."

" It would be the best thing that could happen for the country," said Akram. "Then the people would be able to till their fields and weave their shawls in peace and quiet, afraid neither of foreign invaders nor of oppressive rulers."

As they approachedithe fortress they could see a flag waving over its highest point.

"I thought my uncle would have it up," Percy exclaimed. " It is too far away to see the colours, but I am sure what they are."

Percy rode fast now, walked up the long hill, and then galloped to the gate. It was open and the drawbridge down. He waved his hand to the men who saluted as he rode in, and kept on without drawing rein until he sprang from his horse at the steps, where his uncle, who had been warned of his approach, stood waiting to meet him.

"Welcome back, Percy; welcome back! It is eleven months since you rode out, and you have no doubt gone through much, though I have heard nothing of you."

"There were no means of sending letters, uncle; but I have often thought of you, and wondered how you have been getting on."

"I sent three letters off, Percy. Did you get none of them?"

"None, uncle."

"And you know nothing of what has happened since you have been away? "

"Nothing," Percy repeated, struck by his uncle's grave face. "Nothing serious has happened, I hope?"

"Come in, lad," the colonel said, taking his arm and leading him into the private apartments.

Percy looked round, expecting to see the Ranee appear.

"She is gone, lad."

"Gone, uncle!"

"Ay, lad, she died ten months ago, a month after you left us."

Percy stood aghast. " My dear uncle, how sorry I am ! I never dreamt of such a home-coming as this. My poor aunt! What a terrible loss for you! "

"Terrible, lad. I am getting over it now, but for a time I was crushed, indeed for some days I was myself at death's door, and only pulled through by God's mercy."

"Why, what was it, uncle? Fever?"

"Poison, lad."

" Poison, uncle! " Percy repeated, horror-struck.

"That is what it was, my boy. Ghoolab's work again, I have no doubt, though I cannot prove it. Would to heaven I could, for I would ride to Serinagur with a hundred men, force my way into his presence if need be, accuse him of the deed, and blow out his brains. But I have not a shadow of proof. It happened, as I told you, a month, or maybe six weeks, after you had left. The news had come of the rising at Mooltan and the murder of Agnew and Anderson. We were in great anxiety about you, knowing you were with them, Mahtab especially; but, as I told her, had you been killed also, we should have heard of it, and that you were not the sort of fellow to be caught in a trap, and I had no doubt you had got out of it somehow. A day or two after, she said to me, 'You must be especially careful how, Roland. Ghoo-lab has a hand in every trouble that takes place in the Pun-jaub. No doubt he will do as he did before, play one side against the other, send promises to each and do nothing until he sees how matters go; but he will think that at any rate if there is war and strife he will be free to do as he likes up

here in the north, and he will likely enough try once again to encompass your life." I felt that that was probable enough, and kept a more vigilant guard than usual. One day after dining we were both taken suddenly ill. Two hours later she was dead. I pulled through, but I looked death very closely in the face."

"And did ytm find out who the murderer was, uncle? " " No, my boy, nor have I found out now. I am as sure as to the mover in the plot, but not as to his instrument. I found, as soon as I had recovered, that the cook and other servants had all been seized and caged up. Had I died, no doubt they would all have been tortured and put to death; but the officers knew me well enough to feel sure that I should be angry at it did I recover. I had no ground for suspicion against one more than another. I cross-questioned the cook closely, but beyond protesting his innocence I could get nothing out of him. He had cooked the dinner as usual, but was not, as he said, all the time standing over his pots. Any of the other servants might while his back was turned, or while bringing things up from the cool cellar as he required them, have dropped poison into the cooking pot. There was no denying this. The other servants with equal vehemence protested their innocence. The officers wanted me to use torture, but this I would not hear of. I might have tortured half a dozen innocent men before I came to the guilty one. Besides having an Englishman's abhorrence of such means, I could not rely on anything wrung from a man. A weak man while he is in his agony will acknowledge anything required of him, will confess any crime, will accuse anyone; while a guilty one of stronger nerve will die protesting his innocence. They were all examined closely, but none could say that he saw any stranger, that is, anyone outside the household, enter the kitchen; but as at times the room seems to have been entirely empty, anyone might have slipped in un-perceived."

"And since then you have suspected no one, uncle? " "No one, Percy. None of the sen-ants have left, all are still with me."

"What! have you kept them still about you?" " Yes. All appeared so utterly distressed and broken-down at the death of their mistress, and at the suspicion that rested upon them, that I could not bring myself to discharge them. Indeed, so great was the fury of the people throughout the whole district, that I believe had I turned them out through the gates, their lives would have been sacrificed. Besides, how could I rely upon a fresh set of servants more than upon those who have been with us long, and who apparently cared for us? Moreover, there was a certainty that every one of them would suspect the others, and that each would make every effort to find out the one by whose deed suspicion and disgrace had fallen upon them. They would naturally watch each other as a cat watches mice. The kitchen would never be left empty again. There would be at least two in it, and it would be next to impossible for the attempt to be repeated unseen. The cook himself might indeed have slipped poison into the curry or other dish before compounding it, but I was convinced that whoever was the assassin it was not the cook himself, for he must have known that suspicion would fall upon him, and that had I died his torture and death were certain."

"Then you think that it was someone outside your house, uncle?"

" I do not say that, Percy. I only say that I suspect no one. After the discovery that the rascally steward you shot was a traitor, I can never feel sure of anyone, therefore it may have been one of the sen-ants, it may have been one of the soldiers, it may have been a stranger inside the gates. At any rate no fresh attempt has been made, but it was some time, Percy, before I got to enjoy my food again."

CHAPTER XXI

RETIRED

T)ERCY had felt hungry when he rode into the fortress, but A although he saw his uncle eat as heartily as usual, his appetite seemed to desert him, and he ate very sparingly of each dish placed before him. His uncle smiled.

"You are not such a good trencher-man as you were, Percy."

"Oh, I am all right, uncle; but just at first the thought that any of these dishes may be poisoned is an unpleasant one."

"You will get over it in time. Frankly, I do not think that there is any ground for uneasiness. From the day Gough crossed the Sutlej I felt safe; from the day Gujerat was won I have felt absolutely at my ease. I have no longer the slightest fear of Ghoolab. This district is part of the Punjaub, and the Punjaub will assuredly be annexed to British India." %

"Yes, uncle, they say the proclamation will be out in another fortnight or so."

"That being so, lad, Ghoolab's game is finally up. Did I die to-morrow, surely no nominee of his would obtain the appointment of governor, or whatever your people call him, of a district adjoining Cashmere. He may not like me, he may owe me a grudge for thwarting him so long, but he has no longer the slightest interest in my death; and although Ghoolab would without scruple remove a hundred men who stood in his way, he would not run the slightest risk—and

there is always a certain risk of a tool turning traitor—when there was nothing whatever to be gained by it."

" I hear that you rode into Rawal Pindee to meet General Gilbert's column, as it came through."

"Yes, I took all my cavalry over, but by the time we got there all opposition had ceased, and the sirdars were pouring in to make their submission, and beg for forgiveness. So there was no occasion for their services. Of course he thanked me, and said that he would report my offer."

"I almost thought you might come down and join us, uncle."

" I thought it over, lad, but there might have been trouble here in my absence; but I thought I would keep my force together, so that if there should be any tough fighting in the north, I should be able to march away horse and foot to join our men. I did not calculate upon so complete and sudden a collapse of the Sikhs. Now we have talked enough about myself; it is time that you tell me the story of your adventures, of which as yet I know nothing, and how you came by that desperately ugly wound on your head."

It was late before Percy finished the story of his adventures.

" You have had great luck, lad, to have got so well out of your scrapes," the colonel said.

"Well, it is late now, and we must be off to bed; we shall have plenty of time to talk matters over in the morning."

"I should think, uncle," Percy said, when they had lighted their cigars after breakfast, " that the government will recognize your position, and either grant you the same power over your district that the sirdars have over their estates, or else that they will appoint you as their official over the district."

" I have no doubt they would do so, Percy, were I willing to accept it; but I have quite made up my mind to give it all up and go home."

"You have, uncle ! " Percy exclaimed in surprise.

" Yes, I have stuck here all these years for three reasons:

first, because I am an obstinate beggar, and would not be turned out; secondly, because my wife would not have liked to leave her native land, and would never have been happy in England; thirdly, because the people of my district have been rich and prosperous under me, and I was not going to hand them over to be pillaged and robbed by one of these Sikh harpies. Now, however, the case is altogether changed. If I go, I go of my own free will and choosing. Mahtab has gone, and there is no longer anything to tie me to India. Lastly, I can with confidence hand over the district to English administrators, secure that the people will not be taxed unfairly, and will be safe from all oppression and extortion. During the last two years I have reduced my force here considerably. I was certain that after the lesson we gave them, there was no fear of their ever again making an open assault on the place. I began by not filling up vacancies caused by death or from men being superannuated. Fortunately, there is a good deal of cultivable land down this valley, and, indeed, in other parts of the district, and I have given grants of small holdings to all who were willing to take their discharge."

" I noticed that there was a great change in the valley below, since I went away, uncle, that fields have been marked out, and that there was quite a village down where the Sikhs were encamped when they besieged us."

" Yes, over two hundred holdings have been taken up there. I granted them free of all taxes for the first three years, gave those men who had no savings a little assistance in the way of a loan, and in time there will be a large and, I hope, thriving village there. I have urged the men to keep up a certain organization among themselves,—to form, in fact, a kind of military colony, so as to be in a position to resist dacoits or attacks by the marauding hill tribes. I have similarly settled that other valley three miles to the north; altogether I have given a start to nearly a thousand of the men. They have

served me faithfully, and nothing would induce me to go away and abandon them. I think that it is very likely a force may be formed by our people for the protection of the frontier; and, as you and Mr. Fullarton, with whom I have had a good deal of correspondence, and the Lawrences, are all aware that the men have behaved most faithfully and can be trusted, I hope I shall be able to get all those who wish to continue soldiering to be mustered into the service."

"I should think you might manage that, uncle; one or other of the Lawrences, perhaps both, are certain to be appointed commissioners of the Punjaub. Of course, I am not in a position to speak to them on such a subject, but I am sure Mr. Fullarton would do so. I did not see him after I was wounded, as before I was about he had been taken down to Lahore. I heard that he was recovering fast, and was expected to rejoin the head-quarters camp in a short time. Having been so long on the frontier, I should think probably he will get a large district here, but at any rate he would, I am sure, bring your matter before the Lawrences."

" I should think it by no means improbable, Percy, that they may appoint you district magistrate, or collector, or whatever they call it, of this district; that is, if they keep it as a district."

"I should think they are not likely to do that, uncle. Rawal Pindee will be made, I should say, the centre of a district of which this will form part. Still, possibly I may be appointed an assistant in this district, as I know the country and the people so well; and if so, I will follow up the methods that have made it in your hands the most flourishing little corner of the Punjaub, in spite of the greater part of it being merely hill country."

"Well, Percy, I don't think you can do better than stick to it. You have got a splendid start in the service, and have every chance of rising in it rapidly. It is good for you to work, and the exciting scenes you have passed through dur-

ing the last four years have been a good preparation for making you an active and efficient officer. But what I want to say is this: if your health fails, or if, sooner or later, you marry and would like to settle down at home, or if from any other cause you want to leave the service, remember there is no occasion for you to work for your living. I am a rich man, and, thank God, I do not owe my wealth to grinding the last penny out of the natives. I could have retired and lived more than comfortably in England had I chosen to do so when Runjeet Singh died, for the Old Lion, with all his faults, was the most liberal of masters to those who served him well. Since then I have, of course, largely increased my means. I had but to pay a fixed sum annually to Lahore, and the revenue of the district has multiplied itself by ten since I took charge of it. I could, therefore, give you an income sufficient to keep you comfortably at home during my lifetime, and it will, of course, all come to you at my death. Still, much as I should like to have you with me, I think that, at any rate, it would be better for you to remain in the service of the Company for some years. It is a bad thing for any man to have nothing to do, and there is no better training than that afforded by the civil service of the Company." "Thank you very much, uncle. I like the service greatly, so far as I have seen of it; and I should certainly wish to remain in it. Even if I did not like India, I should do so. I think that a man with health and strength ought to have a career, and not to owe everything to another, however close a relation he may be. I certainly hope to be appointed to the Punjaub, and I should think there would always be a spice of excitement here. There are sure to be constant troubles with the Afghans and hill tribes all round it. I have been awfully lucky in getting noticed so young, and so gaining at least eight or ten years' start of fresh comers of my own age from England; and I feel, above all things, how indebted to you I am for this."

"You are indebted to me that you came out to India, Percy, but almost everything else is due to yourself. The turning-point in your career was when you sat down on board ship to take your first lesson in Punjaubi. It was the steadfastness with which you stuck to your studies during your voyage which won for you the liking and patronage of Mr. Fullarton, and so enabled you to take part in the Sutlej campaign. There you showed pluck and presence of mind, and so gained the attention of Sir Henry Hardinge and of the commander-in-chief. After that it was the fact that you had got up Pathan, which procured for you your early appointment and your nomination to accompany Agnew. Had it not been for that you would have been out of all this last business. I have done what little I could in the way of teaching you to ride well and use your weapons, and have given you the best advice I could; but beyond that everything has depended on yourself. I feel proud of you, lad, very proud of you, and I only wish Mahtab had been here to share-my satisfaction. She was as fond of you, lad, as if she had been your mother. Life here has been altogether different since I lost her; and the sorest point of all is the thought that the blow that struck her was aimed at me."

" I know that you must feel that, uncle. I can quite understand your wanting to get away from here now."

Percy did not take the whole of his leave. His uncle was restless and unsettled, and when, a week later, the news came of the annexation of the Punjaub, Percy said:

"Why should you stop, uncle? The sooner you are away the better, and I do not care to stay here longer. The place is not the same as it was; besides, I cannot help feeling that just at the present time it would be better for me to be at head-quarters. There is nothing like being on the spot when changes are being made."

" I think you are right there, lad. I have been telling my officers what you said about trying to get them into the Com-

pany's employment, and all have expressed their willingness to remain in the district and hold themelves in readiness to join should they receive a message from you. I have but eight hundred men left now, and have given it to be understood that I shall give them fifty rupees each when they are disbanded, and a grant of land large enough to keep them. I have no doubt the grant will be confirmed, as the authoril ties will be glad enough to see a body of men, who might be troublesome if turned adrift, settle down as cultivators, so adding to the revenue. Well, there is nothing to stay for. I will put it in orders this evening, that as the whole country has now been taken over by the British government, the force will be disbanded to-morrow."

The next day the troops paraded for the last time. The colonel made them a little speech, thanking them for the fidelity they had shown, and expressing his deep regret at leaving them. He told them that if a force should be raised by the British for service on the frontier, his nephew would endeavour to procure enrolment in its ranks for such of them as desired it; that he had set aside a tract of land for them, and that Nand Chund had his authority to divide it fairly among them; and that he himself, as a token of his appreciation of their faithful services, had directed fifty rupees to be give,n to each man in addition to the pay due to him, and that his vakeel was writing for each a paper testifying to his services, which he himself would sign, and which they would find useful in their dealings with British officials.

When he had finished the men broke their ranks and crowded round him, tears flowing down most of their faces, calling down blessings upon him, and pouring out their regret

leaving the service of so good and kind a master. It was with some difficulty that the colonel, who was himself deeply affected, extricated himself from them and returned to his residence. The next morning he and Percy started. The colonel had made a very handsome present to Bhop Lai and

Akram Chunder, and they of course accompanied them; but in addition the whole of the cavalry mounted and formed a voluntary escort to them as far as Rawal Pindee.

Travelling quietly they reached head-quarters on the day when the proclamation was read to the troops, amid the booming of cannon, announcing to the Punjaub that it was now an integral portion of British India. Percy introduced his uncle to Mr. Fullarton, and the latter took him to Sir Henry Lawrence, with whom, during a stay of a week in the British camp, he had several long conversations, the chief-commissioner being desirous of ascertaining the views of one of such long experience in the country.

Colonel Groves was strongly of opinion that henceforth there would be no more trouble in the Punjaub. "The Sikh power is altogether broken," he said; "the former danger to India existed in the fact that hitherto they had been so successful in war that they had come to consider themselves almost invincible, and that the great army Runjeet had got together was demoralized by inactivity, and each man thirsted for an opportunity to distinguish himself, and dreamt of a share in the plunder of India. The population in general were, in his opinion, peace-loving and industrious; they had suffered terribly under the exactions of the grasping sirdars, who amassed fortunes out of their toil, and of the tax-gatherers, who had to collect vast sums for the maintenance of the army. That army had ceased to exist—Gujerat and ChiHianwalla had accounted for the greater part of those who had escaped Ferozeshah and Sobraon. I believe," he said, "that in the course of a generation there will be no more orderly or loyal province than the Punjaub. There will be always a certain number of restless and adventurous spirits, but for these there will in time, I presume, be an opening in the regiments which, when you feel that you can trust them, will be raised here as in other parts of India. There is no finer fighting material to be found than among the Sikhs, and

the fidelity with which they have fought to the last for their country is an earnest of that which they will show to our colours when they once take a pride in them."

He then instanced the conduct of his own men, who had proved faithful to him throughout, and had fought as bravely against the Sikh forces as they had formerly done under the Sikh flag. "They were for the most part," he said, "men of hill tribes, and Pathan rather than Sikh by blood, and should you be raising a force for the defence of the frontier against Afghans or hill men, you would find them admirably suited to the service. They are already well drilled and accustomed to discipline, and I promised them, when I disbanded them the other day, that I would speak to you in their favour, and would guarantee their fidelity should they be admitted into the Company's service."

"I will think the matter over," Sir Henry Lawrence said; "a force of that kind, if it could be relied upon, would be of immense service."

" Well, Sir Henry, there is one ready at hand. If I might venture to suggest, I should say, if my nephew happens to have an appointment in the Punjaub, it would be useful he should go for a week or two to the district with the officer charged to raise the force; in a few days he would produce a squadron two hundred strong of well-drilled cavalry, and four or five hundred infantry, with a complement of native officers thoroughly up to their work."

" Your nephew will certainly have an appointment in the Punjaub, Colonel Groves. He has proved himself a most efficient and zealous officer, and his knowledge of Punjaubi and Pathan, and of the country, would be thrown away in any other province. I had his early record in my hands when I was Resident at Lahore. Major Edwardes has written very strongly of the valuable assistance Mr. Groves rendered him, and he has been very useful during the late campaign. I can promise you that his appointment will show that his services

have been thoroughly appreciated. I consider him an exceedingly promising young officer, and shall be glad to have an assistant on whom I can so thoroughly rely in any emergency."

"There is one thing I want to say to you, sir, and that is, that, when I disbanded my regiments, I gave to each man a grant of an acre or two of land in a valley so far untilled, but good land, and capable of irrigation. I had previously planted a thousand of them in two similar colonies, both of which are doing well. I hope that the grants may be confirmed."

"That they certainly would in any case, Colonel Groves; it is a great thing to have so many men, who might otherwise be troublesome, settled on the land; but, indeed, as your grants were made previous to the formal annexation, they would in any case remain good."

At the end of the week Colonel Groves left the camp and took a boat to go down the Indus. The short stay among his countrymen, from whom he had been for many years separated, had done him good, and dispelled the melancholy thoughts with which he had ridden down from the fortress, which had been for some twelve years his home. He had met with great hospitality during his stay in camp, for all were interested in the talk and adventures of one who had been among the best known of Runjeet Singh's officers, and his hearty and genial manner had won for him the liking of all who met him.

Ten days later Percy, who was getting somewhat tired of idleness, received a message saying that he was to appear before the commissioners on the following day. Sir Henry, as president, addressed him when he appeared.

" Mr. Groves, I am happy to say that my brother and Mr. Mansell thoroughly agree with me that at the present moment experience rather than age must guide us in the distribution of our appointments. Although you have been but a short time in the Company's service, you have a wide experience in the country, and your knowledge of its languages is invalu-

able at the present juncture. We feel that you are naturally specially acquainted with the wants and necessities of that portion of the country in which you have lived for upwards of two years, and have therefore determined to appoint you to the charge of the strip of country lying north of Dhangah and running along by the side of the Jhelum. It will be about twenty miles wide, and will extend to the end of the narrow projection of country running up into Cashmere. The line will run to the east of Rawal Pindee, and will include all the hill country, and will touch Torbeylah on the eastern branch of the Indus. It will therefore be about a hundred and twenty miles long, and will of course include your uncle's former district. Your appointment will be that of a deputy-commissioner. It will be a sub-district, either of the district of Rawal Pindee or of Peshawur; that is not settled yet, but at any rate you will communicate direct with me. It is an important appointment for so young a civil servant, but I am sure that you will justify our choice. I congratulate you, Mr. Groves, upon having worthily earned an appointment such as this. You will start within two days for your post, and we think that it will be advantageous for you to make Djarma your head-quarters; there are, of course, several much more important places in the district; but in the first place it is, I believe, strongly fortified, it is distant about midway between the northern and southern points, and it possesses the advantage that in case of need you might collect a force from among the men who served under your uncle, and who are personally known to you. Lieutenant Purchas will accompany you; he is commissioned to raise a police force of a hundred mounted men; he will be stationed at Djarma, and will, of course, be subject to your orders, and responsible for the maintenance of order in the district. We have also decided upon raising a frontier force, and shall, as a beginning, raise two troops of cavalry and six companies of infantry. Major Mellish, who will have the command, will follow you to Djarma in a few

days, and I shall be obliged if you will assist him in raising half that number in your neighbourhood. No doubt the force will be considerably increased later; at present it is but an experiment, and while it is desirable that the corps should start with a number of trained men, we have decided that it would be better to have an admixture of recruits from Pathan tribes on the other side of the Indus, both because they will know the country there, and because it is undesirable that the whole force should be composed of men acquainted with each other."

Percy expressed his thanks to the commissioners for the honour they had done him in the appointment, and especially for having selected him to the post he should have preferred to all others. "I can answer, sir," he said, "that should any emergency ever occur, I could in the course of a couple of days raise a thousand men for any service required."

Ten years later Percy was able to fulfil the promise. He had three years before been removed to a more important appointment, that of the district between the Jhelum and Chenab rivers, when the news of the outbreak of the mutiny sent a thrill through India, and it was evident that it would extend over the whole of the Bengal army. He received a message from Mr. Montgomery, commissioner at Lahore— Sir John Lawrence, who had succeeded his brother as chief-commissioner of the Punjaub, being at the time at Rawal Pindee—saying, "Come to me at once." Ten minutes later he was on horseback, and, accompanied by his two faithful servants, rode to Lahore, and on his arrival was at once received by the commissioner.

"Mr. Groves," he said, "I fear there is no doubt that the sepoys throughout the Punjaub will go with the rest. We have a few days' respite, but I fear that it is certain they will rise. They must be disarmed if possible, crushed if necessary. I think that the Sikhs as a whole will be true to us. They have experienced ten years of good government, and I

believe they appreciate it. If they are faithful, we may not only hold this province, but help the north-west; if they are against us, India is lost for a time. My intention is, as soon as the sepoys have been dealt with, to raise regiments among the Sikhs, and march them south. What do you think? "

" It will depend a great deal on their chiefs, sir; if they are faithful, I believe the people in general will at any rate not take part against us."

" I have received assurances of fidelity from the Rajah of Putiala and many others; some have offered to place their troops at our disposal, others not only troops but money."

"Then I have no doubt of the population, sir; they have always looked to their chiefs, and if they are staunch the people will follow their lead."

"Why I have specially sent for you is this, Mr. Groves. You know your old district thoroughly, and have personal influence there; would you undertake to raise a force at once, whom you could trust to fight against the sepoys? There are the garrisons at Peshawur, Nowshera, Rawal Pindee, and other places."

"I think I can undertake that, sir."

"Then, in heaven's name, start at once. Take a fresh horse from my stable, get remounts wherever you can, and ride as if for your life. The troops at Meerut and Delhi have both risen and massacred the officers and all the Europeans; and although it may be a few days before the news is generally known, you are aware how strangely fast news travels in India, and assuredly this will be the signal for the rising of the sepoys everywhere. I hope to be able to deal with those here and at Mean Meer."

Feeling half-stupefied at the intelligence of the risings at Meerut and Delhi, Percy hurried off.

"I have to ride with all speed to Djarma," he said to his followers; "it is a matter of life and death, and I have not a moment to lose. The commissioner has ordered one of his

own horses to be brought round for me to start with, and I shall change as often as I can on the road. Do you follow on as quickly as you can."

Five minutes later he dashed out through the northern gate of Lahore. He had already performed a long and rapid ride, and had nearly two hundred miles before him; but he made the journey without rest, save to eat something whenever a fresh horse was being procured for him, and in twenty hours from his leaving Lahore he rode into Djarma. The force there had, he heard, been summoned six hours previously by a messenger from Sir John Lawrence to join him instantly at Rawal Pindee. In half an hour after his arrival he had despatched a dozen messengers to the valleys where his uncle's men had been settled; then he threw himself down on a couch, and ordered that he should not be disturbed for four hours.

At the end of that time he was aroused, and going out found that some four hundred men from the valley below had already come in; the greater portion were old soldiers, but some had brought their sons in with them, and all were equally ready to serve. Three hours more, and the force had swelled to twelve hundred men, and included many of the colonel's old officers, among them Nand Chund, who had saved money and settled down quietly after the troops had been disbanded. The old soldiers had all brought their arms with them, and the new recruits had also for the most part arms of some kind; others were found, and distributed among them. The old officers naturally fell into their positions, and the vacancies were filled up by men who had been under-officers.

There were two hundred cavalry-men among them, but of these not more than half had horses of any kind; but messengers had also been sent off to many of the land-owners in that part of the district, begging them to lend horses for the service of the government, and assuring them of payment for

them on a fair scale should they not be returned; and a sufficient number for the unmounted men were now forthcoming. Eight hours after his arrival at Djarma, Percy rode out at the head of two hundred cavalry and one thousand infantry. Nand Chund was left behind, with directions to raise instantly another regiment of infantry and as many horsemen as he could engage in the whole district, and to join him as speedily as possible.

"I could raise five regiments if it were necessary," Nand Chund said; "when the people know that you are to be their leader, every man who can bear arms will be ready to follow you."

"A regiment will be enough for the present, Nand Chund. No one can say how many will be required afterwards. Choose young and active men; we shall have long marches and much to go through. You can say that I have no doubt that all who do faithful duty will be permanently retained in the service if they choose."

Percy did not go to Rawal Pindee, for he knew that there were European troops there, and the place was safe, and he feared that his force might be detained there. His corps made a tremendous day's march, and placed themselves on the main northern road, where, three hours later, the sepoys came along from the Attock and Nusserabad. Warned of their approach by the clouds of dust, Percy placed his troops in a grove, and when they came along, with drums beating and colours flying, poured in a volley and attacked them. Taken by surprise, great numbers were killed, and the rest fled and were pursued by him at the head of the cavalry, and very few of them succeeded in effecting their escape.

The next morning Percy marched his infantry as far as Attock, and leaving them there to prevent the passage of any mutineers, pushed forward with the cavalry to Peshawur. Here he aided the irregular cavalry under Colonel Nicholson in cutting up the sepoys who had mutinied at the frontier sta-

tions. For the next fortnight he scoured the northern district, dispersing bodies of the mutineers and keeping order. His infantry he had sent down to Lahore to be employed as required. At the end of that time he received an order to report himself there with his cavalry.

"You have been doing good service again, Mr. Groves," Sir John Lawrence said; "the prompt punishment you inflicted on the mutineers has had an excellent effect in the north. But you are wanted back in your district; we must carry on things as before, for this will impress the natives more with the fact that we have no fear and anxiety about the future, than if we were ourselves to go south. A tranquil and assured front, a quiet continuance in our usual routine work, will impress them more than anything. Now, as to these men you have raised: first as to the cavalry, I will muster them into the service if they are willing, and the same thing with the infantry. I am raising regiments here as fast as I can, in order to enable the commander-in-chief to take the offensive. Hitherto the population in general seems to have stood aloof, and it is most desirable to show them that we are confident. Do you think your men will all engage? "

"That I cannot say, sir; they all joined me at once from their affection for my uncle and from their personal knowledge of myself. Some of them are well-to-do men; a good many of them are getting past the age for soldiering. They would all be willing, I have no doubt, to serve here in the Punjaub, but many would not care to enlist for regular service. Most of the younger men would, of course, be delighted to do so."

Eventually three strong companies were raised from the infantry and a troop of horse from the cavalry. These were enrolled in the Company's service. Both were at once furnished with officers belonging to the sepoy regiments that had mutinied, and marched away to join the force assembling for an advance against Delhi. Another troop of a hundred

\J-V

men, willing to serve for a year, was officered and sent up to Djarma, together with two hundred infantry, to be in readiness to put down any trouble that might arise with the hill tribes. The rest received two months' pay and returned to their homes, with the understanding that they would, if called upon to do so, rejoin the ranks.

The month that followed was full of anxiety to all. Until Delhi fell the strain was very great, for although the Punjaub was quiet and apparently loyal, the eyes of every native in India were fixed upon the desperate struggle round the city which had for so long been the seat of empire, and it was not until the British flag again floated over the blood-stained city, that India recognized that the British would assuredly emerge victorious from the struggle with the great army it had raised and disciplined.

When at length the strength of the mutiny was crushed by the final capture of Lucknow, and there remained but the work of pursuit and punishment to be carried out, Percy Groves took his leave and went home. He had been fifteen years absent, and was now thirty. He did not go alone, for he took with him a wife and two children, having five years before married the sister of a young civilian in his own district. She had many relatives in the service, and some of these had been among the early victims of the mutiny, and a married sister had been among those so long besieged in Lucknow. The anxiety had told so much upon his wife, that Percy was strongly advised to take her to England directly he could get away from his work, and as soon as he felt that he could be spared he sent in his application, which was at once acceded to. His name had been included by Sir John Lawrence in the lists of those to whose efforts it was chiefly due that the Punjaub had been saved, and when the list of honours came out his name was included in those on whom the honour of C.B. had been bestowed.

Before leaving he had the satisfaction of seeing his two

faithful followers settled down near each other. He had purchased for them of a sirdar, who had impoverished himself by his extravagance, the rights over several villages, and although they lamented Percy's departure deeply, they were both of an age when men view with satisfaction the prospect of a life of ease and comfort.

He embarked this time at Bombay, and returned via Egypt. He was received with delight by his uncle, who had established himself at Southsea, and who looked, Percy thought, but little older than when he had seen him last. When the end of his two years' leave of absence was approaching, his uncle for the first time asked him whether he meant to go back.

" I can only say, Percy, that I shall consider you a downright fool if you do. If you had kept yourself single, it would be a different thing; and if you had an ambition to become some day one of the top-sawyers in the service, a chief-commissioner, and all that, there is no reason that I know of, except that I want you here, why you should not stick to it to the end of your life. Now it is altogether different. You know the doctor has advised that though Annie is perfectly well, she should not return to India. Even if she did, you would not want to take these three little children out with you, and she would not like to go without them. That breaking up of families is the great drawback to the Indian service. Of course, in many cases men must put up with it, because they cannot afford to leave till they have served long enough to get their full pension.

That is not so in your case. You will get a fair pension, of course, because you have held much more important appointments than often fall to the lot of men of your standing; then, too, you were seriously wounded at Chillianwalla. You have been specially reported, and have been made a C.B., all of which will count in the way of pension. However, fortunately that makes very little difference to you; as I told you twelve years ago I have an ample

fortune for us both, and I want you at home. It has been dull work for me since I came back, without anyone to care for here. I am nearly sixty now, and I want a comfortable home for the remainder of my life, and if you go away again I shall be doing something rash, marrying again, or something of that sort. Of course, it is for you to choose; but if you go back to India alone, when you can live here with your wife and children, I shall consider you to be a greater fool than I took you to be."

"Well, you need not consider that, uncle," Percy laughed. "I have been thinking it over myself, and had pretty well come to the conclusion to retire. I have no particular ambition to become a lieutenant-governor, or even a governor; certainly none to be working out there alone, with Annie and the children in England; and the thought that you would like me at home has had its full share in deciding me. To tell you the truth, I have already sent in my request to be allowed to retire, but I had intended to say nothing about it until I could surprise you with the news that it was all settled. I used to think that, did I return, I should have no one I knew in England except you; but Annie's friends and relations, and there are any number of them, have naturally become mine, and I am now thoroughly equipped that way."

"I am glad to hear it, Percy; heartily glad. I reckoned on your good sense as well as upon your affection for me, and I am indeed glad that it is settled. I have had two or three talks on the subject with Annie. She says she hoped and thought you would retire, but that she would not say a word to influence you one way or the other. You are very fortunate in your wife, lad."

" I have been very fortunate all round, uncle; no man has more reason for being thankful and grateful than I have, to God in the first place for all the blessings I have received, and next to him to you."

"Tut, tut, Percy, you have brought as much pleasure into

my life as I have into yours. Now, lad, you must consult your wife, and look about and decide where you would like to establish yourself. We will have a house in London, which I shall call mine, and you shall have a place in the country, with an estate big enough to be an amusement without being a trouble; or if you have no fancy for an estate, we will buy a place here, or anywhere else you and your wife wish to fix on."

"Thank you, uncle; we shall have plenty of time to talk that over. My present idea is that I have no desire whatever to become the possessor of an estate. The life is vastly more cheerful in a town like this, where we have any number of acquaintances, military and Indian, a good club, and something always going on, than it would be in the country, where, as I found while staying with some of Annie's relations, eight miles is considered a reasonable drive to a dinner party."

And so, a month later, Percy Groves retired from the service. His wife, having so many friends in the army, and having been brought up among military men, cordially agreed with him in preferring life near a large garrison town like Portsmouth to settling on an estate in the country, and three months later they were established in a large and comfortable house standing in its own grounds at Southsea. Colonel Groves proposed to Percy to go into parliament, and to take a prominent part in questions connected with India. Percy would not listen to the proposal ^his Indian duties had, however, made him an adept with his pen; and beginning by writing occasional articles upon Indian subjects in which he felt a special interest, he became a regular contributor to one or two of the leading reviews, while his articles on Indian topics in the Times, signed "P.G.," attracted much attention.

This work kept up his connection with India, and afforded just that amount of pleasant occupation that is so necessary to men who, having led a busy and active life, have nothing but their family duties and pleasures and the ordinary routine of

daily life to occupy their minds. Colonel Groves died some five years since, enjoying life to the last, and deeply regretted by his great-nephews and -nieces. Percy Groves is one of the best-known figures at Southsea and at the Oriental Club, and his grandchildren consider it the greatest of treats when they can persuade him to tell them stories of his experiences and adventures in the two campaigns that resulted in the Conquest of the Punjaub.

THE END

"Wherever English is spoken one imagines that Mr. Henty's name is known. One cannot enter a schoolroom or look at a boy's bookshelf without seeing half-a-dozen of his familiar volumes. Mr. Henty is no doubt the most successful writer for boys, and the one to whose new volumes they look forward every Christmas with most pleasure."— Review of Reviews.

CPSIA information can be obtained
at www.ICGtesting.com
Printed in the USA
LVHW062145010421
683279LV00026B/527

9 781537 111827